It Began With a Lie

A Secrets of Redemption Novel

Other books by Michele Pariza Wacek
MPWNovels.com/books

Secrets of Redemption series:
It Began With a Lie (Book 1)
This Happened to Jessica (Book 2)
The Evil That Was Done (Book 3)
The Summoning (Book 4)
The Reckoning (Book 5)
The Girl Who Wasn't There (Book 6)
The Room at the Top of the Stairs (Book 7)
The Secret Diary of Helen Blackstone (free novella)

Charlie Kingsley Mystery series:
A Grave Error (free prequel novella)
The Murder Before Christmas (Book 1)
Ice Cold Murder (Book 2)
Murder Next Door (Book 3)
Murder Among Friends (Book 4)
The Murder of Sleepy Hollow (Book 5)
Red Hot Murder (Book 6)
A Wedding to Murder For (novella)
Loch Ness Murder (novella)

Standalone books:
Today I'll See Her (novella)
The Taking
The Third Nanny
Mirror Image
The Stolen Twin

It Began With a Lie

A Secrets of Redemption Novel

by Michele Pariza Wacek

This book may be purchased for educational, business, or sales promotional use. For information, please email info@LoveBasedPublishing.com.

ISBN 978-1-945363-98-6

Library of Congress Control Number: 2018957813

For my family, for always believing in me.

Chapter 1

"You're right. It's perfect for us. I'm so glad we're here," I said, lying through my carefully pasted-on smile.

I tried to make my voice bright and cheery, but it sounded brittle and forced, even to me. I sucked in my breath and widened my smile, though my teeth were so clenched, my jaw hurt.

Stefan smiled back—actually, his mouth smiled but his dark-brown eyes, framed with those long, thick lashes any woman would envy, looked flat … distracted. He hugged me with one arm. "I told you everything would be okay," he whispered into my hair. His scent was even more musky than usual, probably from two straight days of driving and lack of shower.

I hugged him back, reminding myself to relax. *Yes, everything is going to be okay. Remember, this move represents a fresh start for us—time for us to reconnect and get our marriage back on track. It's not going to happen overnight.*

His iPhone buzzed. He didn't look at me as he dropped his arm and pulled it out of his pocket, his attention already elsewhere. "Sorry babe, gotta take this." He turned his back to me as he answered the call, walking away quickly. His dark hair, streaked with silver that added a quiet, distinguished air to his All-American good looks was longer than normal, curling around his collar. He definitely needed a haircut, but of course, we couldn't afford his normal stylist, and not just anyone was qualified to touch his hair.

I wrapped my arms around myself, goosebumps forming on my skin as a sudden breeze, especially cool for mid-May, brushed past me—the cold all the more shocking in the absence of Stefan's warm body.

He has to work, I reminded myself. *Remember why we're here.*

I remembered, all right. How could I forget?

I rubbed my hands up and down my arms as I took a deep breath, and finally focused on the house.

It was just as I remembered from my childhood—white with black shutters, outlined by bushy green shrubs, framed by tall, gently-swaying pine trees and the red porch with the swinging chair. It sat all by its lonesome in the middle of a never-developed cul-de-sac, the only "neighbors" being an overgrown forest on one side, and a marshy field on the other.

Okay, maybe it wasn't *exactly* the way I remembered it. The bushes actually looked pretty straggly. The lawn was overgrown, full of dandelions going to seed, and the porch could definitely use a new paint job.

I sighed. If the outside looked like this, what on earth waited for me on the inside?

Inside.

I swallowed back the bile that rose in the back of my throat. It slid to my stomach, turning into a cold, slimy lump.

The house of my childhood.

The house of my nightmares.

Oh God, I so didn't want to be here.

Stefan was still on the phone, facing away from me. I stared longingly at his back. *Turn around*, I silently begged. T*urn around and smile at me. A real smile. Like how you used to before we were married. Tell me it's going to be okay. You don't have to leave tonight like you thought. You realize how cruel it would be to leave me alone in this house the first night we're here, and you don't want to do that to me. Please, tell me. Or, better yet, tell me we're packing up and going back to New York. Say this was all a mistake; the firm is doing fine. Or, if you can't say that, say we'll figure it out. We'll make it work. We don't need to live here after all. Please, Stefan. Please don't leave me alone here.*

He half-turned, caught my eye, and made a gesture that indicated he was going to be awhile.

And I should start unpacking.

I closed my eyes. Depression settled around me like an old, familiar shawl. I could feel the beginning of a headache stab my temples.

Great. Just what I needed to complete this nightmare—a monster headache.

I turned to the car and saw Chrissy still in the backseat—headset on, bobbing to music only she could hear. Her long, dark hair—so dark it often looked black—spread out like a shiny cloak, the ends on one side dyed an electric blue.

Oh, yeah. That's right. I wouldn't be alone in the house after all.

Chrissy closed her eyes and turned her head away from me.

It just kept getting better and better.

I knocked on the window. She ignored me. I knocked again. She continued to ignore me.

For a moment, I imagined yanking the door open, snatching the headset off and telling her to—no, *insisting* that—she get her butt out of the car and help me unpack. I pictured her dark brown eyes, so much like Stefan's, widening, her pink lip-glossed mouth forming a perfect O, so shocked that she doesn't talk back, but instead meekly does what she's told.

More pain stabbed my temples. I closed my eyes and kept knocking on the window.

It's not her fault, I told myself for maybe the 200th time. *How would you act if you were sixteen years old and your mother abandoned you, dumped you at your father's, so she'd be free to travel across Europe with her boy toy?*

I squelched the little voice that reminded me I wasn't a whole heck of a lot older than said boy toy, and started pounding on the window. Stefan kept telling me she was warming up to me—I personally hadn't seen much evidence of that.

Chrissy finally turned her head and looked at me. "What?" she mouthed, disgust radiating off her, her eyes narrowing like an angry cat.

I motioned to the trunk. "I need your help."

Her lip curled as her head fell back on to the seat. She closed her eyes.

I had just been dismissed.

Great. Just great.

I looked around for Stefan—if he were standing with me, she would be out of the car and helping—a fake, sweet smile on her face, but he had moved to the corner of the street, still on the phone. I popped the trunk and headed over to him. Maybe I could finally get him to see reason—that it really was a dreadful idea to leave the two of us alone in Redemption, Wisconsin, while he commuted back and forth to New York to rescue his failing law firm. "See," I could say, "She doesn't listen to me. She doesn't respect me. She needs her father. I need you, too. She's going to run wild with you gone and I won't be able to deal with her."

Stefan hung up as I approached. "The movers should be here soon. You probably should start unpacking." Although his tone was mild, I could still hear the underlying faint chords of reproach—what's going on with you? Why haven't you started yet? Do I need to do everything around here?

"Yes, I was going to," I said, hating my defensive tone, but unable to stop it. "But there's a problem I think you need to deal with."

His eyes narrowed—clearly, he was losing his patience with me. "What?"

I opened my mouth to tell him about Chrissy, just as her voice floated toward us, "Can I get some help over here?"

I slowly turned around, gritting my teeth, trying not to show it. Chrissy stood by the trunk, arms loaded with boxes, an expectant look on her face. The pain darting through my head intensified.

"Rebecca, are you coming?" Stefan asked as he headed over to his charming daughter, waiting for him with a smug expression on her face, like a cat who ate the canary. I took a deep breath and trudged over, the sick knot in the pit of my stomach growing and tightening.

What on earth was I going to do with her while Stefan was gone?

Chrissy threw me a triumphant smile as she followed her father to the house. I resisted the urge to stick my tongue out at her, as I heaved a couple of boxes out of the trunk.

Really, all the crap with Chrissy was the least of my worries. It was more of a distraction, than anything.

The real problem was the house.

The house.

Oh God.

I turned to stare at it. It didn't look menacing or evil. It looked like a normal, everyday house.

Well, a normal, everyday house with peeling paint, a broken gutter and a few missing roof shingles.

Great. That probably meant we needed a new roof. New roofs were expensive. People who had to rescue failing law firms tended to not have money for things like new roofs. Even new roofs for houses that were going to be fixed up and eventually sold, ideally for a big, fat profit.

Would there be *any* good news today?

Again, I realized I was distracting myself. New roofs and paint jobs—those were trivial.

The real problem was *inside* the house.

Where all my nightmares took place.

Where my breakdown happened.

Where I almost died.

I swallowed hard. The sun went behind a cloud and, all of a sudden, the house was plunged into darkness. It loomed in front me, huge and monstrous, the windows dark, bottomless eyes staring at me ... the door a mouth with sharp teeth ...

"Rebecca! Are you coming?"

Stefan broke the spell. I blinked my eyes and tried to get myself together.

I was being silly. It was just a house, not a monster. How could a house even BE a monster? Only people could be monsters, which would mean my aunt, who had owned the house, was the monster.

And my aunt was dead now. Ding, dong, the witch is dead. Or, in this case, the monster.

Which meant there was nothing to fear in the house anymore. Which was exactly what Stefan kept telling me back in New York, over and over.

"Don't you think it's time you put all this childhood nonsense behind you?" he asked. "Look, I get it. Your aunt must have done something so dreadful that you've blocked it out, but she's dead. She can't hurt you anymore. And it couldn't have worked out any more perfectly for us—we have both a place to live rent-free right now, while I get things turned around. And, once we sell it, we can use the money to move back here and get a fresh start."

He was right, of course. But, still, I couldn't drop it.

"Why did she even will the house to me in the first place?" I persisted. "Why didn't she will it to CB? He was there a lot more than I was."

Stefan shrugged. "Maybe it was her way of apologizing to you all these years later. She was trying to make it up to you. Or maybe she changed—people said she was sick at the end. But, why does it matter why she willed it to you? The point is she did, and we really need it. Not to mention this could be a great way for you to finally get over whatever happened to you years ago."

Maybe. Back in New York, it had seemed so reasonable. So logical. Maybe the move wouldn't be a problem after all.

But, standing in the front yard with my arms filled with boxes, every cell in my body screamed that it was a really awful idea.

"Hey," Stefan whispered in my ear, his five o'clock shadow scratching my cheek. I jumped, so transfixed by the house that I hadn't even realized he had returned to me. "Look, I'm sorry. I should have known this would be rough for you. Come on, I'll walk in with you."

He rubbed my arm and smiled at me—a real smile. I could feel my insides start to thaw as all those old, exciting, passionate feelings reminiscent of when we first started dating swarmed over me. I remembered how he would shower me with red roses and whisk me off to romantic dinners that led to steaming, hot sex. He made me feel like a princess in a fairy tale. I still couldn't fathom how he ended up with me.

I met his eyes, and for the first time in what seemed like a long time, I felt the beginnings of a real smile on my lips. *See, he does care, even if he doesn't always show it. This is why the move was the perfect thing for our marriage; all we needed was to get away from the stress of New York, so we could rekin-*

dle things. I nodded and started walking with him toward the house. Over her shoulder, Chrissy shot me a dirty look.

The closer we got to the house, the more I focused on my breathing. *It's going to be okay, I repeated to myself. It's just a house. A house can't hurt anyone. It's all going to be okay.*

An owl hooted, and I jumped. Why was an owl hooting in the daytime? Didn't that mean someone was going to die? Isn't that what the old stories and folklore taught? My entire body stiffened—all I wanted to do was run the other way. Stefan hugged me closer, gently massaging my arm, and urged me forward.

"It's going to be okay," he murmured into my hair. I closed my eyes for a moment, willing myself to believe it.

We stepped onto the porch, Chrissy impatiently waiting for Stefan to unlock the door. He put the boxes on the ground to fumble for his keys as I tried hard not to hyperventilate.

It's just a house. A house can't hurt anyone.

After an eternity that simultaneously wasn't nearly long enough, he located the keys and wrenched the door open, swearing under his breath.

His words barely registered. I found myself compelled forward, drawn in like those pathetic moths to the killing flame.

I could almost hear my aunt excitedly calling, "Becca? Is that you? Wait until you see this," as I stepped across the threshold into the house.

It was exactly like I remembered.

Well, maybe not exactly—it was filthy and dusty, full of cobwebs and brittle, dead bugs lying upside down on the floor with their legs sticking up. But I remembered it all—from the overstuffed floral sofa where I spent hours reading, to the end table covered with knick-knacks and frilly doilies, to the paintings lining the walls. I found myself wanting to hurry into the kitchen, where surely Aunt Charlie would have a cup of tea waiting for me. It didn't feel scary at all. It felt warm and comforting.

Like coming home.

How could this be?

Stefan was still muttering under his breath. "I can't believe all this crap. We're going to have put our stuff in storage for months while we go through it all. Christ, like we need another bill to worry about." He sighed, pulled his cell phone out, and started punching numbers.

"Dad, what do you mean our stuff is going into storage?" Chrissy said, clearly alarmed.

Stefan waved his arms. "Honey, look around you. Where are we going to put it? We have to put our things into storage until we get all this out of here."

"But Dad," Chrissy protested. I stopped listening. I walked slowly around, watching my aunt dashing down the stairs, her smock stained, arms filled with herbs and flowers, some even sticking out of her frizzy brown hair, muttering about the latest concoction she was crafting for one of the neighbors whose back was acting up again …

"Earth to Rebecca. Rebecca. Are you okay?" I suddenly realized Stefan was talking to me, and I pulled myself out of my memories.

"Sorry, it just …" my voice trailed off.

He came closer. "Are you okay? Are you remembering?"

There she was again, the ghost of Aunt Charlie, explaining yet again to the odd, overly-made-up, hair-over-teased, forty-something woman from the next town that no, she didn't do love potions. It was dangerous magic to mess around with either love or money, but if she wanted help with her thyroid that was clearly not working the way it should be, that was definitely in my aunt's wheelhouse.

I shook my head. "No, not really. It's just … weird."

I wanted him to dig deeper, ask me questions, invite me to talk about the memories flooding through me. I wanted him to look at me while I spoke, *really* look at me, the way he did before we were married.

Where had it all gone wrong? And how could he leave me alone in a lonely, isolated and desolate house a thousand miles away from New York? Sure, Chrissy would be there, but the jury was still out as to whether she made it better or worse.

The memories pushed up against me, smothering me. I *needed* to talk about them, before they completely overwhelmed and suffocated me. And he knew it—he knew how much I needed to talk things through to keep the anxiety and panic at bay. He wouldn't let me down, not now, when I really needed him.

Would he?

Chapter 2

The empty coffee pot mocked me.

It sat on the table, all smug and shiny, its cord wrapped tightly around it.

I had been so excited after unearthing it that morning—yes! Coffee! God knew I needed it.

The night before had been horrible, starting with the fights. I ended up in the living room, where I spent the night on the couch, a cold washcloth draped over my face in a feeble attempt to relieve the mother of all headaches.

Several times, I'd have just dozed off when the sound of Chrissy's footsteps would jerk me awake, as she paced up and down the upstairs hallway. I couldn't fathom what was keeping her up, so finally, after the fourth or fifth time of being woken up, I went upstairs to check on her. She must have heard me on the stairs, because all I saw was of the trail of her white night-gown as she disappeared into her room. I stood there for a moment, wondering if I should go talk to her, but the stabbing pain in my head drove me back downstairs to the safety of the couch and washcloth. I just couldn't face another argument then, in the middle of the night.

She must have decided to stay in her room after that, because I finally drifted off, only waking when the sun shone through the dirty living room window, illuminating all the dust motes floating in the air.

Coffee was exactly what I needed. Except … I had no beans to put in the coffeemaker. Not that it mattered, I realized after digging through the third box in frustration. I didn't have any cream or sugar either.

Well, at least my headache was gone, although what was left was a weird, hollow, slightly-drugged feeling. Still, I'd take that over the headache any day.

I sighed and rubbed my face. The whole move wasn't starting off very well. In fact, everything seemed to be going from bad to worse, including the fight with Stefan.

"Do you really need to leave?" I asked him again as I followed him to the door. He had just said goodbye to Chrissy, who had immediately disappeared upstairs, leaving us alone. I could see the taxi he had called sitting in the driveway and my heart sank. A part of me had hoped to talk him out of going, but with the taxi already there the possibility seemed even more remote.

He sighed. I could tell he was losing patience. "We've been through this. You know I have to."

"But you just got here! Surely you can take a few days—a week maybe—off to help us unpack and get settled."

He picked up his briefcase. "You know I can't. Not now."

"But when? You promised you would set it up so that you could work from here most of the time. Why can't you start that now?" I could tell his patience was just about gone, but I couldn't stop myself.

He opened the door. A fresh, cool breeze rushed in, a sharp contrast to the musty, stale house. "And I will. But it's too soon. There are still a few things I need to get cleaned up before I can do that. You know that. We talked about this."

He stepped outside and went to kiss me, but I turned my face away. "Are you going to see *her*?"

That stopped him. I could see his eyes narrow and his mouth tighten. I hadn't meant to say it; it just slipped out.

He paused and took a breath. "I know this whole situation has been tough on you, so I'm going to forget you said that. I'll call you."

Except he didn't. Not a single peep in the more than twelve hours since he had walked out the door. And every time I thought of it, I felt sick with shame.

I didn't *really* think he was cheating on me. I mean, there was something about Sabrina and her brittle, cool, blonde, perfect elegance that I didn't trust, but that wasn't on Stefan. I had no reason not to trust him. Just because my first husband cheated on me didn't mean Stefan would. And just because

Sabrina looked at Stefan like he was a steak dinner, and she was starving, didn't mean it was reciprocated.

Worse, I knew I was making a bigger mess out of it every time I brought it up. The more I accused him, the more likely he would finally say, "Screw it, if I'm constantly accused of being a cheater, I might as well at least get something out of it." Even knowing all of that, I somehow couldn't stop myself.

Deep down, I knew I was driving him away. And I hated that part of myself. But still nothing changed.

To make matters worse, it didn't take long after Stefan left before things blew up with Chrissy. I asked her to help me start organizing the kitchen, and she responded with an outburst about how much she hated the move. She hated me, too—her life was ruined, and it was all my fault. She stormed off, slammed the door to her room, and that's how I ended up on the couch, my head pounding, wishing I was just about anywhere else.

Standing in the kitchen with the weak sunlight peeking through the dirty windows, the empty coffee maker taunting me, I gave in to my feelings of overwhelm. How on earth was I ever going to get the house organized? And the yard? And my aunt's massive garden? All the while researching what it would take to sell the house for top dollar, and dealing with Chrissy? My heart sank at that thought, although I wasn't completely sure which thought triggered it. Maybe it was all of them.

And if that wasn't difficult enough, I also had to deal with being in my aunt's home. Her presence *was everywhere*. I felt like an intruder. How could I do all of this, feeling her around me? How could I be in her home, when she wasn't? It wasn't my house. It was Aunt Charlie's. And I wasn't even sure I WANTED it to feel like my home.

Because if it did, then I would probably remember everything.

Including what happened that night.

The night I almost died.

God, I felt sick.

I needed coffee. And food.

Maybe I should take Chrissy out for breakfast as a peace of-fering. We could get out of the house, which would be good for me at least, and then go grocery shopping before coming home to tackle the cleaning and organizing.

I wanted to start in the kitchen. It was Aunt Charlie's favorite room in the house, and I knew it would have broken her heart to see how neglected and dingy it had become. When my aunt was alive, it was the center of the home—a light, cheery place with a bright-red tea kettle constantly simmering away on low heat on the stove. Oh, how Aunt Charlie loved her tea—that's why the kettle always had hot water in it—she'd say you just never knew when a cup would be needed. She was a strong believer that tea cured just about everything, just so long as you had the right blend. And, surprise, surprise, you could pretty much always find the right blend outside in her massive garden, which I had no doubt was completely overgrown now. I didn't have the heart to go look.

I could almost see her, standing in that very kitchen, prepar-ing me a cup. "Headache again, Becca?" she would murmur as she measured and poured and steeped. The warm fragrance would fill the homey kitchen as she pushed the hot cup in front of me, the taste strong, flavorful, and sweet, with just a hint of bitterness. And, lo and behold, not too long after drinking it, I would find my headache draining away.

I wondered if I would still find her tea blends in the kitchen. Maybe I could find that headache tea. And maybe, if I was even luckier, I would find a blend that would cure everything that ailed me that morning.

With some surprise, I realized just how much love encom-passed that memory. Nothing scary. Nothing that could possibly foretell the horror of what happened that dreadful night.

Could my aunt actually be the monster?

My mother certainly thought so. She forbade any contact, any mentioning of my aunt even, refusing to allow her to see me once I woke up in intensive care following the stomach pump. She refused her again when I was transferred to a psych unit, after becoming hysterical when I was asked what had happened that night.

My mother blamed my aunt.

And, I, in my weakened, anxious, panicked state, was relieved to follow her lead. Actually, I was more than relieved; I was happy, too.

But sitting in that kitchen right then, I felt only love and comfort, and I began to question my choices.

My mother had been completely against us moving back here, even temporarily. At the time, listening to her arguments, I had chalked it up to her being overly protective. Now, I wondered. Was that it? Or was something deeper going on?

Chrissy chose that moment to stroll into the kitchen, her hair sticking up on one side. She was wearing her blue and red plaid sleep shorts and red tee shirt—the blue plaid almost an exact match to the blue highlight in her hair. Staring at her, something stirred deep inside me—a distinct feeling of wrongness … of something being off—but when I reached for it, I came up empty.

She leaned against the counter and started checking her iPhone. "How sweet, you're being domestic."

I shook my head—that off feeling still nagged at me, but I just couldn't place it. I really needed coffee. Coffee would make everything better.

She tapped at her iPhone, not looking up. "Anything to eat in this God-awful place?"

I sighed. Maybe I should be looking for a tea that would cure Chrissy.

Chapter 3

Chrissy wrinkled her nose. "What a dump."

She said it under her breath, so neither the bustling waitresses nor the other customers could hear. But I could. I gave her a sharp look, which she ignored.

We were in what *I* thought was a cute little diner called Aunt May's. It felt friendly and familiar and had a respectable number of customers in it for a Monday morning. In fact, on the drive over, I had been amazed at how bright and cheery the town was—it was almost like I had expected to see dark, grimy, stains tainting the buildings, the streets, even the deep green grass. Instead, the sun shone down on clean, well-kept houses and cute stores complete with maintained lawns and pots of colorful flowers.

Chrissy clearly wasn't impressed by any of it.

She poked at her menu. "Do you think anything here is gluten-free?"

I sighed, flipping over my coffee cup. "You'll have to ask."

Chrissy made a face and stared darkly out the window.

Despite the inauspicious start, she seemed to be in a better mood. Well, maybe "better" wasn't quite the right word—"subdued" was probably more accurate. It was almost like our fight had drained vital energy from her, leaving a shell of her former self.

The waitress appeared, coffee pot in hand. "Are you two visiting for the summer?" she asked as she filled my cup. I shot her a grateful look. She looked familiar with her dark, straight hair cut in a chin-length bob and Asian features. Japanese maybe. But I couldn't really place her. Maybe I had run into her years ago, while visiting my aunt.

"No, we just moved here," I said, pulling my coffee toward me, doctoring it with cream and sugar.

The waitress raised her eyebrow at me. "Really? Where?"

"Charlie, I mean Charlotte Kingsley's house."

The waitress set the coffee pot down. "Becca? Is that you?"

Something inside me seemed to twist in on itself, hearing that name out loud. *I'm not Becca*, I wanted to say. *Becca's gone. It's Rebecca now.*

At the same time, I found my brain frantically searching for a wisp of something, anything, to give me a hint as to who this waitress was. "Uh …"

"It's Mia—Mia Moto. We used to hang out, remember?"

I blinked at her and suddenly, it was like the dam opened— memories crashed down into me. I sucked in my breath, feeling physically jolted by the impact. "Mia! Oh my God, I hardly recognized you!"

She laughed in delight and held out her arms. Somehow, I found myself on my feet, swept up in a giant bear hug—impressive, considering how tiny she was. She smelled spicy, like cinnamon and coffee.

"It's so great to see you," Mia said, when we finally separated. "I mean, after that night, we were all so worried, but the hospital wouldn't let any of us visit you."

"Yeah, well, my mom …" I fumbled around, not really sure what to say. The truth was, I hadn't wanted to see them. I had become hysterical again, when one of the nurses said I had visitors. And, until that very moment, I had never even considered how it must have looked from their point of view. They were my friends; they cared about me, and I had almost died. Of course they would want to see me. I felt sick with shame.

"I can't believe it's you," I said, changing the subject. "Who else is still here? Is …"

"Daphne's still here," Mia interjected. "In fact, she's still living in the same house, right by you. She moved in after her mom got sick to help her out. I know she'd love to see you."

"And I'd love to see her too," I said, jolted again by how much I really did miss hanging out with Mia and Daphne.

"And Daniel is still here, too." Mia continued. "He's engaged now."

A rush of conflicting feelings started swirling through me at the sound of his name, anger being the most prevalent. "I'm married," I said shortly, smiling at the last second to soften my tone.

Daniel. God, I had totally forgotten him, too. For good reason, considering he had not only stood me up, all those years ago, but he also had then ignored me completely .... like I didn't even exist. Talk about painful. Snapping back to reality, I turned my attention back to Mia. "In fact, this is my stepdaughter, Chrissy."

Mia turned her 40-thousand-watt, infectious smile on Chrissy. "Great to meet you, Chrissy. Make sure you ask your stepmom where all the hot places are to hang out." Chrissy's lips twitched upward in a semblance of a smile, and her "nicetomeetyoutoo" almost sounded friendly.

I elbowed Mia. "I don't know if that's such a good idea."

Someone near the kitchen yelled Mia's name, but she waved him off. "We definitely need to catch up."

"Yes," I agreed, sliding back into my seat. "I'm really surprised you're here. I thought you would be long gone—California, right? Stanford? Law school?" I had vague memories of Mia going on and on about being the next Erin Brockovich. She had nearly memorized that movie, she had seen it so often.

Mia's smile slipped. "Well, yeah. It's complicated. After that night … you … Jessica …" her voice trailed off and she pulled out her order pad. "I better get your order."

Jessica.

It felt like all the air had been sucked out of the room. I could hear Chrissy asking about gluten-free options, and not getting the answer she wanted, but it seemed like the conversation was taking place outside of the bubble I was trapped in, as I could barely hear anything but a warbling echo.

Jessica. How could I have forgotten about Jessica?

Mia, Daphne, Jessica, and me. We were the four amigos that summer. The four Musketeers. Hanging out at the beach, the mall, at my aunt's house (because she was by far the coolest of all the adults we had to choose from).

Until that night, when Jessica disappeared ... and I ended up in the hospital, broken, mentally and physically.

I rubbed my eyes, the faint wisp of a headache brushing my temples like a soft kiss. I realized that while my memories from that summer were finally returning, that night was still a total blank. Actually, the entire day was a black hole. I didn't even remember taking the first drink, one of many that would put me in the hospital, having to get my stomach pumped, followed by a complete and utter nervous breakdown.

"Becca?" Mia asked, pen poised on her pad. "You okay?"

I reached for my coffee cup, glad to see my hands weren't shaking, and tried on a smile that felt way too small. "Yeah, I'm fine. Just still recovering from moving."

Mia didn't look like she completely believed me, but I could tell she needed to get back to work. I ordered the American breakfast—eggs, bacon, fried potatoes with onions and peppers, and rye toast—even though I was no longer hungry. I knew I had to eat. I had barely eaten anything the day before, and if I didn't start eating, I would probably trigger another headache. I figured chances were decent I'd get one anyway, but at least eating something would give me a fighting chance.

Along with the lack of gluten-free options, Chrissy also voiced her displeasure around the coffee choices, wanting a mocha, or latte, or something, made with some other type of milk than, well, milk from a cow, so she ended up with a Coke. I restrained myself from pointing out that soda was probably a lot less healthy choice than something with gluten or dairy in it. Ah, kids.

She blew the paper off the straw and plopped the straw in her soda, then pulled out her iPhone. "Who's Daniel?"

I didn't look at her as I added a little more sugar to my cup, and carefully stirred. "Just a guy I knew from back when I would visit during the summer."

"Hmmm," Chrissy said, lifting her head from her iPhone to narrow her eyes at me. "Sounded like more than that."

"Well, it wasn't," I snapped. Chrissy looked up at me in surprise, one eyebrow raised. I took a deep breath and reminded myself that I was the grown-up.

"Sorry, I didn't sleep well last night. All your pacing kept me awake." *Oh, great, Rebecca. Fabulous apology right there. Maybe I just should have just cut to the chase and said "Sorry, not sorry."* I tried smiling to soften my words and turn it into a joke.

But, Chrissy was frowning at me. "Pacing? What are you talking about? I slept like the dead."

I stared at her, that sense of "wrongness" I felt in the kitchen that morning rushing through me again. "But, I mean, I saw you …" my voice trailed off as images flashed through my mind.

The white nightgown disappearing into Chrissy's room.

Chrissy standing in the kitchen wearing her red and blue sleep outfit.

I rubbed my temples, the coffee turning into a sick, greasy lump in my stomach. Oh God, I hoped I wasn't going to throw up.

Chrissy was looking at me with something that resembled concern. Or maybe it was alarm. After all, I was the only adult she knew within 1,000 miles. "Are you okay, Rebecca?"

I reached for my water glass. "Yeah, I'm fine. It's an old house. Old houses make all sorts of noises. I'm sure that's what kept me awake."

Chrissy didn't look terribly convinced, but she went back to her iPhone. She was probably texting her friends about how I was losing it. Or worse … texting her father.

I drank some water to try and settle my stomach. I was being ridiculous. Old houses make all sorts of creaks and groans and can sound exactly like footsteps, which is what kept waking me up last night. And as for what I saw … well, clearly, I hadn't seen anything. Just a trick of the light, or the moon, or something. And with the pounding of my head, I really wasn't paying that close attention.

I just needed to get some food in my stomach. And hopefully, some decent sleep that night. Then I could forget about all the house nonsense. Stefan and I could laugh about it … assuming he finally got around to calling me back, that is.

Okay, I so didn't want to go down *that* road. Instead, I sat back in my seat, sipped my coffee, and watched Mia top off the cup of a cute guy who looked like a contractor, laughing at something he said. I still had trouble believing Mia was waiting tables at the diner. Of all of us, she was bound and determined to get out and never come back. I remembered how driven, how passionate she had been about all the injustices in the world, and how determined she had been to right them. She was going to be a lawyer and fight for everyone who couldn't help themselves. What had happened?

A couple of older, neatly-dressed women sitting at a table next to us were staring at me. They wore nearly identical pant-suits, except one was baby blue and the other canary yellow. Their half-eaten food sat in front of them. Taken aback at the open aggression in their eyes, I looked back at them, wondering if I should know them.

Were their stares really directed at me? Did I do something in my youth my traitorous memory had yet to reveal? Maybe they were actually looking at someone sitting behind me. I turned around to look, but no one was there. When I swiveled back, their identical gaze looked even more antagonistic.

I dropped my eyes, only half-seeing the paper placemat covered with local advertising, feeling a growing sense of unease in my belly. They didn't look familiar at all. Who were they? And why me?

"Why did the waitress call you Becca?" Chrissy asked, startling me. For once, I was glad she was there to distract me, even though part of me instantly wanted to scream at her to stop calling me that.

"It was my nickname," I said, willing those older women to get up and leave. Out of the corner of my eye, I saw them lean toward each other, whispering, hostile eyes still watching me. I adjusted my head until I couldn't see them anymore.

Chrissy went back to her iPhone "It's cute. Better than Re-becca."

I ignored the twist of pain inside me and put my hand on my heart. "Wait. Did I just hear an almost compliment there?"

Chrissy rolled her eyes. "I'm just saying. I think I'll call you Becca."

"Don't," I said, before I could stop myself.

Chrissy looked surprised. And, if I didn't know her any better, a little hurt. "What, only people you *like* can call you Becca?"

Cripes. I could have smacked myself. Why on earth wasn't there a manual out there on how to be a stepmom to a daughter who is only fifteen years younger than you?

"That's not it," I said, stalling for time as I tried to put the feelings that had swamped over me into words. "It just … it just triggers bad memories. That's all." I cringed—I sounded so lame, even to myself.

Chrissy gave me a withering look as she furiously pounded on her iPhone. I opened my mouth to say something—I had no idea what … something to bridge the gap that yawned between us—but Mia's voice interrupted me. "Daniel! Look who's here! It's Becca!"

I closed my mouth and turned to look. A police officer was standing at the counter watching Mia fill up a to-go container with coffee. Could that be Daniel? I searched the room, but only saw only a handful of people finishing up their breakfast. It had to be him.

I looked back at the cop. Broad shoulders and dark blonde hair—Daniel. Mia glanced at me and winked. I made a face back at her.

He turned. He was older of course, but yes, it was most definitely Daniel. He wouldn't be considered traditionally handsome—not like Stefan with his almost pretty-boy looks. Daniel's face was too rugged, with sharp cheekbones and a crooked nose. But his lips were still full and soft, and his eyes were still the same dark blue. I found myself suddenly conscious of my appearance. I hadn't taken a shower in two days, and I was wearing an old, faded New York Giants tee shirt. I had scraped my unruly mass of reddish, blondish, brownish hair back into a messy ponytail in preparation for a full day of cleaning and organizing. But I quickly reminded myself that I was being silly.

I was a married woman, sitting with my stepdaughter, and he was engaged.

Besides, he had made it more than clear years ago he wasn't the slightest bit interested in me.

"Becca," he said coming over, his face friendly, but not exactly smiling. "Welcome back to Redemption." It didn't sound much like a welcome.

"Thanks," I said, mostly because I couldn't think of anything better to say. Instinctively, I reached up to smooth out my hair, since as usual, a few curly tendrils had escaped and hung in my face. "Not much has changed."

He studied me, making me really wish I had taken an extra five minutes to jump in the shower and dig out a clean shirt. "Oh, plenty has changed."

"Like you being a cop?"

He shrugged slightly. "Pays the bills."

I half-smiled. "There's lots of ways to pay the bills. If I remember right, you always seemed more interested in breaking the law than upholding it."

"Like I said, things change." He lifted his to-go coffee cup and took a swallow, his dark-blue eyes never leaving mine. "I take it you're still painting then."

I dropped my gaze to his chest, feeling a dull ache overwhelm me—the same pain I felt when I heard the name Becca. "As you said, things change."

"Ah." I waited for him to ask more questions, but instead, he changed the subject. "So, how long are you staying?"

I shrugged. "Not sure. We've actually moved here."

His eyebrows raised slightly. "To Charlie's house? You aren't selling it?"

"Well, yes. Eventually. That's the plan. But, at least for the foreseeable future, we'll be living in it." I sounded like an idiot. With some effort, I forced myself to stop talking. Why on earth did I share so much detail? How was this any of his business?

He looked like he was going to say something more but was interrupted by a loud snort. The two pant-suited women both scraped their chairs back as they stood up, glaring disgustedly at all of us before heading to the cash register.

"What's with them?" Chrissy asked. I had forgotten she was there.

I shrugged, before remembering my manners and introducing Chrissy to Daniel. I made a point of gesturing with my left hand to flash my wedding ring.

His head tipped in a slight nod before looking back at me. "Will you be around later today? I'd like to stop by and talk to you."

There was something in his expression that made me uneasy, but I purposefully kept my voice light. "What on earth for? I haven't even unpacked yet. Am I already in trouble?"

The ends of his lips turned up in a slight smile, but no hint of warmth touched the intense look in his eyes. "Should you be in trouble?"

I let out a loud, exaggerated sigh. "Why do cops always answer a question with a question?"

"Occupational hazard. I'll see you later." He dipped his chin in a slight nod before walking away. I noticed he didn't give me the slightest hint as to what he wanted to talk to me about. That sense of unease started to grow into a sense of foreboding.

"Well, for an old friend, he wasn't very friendly," Chrissy said.

I sipped my coffee. "That's for sure."

She smirked. "He was pretty cute, though. For an old guy, I mean."

Man, she did have a knack for making me feel ancient. But, unfortunately, even that didn't distract my mind from scrambling around like a rat in a cage, worrying about what he wanted to talk to me about.

Chapter 4

After breakfast, we stopped at the grocery store to load up before heading home. It seemed bigger than I remembered, and it clearly had been remodeled in the not-so-distant past, so it was surprisingly nice. As we went down the aisles, the few people we ran into ignored me, which was a relief. Those two disapproving women in the diner still bothered me. I had wanted to ask Mia about them before we left, but she seemed to have her hands full with customers, and the moment didn't seem right.

As we pushed our bagged groceries across the parking lot— well, I pushed, Chrissy interacted with her phone—I noticed a homeless woman at the edge of the parking lot. She was dressed in a colorful array of scarves and jackets (far too bundled up for the weather) and was pushing a grocery cart, crippled by a broken wheel, and heaped high with a variety of bags and other odds and ends.

There was something about her, as she trundled forward, head down low. I found myself watching her as I pushed my own cart, also loaded with bags, to my car.

Suddenly, she stopped. Her head snapped up and she looked at me. I could see her eyes widen, almost like she recognized me.

Luckily, we had just reached the car. I ducked my head and opened the trunk. There was something unsettling about her, something I couldn't put a finger on. I quickly loaded the groceries, not wanting to look at her, afraid if I did, I'd see her hurrying to catch up to me, her cart making a racket on the concrete, that bad wheel spinning out of control, her face a picture of disgust, just like the two women in the diner. Maybe she would even start yelling at me.

I slammed the trunk down and pushed the cart at Chrissy to put away while I unlocked the car. To my surprise, she took it to one of those little cart corrals, while I got into the car. I needed to be safely inside before I looked at the homeless woman again.

But she wasn't looking at me anymore. She was moving away from us, head down, lips moving like she was muttering to herself.

As Chrissy got into the passenger seat and slammed the door, I watched the homeless woman go, wondering if she would look at me again. But she didn't. She seemed completely oblivious.

Had I imagined the whole thing?

I shook my head to clear it, and drove home. Chrissy immediately jumped out of the car and disappeared, so I found myself tackling the groceries and the kitchen by myself, which actually turned out to be okay—I dug out my iPod and mini speakers and got some music going, rolled up my sleeves, and dug in.

Seeing my old friend Mia and getting some food into my stomach (and coffee, of course, oh thank God for coffee) had put me in a much better mood. I was ready to make the best of a bad situation … well, maybe "bad" was too strong a word. Maybe "difficult" was more fitting. Either way, I was excited to turn the house into a warm and loving home—the perfect nurturing cocoon to reconnect our little family.

I was knee-deep in dust and grime but making pretty good headway on organizing and sorting and cleaning when the doorbell rang, startling me, causing me to nearly drop a delicate wine glass etched with green vines and tiny purple flowers.

Oh God, that's probably Daniel. I carefully put the wine glass down and rubbed my hands against my old jean shorts as I glanced at the clock. It was a little after one o'clock. Why on earth had he come so soon? I looked helplessly around the kitchen—it was a mess. I was a mess. Well, there was nothing to be done about it, and besides, he had already seen me in the same outfit at the diner, albeit less filthy than it was at the moment.

But it wasn't Daniel. It was a woman. She was tall, as tall as I was, and slender to the point of being straight up and down. Her reddish-brown hair was pulled back haphazardly and stuffed into a clip; a few wisps had escaped and framed a strong, plain, but not unattractive face. She wore round, red glasses that matched the splatter of freckles across her cheeks and nose.

When she saw me, her face broke into a huge smile that completely lit her up, making her almost beautiful. "Becca! It really is you!"

There it was again. That twist of pain inside me, the automatic denial rising to my lips. *I'm not Becca anymore. Becca died when I was sixteen.*

I opened my mouth, and found myself asking "Daphne?"

She grabbed me in a big hug.

"I missed you," she said into my ear. I hugged her hard as an answer. She had a comforting smell, like lavender and lemongrass.

She let go and squeezed my arm. "I know I just dropped by, but do you have a minute to chat? We have so much to catch up on."

"Of course, just as long as you can excuse the mess." I led her back into the kitchen. Just like old times.

She stopped at the doorway. "Wow. Nothing much has really changed, has it?"

"No, it really hasn't," I agreed. Even with the clutter and dust, it still felt like Aunt Charlie was going to swoop in any moment, offer us tea and maybe cookies, and tell Daphne she simply MUST stay for dinner. A sharp and intense wave of sadness flooded over me, taking my breath away for a moment.

Could my aunt really have been a monster?

As if reading my mind, Daphne said "I'm just waiting for her to offer me some tea."

That snapped me out of my thoughts. "Is that a hint?"

Daphne laughed. "Well, I wouldn't say 'no'."

I filled up the teakettle and put on the stove, then started hunting through her drawers. "I haven't actually found her special tea blends," I said apologetically. "Although I did buy some tea today."

"Whatever is easiest," Daphne said, picking her way over to the butcher-block kitchen table and sitting down. Thank goodness I had already scrubbed it down. "Although she may roll in her grave if you serve supermarket tea from her tea pot."

"Lucky for me, the graveyard is a good distance away from here, so I won't see the damage." I dug the wild orange herbal tea out of the cupboard.

"You know," Daphne said, staring at the kitchen window. "All her tea blends are probably out there." She waved to the garden. "Even if you can't find anything in here, she may have notes somewhere. Maybe you could recreate them."

I plucked out a couple of mismatched mugs, a red one covered with flowers, and one with the cartoon character Maxine on it that I recalled Aunt Charlie getting as a joke from one of her clients. I quickly washed them. "Yeah, I'm sure that's true. Too bad I have a black thumb."

Daphne laughed. "You do not. You spent your entire summer out in that garden. Well, when you weren't painting, that is."

That stopped me short. Me, garden? In New York, I couldn't even keep a houseplant alive for more than a few weeks. My mother used to sigh with displeasure when she came to my apartment—she was a big believer in having something living and green to complete the design of a living space. I didn't even want to think about how many plants I had sent to an early grave in my attempts to please her. I had finally broken down and bought a few plastic plants.

Which I would then forget to dust.

Putting my New York mishaps aside, now that Daphne brought it up, I could remember digging in the garden, the warm soil between my fingers—the rich, almost green smell of things growing and blooming.

Aunt Charlie had shaken her head in amazement when I coaxed a few of her herbs back, after a particularly destructive thunderstorm. I remembered her telling me I had a green thumb. And it seemed I did.

Until I returned home from the hospital. After that, I couldn't grow a weed.

I gave my head a quick shake, finished the tea, and sat at the table with Daphne.

"So, tell me everything," she said.

I shrugged, blowing on my tea to cool it. "Not a lot to tell, I'm afraid. I'm married and have a sixteen-year-old stepdaughter."

"What made you come back here?"

I was silent. Behind Daphne, I could see the wind tossing the leaves and branches in the overgrown garden. I opened my mouth and found myself telling her everything. How after I divorced my first husband, I had to go back to work and ended up in Stefan's law firm, which is how we started dating, and eventually married nine months ago. How the firm was struggling financially, and how Stefan suspected an embezzler, but couldn't prove it yet, so he was working extra-hard and extra-long to save the practice and build a case against the embezzler. How Aunt Charlie willed me her house free and clear, and as Stefan hadn't taken a paycheck for months, we had no choice but to move.

Daphne laid her hand on mine. "He didn't tell you." It wasn't a question.

I shook my head. "Not until it was too late, and we had lost our apartment. He said he didn't want to worry me, and he thought it was temporary. He thought he'd be able to fix it, but ..." I sighed. "It's not like I could support us in New York. Assuming I even could get hired, after not working for a year."

Daphne sipped her tea. "So, I take it you aren't painting, either."

I felt that same stab of pain in my gut I'd felt when Daniel had mentioned painting, and gave her a twisted smile. "I haven't painted in years. And now that I'm here, I have all of this," I waved my hand around the kitchen, "to clean and organize, and once that's done, I'll have to figure out what needs to happen to sell the house. If it turns out we're going to be here for a while, I may also have to start looking for a job." My stomach twisted inside at the thought. I had never liked any of the jobs I had, even though I had tried many different things over

the years—everything from waitressing to bartending to department sales clerk to legal secretary. I even had a stint working as
a stagehand in an off-Broadway production. But, every job I had
made me feel like I was slowly suffocating … like I was a butterfly trapped in a killing jar, frantically beating its wings against
the glass. And the only way to wash that feeling away? With
copious amounts of wine. Every day.

Oh God, I so didn't want to go back to that.

I swallowed hard, and pushed that thought down—if that's
what it came down to, I could handle it for a short time. It was a
small price to pay to keep Stefan happy and our family financially secure. Stefan was working so hard, he likely needed a little
break, and if my small income helped put food on the table,
then I could do that. It wouldn't be a big deal, and I'd only need
to do it until we got our feet back under us. After all, Stefan
didn't want me working either. He liked having me available to
host client dinners and accompany him to parties and events,
which would be more difficult to do if I had some other job.

No, IF (and it was a big IF) I had to go back to work, it
wouldn't be for very long.

Daphne stirred her tea and looked out the window. "That's
a bummer you aren't painting. I always loved your work. But, I
guess I shouldn't be surprised you aren't. None of us are doing
what we thought we would be. Everything changed that night
you … Jessica …" she trailed off.

"Oh God, Daphne." I dropped my mug with a clatter, my
hands rising to cover my mouth. "What must you think of me?
I'm so sorry I never reached out to let you know I was okay after
that night. I should have …"

"I'm not here for an apology," Daphne gently interrupted
me. "Besides, there's nothing to be sorry about. We knew you
were alive; your aunt told us. And, after that night, I don't think
anyone blamed you for not coming back. Especially with all the
questions swirling around about what happened to Jessica."

"So, no one knows what happened to her *still*?"

Daphne shook her head. "Nope. But that doesn't mean everyone doesn't have an opinion. There are those, not many but

a few, who still believe she just ran away and someday will just reappear—walk into Aunt May's with some really good explanation about why it's been fifteen years and she couldn't pick up the phone or drop a postcard into the mail to let everyone know she's okay. But they're the minority. Most people don't think she's coming back."

She paused, and her eyes drifted to the window. I found myself wanting to ask what she thought happened to Jessica, but the words seemed to stick in my throat. The silence stretched out into something unrecognizable. As much as I wanted to break it, a part of me felt like I would be intruding on a deeply-private and personal pain, so I stayed quiet, instead picking up my cup to swallow some rapidly-cooling tea. Right as it touched my lips, a particularly loud creak from above startled me, and I spilled it instead.

Daphne looked up at me, the strange spell seemingly broken, a mischievous grin on her face. "I see Mad Martha is still alive and well."

Something dreadful stirred inside me. I sucked in my breath. "Mad Martha?"

She looked at me incredulously. "Don't tell me you don't remember? We have our own little haunted house here in Redemption, and you're living in it!"

A wisp of white nightgown disappearing into Chrissy's room.

All of a sudden, pieces began to click together, and I really didn't like the picture they were creating. I especially didn't like all the holes in that picture. I needed someone to help me fill in those holes and tell me what I had forgotten.

I eyed Daphne. Could she be that person? I wasn't particularly proud of what had happened that night, nor did I like talking about it, but if I wanted help with the holes in my memory, I was going to have to tell someone.

And, besides, with the way Daphne and I were connecting right now, it was like we had picked up exactly where we had left off fifteen years ago. "I lost my memory."

Daphne blinked at me. "You what?"

I smiled self-consciously. "Yeah, sounds sort of stupid, out loud like that."

"Not stupid," Daphne corrected, pressing her lips together thoughtfully. "Just … surprising. I wasn't expecting you to say that. How much do you remember?"

"It's slowly coming back. In bits and pieces."

"What happened?"

I swallowed. "After that night," I didn't need to tell her which night I was talking about, "after they … stabilized me, they ended up moving me to a psychiatric ward." I couldn't meet her eyes. I was still pretty humiliated about that time in my life. "I was … pretty hysterical. I'm not sure how long I stayed in the hospital, but by the time they discharged me, I had blanked out the entire summer. Actually, I pretty much lost all memories of all my visits here."

I sneaked a glance at Daphne. She was looking at me with such compassion, I could feel my eyes start to tear up. I hurried to continue my story. "The doctors said the amnesia was probably temporary and my memories would eventually return, but they recommended I work with a therapist. My mother, on the other hand, thought my amnesia was a gift from God, and did everything she could to keep my memory blocked. Everyone was forbidden to talk to me about that summer, or my aunt, or really anything that could trigger my memory. I wasn't shown pictures. I was told to put it all out of my mind."

I paused, drew my finger through the puddle of my spilled tea on the table. "And, God help me, a part of me wanted that, too."

Daphne reached out and squeezed my hand. "So, you went along with it."

I nodded. "It wasn't until we got back here that my memory started returning. I thought it had all returned, except for that night, but I guess there's still some holes."

"You must remember that one party by the lake, right? The one where we went through a couple of cases of beer and ended up skinny-dipping?" She took one look at my face and burst out laughing. "No, that never happened. At least, not the skinny-dipping part."

I sagged in my seat. "I can hear everyone in Redemption breathing a sigh of relief."

She laughed. "Oh stop. You were so cute. No one would be breathing a sigh of relief."

"Not like if it happened now, of course."

Daphne playfully punched me in the arm. "That's not what I meant. Anyway, I'm not entirely surprised you don't remember that night. You were pretty wasted the last time I saw you. But I didn't know you had blanked out the whole summer as well."

I blinked. "You were with me that night?"

She nodded. "We all were. We were having a farewell party. Summer was pretty much over. You were going back to New York in a few days. Jessica and Mia were supposed to leave the next day for California. They were going to be staying with some of Jessica's cousins. I think they were cousins—they were related somehow to Jessica. She wanted to scope out the modeling scene. Remember how much she wanted to be a model? And Mia was going to go to school at Stanford. I'm still not sure how they actually planned to be in California together, since Jessica really needed to be in LA for modeling and Stanford is up in the Bay area, but they had some complicated plan worked out."

"And then Jessica's mom cancelled the trip," I said suddenly.

Daphne half-smiled. "Ah, so you remember."

I shook my head. "No, not really. It's still a black hole. But, I can remember that. How furious Jessica was."

And, boy, was she furious. Jessica was drop dead gorgeous—long, silky blonde hair with the perfect peaches-and-cream complexion and large, green eyes fringed with long, black lashes. But that day she was in such a rage, her skin was colored by two spots of red, high up on her cheekbones. I remember thinking how unfair it was that even a furious Jessica was a beautiful Jessica.

"Why did her mom cancel?" I asked.

Daphne shook her head. "I don't know. I think it had something to do with Jessica's uncle leaving town without a word all those years ago. We must have told you about that, how Jessica's mother had a huge fight with her brother and he just up and left. Never heard from him again. Anyway, I can't quite remember exactly what happened—I wish I did, but after the entire night blew up with you almost dying, and Jessica disappearing, and Mia upset, it went out of my head."

The pieces continued to click together inside my mind, and I found myself saying, "And then, when Jessica didn't show up at her cousin's ..."

Daphne nodded. "You got it. Then, we knew something happened to her. But what? Was it as simple as her not going to her cousin's after all? Or did something happen to her while she was on the road? And why didn't she at least tell Mia she was leaving?"

I fiddled with my mug. "So, what happened then?"

"We got the police involved, and they investigated but didn't find anything. It certainly looked as if she just up and left—her clothes were gone, but where she went, no one knows. Her mother hired a private investigator as well, but he didn't have any more luck than the police. It was like she just vanished into thin air."

There was another creak upstairs, this one sounding exactly like the footsteps that had kept me up the night before.

Footsteps.

A wisp of white nightgown disappearing into Chrissy's room.

Mad Martha.

Jessica vanishing.

I shivered. "Maybe a ghost got her."

Daphne smiled. "Don't think that wasn't a popular theory back then. Actually, come to think about it, there's probably more than a few folks who still believe that's what happened to her. Mad Martha on the prowl, or maybe Nellie."

"Nellie?"

Daphne shook her head. "I guess you really don't remember." She sat back in her chair, straightened her back and got a serious look on her face. "Listen up. It's story time and Aunt Daphne is going to tell you all about it."

I smiled despite myself, even though on the inside I was feeling colder and colder.

"A Mr. Edward Blackstone built this house for his lovely, blushing bride, Martha. Edward had made a bunch of money in something, manufacturing? Or maybe it was railroads? I can't remember. Anyway, Martha and Edward moved in, and all seemed well for years, until they hired a young maid named Nellie. By all accounts, Nellie was strikingly beautiful, and it didn't take too long for her to catch Edward's eye."

Daphne paused for effect and swirled the leftover tea in her cup. It was probably as cold as mine, but I was too transfixed to get up for more hot water. "It's not really clear what the relationship was between Nellie and Edward. Some say they were having a full-blown affair; some say the attraction was all on Edward's side and Nellie didn't return Edward's, ahem, *affections*. Still others say Nellie was the one who was doing all the flirting, to get Edward to leave his wife for her. And some say absolutely nothing was going on, and it was all in Martha's head."

"But, regardless of what the truth was between Edward and Nellie, everyone agrees that one night, Martha just snapped. She killed Nellie. Stabbed her with a kitchen knife in one of the rooms upstairs. Then she killed herself."

I sucked in my breath, the cold inside me shifting to something dark and nasty. "Killed herself?"

"Hung herself."

I closed my eyes briefly. "Oh God, that's horrible."

Daphne nodded. "And ever since, both Martha and Nellie are said to haunt this old place." She made a broad, sweeping gesture with her hand.

I shivered again, seeing what I thought was a white nightgown disappear into Chrissy's bedroom.

She noticed my shiver and smiled. "And that story is even spookier at night."

I half-smiled, trying to shake the sense of uneasiness that was growing more intense by the minute. I was missing something, something big—I could feel it. It was right there on the tip of my tongue, like a word that kept sliding out of my mouth's grasp, but I just couldn't put my finger on it.

Maybe Daphne would know—after all, this could be another lost piece of my memory that my mind hadn't decided to cough up yet. Maybe I should ask her, and while I was at it, I could even tell her about the pacing I heard, and what I saw disappearing into Chrissy's room. If nothing else, maybe we could have a good laugh over it, and that would deflate the anxiousness inside me.

But as I was opening my mouth to tell her, she glanced over at the clock above the stove. "Oh, I didn't realize it was so late. I should probably get going—my mom will wonder what happened."

I got up with her, not sure if I welcomed or resented the distraction. Did I really want to talk about it?

At the door, she hugged me again. "I'm really glad you're back. Come by anytime. I'm still just around the corner, practically your neighbor."

Neighbor? Suddenly I remembered what Mia had said this morning. "Wait a minute. You're still living at home with your mom?"

I regretted my words the instant they were out of my mouth, but Daphne simply smiled sadly. "Yeah. What would our sixteen-year-old selves have thought if they could see us now?" She squeezed my arm. "I really do need to get going. My mom, well … she's not well. It's easier if I'm home."

Daphne living at home … Mia a waitress at a coffee shop … Daniel a cop. The weight of that night, the night Jessica disappeared, draped over me, suffocating me. I had thought that night had ruined *my* life.

Jessica's disappearance had ruined an entire town.

I looked at Daphne, her plain face full of compassion and sadness, her kind eyes, and at that moment I felt like I was exactly where I was supposed to be. "I'm glad I'm back, too," I said, and I meant it. Even though I knew it was only temporary, it didn't mean I couldn't connect and rekindle our friendship while I was here. "And the next time we talk, I definitely want to hear what happened to everyone. Although today I guess I'll get a head start with Daniel."

Daphne cocked her head. "Daniel? What do you mean?"

"He's stopping over, later today. Wants to talk to me. Wouldn't say about what." I rolled my eyes as I said it. "We just got here yesterday, so we couldn't possibly have done anything wrong. At least not yet."

She stared at me, her eyes suddenly serious. "He's coming here? No, he couldn't possibly ..." She looked away as her voice trailed off.

Suddenly, I had trouble breathing. The sick, uneasy feeling rose up like bile in my throat, and I forced myself to swallow it back down. "What? Do you know something?"

She squared herself and looked back at me. "I keep forgetting—you don't remember. Becca, Jessica was here that night. Our farewell party was here."

The room suddenly shifted. I felt dizzy and lightheaded. "Here?" I found myself asking, my voice sounding far away.

Daphne nodded slowly. "Yes. This was the last place she was seen before she disappeared. And you were the last person to see her."

Chapter 5

I sat on the couch for a while after Daphne left, trying not to hyperventilate or pass out. I was dizzy and nauseous, and could feel the edges of a panic attack starting to overwhelm me. Worse, my head was beginning to pound again.

What did it mean that Jessica was at the house that night? And that *I* was the last one to see her?

It certainly couldn't mean I had anything to do with her disappearance ... could it?

Absolutely not, I told myself firmly. After all, according to Daphne, I had already been pretty wasted. For heaven's sake, I had ended up in the hospital almost dying from alcohol poisoning. I wouldn't have been in any shape to do anything to anyone.

Then why were you hysterical in the hospital anytime anyone brought up that night? a little voice asked (a pretty nasty little voice, I might add). *What would you have to be hysterical about?*

I had no answer. Just that growing sense of unease—that there was something very wrong going on, along with that gnawing feeling that I was missing something important.

What I probably needed was some food. It was well past lunchtime, after all. Food and maybe another cup of tea. That would help me get back on track.

I went into the kitchen, put the kettle back on and pulled out the gluten-free wraps Chrissy had talked me into buying at the store. I had no idea what they would taste like but, well, they were gluten-free, which seemed to satisfy Chrissy. I assembled turkey, provolone, avocado, lettuce, and tomato for two—even if Chrissy didn't want something, we could have it later.

I called Chrissy, made tea, and sat at the kitchen table to eat.

Chrissy eventually appeared, wolfing down her wrap and announcing she was going out. As I tried to decide on the correct response—do I insist she stay to help me unpack, or grill her on where she was going and when she would be back? —she disappeared out the door.

I sighed. Maybe it was easier that way.

I finished my wrap (feeling a lot better once I had some food in my stomach) and jumped back into cleaning with my music turned up.

A sudden pounding startled me, and I banged my head against one of the cabinets. Swearing under my breath, I sat back on my heels and realized how late it had gotten. The sun was setting, and dark shadows stretched across the kitchen.

The pounding started up again, and I almost fell over trying to get to my feet.

It was Daniel. He was standing at the backdoor, rapping on the glass, his face shadowed by the setting sun. I turned off the music and flipped on the light before heading over to let him in. The backdoor was in the mudroom, which housed a big, rust-stained sink and the ancient-looking washer and dryer—hopefully they both still worked. While I could hang things outside in a pinch, I really didn't want to buy a new washer right now. The working surface still had traces of dirt and extra plant pots stacked on it.

I kicked a bunch of mismatched boots and shoes out of the way before reaching for the knob. The door stuck, and I had to fight with it for a few long seconds before wrenching it open. A cool breeze blew in, making me feel grimy. I was again aware of the fact that I was in need of a shower. It didn't help that Daniel looked pressed and composed, in his clean uniform.

"You didn't answer your front door," he said.

I held the door open even wider, gesturing him inside. "Sorry, I didn't hear it. Unpacking."

I led him back through the mudroom, past the closed door to the basement, and into the kitchen, where he stopped in the doorway. "Wow," he said, looking around. "Feels like old times."

I looked around myself, and was actually pretty impressed by what I had accomplished. The kitchen virtually sparkled in the late afternoon sun—predominantly white and grey with cheery accents of red, yellow, and happy sunflowers. Aunt Charlie loved sunflowers, and they were everywhere—on canisters, decorative plates, a glass pitcher, and salt-and-pepper shakers. You could always count on a few real sunflowers from her garden in a vase, as well, when she had been there to cut them. During my organizing, I had found and washed the vase. Maybe at some point, I'd venture outside to see if there were any still growing.

I had kept more of my aunt's things than I had expected to. As I went through them, I realized I liked Aunt Charlie's mismatched dishes and utensils more than the elegant, yet coldly-impersonal items Stefan and I had brought from New York.

I wasn't sure if Stefan would approve.

He will, I said firmly to myself. *He just needs to see how warm and cozy it is for himself.* I made a mental note to fill the kitchen with sunflowers before he came home. Nobody could resist sunflowers.

"Do you want to sit down?" I waved to the butcher-block table. "Can I get you something to drink?" As soon as I said it, I wanted to stuff it back in my mouth. This wasn't a social call. Daniel still had his uniform on, which had to mean he was there as a cop. And that couldn't be a good thing.

His eyebrows quirked up. "Are you offering me tea?" A ghost of a smile was on his lips.

I found myself starting to smile in response. "That IS what this kitchen is known for."

"If it's not too much trouble." He sauntered over to sit at the table.

A wave of self-consciousness washed over me as I started heating the water and pulling the cups out of the cupboard. I still had no idea why he stood me up all those years ago. Part of me wanted to say something. But what if we had talked about it, and I just didn't remember? From the looks of him, it certainly didn't appear that he felt we had any unfinished business. In fact, he'd probably completely forgotten about the whole encounter. I pictured myself casually asking, "So, since you're here, I always wondered why you stood me up fifteen years ago?" and having him stare at me in complete befuddlement. "What?

I don't remember … oh, that's right. Sorry about that. I had forgotten all about it."

Yeah, I was definitely keeping my mouth shut.

Instead, I busied myself with the task of tea making, keeping my head down so I didn't have to look at him. "Unfortunately, the tea is store bought—I haven't found her blends yet," I said, keeping my voice light.

He didn't answer, so I chanced a quick peek from under my lashes. He was standing by the window, staring out into the overgrown garden, probably remembering "the good old days" with Aunt Charlie—all the fresh fruit and veggies and tea from her famous garden. Probably wishing she were there instead of me. "I'm sure it's fine—even if Charlie would have found it blasphemous."

"Yeah, that's what Daphne said, too."

He turned to look at me. "Oh, was Daphne here?"

I mentally kicked myself. *Daniel isn't your friend,* I reminded myself. *He's a cop.* Never mind whatever happened to us as kids. It didn't make him any less of a cop. And after all these years of living with attorneys, one thing that had been drilled into me was to say as little as possible to anyone opposing you. Especially if that person's a cop. The less Daniel knew about my life, the better. I didn't want to give him any ammunition to weasel more information out of me than what I wanted to share. "Yeah, she stopped in to say 'hi.'" I carried a tray loaded with tea, sugar, and cream over to the table, and plunked it down in the center.

He accepted the mug, and I chose a seat across from him, trying not to focus on the silence of the house. "Are you stopping in to say 'hi,' too?"

He put the mug down. "Not exactly. I have a few questions for you."

My heart started pounding. I took a sip of tea to compose myself. "Questions? You do know I just got here yesterday, right?" Was he going to bring up why he stood me up?

"This isn't about anything recent. I want to ask you about the night Jessica disappeared."

I put my mug down carefully, alarm bells going off inside me. This couldn't be good. "That was a long time ago."

He nodded. "Yes, but we still don't know what happened to her."

I played with my mug, spinning it around on the table. "I don't know how I could possibly add anything new at this point."

"You may be surprised. Sometimes just talking about it can shake something loose."

I shook my head. "I don't think that's the case with me. I haven't thought about that night in years. And don't forget I almost died."

"I remember." His voice was short, clipped. I finally raised my head and met his intense, flat stare. He was judging me. I could feel a spark of anger start to glow inside me.

"I was sixteen," I made my voice match his short tone. "I was stupid and had too much to drink. That hardly makes me a reliable witness, even if it wasn't fifteen years ago."

"We were all sixteen. We were all stupid. But, one of us is still missing."

What was that supposed to mean? "You think that's my fault?"

"*Is* it your fault?"

Rebecca, get a hold of yourself. Remember, you're talking to a cop. I sat back in my chair and folded my arms. "Don't give me that cop double talk. You wouldn't be here if you didn't think I knew something."

He shifted in his chair, leaning back as well. "Maybe I do. But I never said I think it was your fault."

There was something in his tone, in the way he watched me, that made me want to defend myself, to explain why I went back to New York without another word. *I shouldn't need to explain myself to Daniel, he's the one who should be apologizing to me. He stood me up after all.* Instead, I focused on picking up my tea and attempting to drink, but my throat had closed, and I almost choked.

Daniel looked at me with a strange mixture of concern and suspicion. "Are you okay?"

I wiped my mouth with the back of my hand. "I'm fine. It's just ... look, I really don't think I can help."

He studied me in silence, his expression unreadable. The late afternoon sun slanted across his face, highlighting the gold in his dark blonde hair, and turning his eyes an even deeper blue. The silence of the house seemed to press against us, and I was suddenly aware that we were alone.

He pushed his mug across the table, the grating sound breaking the spell of the moment. "Think about it. I've read the police report from that night, so I know what you told the cops at the time. I just have a few more questions."

I blinked at him stupidly. Police report? What I told the cops? I didn't have any memory of telling the cops anything. In fact, what I did remember was quite the opposite. I had a very clear memory of my mother blocking the door to my hospital room with her body, ordering the cops to leave me alone—that I needed time to recover, and she would NOT let them upset me.

What the hell was going on? Did I talk to them later and I blocked that out, too? And what *did* I tell them?

He was clearly waiting for me to say something, still watching me with that unreadable expression—did I look guilty to him? I nodded, and agreed to think about it.

He thanked me for the tea and I saw him to the door. He left without a word or a glance. I returned to the kitchen, thinking that I probably should figure something out for dinner. But instead, I found myself mulling about the festering nature of secrets, as I stared out the window at the garden. I watched the shadows start to deepen and lengthen, until it resembled something more twisted, like a nightmare's garden.

What secrets had I buried there, years ago?

Chapter 6

I texted Chrissy to find out where she was, and if she was coming home for dinner. Even as I was typing, I felt like I was giving away my power, *asking* her to come home rather than telling her. But what on earth could I do? I didn't have a clue where she might be, or who she could be with, so it wasn't like I could physically go get her and drag her home. And she *was* sixteen, after all. Yet, that didn't change how I felt like a whiny stepmother with every keystroke.

It was going to be a really long summer.

I thought about texting or calling Stefan, but kept stopping myself. He had said he would call me, and he tended to get irritated when I didn't wait for him to reach out first. Plus, he was already frustrated with me when he left, and I didn't want to make things worse. Part of the point of being here was to turn our marriage around, and the best way to do that was to focus on what I could actually do—namely, turn this house into a beautiful home he would love living in.

Until we sold it, that was.

Well, regardless, living in a cozy, warm home even temporarily would be a good start to fixing our relationship.

Besides, I had more than enough on my plate already, between getting this house in shape and Chrissy.

God, what was I going to do with her?

While I was staring at my phone wondering what to do next, Chrissy texted back, asking what I was making for dinner.

What the hell? What am I, a short order cook?

Enough of that, Rebecca. I took a deep breath. *Remember who the grown-up is here.*

Too bad I didn't feel much like one.

I typed back *I'm thinking something light, like a Cobb salad,* which I knew was her favorite. Apparently, I wasn't above bribery to get her home without a fight.

I stared at my phone, willing her to text back. No response.

So much for bribery.

I sighed, and went into the kitchen to start pulling the Cobb salad together. I poured myself a glass of wine while I was at it. It'd been a hell of a few days.

In the middle of chopping tomatoes, my phone rang. Was it finally Stefan? I wiped my hands down and hurried to the phone. No, not Stefan. But my disappointment quickly evaporated.

"CB! Is that really you?"

"The one and the same," my cousin's voice answered, sounding faintly amused.

I gripped the phone tightly. "Oh my God, I can't tell you how happy I am to hear your voice."

CB was my only cousin on my mother's side. He was also my biggest supporter and cheerleader, always managing to show up at the perfect time with a bottle of some sort of alcoholic beverage, getting me to laugh, even during the darkest of times. Although, in the case of this move, there had been no laughter—only fighting about the massive mistake he said I was making. It was one of the only times he and my mother had been in perfect agreement.

"Are you finally seeing the light? Ready to admit that your favorite cos was right when he told you it was a bad idea to move to Hicksville?" He paused to sigh dramatically—I could almost see him rolling his eyes—"Alas, you just wouldn't listen."

I sighed. "Oh, CB don't start. I've had a dreadful time out here."

His voice softened. "That bad, huh?"

"The worst." I picked up my glass of wine and carried it over to the kitchen table.

"Tell your cousin all about it—I'm ready for all the gory details. And don't hold back—especially on any juicy bits of gossip."

Aunt Charlie never had children of her own, but her two sisters liked to unload their children on her during the summer, so they could jet off to their lavish European vacations. CB was an only child, but I had two older brothers, both of whom hated it in Redemption, and did everything possible to stay in New York. I, however, had always been more comfortable with Aunt Charlie than I was with anyone else in my family, so much to my mother's chagrin, there came a time when I preferred being with Aunt Charlie and didn't even want to return to New York. After *That Night*, I sometimes got the feeling my mother was glad it happened—not because she wanted me to suffer, but because she didn't want Aunt Charlie influencing me anymore.

I settled myself in a position that allowed me to watch the daylight drain away, and took a sip of my wine. "Well, I saw Mia and Daphne. Mia is a waitress at Aunt May's Diner. And Daphne is still living at home, taking care of her mother."

"Really?" CB sounded surprised. "Mia and Daphne are still there? I was sure both of them would fast-track it out of that town."

I found myself strangely reluctant to talk about how Jessica's disappearance seemed to have left this town frozen in grief and pain. "They're not the only ones. Daniel's here too—he's a cop."

"Daniel is a cop? Did you ask to see his handcuffs?"

"Very funny. No, but he did come here to ask me a few questions." Crap, why did I say *that*? I didn't want to talk about my conversation with Daniel at all, and now here I was, setting myself up to talk about it.

"What questions? Was there a strip search involved?"

"Very funny. No, he wanted to talk about Jessica."

There was a pause. "Now, there's a blast from the past. Why did he want to talk about her?" His voice had shifted, was no longer teasing.

"He didn't tell me, but I think he's still investigating her disappearance."

"So, there's no new information."

I swirled my wine around. "Nope."

"Then why did he want to talk to you?" Now there was an edge in his voice, exactly the way he sounded back in New York, when we were fighting about my pending move.

"He wanted me to tell him what I remembered about that night."

"And, what do you remember?"

What on earth was going on with him? "Christ, CB. You *know* what I remember. Nothing. Why the inquisition?"

He growled. "Because this whole thing was a really bad idea. The last thing you need right now is to be interrogated about that night. I can't believe Stefan did that to you. Is he even there?"

I was silent.

He made a disgusted sound. "I knew it. I gotta go."

"CB, wait." I didn't want him to hang up angry. Suddenly, I just couldn't stand it. Everyone I had talked to from home the past couple of days—Stefan, Chrissy, and now CB—I somehow managed to fight with, and I just couldn't take another one. "Don't be mad."

He took a deep breath. "It's not you. I just … well, you know what I think about this. Look, I really do have to go. I'll call you soon."

I heard voices in the background. Clearly, he was out on the town, which was par for the course for CB. He'd probably called me on his way to the latest trendy bar or club. I was hit with a sudden wave of envy—why, oh why couldn't I be back with him in New York, getting ready to have a mindless night of fun, instead of stuck in the awful mess I had stumbled into? "You promise?" I asked.

Now his voice sounded almost normal again. "When have I ever let you down? Be good."

He hung up. I stared at the phone for a long minute before putting it down. I felt even more depressed than I had before CB had called.

I was contemplating reaching out to Stefan when the phone rang. Finally, was it him? I eagerly looked at the screen only to feel my heart sink again. It was my mother.

Well, it's not like this day could possibly get any worse.

"Hi, mom."

"You were going to let me know you arrived there safely," my mother said, her voice faintly accusatory.

Deep breath. Maybe another sip of wine. "Sorry. It's been hectic."

"I can imagine. Moving halfway across the country is very stressful."

I closed my eyes. "Mom, don't."

"Don't what?"

"You know we didn't have much choice."

"Of course you had a choice! You could have moved in with us. We could have made it work."

Stefan would never agree, I wanted to say. *His pride wouldn't allow it.* I took another drink of wine. This was precisely why I hadn't wanted to talk to my mother. I hated fighting with her. I wanted to tell her the truth. That not only would it be too painful for Stefan, but it would also likely derail our already shaky marriage. But it also felt disrespectful to Stefan to share something that personal.

Instead, I repeated what Stefan had said when my parents had first brought up the option to move in with them. "But, this is a much more practical solution. There's a lot we have to do to get this house ready to put on the market, and it makes far more sense for us to live here while we do the work."

"It doesn't make any sense to commute between Wisconsin and New York."

"That's just temporary. Stefan will be able to set up a home office in a few weeks."

"Is he there now?"

My hand squeezed the wine glass so tightly I thought I might break it. I forced myself to breathe as I loosened my death grip. "Mom, we talked about this. He still has some things to finish up before he can work from here."

"I don't like the thought of you all alone out there."

I didn't either. But, there was no sense agreeing with her; she would just use that as a wedge. "Chrissy is here. Plus, some of my old friends still live in Redemption. So, I'm not all alone."

"He shouldn't be leaving you alone," she said firmly. "It's not right."

Again, I found myself agreeing with her. "It's only for a few weeks," I said again, wondering who I was actually trying to convince. "Then, he can work from here. And, if all goes well, we'll hopefully be back in New York before Christmas."

She sighed. "I just worry about you, Rebecca."

"I know." I was a little bit worried about me, too.

She continued like I hadn't said anything. "Out there, all alone, in that … *that* house. Rebecca, are you sure you're okay? Are you having nightmares?"

"Nightmares?" I blinked, startled at the change of direction. "Why would I have nightmares?"

She seemed flustered. "Well, because of what happened, of course. Who wouldn't have nightmares after what you went through? You shouldn't be alone in that house. It's just not safe. Stefan should be there with you. That's what husbands are supposed to do; they're supposed to be there with you. What about …"

This was not going well. "Mom," I cut her off. "I gotta go. Chrissy just walked in."

"Okay, but Rebecca, call me. I mean it. Especially if anything happens. I worry …"

"I really have to go. I promise, I'll call."

I quickly hung up before she could protest, sucking in deep breaths to try and calm myself in between gulps of wine. I checked my phone one more time, even though I knew it was a futile gesture, to see if either Stefan or Chrissy had tried to contact me.

No missed calls. No texts.

I rubbed my forehead, trying to force down all the doubts and worries that squirmed under the surface.

Stefan loved me. He was as committed to making our marriage work as I was. We just hit a little rocky patch. Nothing to be worried about. All normal couples hit rocky patches. It didn't mean they were headed for divorce. And, besides, Redemption was to be a fresh start to getting our marriage back on track. Right?

I blew the air out of my cheeks and stared at my empty wine glass, feeling completely, utterly alone.

Chapter 7

Shortly after I finished assembling the Cobb salad, Chrissy appeared. She gave me one-word answers to my questions as she wolfed down the salad, and then disappeared to her room, leaving me to clean up the kitchen alone.

Well, at least we weren't arguing. Finally, we'd had one conversation that didn't end in a fight. Chalk one up for the good side. Maybe I was on a roll.

I poured myself another glass of wine and cleaned up the kitchen. Eventually, Chrissy and I were going to have a little chat about household duties, but that would have to wait for another day. Today, all I wanted to do was crawl into bed with my book and my wine.

I had just finished loading the dishwasher when Stefan finally called.

It was a short conversation. He apologized for taking so long to get in touch with me, said things were pretty hectic at the office, and that he wasn't sure when, exactly, he'd be able to fly back, but assured me it would be as soon as he possibly could. He asked me a few questions about the house and Chrissy, before telling me he had to go, but would call again soon.

All in all, I found the conversation pretty dissatisfying.

I stood in the kitchen holding my wine, staring out the window, suddenly overwhelmed and exhausted by all the events over the past few days. I really should just go to bed. Start fresh tomorrow.

Except … I had yet to sleep on a bed in this house. I hadn't had the courage yet to venture up the stairs.

I left the kitchen and studied the couch. It didn't look all that inviting, and I didn't want a repeat of last night.

But, did I really want to be upstairs? Where I saw … absolutely nothing. A figment of my imagination.

Clutching my wine, I looked at the stairs, squared my shoulders and slowly started climbing.

I surveyed the hallway when I got to the top. Chrissy had taken the room at the far end of the hall—the room CB always had when he visited. It was next to the staircase that climbed to the loft-like space, which Aunt Charlie always called "The Studio," which was also where I used to spend most of my time, painting. On the other side of Chrissy's bedroom was the room Aunt Charlie called her "Magic Room," where she jokingly cast her spells, but in reality, was probably more like an office. If it was as I remembered, it would be full of herbs and dried flowers, complete with a mixing table and stacks of files and recipes. Maybe *that* was where I would find the recipe for the headache tea.

The next room, directly in front of the stairs, was a fairly-spacious bathroom with both a large tub and a shower, and next to the bathroom was "my" room—or at least, the one I always stayed in. At the end of the hall was Aunt Charlie's bedroom, which also had an adjoining bath.

All the doors were closed. The hall was silent. I couldn't even hear anything from Chrissy's room, although I could see the light on under the door. I figured she was listening to music on her headphones.

I studied the door leading to Aunt Charlie's room. Clearly, it was the master bedroom. It should be our room—mine and Stefan's. I was sure Stefan would expect me to set it up for us.

Yet, I hesitated. It still felt like Aunt Charlie's room to me, and I hadn't sorted out my feelings about her yet. If anything, the longer I was in her house, the more confused I became. If only I had the clarity I had felt back in New York, when I was fairly confident that she was the cause of all the bad things that had happened to me that summer. To my own surprise, I found myself … conflicted. My emotions didn't match what I had been told. And, with no memory of that night, I didn't know what was right.

I opened the door to my old room, instead.

Other than the dust, grime, and overall stuffiness, it was exactly how I remembered.

One big (filthy) window overlooked part of the backyard. Dusty purple curtains matched the purple and blue log cabin quilt that made up the queen-sized bed. Two nightstands with matching blue pottery lamps, a dresser, and a bookshelf completed the furnishing. Standing there, I smelled the dust burning on the hot light bulbs.

I went to the window, and coerced it open with a bit of forceful yanking, allowing the fresh, cool breeze to rush in.

I could sleep here, I thought. I needed to wash the sheets, but was ok with throwing a clean blanket over the quilt for the night, and using pillows from the couch. That would work just fine.

I went back downstairs, grabbed the pillows and some of my personal items, and quickly made the bed. Then, I took a long, hot, much-needed shower, feeling the tension in my neck and shoulders dissolve in the steamy heat.

After my shower, I knocked on Chrissy's door to say goodnight. She was laying on her bed, headset on, phone in hand. She barely acknowledged me, and I closed the door.

One of these days, I knew I'd need to reach out to her—to try and have a conversation. One of these days.

I got into bed with my book, but only read a few sentences before I found myself drifting off, unable to concentrate on what I was reading, my eyes closing.

I forced myself to open them to turn out the light, and found myself in the kitchen, the light of the moon spilling in through the windows, filling the room with an eerie, soft, white glow. Aunt Charlie was busy at the stove.

"About time you came back, Becca," she said, adjusting the teakettle. "And I must say you did a splendid job cleaning the kitchen. Definitely worth the wait."

I blinked. "Aunt Charlie?"

She made a "tsk tsk" sound. "No question you've been gone too long. Of course, it's me. Where else would I be?" She hummed to herself as she started preparing tea. I could hear the clanking of the cups and saucers, as she stirred and measured and poured.

"But … aren't you dead?"

She laughed. "What a question! Is that the best you can ask me, dear?" She brought the tea to the butcher-block table and set the cup in front of me.

I stared at the blue, chipped pottery mug filled with tea. It was my favorite when I was growing up. I loved the play between the clay texture and elegant shape. Even the chip in the handle somehow added to its charm. Of course, Aunt Charlie would remember it as my favorite.

I could actually smell tea—the aroma of flowers and herbs, and feel the heat rising from the cup. Somewhere inside me, I knew it had to be a dream … it *had* to be … but all my senses made it seem so real.

"Drink up, Becca," Aunt Charlie said, picking up her own tea. "You're going to need it."

Something in her tone stopped me. I could feel the hairs on the back of my neck raise. I looked at her. She was watching me, carefully, over her tea. But there was something in her gaze, something flat and hard, glinting like polished stones. It felt predatory. I shifted away from her. "What do you mean, I'm going to need it?"

She nodded to the cup. "Drink first."

I looked back down to the tea. It looked darker than before—almost black. The smell was so strong, it was almost overpowering. "What's in it?"

She smiled, showing a hint of very white teeth—far whiter than I remembered them. "Oh, you know me. A bit of this, a bit of that. It's for your own good."

Something clicked inside me. *It's for your own good.* Where had I heard that before? And why did it make me instantly afraid?

"I don't want any tea."

She sighed. "Always a stubborn one. I blame my sister. She was stubborn, too. And about all the wrong things."

The smell of the tea was making me dizzy. Even odder, I was starting to feel an overwhelming urge to drink it. I closed my eyes and tried to take a deep breath, but the smell overwhelmed me. I could almost taste it—strong with a hint of bitterness and a touch of sweetness. Oh God, did I want to drink it.

I opened my eyes. Aunt Charlie was staring at me, that slight smile back on her face, those white teeth gleaming in the moonlight. "You want to, don't you?" Her voice purred low and deep in her throat, like a soft seduction.

I shook my head fiercely. Her smile grew wider, showing more of those white teeth.

White, pointed teeth.

I blinked hard, and tried to get up—to push away from the table and that tea that was compelling me to drink against my will, away from that sly, predatory smile with all those sharp, pointed teeth. But I couldn't move. My limbs felt thick and heavy, like I was underwater.

I heard a crash from above.

Aunt Charlie stopped smiling and looked at the ceiling. "Oh dear," she said. "Mad Martha again."

Another loud, hard crash.

I stared at Aunt Charlie, who was suddenly Aunt Charlie again. The predatory, toothy smile was gone, and there she was, looking old and worn out, her face seeming to fold in on itself. She stared at the ceiling, her eyes sad, and sipped her tea. "Mad Martha?" I asked.

She turned her gaze back to me. "The house is haunted, you know. Haunted in more ways than one." Her voice was sad. "We struggle and we fight, but in the end, it consumes us. It always does."

I opened my mouth to ask what she was talking about, but was silenced when all hell broke loose above me. Crashing. Screaming.

Aunt Charlie shook her head. "I really ought to make her some tea," she murmured to herself. "Chrissy, too."

Chrissy!

I sat straight up in bed, sweating, breathing heavily, a terrible scream trapped in my chest. Moonlight streamed through my window, cutting a swatch of pale light across the dark-blue carpet, leaching the color from it, and turning it a dark grey. The lamp next to my bed was off. I must have turned it off in my sleep.

I gulped down air and tried to slow my breathing. *It was a dream*, I told myself. *Only a dream.* I rubbed my chest, my memory showing me Aunt Charlie's sharp, predatory eyes in the moonlight, watching my every move, as if she were ready to pounce the moment I showed weakness ....

Crash.

Chrissy! I bolted out of bed and ran out of the room.

Her door stood wide open, moonlight pouring out and pooling in the hallway. I ran to her room, feeling my breath hitch in my chest, my sleep shirt sticky with sweat.

Her room was empty.

For a moment, all I could do was stand there, trying not to drown in the waves of panic that smashed against me. Oh God, where on earth was she? And what was that crash? Nothing in the room was touched. Did it even come from there?

I wheeled around and started flinging open doors, calling her name. She couldn't be downstairs. Not in the kitchen, sitting at that table with my aunt across from her, that *tea* in front of her.

She wasn't in the Magic Room or the bathroom. My aunt's room? Could I even open that door? Did I even want to? Oh God, what if it wasn't Chrissy in that room? What if there was … someone else waiting for me there?

I had no choice—I had to find Chrissy. I was just reaching for the knob when I heard another crash, echoing up from downstairs.

I bolted down the stairs, part of me relieved, because I didn't have to open that door after all.

I found Chrissy—standing in the part study, part library, part family room. It was a huge, strange, L-shaped room, having once been two separate rooms—a dining room and a family room/den. But Aunt Charlie couldn't stand the thought of a formal dining room, so she knocked the adjoining wall out and combined them. Lined with bookshelves holding dozens and dozens of books, the room housed two overstuffed couches, a big stone fireplace, a television that never seemed to work (Aunt Charlie wasn't much into television), and a sewing machine complete with a pile of my aunt's half-finished sewing projects.

Chrissy stood in front of the bookshelves, mindlessly yanking books out, dumping them on the ground and muttering to herself. The room was in chaos, as if vandals had been there—books strewn everywhere, tables turned over, lamps, picture frames, knickknacks, and more tossed about.

I opened my mouth to ask what in God's name she thought she was doing, but something about the numb, mechanical way she was moving made me close my mouth, and study her more closely. Her eyes were half-closed, her face smooth and pale, almost statue-like in the cold moonlight. Could she be sleepwalking?

I picked my way gingerly through the debris and broken glass, trying not to think about what had broken, to touch Chrissy's arm. She ignored me, but now that I was closer, I could hear the words she was muttering.

"Where is it? Where did it go? I know it's here somewhere."

I gently shook her arm. "Chrissy, let's go to bed."

Chrissy didn't really resist, but neither did she stop what she was doing. She continued muttering.

I grabbed her arm to stop her. She pulled against me, but without any real strength. "Chrissy," I said, trying to keep my voice calm. "You're sleepwalking. Let's go to bed."

She stopped and turned. Her half-lidded eyes were empty.

"You know."

Her voice was clear and sharp, a knife cutting through the stillness.

I felt a chill go down my spine, and shivered. "I know what?" I asked, realizing even as I said the words that it didn't make sense to have a conversation with a sleepwalker. Not to mention being dangerous. Hadn't I read somewhere that, if you woke a sleepwalker, something bad would happen to her?

She cocked her head. "The evil that was done."

I froze. Every hair on my body stood on end. The icy touch of fear crawled down my spine and into my stomach. I licked my lips, my mouth dry. "What are you talking about?" I asked, my voice barely above a whisper.

She kept staring at me, her eyes still empty, the moon casting dark shadows on her face. "Does it matter?"

My eyes widened. "Of course it matters," I said. "What evil? What was done? What are you talking about?"

She smiled at me then, and it was as empty and hollow as her eyes.

"It's right in front of your nose."

As I opened my mouth to question her again, her eyes suddenly rolled up into the back of her head, and she collapsed into my arms.

Chapter 8

I rocked gently in the porch swing, sipping my wine and watching the sun slowly set, turning the sky a fiery red. My hair was still damp from the shower, and since I had left it loose to dry, it curled around my face. I was wearing a dark yellow floral jumpsuit I always liked, because it turned my hazel eyes gold, and brought out the blonde highlights in my hair.

In that moment, I was pretty desperate to find something, *anything*, about myself that I could feel good about.

It had been a grueling two days. After Chrissy collapsed just two nights before, I nearly had a heart attack, sure I had some-how killed her. I held her on the floor, calling her name, strok-ing her hair, frantically trying to decide if I should leave her on the floor while I called 9-1-1, or stay with her, when she finally stirred, her eyelids fluttering, revealing those deep brown eyes that so reminded me of her father. Bedroom eyes. He had it in spades, and so did his daughter.

"Mom, is that you? What … what happened? Where am I?" It was like ten years had melted away—all her teenage bra-vado gone, leaving in its place a hurt, frightened child. My heart broke for her.

"No sweetheart, it's me. You were sleepwalking."

"Sleepwalking? What? Rebecca?" Her eyes started to focus, and she pushed away from me. "I don't sleepwalk. What are you talking about?"

"You don't remember anything?"

She shook her head, then winced. "Ouch. My head hurts."

I decided it wasn't the time to try and convince her she had indeed been sleepwalking. I helped her up and got her into bed. As much as I wanted to push, I knew it also wasn't the time to ask her what she had been talking about.

You know.

After tucking her into bed, I fetched some water, aspirin, and a cool washcloth. She docilely accepted my mothering, closing her eyes submissively and relaxing against me. For the first time, I could see in her the child she once was—trusting, sweet, obedient. I wondered what had happened to her—how her parents had shaped her, warped her—how they had changed her. A beautiful, shallow mother who was more focused on herself than her daughter, and a workaholic father who cycled between doting on her, and being completely unavailable, physically and emotionally.

Would I be having so many problems with her now if she had had a more normal childhood?

After turning off the lights and closing the door to her room, I headed to my own bed, in the hopes of salvaging a few more hours of sleep myself. But every time I closed my eyes, I saw either Aunt Charlie, all sharp, pointed teeth and predatory smile, foisting a cup of black, tar-like tea on me, or Chrissy in the den, all empty eyes and hollow smile, talking nonsense.

(And then I had to listen to a nasty little voice inside me questioning—*was it nonsense?* I squashed it down. Of course, it was nonsense. What else could it be?)

The sun had just started to peek above the horizon when I finally gave up on sleep altogether. Chrissy's door was still closed, and when I checked on her, she appeared to be totally out. I went downstairs and brewed a strong pot of coffee before wading in to the den to begin cleaning up the wreckage.

I took a break around nine and started making Chrissy's favorite breakfast— gluten-free pancakes. I hadn't heard a peep from upstairs, and thought I'd prepare a tray to bring up to her, but just as I was flipping them onto a plate, she appeared in the kitchen.

"Hey, you didn't have to come down," I said. "If you want to go back to bed, I'm happy to bring you breakfast in bed."

She looked at me suspiciously. "Why would you do that?"

"Well, ahhh, after last night, with the sleepwalking ..."

"I don't sleepwalk," she interrupted, her voice flat. "Are those gluten-free?"

"What? Yes, they're gluten free, but Chrissy ..."

She took the pancakes and poured syrup on them. "I don't know what you're talking about. I don't sleepwalk. I never have." With that, she put down the syrup, picked up a fork and the plate, and walked out of the room, leaving me standing in the kitchen alone, my mouth hanging open.

You know. The evil that was done.

I shook my head to clear it. So much for any trace of closeness I had felt with her, the night before. Everything seemed to be back to the way it always was.

You can't ask her now, can you? About what she was talking about, the nasty little voice inside me questioned.

I pushed the voice down again, and focused on forcing myself to eat some pancakes, even though I had completely lost my appetite. I supposed I should be grateful Chrissy's appetite hadn't been affected.

After breakfast, I went right back to cleaning. Cleaning was something I could control. And, besides, it felt like the best thing I could do for Stefan and Chrissy in this moment. I opened every window, vacuumed, dusted, scrubbed floors, scrubbed windows, and even walls. I stuffed towels and sheets into the tired old washing machine (which still worked amazingly well, thank God), and scoured both bathrooms. I even dragged the curtains and the quilts out of Chrissy's and my rooms, to air outside.

The only rooms I didn't touch were Aunt Charlie's bedroom, the studio on the third floor, and the basement.

I also re-packed most of our belongings and stacked them in the garage with intent to eventually put them into storage when we were ready to show the house. Yes, it was an additional cost we couldn't afford, but didn't it make more sense to keep everything in boxes, so we'd be ready to move back to New York when we could? Surely Stefan would agree that made more sense than unpacking everything only to re-pack it after we sold the house.

Stefan still hadn't called or texted, and for once, I was relieved. I had absolutely no idea how to handle the sleepwalking incident. Do I tell him over the phone, when he was in New York and couldn't do anything, which would just worry him and make it more difficult for him to get things done? Do I wait until he's here, so I could tell him in person (and he could see for himself that Chrissy was fine)? If I waited, did I risk him getting upset for not telling him sooner?

It was easier to just do nothing—to not make a decision. If he didn't call or text, the decision was out of my hands. Which may have been why, subconsciously, I had left my phone upstairs on my nightstand, next to my book.

The only person who called was Daphne. "You want to go out with the 'gang' on Friday?" she asked. "Everyone would love to see you."

I hesitated. Was it right to leave Chrissy alone while I went out? Of course, she was sixteen years old, and Stefan and I had certainly left her alone in New York. But still, it felt strange leaving her in the house, and Stefan wasn't there to help make the decision. And it wasn't like I was going to be staying in Redemption permanently. Should I really jump back into relationships I would eventually leave, yet again? Was it fair to everyone else for me to do that to them? And besides, shouldn't my energy be focused on Stefan and Chrissy? On fixing my marriage rather than starting up relationships that were destined to be temporary?

On top of all of that, I wasn't looking forward to explaining to everyone how there was no "Becca" anymore. I was Rebecca now—responsible, sophisticated New Yorker with a husband and stepdaughter.

Would they even like Rebecca?

The smart decision would be to decline. But, a part of me wanted to go—wanted to renew my friendship with Daphne, even if it wasn't going to last. I had loved spending time with Daphne and Mia fifteen years ago. And, I missed going out. Back in New York, I was busy every night. I missed that, too. I missed being around friends.

"It will be fun," Daphne pressed in the silence, interrupting my thoughts.

Fun. God, I *so* missed having fun. It felt like forever since I had had any fun. I practically owed it to myself. Despite my misgivings, I agreed to go.

I wondered again about that decision as I sat on the porch, sipping my wine and rocking, smelling the fresh, cool breeze as it played against my hair and skin, watching the sun sink lower in the sky, transforming into a bright-orange ball. Hopefully, I'd get a good night's sleep, and then, I could re-evaluate everything—the night out and what I should do about Stefan—with a much clearer head. And maybe I'd try talking to Chrissy again, about her sleepwalking ....

A police car pulled up slowly, and parked by the curb, interrupting my thoughts. The driver's side door opened, and out stepped Daniel. I sighed and took another drink of my wine. Great. Just great. At least this time, I had showered and was wearing something decent.

"Evening, Officer," I called out, as he sauntered over. "I must say, as flattered as I am with all the personal attention, there must be some actual crime in Redemption that requires your focus."

He looked up at me, unsmiling, and stopped at the bottom of the steps. The sun glinted off his hair, making it look reddish-blonde. His brown uniform shirt strained against the muscles of his chest.

"Your stepdaughter, is she here?"

Uh oh. I frowned. "No, is there a problem?"

He rested one hand on the railing. "Maybe. Maybe not. Earlier today, there was a group of teenagers drinking beer by the lake. Your stepdaughter is underage, isn't she?"

I gritted my teeth. Just what I needed. She *had* been gone all day, so she very well could have spent the day drinking by the lake. Although, on second thought, we had only just moved to Redemption! How was she able to make friends so quickly? Was she like this in New York too? God, there was so much I didn't know about my stepdaughter.

"She's sixteen."

He nodded. "You may want to have a talk with her about underage drinking."

I snorted. I couldn't help myself. "And feel like the biggest hypocrite on the planet?"

His eyes narrowed. "What she's doing is illegal."

"Assuming she's actually consuming the alcohol—do you have proof of that? But, regardless, geez, Daniel. When I think about the amount of beer you and I both drank out on that lake that summer when we were sixteen, how on earth can I possibly tell her not to do that?"

"You of all people should know the dangers of underage drinking."

I looked away. He was right. I *should* talk to Chrissy about it. A responsible stepmother would. And, knowing Chrissy, she would probably laugh in my face. Where oh where was Stefan?

"I still can't believe you're a cop," I said. "You weren't exactly the most law-abiding citizen when we were sixteen."

He leaned against the post. "Like I said, people change."

Does that mean you don't stand people up anymore? I clamped my jaw shut to keep that question from falling out of my mouth. Did I even want to know the answer?

"They usually don't change that much," I said instead. "If I recall correctly, you were the one instigating most of that *illegal* stuff we did."

"Maybe I learned my lesson. Speaking of that summer, did you give any thought to answering a few questions about the night Jessica disappeared?"

And there it was. I tilted my head and smirked. "Ah, perhaps we've come to the real reason you've stopped by?"

He crossed his arms across his chest, ignoring my comment. "Some things don't add up. I think it could help a lot, if you would answer a few questions."

I sipped my wine. "It was fifteen years ago. Did it occur to you that perhaps Jessica doesn't *want* to be found?"

"Maybe. But it still would be helpful to have some answers. It might help bring some closure to this town." He paused, staring intently at me. "Maybe it would even give *you* some closure."

I dropped my gaze, shaken by his comments and his penetrating blue eyes. I felt like they had looked right through me ...
seen all my secrets laid bare.

"I just don't know how much of a help I can be. You have
my statement. I really doubt I would remember anything more
after all this time."

"You were the last to see her that night. That alone is worth
talking about some more. Make sure the cops asked all the right
questions."

I shivered. The last to see her. Suddenly, a piece clicked into
place, and I looked up. "How do you know I was the last to see
her?"

A trace of surprise wafted across his face, and disappeared
so quickly, I wondered if it had actually happened. His face
smoothed back into its unreadable expression. "We have a witness."

"But if you have a witness," I said slowly, thinking aloud,
"Doesn't that mean the witness was also there, and also last to
see Jessica?"

"The witness left."

"Left." I rolled the word around in my mouth. "So, if the
witness left, then we don't know if I was the last to see her or
not."

"That's why I want to ask you more questions about that
night."

I took another sip of wine. "But, it seems to me, as I've
mentioned, that I'm not very reliable. I ended up in the hospital with alcohol poisoning. Wouldn't your other witness know
more than me? And, who is it, anyway?"

"I'm not expecting miracles," Daniel said, sounding a little
frustrated. "I remember how drunk you were that night ..."

I stared at him in surprise. "You do?"

He looked at me like I had slapped him. "It was a party. I was
there. You don't remember?"

I clicked my jaw shut. Now what did I do? I really didn't want
to admit to him that the entire night was a black hole. What
would he think of me? Would it make me look more, or less

guilty? And yet, there was something about the way he was watching me. Did something happen between us that night? Did we have a conversation about why he had stood me up? And why *was* I so drunk, anyway? I certainly got myself tipsy on more than one occasion that summer, but drinking so much that I ended up in the hospital getting my stomach pumped? It didn't make sense.

Could something have happened that night with Daniel?

I opened my mouth, still not sure what I was going to say, when a voice behind me said "Well, isn't this cozy?"

I closed my eyes. Chrissy. Great. Just great. How much did she hear? I half-turned in my seat. "Chrissy, how long have you been standing there?"

"Long enough."

"Chrissy, were you at the lake earlier today?" Daniel asked.

She leveled a stare at him. God, she looks just like her father. "Why are you asking?"

"Just answer the question."

"Is it a crime to be at the lake?"

"Depends on what you were doing."

"Am I under arrest?"

"Chrissy," I gasped. "What the … "

Daniel stared hard at her. "Not at the moment."

"Okay, then," she said. "I know my rights. I don't have to answer your questions."

Daniel gave her one final stare before pushing off from the stairs. "Thanks for your time, Becca. I'm sure I'll be seeing you around." He shot me a meaningful look that was as clear as if he had voiced the words. *This isn't over.*

"Oh, don't leave on my account, Officer," Chrissy said, her voice dripping with innuendo.

Daniel didn't respond. He simply nodded his head to both of us, and sauntered back to his car.

Chrissy moved to stand by the swing, watching him walk to his car. "So, what did *he* want?"

"To let me know you may be illegally drinking. Are you?"

She shot me a disdainful look. "That doesn't sound anything like what you two were talking about."

"Oh, so you *were* listening to our conversation?"

"Should I not have been? Do you have something to hide?"

Great. Now I was getting the same interrogation. Chrissy had definitely learned well from her father. "Don't change the subject. You're sixteen—are you drinking?"

Her phone beeped, and she studied it. "I think you're the one changing the subject. Did he stop by on Monday, too? When I wasn't here?"

I stood up abruptly, knocking the swing so it jangled. "Don't think this is over—I'm planning to have a talk with your father about this." I moved toward the house.

She looked sideways at me, a calculating and faintly-accusatory expression in her eyes. "Maybe I'm going to have a talk with my father as well," she said darkly.

Silently, I opened the door and stalked into the house. I was already feeling out of sorts after the conversation with Daniel, and the last thing I wanted was to get into a war of words with my sixteen-year-old stepdaughter.

Still. A tiny voice inside me warned that I should say something to her immediately. There was something very unsettling in the way she watched me, and I realized it made sense to have a conversation with her before her feelings further hardened against me. Even though I knew it, I was just too tired and too drained to deal with it right then.

Tomorrow, I promised the little voice, as I trudged upstairs to bed.

Unfortunately for me, that little voice turned out to be right on the money.

Chapter 9

Chrissy poked her head into my room as I was getting ready for my night out and mulling over the choices my closet offered. "I'm inviting a friend over tonight," she announced.

Surprised, I looked at her. "A friend? Who?"

"What, you don't think I can make friends?"

Oh God, the teenage logic. "Of course, that's not what I meant. We've only just moved here."

Chrissy made a face and drifted away from my door. "Whatever."

I tried again, softening my tone, as I followed her into the hallway. "So, who is it?"

"You wouldn't know her anyway," she said over her shoulder, heading to her room.

I kept following her. "Well, I'd like to know her. And meet her before I leave."

"She won't be here before you're off to have fun with your *friends*." The sneer on her face said it all, as she threw herself on her bed, wrinkling up the grey, blue, and white goose down quilt, tapping on her phone.

"Why do you care if I go out tonight? Your dad and I used to go out all the time."

She glared at me. "Exactly. You AND Dad went out. Now you're going out by yourself."

"Do you see your father here?" I snapped, feeling both guilty and defensive. Why on earth did I have to justify my decisions to a sixteen-year-old girl? I was the adult. "He left me alone here, too, you know."

She looked back at her phone, shaking her head. "Whatever."

I clenched my jaw, swallowing the words that were fighting to come out. Actually, even more than yelling at her, what I really wanted to do was to shove my phone in her face and *prove* it to her. Show her the single, lonely text I'd gotten from her father that entire week that said, "Sorry babe, work is a zoo. Will call when I can." *You see, he's the one ignoring me!*

I took a deep breath, reminding myself once again that I was the grownup; I certainly didn't need to get into a pissing contest with my sixteen-year-old stepdaughter.

I decided to switch to safer subjects. "Okay, so what is your friend's name?"

For a moment, I didn't think she was going to answer me, but then she surprised me. "Brittany. Happy?"

"Happier. What's Brittany's last name?"

She texted furiously. "What does it matter?"

I sighed. Chrissy probably didn't know Brittany's last name, either. "Okay, so don't stay up too late, no boys, and no getting into anything you know your father and I would disapprove of. Okay?"

She muttered under her breath. I took it as a "yes," and headed back to my room to finish getting ready.

I wondered if I should cancel. Was this a good idea, especially knowing Chrissy was having someone over I hadn't met yet?

On the other hand, I reminded myself, she's sixteen. She's clearly been hanging out with this girl somewhere, and she would probably get into less trouble at the house than she would going out on the town on a Friday night.

Besides, I was tired of spending my days with a sullen teenager while trying to distract myself from thinking about Stefan not texting me or calling me, spending his nights alone in New York with the blonde and elegant Sabrina … NO! Not going there. Stefan was in New York to work. Period.

And, I *was* going to have some fun.

I went back to my closet, poked at it some more, and decided the tight jeans and dark green v-neck silk top I had on was the winning outfit. Green was one of my favorite colors to wear. It brought out the green in my eyes and the red in my hair. Plus, this particular top clung in all the right places, making me look thinner and more well-endowed than I was. Why shouldn't I look nice? Even if Stefan was in New York? And, so what if I ran into Daniel? He was engaged anyway. I wasn't wearing it for him. I was wearing it because I was going out with my friends, and I wanted to look good—to FEEL good.

I left my hair loose so it framed my face, and admittedly, it was a bit of a wild mess. I dusted on a bit of makeup, trying (and failing) to make my unremarkable face look, well, more remarkable. Remembering the hours I had spent in New York trying to make my hair and makeup look like all the chic, smooth, perfectly-put-together wives we knew, I decided to just forget it, and embrace my wild, messy side instead. I added some extra-large gold hoop earrings before grabbing my keys, purse, and cell phone, and I headed out. Chrissy grunted in response to my goodbye.

I was meeting Daphne at The Tipsy Cow, one of the main hot spots in Redemption. It was a huge, cavernous bar with wooden beams and posts, and a wood floor. It smelled like a mixture of beer, wine, perfume, cigarettes, and, as it was actually a bar and grill, fried food.

It was packed. It took me a few minutes to weave my way through the crowd, avoiding the laughing, oblivious people holding full glasses of beer and wine. I scooted between tables, chairs, pool tables, and dart boards before I saw Daphne waving at me from one of the big corner booths.

"You made it," Daphne exclaimed, sliding over to make room for me. Mia was there too, along with another woman I didn't recognize.

"This is Celia, Barry's wife," Mia said. "You remember Barry, right?"

A vague memory of a tall, scrawny joke teller with red hair, freckles, and bad acne floated through my mind. I also recalled that he was a good friend of Daniel's.

"Is he here?" I asked.

"Oh, he's around here somewhere," Celia answered, eyeing me. She had a sharp, heart-shaped face that reminded me of a fox, with thick black hair pulled back into a ponytail. She also wore lots of makeup. Her black, boat-neck top clung to her well-endowed breasts, which she further amplified by draping herself with lots of silver jewelry, including big silver hoops and jangling silver bracelets. I caught a whiff of her perfume, which smelled almost (but not quite) like Calvin Klein's Euphoria. Probably one of those designer knock offs. She quickly dismissed me and turned back to her drink, which looked like a Cosmopolitan.

On second thought, maybe I was better off at home with Chrissy.

Mia flagged down a server so I could order a glass of wine, after briefly considering something stronger. Redemption was a bad influence on me—wine would be more than sufficient.

"Soooo," Mia said with a wicked grin, after the server had dropped off my wine. "Have you run into Mad Martha yet? Or maybe," her voice dropped to a whisper, "Aunt Charlie herself?"

I nearly spilled my drink in my shock. Mia gasped and leaned forward. "You did! I knew it!"

Daphne shook her head. "We all should have known it. Charlie wouldn't leave quietly."

Mia was nearly bouncing up on the bench seat. "I can see it all over your face. Spill it."

I took a long sip, watching Celia out of the corner of my eye. How much should I tell? Celia seemed irritated at my presence, studying her Cosmo with an almost bored expression on her face.

I had a sudden flashback to the dreadful work parties I had to attend with Stefan back in New York. I would keep a plastic smile plastered on my face as those brittle, beautiful, pampered attorney wives would size me up and dismiss me with the same expression currently on Celia's face—barely making small talk in the process.

I was so tired of seeing that expression, so tired of women more beautiful and more elegantly and effortlessly made up judging me—the one who struggled to keep her lipstick from smearing, and her clothes from wrinkling. I knew they all wondered what on earth Stefan saw in me, when there were so many far more acceptable choices around him. I was suddenly just ... *done*.

I leaned across the table, looking around in mock conspiracy. "Well," I began, drawing out the word. Mia and Daphne leaned in closer. Even Celia glanced up, interested despite herself. I told them about that first night, seeing what I thought was Chrissy disappearing into her room wearing a white nightgown, and the next day seeing her in red and blue.

Mia and Daphne both wore suitably-horrified expressions on their faces, but Celia simply looked disgusted. "You didn't see anything. It was all in your head."

I took a long swallow of my wine. "How do you know I didn't see anything?"

Celia pursed her lips. "I don't care if you *are* living in Crazy Charlie's house. There's no such thing as ghosts."

Crazy Charlie. The name thudded inside me, reverberating like the old, bent cow bell Aunt Charlie had on her desk, bringing up all the shame, anger, and embarrassment I had thought I was long done with. I had forgotten about that horrid nickname. Aunt Charlie used to laugh about it, but it had made me silently seethe.

"I don't know what you heard, but my aunt wasn't crazy," I said, surprising myself with how loyal I sounded, considering I hadn't sorted out my feelings for Aunt Charlie. But there was no way I was letting this smug fake get away with calling her names. "Forgetful. Unconventional. Even a bit weird. But, she wasn't crazy."

"Says the woman talking about seeing ghosts in her house," Celia said.

"God, Celia, you don't know what you're talking about," Mia returned. "*You've* never been inside that house. It really is haunted."

Daphne shivered next to me. "I've felt it."

Celia snorted. "You were probably drinking too much of that famous tea. I heard she was growing pot in that garden of hers to put in it."

Mia scoffed. "You are such an old gossip. She did no such thing."

"How would you know? You were too busy drinking it," Celia retorted, tossing the last of her Cosmo down, her silver bracelets jangling.

"I never saw pot in her garden," Daphne said. "And I never felt high after drinking her tea."

"You probably didn't even know how high you were," Celia said, darkly.

"God, Celia, what the hell is your problem?" Mia said.

"If you really think you saw ghosts, you were definitely high, whether you knew it or not," Celia said stubbornly.

"This is a stupid argument," Daphne said. "I know that house is haunted, and no, there wasn't any tea involved."

I looked at her in horror. Was she talking about that night Jessica disappeared? What did she see? I was almost afraid to ask when Mia beat me to it.

Daphne didn't answer, instead playing with her wine glass. She didn't look at me.

"It was a couple of days before ... well, you know. Becca had been ... hearing things, especially at night." I looked sharply at Daphne. Hearing things? At night? I didn't remember that.

Daphne didn't look at me; she didn't look at anyone. Instead, she kept her gaze focused on her wine glass as she spun it on the table. There was something about her manner, the way she hesitated as she talked, and her fixation on her wine glass that made me feel like if she wasn't actually lying in that moment, she wasn't telling the whole truth either.

"It started as a big joke. Maybe it was Mad Martha after all, trying to communicate with us, but we weren't getting the message." Daphne paused, and looked up. "So, we decided to make it easier for her."

"We had a séance," I breathed. Suddenly, that afternoon flashed in my memory, the two of us sitting in the kitchen, talking about Mad Martha, the late afternoon sun streaming through the windows, the kitchen so white and clean and bright that the idea of something dark and disturbed dwelling in the shadows seemed nothing short of silly.

Daphne looked straight at me. "Yes, in our teenage stupidity, we decided it would be funny to have a séance." She picked up her glass and finished her wine. "Oh, and Charlie wasn't there, so no, we hadn't had any tea." She shot Celia a look.

"We were drinking Cokes and eating potato chips. Out of a bag," I said, and then wondered why I felt the need to explain myself. Especially to New-York-Wanna-Be Celia, with her cheap jewelry and even cheaper perfume. She would immediately be sussed out as a fraud, if she actually did ever make it to New York.

And boy, would she get a wakeup call, then.

Daphne continued the story. "So, we collected candles and incense, went upstairs, and closed the windows and blinds to make it as dark as possible." She lowered her voice and we all leaned in closer. "We lit the candles and sat on the floor facing each other, holding hands."

She paused, and I found myself picking up the story, just like old times. "We had no idea *how* to do a séance, so it was a bit of a slow start, but we finally asked if Martha was there."

I stopped talking, suddenly overwhelmed by memories of that afternoon. The smell of the sandalwood incense mixed with the burning candles, the darkness of the room even though I knew the sun was still shining brightly outside, the oven-like heat, Daphne's sweaty hands in mine.

And then the sudden, sharp, sick sensation that we were absolutely not alone in that room.

Mia and Celia were now both staring at us, completely transfixed. Celia's mouth even hung slightly open. "So, what happened then?" Mia breathed.

Daphne took a deep breath. "It's hard to explain, but there was this feeling. Like a presence hovering near us. You could almost feel it breathing. I asked who was there, and there was this whoosh of air."

"All the candles blew out," I said. "A couple even fell over."

"And then, on the mirror," Daphne continued. "We saw this flash of words."

"Words?" Mia said. "What did they say?"

Daphne didn't answer, just picked up her wine. Instead of drinking it, she held it in front of her, staring into it.

I was the one who answered, my voice quiet and dreamlike, almost like I had slipped back in time into my sixteen-year-old self, in that hot, sweaty room with Daphne, terrified about what we had somehow conjured up.

"It's coming. Beware."

Chapter 10

Nobody spoke. In my memory, I could see the words, clear as day, in smoke and blood, reflected deep in the mirror. A blink, a second look, and the words vanished.

Then Mia burst out. "No freaking way! And you didn't tell me?"

"We never even talked about it ourselves," Daphne said. "Just ran out of the room. Charlie was just coming home, and I decided I needed to leave too. I think we eventually would have talked about it, and told you too, but then a couple days later, Jessica disappeared."

"What a bunch of bull," Celia said. "That whole story is a crock."

"What's a bunch of bull?" A guy who looked vaguely familiar with his longish, reddish-brown hair, dash of freckles, dark-brown eyes, and crooked, sexy smile asked, as he slid into the booth next to Mia. He nodded to me. "Barry. And you are …?"

"It's Becca," Mia chimed in before I could say anything. "Don't you recognize her?"

Barry did a double take. "Becca? Oh wow—all grown up. I didn't realize you were back in town. How long are you here for?"

More people were crowding into our booth, and rather than correcting everyone about my name, I found myself sliding over to make room. I also found a new glass of wine in front of me. I hadn't even realized I finished the last one.

"Becca is staying in Charlie's house," Mia was saying, as I officially gave up on trying to get my name corrected, and instead got my bearings with all the new faces. There was Barry, who was now married to Celia, and Rich, who was now with Janey. I remembered both Rich and Janey—Rich had blossomed from a geeky, skinny nerd of a teenager into a big, muscular guy, with a broad, square jaw, traces of a beard, and very dark eyes. Janey didn't hang out with us much. She seemed closer to Jessica.

"Really?" Barry asked, drawing the word out. "Any sign of ghosts?"

"We were just talking about that," Mia exclaimed at the same time as Celia glared at him. "Don't even get them started again."

"Get what started?" Daniel asked, sliding into the booth. He wore a Brewer's tee shirt, which just happened to be the right shade of blue to match his eyes.

"What did we miss?" asked an absolutely gorgeous blonde next to him. His fiancée, I presumed. I felt a bit sick to my stomach and reached for my wine.

"Becca, I don't think you've met Gwyn yet," Mia chimed in.

I shook my head and Gwyn and I nodded to each other. Daniel concentrated on refilling his beer from the pitcher sitting in the middle of the table.

"So, let's get back to the ghosts," Barry said.

"There are no ghosts," Celia snapped. "Ghosts don't exist. Just a couple of drama queen teenagers who forgot to close a window."

"Teenagers? What are we talking about?" Daniel asked.

"We didn't forget to close the window," Daphne said. "In fact, we double-checked all the windows."

"Well, clearly you must have missed something," Celia said. "Or you imagined the whole thing. Or you were high on whatever Charlie was growing in her garden. Or … you're exaggerating." I had the distinct impression what she really meant was "lying."

Barry rubbed his hands together gleefully. "Oh, this is getting good."

Daphne sipped her wine. "Or, it happened exactly as we said."

Celia snorted as she drained her drink.

"Enough already," Janey said. "What are you guys talking about?"

While Mia and Daphne filled the rest of the table in, I focused on my wine and studied Gwyn out of the corner of my eye. She was like blue ice—white-blonde hair cut short and asymmetrical, a flawless porcelain complexion, and pale-blue eyes that matched her pale-blue top. While I watched, she tucked her hand under Daniel's arm. I glimpsed a flash of a sparkle, most likely from a diamond engagement ring, before quickly looking away, feeling a hot surge of mixed emotions—regret, guilt, and something that felt awfully close to jealousy, even though I had absolutely no right to that emotion. I swallowed some wine, and turned my attention back to the conversation, which had gotten loud as the table had broken out into a friendly (well mostly friendly) debate about whether or not Daphne and I had really seen a ghost that night, and what the mirror message meant.

"It's pretty obvious what Mad Martha meant," Mia was saying. "It was a warning."

"Well, duh," Barry said. "But a warning of what?"

"Jessica," Mia said.

The table fell silent.

"It was NOT a warning," Celia spat into the silence. "Jessica ran away from home. That's it."

"Jessica did NOT run away from home," Mia snapped. "I was her best friend. She would have told me."

Celia's whole attitude suddenly shifted—softened—as she backpedaled. "Look, I'm sure she didn't mean for it to happen like that. She probably got mad that night and left without thinking. We didn't have cell phones and text messages back then the way we do now. It doesn't mean anything."

Mia was shaking her head. "No, something happened to her. It's not like she was the first to disappear from this town."

Celia's mouth flattened in a straight line. "People don't disappear from this town. They leave. Pure and simple." She dropped her eyes, looked down into her empty glass. "And I don't blame them," she muttered.

Mia looked like she was about to argue, but Barry interrupted. "What I don't understand is why you'd think the message was a warning for Jessica." He put his hand on Celia's arm, giving her a look. She glared at him, but kept her mouth shut.

Mia looked around the table in surprise. "Oh! Did I forget to share that part? This happened a couple of days before Jessica disappeared."

Daniel lowered his beer onto the table with a thunk. "Is this a joke?"

"No joke," Daphne said. "It happened two days before that night."

Daniel narrowed his eyes at Daphne. "Why didn't you say something sooner?"

"What, you think the ghost did it?" Barry asked lazily, winking at the waitress and gesturing for another round. Beside him, Celia looked like she was about to blow a gasket.

Daniel narrowed his eyes ever so slightly. "Don't be ridiculous. But the timing is awfully coincidental, and I don't believe in coincidences. Did you say anything to Jessica?"

Daphne frowned. "Jessica? Why would we tell Jessica?"

"They better NOT have told Jessica," Mia jumped in. "It's bad enough I'm just hearing about it now."

"Did you tell anyone else?"

"Boys and girls, we have an interrogation on our hands," Barry said. "Where's the popcorn?"

Daniel slid back in his seat, his face expressionless, and took a long swallow of beer.

"Daniel's right. Maybe there IS something to this," Mia said. "I mean, it's hardly the first time someone has disappeared from this town. Maybe we should have another séance."

I started choking on my wine. Daphne pounded me on the back.

Barry banged the table with his hand. "Now there's an idea! Let's interrogate a ghost."

"That's a horrible idea," Daphne said.

"Finally, we agree on something," Celia said. "Stupid idea and a complete waste of time."

"I think it would be fun," Gwyn said enthusiastically, one hand on Daniel's arm.

I finally got my breath under control. "Hold on," I said, starting to feel a little panicked. Oh God, what have I gotten myself into? I can't possibly have a séance in that house. *What on earth would Stefan say?* "I'm the one who would need to coordinate it, and I don't think it's a very good idea."

"Why not?" Mia asked. "It may be good for you, too."

There was a full glass of wine in front of me. I seized it and drank a little frantically. Again, I didn't remember the waitress bringing me a new glass. How many had I drank so far? "I have a sixteen-year-old stepdaughter."

"So, what?" Barry said. "You were sixteen when you did the first one."

I made a face. "I'd rather not put ideas in her head."

"We could plan around your stepdaughter," Mia said. "Your husband too, for that matter."

I didn't like this direction at all. "More importantly, I'm with Daphne. I don't really want to go through that whole experience again either."

"Let's talk about it later," Daniel said in his no-nonsense, I'm-taking-no-argument cop voice, firmly putting his beer down. After a pause, the conversation shifted to sports. Gwyn gave him an adoring look. I couldn't help myself—I rolled my eyes, before I noticed Mia looking at me. She grinned and winked at me. I started to make a face at her, but instead I found myself grinning back.

Man had I missed her.

The conversation moved on from sports to even lighter topics. Barry had the whole table laughing with a few of his work stories—he was the sales manager at a local car dealership that his dad owned. I chimed in with a couple of stories from New York. I lost track of both the time and the number of drinks I had, until I stumbled to my feet for a trip to the ladies' room.

"What happened to you in New York?' Barry asked as I struggled to keep myself upright. "You used to be able to hold your liquor. You turn into a lightweight?"

"Yeah, well, we're *sophisticated* back in New York," I said, nearly falling as I got out of the booth. "We don't drink just anything. We're refined, in our alcohol tastes."

The table hooted. "You can't even *say* 'sophisticated,'" Barry laughed.

A strong, warm hand grabbed my arm and steadied me. Daniel. "You okay?" he asked.

The place he touched on my arm felt warmer than it should have. My emotions churned confusingly in my gut. I pulled my arm away and straightened up. "Yes, thank you." Did he let go of my arm a little reluctantly? Of course not. I was being ridiculous. I shook my head to clear it, as I headed for the bathroom.

I took a few moments pretending to fix my appearance, but really, I just needed to pull myself together. I had a bit too much to drink, that's all. In fact, I realized I probably needed to go home and sleep it off.

Home. Chrissy. Oh God, I'd totally forgotten about her. I hurriedly dug around in my purse for my cell. No messages—was that good? Or bad? It was a lot later than I had expected. Would I be able to drive? If I couldn't, would I be able to get a taxi? And how would I explain that to Chrissy?

I really sucked at being a stepmother.

The bathroom door opened, and a woman a few years older than me tottered in. She was stuffed into tight jeans and a tight, red top that was cut low, showing off her ample cleavage. Her dyed blonde hair was piled high on her head in a messy bun that was beginning to unravel. High-heeled, sexy red shoes completed the outfit.

"Oh," she said, when she saw me. "I didn't think anyone was in here."

I smiled wanly back at her. It was clear she had had a bit too much too, and I wasn't really in the mood for conversation.

She tottered a few steps closer, peering at me. Suddenly, she frowned. "Wait. You're Charlie's niece, aren't you? From New York." She didn't make it sound like a good thing.

"Um, yes," I said. Maybe she was just a little drunk and didn't mean to sound unfriendly. "And you are ...?"

She straightened up, glaring at me. "Why don't you go back to New York? No one wants you here anyway." She turned on her heel, nearly twisting her ankle in the process, and stomped into one of the stalls.

Shaken, for a moment all I could do was stand there. Where was the hostility coming from? Did I do something to her fifteen years ago I couldn't remember?

I definitely needed to get out of that bar. Immediately.

I took a deep breath to steady myself and opened the door.

Daniel was waiting for me, arms crossed, leaning against the exposed red brick wall. He did not look happy. "Took you long enough."

And the night just kept getting worse and worse. "Is that a crime?" I snapped. I wanted to get out of there before that woman came out of the bathroom. I didn't feel up to another confrontation.

He glowered at me. "I want to talk."

"That's too bad, because I don't." I started to walk past him, but he moved to block me. My reflexes were slowed because of the alcohol, and I was almost on top of him before I stopped myself. I was so close I could smell his soap, clean and woodsy, mixed with beer, and the musky scent that was him, and for one wild moment, I thought he might kiss me. His dark-blue eyes stared into mine, and a spark of shock, frustration, and desire sizzled between us.

I took a step backward before I embarrassed myself by instinctively leaning in for that unwanted kiss.

"Why didn't you tell me about the séance?" He took a step backward as well, and a cool rush of air kissed my face instead, the coldness jolting me back to my senses. God, I had definitely had too much to drink.

"Why on earth would I? We were couple of dumb teenagers who managed to scare the crap out of ourselves. How would knowing that help you find out what happened to Jessica? Are you seriously thinking about interrogating a ghost?"

His mouth pressed into a line. "Don't be stupid. This is exactly why I want to talk to you about that night. Who knows what else you haven't shared because you don't think it's important."

"Maybe I don't think it's important because it *isn't* important."

He shook his head. "You don't know that."

"And you know better? Why? Because you're a cop?"

"Because I have more of the bigger picture than you have."

"Then why don't you tell me this *bigger* picture? Maybe then I could help."

He paused, his eyes narrowing. "Does that mean you'll answer my questions?"

I bit my lip and looked away. How could I respond to that? As much as I would love to get some of *my* questions answered—like what *did* I actually say to the cops back then? And who *is* this witness, and what did he or she see? —how could I admit to him I really couldn't answer his questions? That I didn't have the ability? Wouldn't he think my patchy memory made me look guilty?

I turned back to Daniel. The cop was back—he was simply standing there, watching me. Like a predator. Waiting for me to respond. But, even in my inebriated state, I could see something beneath the cop—something hopeful, almost eager, even boyish.

And, below that, a glimmer of something else. A spark. Desire. For something that could have been, and never had a chance.

Or maybe it was all just wishful thinking, on my part.

I opened my mouth, to say what, I'm not sure—the truth, a lie, something in between. But I never got the chance.

A bright, cheery voice interrupted the moment, saving me. "Oh, there you two are."

Gwyn rounded the corner, smiling and reaching possessively for Daniel's arm, angling her hand in such a way that I had no choice but to notice the diamond ring prominently displayed on her ring finger. I quickly dropped my gaze. Man, she was annoying.

Was it my imagination, or did Daniel's face flatten with disappointment, right before he plastered a plastic smile on his face? "Just asking Becca a few follow-up questions about the séance," he said lightly.

I seized my chance. "I've got to get home anyway. Gotta check on the stepdaughter." I hurried past them, firmly telling myself I was relieved, happy, we were interrupted. There was absolutely nothing to be disappointed about. Gwyn had just saved me from saying … well, likely something I shouldn't.

"I hope you're not going to drive," Daniel called to me.

"Of course not," I said over my shoulder, although at that point, I didn't know what I was going to do. All I knew for sure was that I couldn't get out of there fast enough. Besides, after that encounter with Daniel, I was feeling pretty sober. Maybe I just needed some fresh air to finish clearing my head. If nothing else, I'd stand outside and wait for a cab.

Luckily, Daphne saved me. "You leaving?" She slid out the booth. "I'll go with you. In fact, I can drive your car if you want."

"Really? But don't you have your own car?"

She shook her head. "Mia picked me up after work. My mom doesn't like me leaving her home without the car unless I absolutely have to. As for drinking, I never have more than a glass."

I couldn't believe my good luck. I agreed before Daphne could change her mind, and started digging some money out of my wallet to pitch in for the tab before Mia waved it away.

"It's our treat. We're celebrating! You're finally back where you belong."

Where you belong. The words thudded sickly inside me. The woman's voice in the bathroom—"Go back to New York. No one wants you here, anyway." Chrissy's blank eyes staring at me from the study. *You know. The evil that was done.*

Shaking my head to clear it, I opened my mouth to protest— to remind everyone that this wasn't permanent, that I had every intention of selling the house and moving back to New York— but no words came out. Instead, I found myself fumbling with my wallet as I put it away, saying my goodbyes.

Daphne said she had to use the bathroom and told me she'd meet me outside. I quickly headed for the door.

Outside the air was fresh and cool, a welcome respite from the bar's sweaty staleness. I took a deep breath, feeling my nervous system start to relax, and my overheated cheeks cool down.

Out of the corner of my eye, I saw a shadow detach itself from the wall, like a ghost rising from the dead. *Oh God, it's Mad Martha.* I jumped back, my heart in my throat, even though my rational mind interjected immediately, assuring me there was no way it could be Mad Martha, or any ghost for that matter.

The shadow shambled forward, crouching, limping. Was it an animal? Instinctively, I took a few more steps backward. If it was an animal, it didn't look well.

The shadow shuffled a little closer into the pool of light from the streetlamp, revealing a face peering out from a lump of mismatched clothes and scarves. I gasped. It was the homeless woman from the supermarket.

She saw me, her eyes like black holes in her sockets, and hissed. "You."

I backed away. "What?? What do you want?"

She inched forward, greasy hair falling across her forehead. "You know, don't you?"

You know. About the evil that's been done.

My blood turned to ice. I couldn't move, couldn't breathe. She sounded exactly like Chrissy had, that night in the library.

She smiled, revealing gaping holes where teeth used to be. "Yes, you know, don't you?"

I tried to catch my breath, but it felt like every organ in my body had frozen solid. *Oh God, what's happening to me?* Am I having another breakdown? Another overdose? A part of me wanted to ask her, no scream at her, "What?? What do I know?" I wanted to shake her until the answer popped out of her mouth and I would …

"Okay I'm ready." Daphne appeared beside me.

I blinked, turned my head toward Daphne, then looked back. The homeless woman was gone.

I jerked my head around. Where did she go? The street was empty, except for Daphne and me.

"Becca, are you okay?" Daphne was looking at me strangely.

"I'm … ah … I'm fine. Just, well, I think I had a little too much to drink," I said weakly. A part of me wanted to tell her, wanted to ask her about the strange homeless woman, but what could I say that wouldn't make me sound crazy?

I handed my keys over and pointed Daphne toward the car. As we walked, I looked back over my shoulder one more time. Was it my imagination, or was there a shadow by the wall again?

I gave myself a shake, and focused on getting into the car. I had to stop this thinking. I was letting my imagination get the best of me. All that was happening was a combination of too much wine and too many ghost stories.

Daphne talked lightly on the way home, mostly filling me in on some of the history of the gang since I last saw them. She kept everything light—nothing about Jessica or séances. I didn't say much, content to let her talk.

Despite my protests, she pulled into my driveway and parked. The garage was still stuffed with boxes. "It's a fast walk to my house," she said. "I don't mind."

I was going to argue more. I was certainly sober enough to drive myself around the block, but I suddenly realized the house was ablaze with lights. It looked like every single light was on, in every room.

Why did Chrissy turn on all the lights? What was going on?

Daphne noticed it, too. "Well, it looks like someone wanted to welcome you home."

I mumbled an agreement, but something didn't feel right. Back in New York, if Chrissy went to bed before we got home, she would turn everything off, leaving us to stumble around in the half-dark so we wouldn't wake her.

Daphne hugged me, told me she'd call soon, and headed down the street. I watched her for a few moments before turning back to the house, just in time to see a curtain flutter.

Had I made a mistake? Was Chrissy more nervous about being left alone in that house than I had thought? Or worse, what if she HAD gone to bed, and sleepwalked again, and I wasn't home to help? Oh God, what if she really hurt herself, and I wasn't there? I hurried up to the front door, pulling my keys out with shaking hands. I would never forgive myself if something happened to her while I was out at a bar.

I finally got the door unlocked and flung the door open. "Chrissy," I called, "Are you …"

My voice died in mid-sentence. Stefan was there. On the couch. Looking quite displeased. Next to him, Chrissy was curled up, smug as a cat full of cream, her hand possessively tucked around his arm, reminding me of how Gwyn had reached for Daniel earlier.

He fixed me with a careful, even stare. "Where," he began, his voice dangerously soft, but each word was spoken with the sharp precision of a lawyer, "have you been?"

Chapter 11

My mouth went dry and I tried to swallow. "Out with some old friends," I managed.

His gaze narrowed. "Where exactly?"

I shifted my balance from one foot to the other. A part of me was thinking how ridiculous his little inquisition was. I was a grown woman, and I certainly didn't need permission from my husband to go out to a bar. But then the scene outside the bathroom with Daniel shot through my head, and guilt stabbed through me. "At a bar," I muttered.

Stefan stood up and walked over to stand in front of the living room window. "Chrissy, go to bed. We can talk more in the morning." Chrissy slid off the couch, gave me a secretive smile, and kissed her father on the cheek, before sashaying up the stairs.

He waited until we could hear the click of her door closing before turning to me. "You're drunk."

I straightened my back. "I am not."

He pointed to the window. "Then why did you let someone else drive you home?"

"I ... ah," I fell silent.

He took a step toward me. "What the hell has gotten into you, Rebecca? I come home early to surprise you, only to find you've left Chrissy all alone to run off to a bar to get drunk? You haven't been in Redemption for a week! And what you're *supposed* to be doing is getting us settled in." He flung his arms around the living room. "What have you been doing with yourself all week?"

I gasped at him, wordless, my mouth falling open in shock. How could he so quickly dismiss my hours and hours of hard work on the house? I could feel tears prickle the back of my eyes. All of the love and care I had put into creating the perfect environment where we could reconnect again as a family ... and he just shot it all down.

I sucked in my breath and managed to get my mouth working again. "You can't see all the cleaning and organizing I did?" I squeaked, my voice as small as I felt.

"What I see is your aunt's ... *things* all over the place. You were *supposed* to be boxing all of that up and unpacking *our* belongings. How are we supposed to live here with everything we own still in boxes? And, how are we supposed to sell the house with this ..." he waved his hands in frustration. "This ... mishmash everywhere? Do I have to do everything? I'm working my butt off trying to save the firm, and *all* I asked of you was to create a home for our family. It appears you can't even do that."

"That's not fair," I burst out, my voice finally working. "I *was* creating a home for us. Look at what I did. How can you not see it?"

He stared at me incredulously. "See what? Let's talk about what I *don't* see. I don't see our furniture in this room. I don't see our dishes in the kitchen cabinets. Nor, when I walked through the door, did I see YOU. YOU weren't here. YOU were at a bar. How do you think it makes *me* feel when I move heaven and earth to sneak away for a weekend and you're not even here? Do you have any idea how much is on my plate right now? The longer it takes me to get to the bottom of the embezzlement at the firm, the longer I'm away from you and Chrissy. And that's just my time! Let's not forget I just spent money *we don't have* to see you, and you're off at a bar getting drunk."

"I ..." Oh, God. What have I done? I knew I shouldn't have gone out. I felt physically sick as shame and guilt started seeping through my pores. "Stefan, I'm ... I'm sorry." I tried to go to him, but he turned away from me in disgust. "I just wanted to go out with my friends and have a little fun. Is that so wrong?"

"You're drunk," he said, his voice flat. His entire body was stiff and unyielding. I could feel how repulsed he was by me. "It's pointless to talk about this now. Let's go to bed."

I wanted to protest more. He wasn't being fair. I just went to a bar with some friends, that was it. That wasn't a crime.

An image of Daniel stopping me in front of the bathroom popped into my head.

I squashed it down. *I didn't do anything wrong*, I told myself. *Other than wanting him to kiss me.*

I could feel the hot burn of a flush start to creep up my neck. I turned away quickly before Stefan could see it and, heaven forbid, ask me about it, and started up the stairs.

"Why are you going into this room?"

I jumped—I was so deep into my own thoughts, I didn't even realize he had stopped in the hallway.

"I thought you wanted to go to bed," I said.

He peered inside the room, still not walking in. "I did."

"Well, then, let's go." I opened my arms and gestured around the room with a flourish.

He frowned. "Why aren't we in the master bedroom?"

Oh. Crap. My arms dropped to my sides. "Well, that's my aunt's room." My voice sounded lame even to me.

He stared at me. "Are you serious?"

I gazed down at the floor, wishing it would open it up and swallow me whole. God, would the night ever end?

He sighed heavily. "Fine. We'll stay here tonight. But, Rebecca, you've got to get it together. This is ridiculous. You're being ridiculous."

I nodded, too embarrassed to defend myself, and slunk off to the bathroom. He started undressing, muttering to himself as he opened the closet and peered into drawers.

God, I *was* a mess. Stefan was right. I could barely meet my own reflection in the bathroom mirror. Makeup smeared, eyes puffy and bloodshot. I sighed. What a disaster.

I cleaned myself up and got ready for bed. All I could think about was pulling the covers over my head, hoping the next day would be better.

Stefan was already in bed, lying on his side, light off. I fumbled my way to my side, trying not to disturb him, or bang into anything in the dark. Crawling into bed, I listened to Stefan's steady breathing as he slipped into sleep, and replayed the evening over and over again in my head.

It took me a long time to fall asleep.

***

The sun was streaming through the window when I finally awoke. My head was foggy and congested, and I had a slight headache. At first, I couldn't remember why I had a headache. What did I do last night? How much wine did I drink?

Then I saw Stefan's clothes strewn across the floor, just like they always were back in New York, and the memory of the entire night crashed into me. And, with it, all the guilt and shame.

What have I done?

What do I do now?

I threw the covers back. It was after ten in the morning. I couldn't believe I had slept so late. I hurriedly pulled on a pair of yoga pants and a tee shirt before heading downstairs.

Chrissy's door was open, so she was clearly up. I closed my eyes briefly. Of all days for her to be up before me. Why couldn't she have slept in until eleven, like most days? How on earth was I supposed to have any sort of conversation with Stefan about what happened last night with her in the room?

I hurried to the kitchen, still not sure what I should say or not say. I had so wanted this move to be a fresh start—financially, yes, but more importantly, for our marriage—and instead I felt like it had been one disaster after another. How could I turn things around?

I was still mulling my options when the scene that greeted me in the kitchen stopped me short. Chrissy and Stefan were standing very close—too close—as they both leaned against the counter, heads together, obviously talking. As I watched, Chrissy let out a little breathless laugh, throwing her head back, tossing her shiny black and blue hair. She wore a white, silky shirt that exposed one shoulder and half her white, lacy bra that looked pale and innocent against her black hair.

"Good morning," I said.

They both jerked their heads up to look at me. "Good morning," Stefan said, before turning to glance meaningfully at the cheery sunflower kitchen clock. "Or maybe I should say good afternoon?"

A fresh wave of guilt flooded my veins. "Sorry," I said. "I normally don't sleep so late."

Stefan picked up his coffee mug. "Well, it's not terribly surprising after your late night."

I flushed. Even though his tone was neutral, I could still hear the reproach underneath. He was up late, too. And so was Chrissy. Yet, both of them were awake before me.

"Chrissy, can you leave us for a moment?" I asked. The last thing I wanted was to have this conversation in front of her.

She turned her head to look at her father. As she did, her shirt shifted so her entire white lacy bra became exposed. I wanted to add that she could stand to put some more clothes on, while she was at it, but I held back.

Her father nodded to her. She glanced at me, a lazy smile playing on her lips as she pushed away from the counter, arching her back like a cat. "Of course, Rebecca," she said, as she sauntered out of the kitchen, her hips swaying more than I liked to see. Did she always walk that way? Chrissy definitely had a seductive edge to her, but this seemed a little … over the top.

But, enough of Chrissy. I faced my husband. Even at home on a Saturday morning, he still looked pressed and put together, while I felt like a wild mess in my yoga pants. He leaned back against the counter, crossing his arms across his chest.

"I'm sorry about last night," I said. "I'm really glad you're here and I wish I had known you were coming so I could have been waiting for you."

He tilted his head. "Sort of wrecks the whole point of surprising you."

I squirmed a bit. "Yes, but … isn't that kind of part of the risk you take when you decide to surprise someone?"

He lifted an eyebrow. "Are you saying this is my fault?"

"No, that's not …" My voice trailed off. Sometimes I really hated being married to a lawyer. I took a deep breath and tried again. "You know, whenever I've thrown one of my friends a surprise party, I've always made sure there was someone assigned to making sure my friend showed up. You barely reached out last week." I wanted to ask him about Sabrina. It was on the tip of my tongue, but at the last moment, I stuffed it back and went a different route. "You only texted me twice and called me once. For the entire week. If we had been talking regularly, then maybe ..."

"So, you *are* blaming me," he said. "It's my fault because I was buried in work and didn't text you enough for your satisfaction."

Oh God. I was just making this worse and worse. "No, I'm not trying to blame you. I'm just trying to explain. I was lonely and wanted to have a little fun. I know you're working hard and I didn't want to bother you. I didn't think it would be that big of a deal."

I dropped my gaze to the floor, unable to look at him, feeling more and more deflated. *What happened to us*, I wanted to ask. *How had we managed to drift apart so far and so fast that even something like this turns into a major issue?*

He sighed. "I'm sorry, too, Rebecca." I peeked up at him from behind my lashes, but he had turned to the coffee pot and was busy pouring. "You're right. I shouldn't have gotten so angry when you weren't here. You didn't know I was coming. How could you?" He turned back to me, smiling, and held out a cup of coffee. "A peace offering?"

I smiled back and reached for it. He had made it precisely the way I liked it. "I overreacted," he continued. "Partly because I was upset that you weren't here when I had wanted so badly to surprise you, but also because I was disappointed with the house."

"I know, but don't you think it makes sense for us to stay packed? It will make it so much easier for us to move once we sell the house."

He sighed again, casting his eyes around the warm, homey kitchen. "I see what you're saying, but it doesn't feel like home without our things," he said.

I opened my mouth to protest. I wanted to protest. But, he sounded so sad, so resigned, I couldn't.

"This is our fresh start," he continued. "And I was hoping to do it in a way where we both felt comfortable. Was that so wrong?"

"No," I said. It hadn't occurred to me that Stefan would feel more cared for in the nest I was trying to create if I unpacked. I felt stupid for not realizing that sooner. "I'll start unpacking next week. I promise."

He waved one hand. "Let's not worry about that now. What's important is we're together. As a family. Shall we go out to breakfast?"

"I can make us something," I said quickly, putting down my cup. I wanted to do something to assuage the guilt I was feeling, but he picked it up and pressed it into my hands. "Let me do something nice for you," he breathed into my ear, and I felt a shudder run through me. "I was a jerk yesterday. I totally overreacted, and I'd like to make it up to you. I'd like to take you and Chrissy out to breakfast. Treat you a little. Remember how we always used to go out to breakfast every Saturday morning together?"

"I remember," I said. After making love Saturday morning, he would always sweep me off to breakfast at one of our favorite little restaurants.

He nibbled my ear. "It won't quite be the same with Chrissy, but maybe we can make up for that later."

"I'd like that," I said. It had been months since he had shown any interest in me sexually—since the day he came home to tell me the law firm was failing.

See, this move would be a good thing after all.

"Go get ready," he said, swatting me gently on the behind. "And hurry up. I'm starving." He winked at me, making his intentions clear as I left the kitchen.

Chapter 12

Stefan drove us to Aunt May's Diner. "Chrissy said this place was great," he said as he parked in front of it.

Chrissy said what?

"Ah, well, yeah I liked it," I said cautiously. "But it's just diner food, which I know you're not a big fan of. The Terrace isn't that far away and has a really nice brunch, at least from what I remember …"

Stefan turned the car off and removed his seatbelt. "No, I'd like to try this place. Chrissy said your friends were here last time. I'd like to meet them. Especially if you're going to be spending time in bars with them." He shot me a sideways smile—a smile that didn't quite meet his eyes.

I felt myself grow cold. What did he mean by that? Was it another dig? Did this mean he was still upset with me? And why did he suddenly want to meet my friends? He hadn't shown much interest in meeting my New York friends.

Or did he mean Daniel?

As if reading my thoughts, he continued. "Chrissy told me you're old friends with a cop here. What was his name, David? Darrell?"

"Daniel," I said, through numb lips. *What else has Chrissy been saying?*

He snapped his fingers. "Of course. Daniel. So, was he out at the bar too last night?" On the surface, his voice was casual, bored even. But, underneath I detected an edge.

Was he jealous? He never had acted the least bit jealous before. *What the hell has Chrissy been saying to him?*

I made a point of meeting his eyes. "Yes," I said coolly, matching his flat tone. "Along with Gwyn, his fiancé. Shall we go in?" Without waiting for an answer, I opened the door and stepped out of the car.

What the hell was that all about? I made sure I kept my back to Stefan, raising my face to the sun and allowing the wind to tousle my hair. I wanted a moment to pull myself together. I could feel my head starting to throb.

"Aren't you coming?" Stefan asked, his voice right behind me, startling me. Chrissy was next to him, her eyes bright. She had been conspicuously silent in the backseat when we had pulled up at the diner, which might mean she had been busy with her phone, but I had a feeling she had been hanging on our every word.

I nodded, as I started trailing after them. Chrissy had started chatting with her father and as I watched them, I somehow felt uninvited … unwelcome.

Aunt May's was crowded with other families who clearly had the same idea we had. Mia waved to me from across the room. I waved back. "That's Mia," Chrissy said, before I could. "She's pretty cool."

"I'd love to meet her," Stefan said. "Rebecca, can you introduce us?"

"Well, I can try, but she's probably pretty busy," I said hesitantly, not at all sure about how I felt about Stefan meeting my friends. The bar comment still hovered between us, like an unwelcome cloud of noxious gas.

Mia waved as she wound her way toward us. "You must be Becca's husband," she said, holding out her hand. "I'm Mia. I'm so happy to meet you."

"Stefan," he said, shaking her hand. "It's great to finally meet one of *Rebecca's* friends." Was it my imagination, or had he just emphasized "Rebecca"?

She stuck her pen behind her ear. "Well, if you hang out in here long enough, they'll all stop by eventually. Let's get you a table."

I trailed after them, my head continuing to pound, my stomach suddenly queasy, with all the smells of bacon, coffee, and pancakes in the air. Was this some sort of delayed hangover? I hadn't felt all that bad when I woke up that morning. I fumbled for a tissue to blow my nose, trying to clear the stuffiness from my head.

"What's good here?" Stefan asked, as Mia handed us menus, poured coffee, and got us water. I drank some of the latter, hoping it would settle my stomach, as Chrissy talked to him about the food. I glanced furtively around the diner, hoping Mia was wrong, and that none of my friends were there. Especially Daniel. My stomach rolled inside me.

"You know what you want?" Mia was back, pen poised on her pad. Stefan nodded at me. I swallowed, trying to quell the sickness inside me, and ordered a couple of eggs and toast. Maybe if I ate something I would feel better.

"That's it?" Stefan asked.

I drank more water. "I'm not that hungry. Actually, I think I'm going to go to the restroom for a minute." Maybe I just needed a few minutes by myself to splash some cold water on my face.

Luckily, the restroom was one of those one-room stalls, and it was empty, so I didn't have to worry about someone walking in. My head didn't feel any better after the cold water on my face. In fact, I then started to feel a bit dizzy. I swallowed a couple of ibuprofens, hoping they'd take the edge off.

I leaned against the sink, pressing a cold paper towel against my eyes. I wanted to think, to try and figure out what was going on with Stefan, but it felt next to impossible to sort anything out while dealing with the dull pounding in my head, a stuffy nose, the faint dizziness, and the nausea. I spent a few more minutes breathing into the pain and sickness, giving the ibuprofen more time to kick in.

It occurred to me that, while I appreciated not having to worry about another person coming in to the one-person bathroom and asking me a lot of questions I didn't want to answer, it also meant I was holding up the bathroom. Reluctantly, I dried my face, cleaned up my makeup and combed my hair out.

I surveyed the results in the mirror. Not great, but not terrible either. It would have to do.

I opened the door and started to head back to the table, when someone called me from behind. I turned around. Daniel.

"I was hoping to catch you," he said. The cop was back—literally. He had his uniform on, and I noticed a strain around his eyes I hadn't seen before. My stomach clenched tightly. Oh God, I did NOT want to deal with anything else—especially Daniel, and his questions.

And the memory of wanting him to kiss me last night.

"Don't you have something better to do?" I asked, my tone snappier than I intended, as I felt the warmth of a blush creep up my neck. I prayed no one noticed. "There's got to be a real criminal somewhere in this town you could be harassing. Hell, you could probably go outside and write some parking tickets, at the very least."

His mouth twitched. "Believe it or not, we're having a slow crime day. And, I don't write parking tickets anymore. I've been promoted."

"A cat to save, maybe?"

"That's the fire department."

"What about another town? Like Janesville? Or, better yet, Milwaukee? I bet their criminals aren't taking the day off. They could probably use your crime-solving skills."

He smirked. "Not my jurisdiction. So, I guess you're stuck with me."

"Anything wrong, Officer?" I jumped. Stefan had come up behind me. I had forgotten he was even there, in the diner. How much of our conversation had he heard? My stomach twisted into even more knots.

Daniel straightened, his face instantly smoothing into an unreadable, professional mask. "And you are?"

Stefan held out his hand. "Stefan McMurray. Rebecca's husband." He casually—and protectively—wrapped his other arm around my waist.

Daniel introduced himself and shook Stefan's hand, his eyes flicking across Stefan's arm holding me firmly against him.

"I hope there's not a problem, Officer," Stefan said, tightening his grip and pressing me against him. I was having trouble breathing—whether it was from the pressure of Stefan's arm or that he was talking to Daniel, I couldn't tell.

Daniel paused, studying both of us, face betraying nothing. "Of course not," he said smoothly. "I just had a few questions for Becca."

"Questions about what? Has *Rebecca* been caught doing something naughty?" There was that slight emphasis on my full name again. His voice was teasing, playful, but there was definitely an edge to it. *I've got to find out what Chrissy has been telling him.* I felt like I was going to throw up.

Daniel's eyes continued to flick back and forth between us. "What makes you say that?" he asked smoothly.

Stefan squeezed me so tight, I started to gasp. "You're the one with questions for *my* wife. Maybe you ought to tell me, *Officer*," Stefan answered, just as smoothly.

Cat and mouse. Lawyer and cop. I felt like I was being pulled between them, like some sort of plaything. The tension was so thick I could barely breathe. I opened my mouth to stop them, to say we should go back to our table, our food was likely there, but nothing came out.

It was Mia who came to my rescue. "Hey, you guys," she said. "I've got your food right here." She showed us her tray. "More importantly, you're blocking the way to the bathroom. Daniel, if you want to join them and finish your conversation, I can bring you a cup of coffee."

Daniel paused, eyes locking with Stefan's. "No thanks, Mia. I've got to get back to the station." His voice was pleasant, even friendly, but the look in his eyes was hard.

Stefan smiled, icily. His eyes narrowed. "We wouldn't want to keep you from your job," he said, his voice equally pleasant, but with an underlying frigidness. "It was great meeting you, *Officer*."

Daniel nodded briefly. "Yes, I'm glad I was able to finally meet *Becca's* husband. I trust we'll be seeing you around more." It was less of a question and more of a statement.

"I'm sure you will," Stefan said. Daniel nodded briefly to both of us and turned to walk out, when Stefan called out to him. "Officer Shafer."

Daniel turned. Stefan smiled that cold smile again. "If you have any more questions for my wife, please address them to me. I don't know if *Rebecca* told you, but as an attorney, I'll be happy to answer whatever questions you may have. I'll have my secretary leave a message for you at the station to make sure you have all my contact information."

Daniel paused and just stared at him. Then, he smiled. A wolfish, predatory smile that said, *"So, this is how you want to play it? Game on."* Without another word, he turned and exited the diner.

Stefan waited until he was gone before he let go of me. The air rushed back into my lungs as I took a welcome deep breath. The tension around him dissolved.

"Stefan," I hissed, conscious of the eyes of all the diners on us, feeling mortified by the whole exchange. "What the hell was that all about?"

He looked at me, his gaze faintly narrowing. "I know he's an old friend, but Chrissy made it seem like he was harassing you. I wanted to see what was happening for myself, and if he was harassing you, put a stop to it. Come on, let's get back to our table and eat. I'm starving."

I wanted to protest—no, what just happened wasn't about protecting me from harassment. There was something else going on, something deeper. Was it jealously? Could it be as simple as that? But Stefan was already heading back to our table. I watched him walk away, as a wave of dizziness engulfed me.

"Miss? Are you okay?" One of the diners, an overweight balding man with black-rimmed glasses asked me, looking concerned. He slid his chair back and started to get up.

I waved him off. "I'm fine, thank you," I managed, even though I was far from it. My head was pounding, and I still felt lightheaded and nauseous. At the same time, I didn't want to add any more fuel to the gossip fire in the diner. What was it about this town that always seemed to make me the center of a big, fat drama? First, my aunt as the eccentric old witch in the haunted house, and now, this. I took a deep breath and managed to totter my way back to the table where our food waited.

Stefan and Chrissy had already started to eat. I sat down and drank some more water.

Stefan studied me. "Are you alright? You're looking a little pale."

I picked up a piece of toast and nibbled it. "I'm fine." All I wanted was to go home and lay down.

Stefan continued to watch me. "Are you sure? You're not eating much."

"I'll be fine. It's just a headache. I just need to lie down a bit when we get home."

Chrissy smirked, but kept her mouth shut. Thank God.

Stefan frowned. "I'm sorry to hear that. Make sure you eat. You know your headaches always get worse when you don't."

I nodded and took a bite of eggs, chewing very slowly and willing my stomach to stop rolling around so I could swallow.

Stefan picked up a piece of bacon. "Rebecca, why is everyone calling you Becca?"

"Because that's what her *friends* are allowed to call her," Chrissy answered, scowling at her food.

I looked at her in surprise. She was still upset by that? "That's not true," I said. "Well, not entirely true. It's what everyone here used to call me, when I came here. But, that was a long time ago. I've been Rebecca for years. It'll take some time, but they'll get used to it."

Chrissy viciously stabbed her fork into her hash browns. "Whatever," she muttered.

"Becca is a name for a child," Stefan remarked, forking up some eggs. "The sooner they start calling you Rebecca, the better."

I stared at him in disbelief. Becca is a name for a child? While I agreed with Stefan that I preferred Rebecca now, it wasn't because Becca was a childish name. It was because every time I heard it, I felt that familiar knife twist in my stomach.

Becca was a different girl. She was full of hopes and dreams, and didn't give a damn what her family—or anyone else—thought. She was going to live her life *her* way.

But, Becca was dead. She died of alcohol poisoning when she was sixteen. And, maybe it was for the best that Becca DID die—otherwise, I never would have met and married Stefan. Sure, we still had some work to do (okay, a lot of work) to fix our marriage, but it would happen. Stefan would eventually turn the law firm around, we'd sell the house, and before we knew it, we'd be back in New York, our marriage and lives back on track. Maybe even stronger than ever, having overcome this dip.

Everything would be fine. It was just a matter of time.

Chapter 13

After resting for a while (Stefan had insisted I go right to bed as soon as we got home, assuring me he and Chrissy would be fine), I got up and took a quick shower, spending a little extra time on my hair and makeup. I wanted tonight to be special.

I was going to make dinner. Not that I was much of a cook, but since we had to lay off our cook/housekeeper in New York, I had learned a few dishes, beef Stroganoff being one of them. I had gotten all the ingredients at the grocery store, including gluten-free pasta and gluten-free breadsticks, intending to make it for Chrissy and me this weekend, for what I hoped would be the start of a "girl's night in" and some bonding. Now, I'd make it for all three of us.

I put on an emerald green tunic dress that I knew Stefan liked because it brought out the green in my eyes and the red in my hair. Plus, it was short and showed off my legs.

As I headed downstairs, I could hear the low murmur of voices, but at first, I couldn't find them. They weren't in the living room or the kitchen. Finally, I found them in the family room, sitting on the couch, speaking quietly. Stefan had his laptop open and propped up on a tray table. Chrissy, wearing faded jean short shorts (*very* short shorts) and a cutoff cream tee shirt with the words "Raw Power" on it, had her bare legs in Stefan's lap.

I stopped short in the doorway, staring at them.

Something didn't feel right. I felt like I was interrupting an … *intimate* moment.

I cleared my throat. They both looked up and noticed me. "Oh, there you are. Feeling any better? You look better," Stefan said, looking at me with distinct male appreciation. I could feel myself respond to that gaze—it'd been a long time since Stefan had looked at me like that.

Chrissy gave me a lazy smile, looking like a very-pleased-with-herself cat. She didn't move her legs. She twined one of her fingers in her dark hair.

I took a step into the room. "Yes, I am. In fact, I thought I'd make dinner for all of us."

"Oh, you don't have to do that," Stefan said. "We could go out, or I could make something, maybe with Chrissy's help." He smiled at his daughter, who practically glowed as she smiled back.

There was something about that smile. It was like a secret between them. I didn't like it. I fought the urge to push Chrissy's legs off his lap. I took a step closer to them.

"No, I'd like to make it. You've done enough. I'd like to do something special tonight. For both of you."

Stefan gave me a slow, seductive smile. "That would be nice. Thank you. Let me at least help get you started." Stefan moved the tray table out of his way and Chrissy finally, reluctantly, moved her legs. He stood up and crossed the room to me, engulfing me in a quick kiss and a hug. "You smell great," he whispered in my ear. "You look great, too. We still have some … unfinished business from this morning, don't we?"

I hugged him back. "Yes, we do." He smelled great, too—I breathed in the clean, sharp scent of his expensive aftershave.

"Oh my God, get a room, you two," Chrissy snapped from the couch.

"Careful what you ask for," Stefan said to his daughter while nuzzling my neck. "We may just do that."

"Disgusting," Chrissy muttered.

I laughed, a mixture of relief and desire flowing through me. Everything was fine. I have no idea what my issue was with what I saw, or thought I saw, but I had to get my head on straight. I never saw anything even remotely inappropriate between he and Chrissy in New York. Plus, I knew Chrissy missed her father. She probably just wanted to be close to him while she had the chance, which is why she had her legs in his lap.

I glanced over at Chrissy and saw her staring at me, her face full of anger, her eyes like daggers.

If looks could kill …

Stefan let go of me. "Here, let me help get you started. I can pour us some wine. It's definitely five o'clock somewhere." He took my arm to lead me into the kitchen. I let him, feeling a little shaken by how Chrissy was glaring at me.

Almost like a jealous lover.

No! It couldn't be that. I was the hated stepmother—competition for her father's attention. That's all.

Stefan went to open the bottle, his manner entirely relaxed as he chatted with me. I pulled the ingredients out of the fridge, trying to listen to him as my head whirled. What did I see? Nothing, really. Chrissy wearing inappropriate attire that morning while they were in the kitchen together, Chrissy still wearing inappropriate attire (did she have that on when we went to breakfast? Did she change? I couldn't remember), her legs in Stefan's lap, glaring at me when Stefan hugged me.

But Stefan wasn't touching her back. He wasn't touching her when I walked in the kitchen that morning. And he wasn't touching her just now. He had his computer on a tray table and both hands on his keyboard.

I had to get it together.

"I'm going to wrap up what I was working on, so we can spend the whole evening together, uninterrupted," Stefan said, caressing my back and kissing my neck.

"Hmmm … be careful you don't start something you can't finish."

"Oh, I'll definitely be finishing this," he said as he kissed me one last time before letting me go. "I better get out of here before I can't."

I laughed.

After he walked out of the kitchen, I took a sip of wine and began washing and chopping. I was sautéing beef and slicing vegetables for a salad when I heard the dim chirps of my cell phone buried in the depths of my purse. Oh geez, it was probably Mia, wanting all the details of what happened between Daniel and Stefan. I didn't want to talk to her right then, but for all I knew, she had been trying to reach me all day. Maybe it would be best to talk to her briefly, and then I could turn the phone off for the night.

I dug my phone out of my purse and my heart sank. It was CB. As anxious as I was to talk to him to smooth things over after our last conversation (I had sent him a couple of texts, but he had been short in his responses), it just wasn't the time. Stefan ... *tolerated* CB. Barely. Things had gotten even more strained between the two of them after CB had made his feelings known about how big of a mistake he thought this move was.

I considered not answering, but that would mean more explanations when we next talked, which would likely end in another fight. Maybe just a fast conversation while I cooked. Stefan was in the other room working anyway.

"Cos! Sorry I didn't call you back sooner. It's been a week, I tell you." He sighed dramatically. "I have so much to share. Marguerite's last nip and tuck did NOT go well, she looks a fright. Now she's talking lawsuits." Marguerite was his mother, my aunt, but he always called her by her first name. "But, before I get into all of that, I want to hear about you. What's the latest and greatest in Hicksville? Have you seen Daniel again?"

I winced, tucking the phone between my shoulder and neck as I kept chopping. "Actually, this isn't a great time. I'm in the middle of cooking. Can I call you back tomorrow?"

CB was silent for a moment. "Is Stefan *finally* there?"

I started rattling in the cupboard for a large pan. "Yes."

"Permanently?"

I banged the pan on the stove and turned up the burner. "Well, no. Not yet. Look, let me call you back."

CB muttered something.

"Don't start," I said. "I really do want to talk to you. I'll call you back."

"Fine. Call me back." The line went dead.

I put the phone down and picked up my wine, taking a long drink to center myself before getting back to cooking.

"Who was that?"

I jumped, spilling my wine on my dress. "Jesus, Stefan, you scared me. Why did you sneak up on me like that?" I grabbed a washcloth and soaked it in cold water to dab at my dress. Thank God it was white wine.

Stefan came closer, his manner still relaxed and friendly ... but there was a tension about him that made it seem forced. His eyes were watching me carefully.

I dabbed furiously at my dress. "No one important."

He cocked his head. "Then why did you say you'd call him back?"

I opened my mouth to ask why he was assuming it was a "him," but gave up before uttering a word. Why fight it? He was going to drag it out of me sooner or later. And if I told him now, maybe it wouldn't lead to a fight and I would still be able to salvage the nice, romantic night I had planned.

I sucked in my breath. "I just ..." I threw the washcloth in the sink and sighed. "It was CB."

I didn't look at him, but I could feel the tension vibrate. "You know how I feel about him."

"Yes, but he is my cousin."

"Is he planning to come out here?"

I looked at him in shock. "CB? Why would he come out here? He hates it here."

"You're here. Why wouldn't he visit?"

I shook my head. "CB had his fill of this place when we were kids. He's not going to come here by choice."

Stefan studied me for a long moment, his eyes narrowing slightly. Then, he breathed out in a long sigh and smiled—a smile that didn't reach his eyes. "I know he's your cousin, but you know how I feel about him. He's too ... attached to you. I don't think he's a good influence on you or Chrissy. He should stay in New York."

A part of me wanted to defend CB, and my relationship with him. It wasn't the first time Stefan accused CB of being overly interested in my life. But I forced it down. Did I really want to start a fight about my cousin? Or would I prefer to fan some of the closeness we had just rekindled into a nice, hot flame? "Of course. Want to top off my wine?"

Stefan leaned over to kiss me on the head as he took my glass.

I accepted the wine and gave him my most seductive smile. There would be plenty of time to discuss CB once our relationship was on stronger footing.

He smiled again, more genuinely. "It smells wonderful. I can't wait to dig in," he said. His eyes heated up. "I'm definitely *very* hungry."

I dropped my gaze demurely. "It won't be too much longer."

"Is that a promise?"

I fluttered my eyelashes. "Absolutely."

From the family room, I was sure I heard the sound of retching.

Stefan sighed and retreated to the living room while I went back to cooking.

Chapter 14

Lying in bed later that night, with Stefan's arm flung over me, I drowsily watched the curtains flutter against the open window and listened to Stefan's heavy breathing beside me. The moon shone through the window, bleaching the color out of everything it touched.

It had actually ended up being a relaxing, fun evening. My headache was pretty much gone, although I was still stuffed up. The beef Stroganoff was perfect—both Stefan and Chrissy had second helpings. Stefan was charming and engaging, talking to both of us and sharing funny stories. Even Chrissy was well-behaved, treating me like I was a real person, instead of someone she was forced to deal with.

After dinner, we dug through my aunt's impressive collection of games, and finally decided on Scrabble. None of us had played in years. Actually, I wasn't sure if Chrissy had ever played it, so we ended up laughing a lot as we got the hang of playing.

At ten, Chrissy decided to head off to bed and wished us both a good night. As soon as she disappeared upstairs, Stefan turned to me, desire dark in his eyes, and nuzzled my neck. "I think we have some unfinished business upstairs," he said, his voice husky as he nibbled at my ear.

"I think you're right," I said, letting him lead the way.

Now, cuddled against him in the afterglow and listening to him sleep, my eyes slowly drifting closed, I began to think that maybe everything really was going to be fine—that despite the rocky start of his surprise visit, we had finally started to reconnect.

I heard banging downstairs in the kitchen, and my eyes flew open. "Stefan," I whispered, shaking him. "I think someone's in the house!"

Stefan muttered in his sleep and rolled over.

"Stefan," I said a bit louder, and shook him harder. He opened his mouth and started to snore.

Maybe it was Chrissy sleepwalking again. Of course, I hadn't yet told Stefan about the first incident, so perhaps it would be more prudent to simply deal with it myself than try to explain all of it to a half-awake, and probably pretty irritated, husband.

I slid out of bed and made my way down the stairs, all the while listening to the banging. Man, I really hoped Chrissy wasn't destroying the kitchen the way she had the living room.

But it wasn't Chrissy in the kitchen. It was Aunt Charlie, opening and closing cupboards and banging pots on the stove. "Oh, there you are. I didn't think you were ever going to get down here."

I stepped into the kitchen. "Why are you making such a racket?"

She picked up the kettle from the stove and poured water into the teapot. "To get you down here, silly. Why do you think?" She put the teapot and two mugs on a tray and carried them both to the table. "What are you waiting for? An engraved invitation? Sit down, we have to talk."

I wasn't so sure I wanted to sit down at the table with her, but somehow, my body carried me to the chair opposite her. "This is a dream, isn't it?"

Aunt Charlie let out a guffaw as she poured the tea. "Of course it is. I'm dead—how else am I supposed to have a conversation with you?"

"Séance?"

Aunt Charlie put a mug in front of me. "That's Mad Martha's deal. Can't make tea in a séance."

I stared down into the tea. This time she put it into a sunflower mug, all bright and yellow and cheery. Aunt Charlie caught me staring at the mug. "You're going to need all the cheer you can get." She nodded to the mug. "Dark days are ahead. Dark days, indeed. Drink up."

Dark days. An ominous feeling, as thick and heavy as a cloak, settled around me. I swallowed hard, trying to push it down, and looked into my cheery, happy sunflower mug. It certainly looked like tea. I could smell the aroma of flowers and herbs—it was one of Aunt Charlie's favorite blends. "What do you mean, 'dark days are ahead'?"

Aunt Charlie paused, her mug by her mouth, and sighed. "It's started. I had hoped ... well, I couldn't reach her in time. I tried. I had thought I might have more time. But ..." Aunt Charlie shook her head. "No sense crying over spilled milk. What's done is done. All we can do now is mitigate the damage as best as we can. And that starts with you drinking your tea." She nodded at my mug.

What's done is done? Reach her in time? Reach *who* in time? In time for what? I had so many questions, but when I opened my mouth to start asking them, my senses were overwhelmed by that tea. It called to me, seduced me, completely overpowered me.

Maybe one sip wouldn't hurt. I looked down into the mug. The tea looked like tar, thick and black.

I glanced at Aunt Charlie. She was sitting very still, watching me. The moonlight slanted against her face, making her nose and chin seem far more pointed than I remembered as a child. Her eyes were black pools of nothingness, as black as that tea. Those eyes ... just like the homeless woman under the streetlight ...

Aunt Charlie smiled. The moonlight glinted off her teeth.

Sharp, pointed teeth.

I jumped backwards, knocking my chair to the ground as I backed away from her. Aunt Charlie sighed. "You really ought to trust me. If you don't, you're going to make this so much more difficult for yourself."

"You're not my Aunt Charlie," I gasped, backing up against the wall.

She chuckled. "Of course I am. Who else would I be?" And then she smiled.

Her smile grew wider and wider, revealing rows and rows of teeth. It kept growing and stretching, nearly swallowing up her entire face, until all that was left was a giant open mouth and sharp teeth.

I sat up with a gasp. I was back in bed. Stefan was in a deep sleep next to me, laying on his side away from me.

I rubbed my chest, trying to get my breathing under control. I was soaked with sweat, my black satin negligee sticking to me.

I listened to Stefan's peaceful, deep breathing next to me as my own began to slow down, feeling the cool night air against my soaked skin. I had just started to consider laying back down again, when I heard a crash. *Oh God, it's Aunt Charlie.* I wanted to crawl under my bed, my terror a living beast inside me, *No, I don't want any tea!*, but then I realized it hadn't come from downstairs.

Chrissy!

I leapt out of bed and ran to her bedroom. For a moment, I thought maybe I should wake Stefan, but that thought was quickly overruled. I had to make sure she was okay.

You should also be waking Stefan, a little voice deep inside me scolded. *He's her father, you know. You're just the step-mother. And a pretty sorry one at that.*

That was true. But, it was going to take too long to get him up to speed. Right now, making sure Chrissy was safe was my biggest priority.

Her door was closed. I skidded to a stop in front of it. Should I just go in? My heart was pounding in my head and my breathing sounded loud and harsh. I leaned over to press my ear against the door, but I couldn't hear anything other than my own panic.

I gently grasped the doorknob and turned.

Chrissy stood in the center of the floor, completely bathed in the light of the moon. She looked like a statue, with her long black hair hanging straight down her back, in total contrast with her white nightgown that practically glowed in the light. I couldn't tell if she was awake or not.

"Chrissy," I said softly, trying for the perfect volume—loud enough to get her attention if she was awake, and quiet enough to NOT wake her, if she was sleepwalking.

She turned to me, her face smooth and pale. Her eyes were open, but I still couldn't tell if she was actually awake or not—

they looked like bottomless dark pools in her face. "I've looked everywhere," she said. "I can't find it."

I took a step into her room. "Can't find what?"

She cocked her head, as if she was listening to unseen voices. "What you want. Or, at least, what you think you want."

I took another slow step into her room. I was pretty sure she was sleepwalking. "What I want?" I asked cautiously.

A shadow of fear rippled across her otherwise expressionless face. "Please don't hurt me. I'll do better."

Another step. I had almost reached her. "I'm not going to hurt you. I'm here to help you."

She looked like marble in the moonlight. "Then, why did you kill me?"

I jerked to a stop. "Kill you? Chrissy, what are you talking about?" I struggled to keep the edge out of my voice, so as not to wake her. She had to be dreaming.

Her face changed ever so slightly, like something not quite right was crawling right beneath the surface of her skin. "You know," she hissed. "The evil that's been done."

My terror crawled up into my throat and then my mouth—I could taste it— cold and metallic. *Keep breathing*, I told myself. *Don't startle her. You don't want to accidentally wake her. And whatever you do, don't throw up.* I took a step closer and slowly reached out my hand to touch her arm. "Chrissy. What are you talking about? *What evil?*"

Suddenly, her eyes rolled into the back of her head, and her legs started to fold underneath her. I darted forward and caught her before she fell. She hung limply in my arms, and was much heavier than she looked, so I awkwardly rearranged her to cradle her head as I lowered her to the ground. I caught a glimpse of us in the mirror above the dresser—Chrissy, smooth and pale in her white sheer nightgown, her black hair cascading like a waterfall past her shoulders, emphasizing her porcelain complexion. Me, a half-crazed freak with my wild, tangled hair going every which way, looking old and "used up" in the (unflattering) black negligee Stefan had bought me on our honeymoon.

Why did you kill me?

An evil stepmother with her innocent, virginal princess step-daughter she had just killed.

I felt cold and shaken by the thoughts, and shifted my attention to making Chrissy as comfortable as possible on the floor. Her eyes fluttered open.

"What's going on? What happened?"

I smoothed her hair back from her forehead. "You were sleepwalking again. Can you remember anything?"

Her eyes finally focused on me. "Wait … what? Rebecca, what's going on?" She struggled to sit up and I gently pushed her back down.

"Don't try and get up. Just rest for a minute."

She lay back down weakly. The moonlight slanted across her face, making her look a lot younger than her sixteen years. "What's going on? Why are you in my room? Why am I on the floor?"

"You were sleepwalking again."

She stared at me. "I don't sleepwalk."

"Well, you do now."

She started to get agitated. "You're lying. I don't sleepwalk."

I started to get exasperated. "Maybe I should get your father …"

"No!" She reached up and grabbed my arm.

Startled, I stared at her. She looked … scared. About me getting her father? Nervously, she licked her lips. "I … don't want to worry him. I know he has to go back to New York and I don't want him worried about me."

"Okay, I won't get him," I said, not wanting to agitate her any further.

Her fingers dug into my skin. "You won't tell him. Right?"

I looked at her uneasily. Was this really something I wanted to keep from Stefan? "I don't know …"

She squeezed my arm even more tightly. "No. You mustn't. At least, not now. Please?"

I stared down into her pleading, desperate eyes and sighed. "Okay, I won't tell him. At least for now."

She closed her eyes. "Thank you, Rebecca."

"How are you feeling? Should we get you back in bed?"

She whimpered. "My head hurts. A lot."

"Let's get you in bed, and I'll get you some ibuprofen." She nodded, and I carefully helped her stand.

As I tucked her in, I asked her, as casually as I could, "Do you remember anything? Anything at all?"

She shook her head. "No … just … no. I don't remember."

I smoothed the covers back, wondering about the hesitation. "Oh, it's not important, it's just you said …"

She then looked terrified. "I *said* something? I talked?"

"Yes," I said, confused by her reaction.

She gripped my arm again, practically clawing at it, in her agitation, half sitting up, her eyes wild. "What did I say?"

"Uhhhh." What do I tell her? That she told me I know something about the evil that's been done? That she asked me why I killed her?

Yeah, that's the ticket. We should have no trouble bonding after *that* conversation.

She started shaking my arm. "Rebecca, tell me! What did I say?"

She was so upset, I couldn't tell her the truth. At least, not the whole truth. What if it made everything worse? "Just that … you were looking for something. You couldn't find it."

She looked confused. "Looking for something? What was I looking for?"

I gently disentangled her arm and guided her back down to her bed. "I don't know. Did you lose something in real life?"

She shook her head, still looking puzzled.

I tried a reassuring smile, but it felt fake on my lips. "Well, it was probably nothing."

She allowed me to tuck her back into bed, her body limp. Her hair stuck in clumps to her face and neck, and she stunk of sweat. The agitation having drained from her body, she seemed completely exhausted. "Did I say anything else?"

"Nothing that made much sense," I said lightly, stroking her hair. "Let me get you something for your head."

She nodded, and I started to get up when the corner of my eye caught the mirror above the dresser. My mouth went dry. The moon reflected in the glass, and just like that, I was sixteen, standing there with Daphne, staring into that exact mirror, terror crawling inside me like a living thing.

It's coming. Beware.

Chrissy was sleeping in the room we had done the séance in.

Chapter 15

"Do you really have to fly back today?"

We were in the kitchen. Stefan was organizing his briefcase, and I was pouring coffee. Chrissy was presumably still asleep.

I was tired and grumpy, and still stuffed up. After getting Chrissy settled with ibuprofen and a cool washcloth on her forehead, I had returned to bed, needing a few more hours of sleep. Stefan hadn't seemed to stir as I crawled in next to him, idly wondering how on earth he could possibly have slept through all the commotion.

But I couldn't sleep. Images of Chrissy asking me why I killed her, and how I had known about the evil that was done swirled together with images of that ill-fated séance.

How could I have forgotten about the room? How could I have let Chrissy choose that room?

And why HAD Daphne and I picked that room to do the séance in, in the first place?

I needed to talk to Daphne. Immediately. Well, maybe not immediately—it *was* the middle of the night—but as soon as possible.

I finally dozed off and slept fitfully, waking when Stefan's travel alarm went off. He got ready while I headed to the kitchen to make coffee.

Stefan sighed as I handed him a mug. "Look, I know this wasn't ... well, it didn't turn out exactly as I had planned. But, you know I have to go back."

I did know. And, if I were being honest, a part of me wanted him to leave. I needed to get to the bottom of what was going on in the house, and my gut said he'd just get in the way if he was around. Once all of that was taken care of, then I could focus all my time and attention on reconnecting.

Besides, it was still bothering me, the way Chrissy had been behaving around him. Him being in New York seemed like the best option for everyone right now.

So, why was I feeling so grouchy?

"I know you need to go back. I guess it's just …" I trailed off, not really sure how to finish that sentence.

He put his coffee down and reached over to rub my back. "I know it's been difficult for you. It's been difficult for all of us. I'll try and make it back in a couple of weeks—maybe sooner if I can swing it. Okay?"

I nodded. I wondered if part of the reason I was feeling so out of sorts was the gnawing, uncomfortable sensation I had that kept pushing me to tell him about Chrissy. Despite my late-night promise, I knew I shouldn't keep Chrissy's sleepwalking, and sleeptalking, from him. While I was at it, I could talk to him about her clothing choices over the weekend, too. "Stefan, we really should talk about Chrissy …"

He interrupted me. "I really have to get to the airport. Is this something we can talk about later? Chrissy told me you two were getting along better than ever. I thought you were too, watching you this weekend. Is that true?"

Crap, why did he always do that to me, when it came to Chrissy? "Well, I guess, that's true, but that's not …"

He picked up his coffee. "Then, what's the problem?"

Did I really want to start? Me already on the defensive, and him about to run out the door? "I … I guess it's nothing. We can talk about it later."

He swallowed his coffee. "I know she can be a handful—she's a teenager, after all. I know I gave my parents hell when I was that age. I also know how difficult it must be for you to parent her without me. I talked with her and asked her to be on her best behavior, and to start helping you out more. I'm sure part of the reason we're not fully unpacked yet is because she's not helping you like she should be. She promised me she'd do better." He put his mug down and smiled at me. "I really do appreciate everything you do. I know I don't always show it, but I do."

It felt like my heart had stopped beating for a moment. Stefan almost never said things like that. "Ah … You can count on me. We're a family."

He leaned over and kissed my cheek. "We'll get through this," he whispered in my ear. "I promise."

I nodded. He smiled again and went back to packing up his briefcase. "With Chrissy's help, you should have no trouble whipping this house into shape, so you can get it on the market. Especially if you focus a hundred percent of your attention on it."

"Of course," I said, not really sure where he was going.

"Because, the sooner we sell it, the sooner we can move back to New York and get back to our lives."

"Right," I agreed.

"I know how much you want to get back to New York and your friends there," he continued. "Which is why I think it makes sense to … maybe not waste your time seeing old friends here."

My good mood soured. I tried to swallow my coffee and it tasted like ash in my mouth. "Why can't I do both?" I asked.

He paused for a moment, resting his hands on his briefcase. "Rebecca, do you really think that's smart? Why do you want to waste time getting to know people you'll never see again after a few months?"

Never see again? I could feel my eyes widen. "That feels a little harsh, doesn't it? Especially in this age of email and social media …"

"Do you really think that's wise? Especially with everything that's happened to you here in Redemption? It's not like your friends here are a …" he paused delicately. "A terribly good influence."

I couldn't believe what I was hearing. "What?"

"Let's look at the facts," he said soothingly. "What happened fifteen years ago? You nearly died of alcohol poisoning. And that near-death event triggered years of suffering for you. You even lost your memories! Then, what happens? You're not even in Redemption for a week and you're already at a bar with your old friends getting drunk. Much drunker than you ever were back in New York."

"I drink in New York," I said, stung. "I've gotten drunk, too."

"Well, I've never seen you as drunk as you were Friday night," he said firmly.

I wanted to argue. That wasn't true. Or fair. I wasn't *that* drunk.

"Besides," he continued. "Don't you think it would make more sense to cut off all contact? Aside from the bad influence aspect, Redemption is your past, not your future. Now that you've come back and made peace with it, all that's left is to sell the house and move on with our lives. It's not like you don't have your hands full with all the unpacking. Wouldn't it make more sense to spend your time getting the house in as perfect shape as you can to sell it for top dollar?"

I dropped my eyes to my coffee. "I suppose," I said miserably. I didn't like anything he was saying, and was trying to think of another way to get my point across when I realized which mug I was holding.

It was the sunflower mug—the same one Aunt Charlie handed me last night in my dream. Of ALL the mugs in the cupboard, I had chosen *that* one. I carefully put it down.

Stefan had started talking again, oblivious to my focus on the mug, and the fact that I hadn't been listening. "… better this way. I'll need an office, too, once I'm working from home. Maybe you can set up that bedroom as my office once you move us into the master bedroom?"

I felt my heart sink even further. I had forgotten about the bedroom. But before I could figure out how to respond, Stefan was kissing my cheek, promising he would let me know when he landed, and walking out of the house.

Crap.

I rubbed my face. Coffee. I needed more coffee. And *not* coffee from the sunflower mug. I went to the sink to rinse the cup out, then fished out a new one—one with yellow daisies on it—and poured fresh coffee into it. I leaned against the counter, sipping, and tried not to sink too deeply into despair.

My life, for the near future at least, was going to be spent turning this warm and comfy house into a mirror image of our

New York apartment, having no contact with anyone other than Chrissy and eventually, Stefan.

Is this what I really wanted?

No. It wasn't. But, I did want to save my marriage.

Was doing this worth my marriage?

Or was the price too high?

No. I didn't want to go there. I *couldn't* go there. The idea of ending my marriage … my *second* marriage … it was too much.

My family had been supportive when my first marriage ended. I could tell my mother had been disappointed, but she had stood by me. He had been cheating on me after all. She agreed I needed to divorce him.

One mistake was unfortunate.

But, two mistakes?

My mother had taken me out to lunch a few days before the wedding to have a heart-to-heart with me. "Are you sure?" she kept asking. "I know he's a catch. But, Rebecca. It's just so fast. Are you sure?"

"I am Mom," I kept reassuring her. "I know it's fast, but he has a sixteen-year-old daughter. He wants us to be a family and give her a solid foundation. Besides, his wife cheated on him, too. He won't do that to me."

I could tell my mother still hadn't been that convinced. As much as she wanted me married to a man like Stefan, a man who could take care of me properly and who didn't need the trust fund waiting for me when I turned fifty-five, she still wasn't convinced that I wasn't making another mistake.

How could I possibly face her if I got a second divorce? How could I possibly admit to her that yes, she was right … I had rushed into it too fast?

Would she cut me off? Sure, I had the trust fund, but I had to wait almost twenty-five years before I could access it. How would I support myself in the meantime? New York was expensive. And, as hard as I had tried, I had yet to find a career path that I could both excel in and that would allow me to pay all my bills.

No, I couldn't face her with a second failed marriage. Nor could I face myself. I needed to make this work.

Whatever the cost.

Chrissy walked into the kitchen then, interrupting my thoughts, hair mussed from sleep, wearing her usual red and blue sleep outfit. "Dad leave already?" she asked, yawning.

"Yeah, he's got to get back to New York. Early meetings to-morrow. How are you feeling?"

"Okay." She paused, awkwardly shifting from foot to foot, not meeting my eyes. "Did you tell him?"

I shook my head as I sipped my coffee. "No. He doesn't know."

She looked relieved—a little too relieved actually. "Thanks, Rebecca."

I nodded, wondering why she was so insistent that I not tell her father. Should I ask? Maybe it would be better if I just kept my mouth shut. Maybe this would help us finally bond. "Want some breakfast? We can go out, or I can make you something. Gluten-free pancakes?"

She moved to the kitchen, pulling her long black hair back from her face and securing it into a ponytail. "Actually, let me make breakfast. You just enjoy your coffee."

I looked at her, in shock. Chrissy actually could cook—she had had lessons at one point. Maybe it was a summer camp thing or when she was at boarding school, I couldn't remember. Every now and then, when we were in New York, she would make us all dinner. She had even given me some tips when I was struggling to learn after we let our housekeeper go. But she had never offered to cook for just me.

"Thanks. That would be nice."

She looked up at me and smiled. An actual, genuine, hon-est-to-God smile. But, then, almost as if she were embarrassed, she ducked her head. "It's no problem," she mumbled. "I like to cook."

I quietly moved away from the counter, smiling inwardly as I carried my coffee to the table. Maybe this would all work out after all.

Chapter 16

"So, what was all that about between your husband and Daniel?" Mia asked me, tearing open a couple of pink packets of sugar substitute and pouring them into her iced tea. "Spill it, sister."

Daphne, Mia and I were all meeting for lunch at The Tipsy Cow. I was feeling a little pang of guilt being here after my conversation with Stefan. But, I told myself it was just lunch, and besides, didn't I owe them an explanation rather than simply disappearing? It was much better to explain in person. Plus, I knew Mia was dying to hear about the diner incident, and I definitely wanted to get to the bottom of why we had done the séance in Chrissy's room. Stefan would also want that cleared up as well. It was a good thing I was here.

I blew my nose. "Stefan doesn't want Daniel to talk to me anymore. At least not in any official capacity."

Mia raised her eyebrow. "Really? And how is he going to stop that?"

"He's a lawyer, remember? He wants Daniel to funnel his inquiries through him."

Mia half-smiled. "Well, well, well. I can see why that didn't go over so well."

Daphne studied me. "Did you ask Stefan to do this for you?"

"Ah …" I looked down at the table, studied a scar in the wood, suddenly wanting to squirm. "Well, no."

Daphne looked like she was going to say something more, but changed her mind, taking a drink of her iced tea instead.

I jerked my head up to look at her. "What?"

She shook her head. "Nothing. It's none of my business."

"What?" I said again, a little impatiently.

Daphne hesitated. In the silence, I could hear the clatter of dishes from the kitchen and the murmur of voices from the door as the hostess sat a group of three women, one with a baby in a carrier.

"It's just," she finally said. "It's just ... surprising to me. That's all. I can't see sixteen-year-old Becca taking that."

I sucked in my breath, wanting to scream, "That's because Becca is DEAD." I didn't want to talk about Becca anymore—it was too painful. Instead, I played with my glass, knocking the ice cubes together so they made little clinking noises. "That was a long time ago. People change."

"That's for sure," Mia piped in.

"Stefan isn't trying to control me," I continued. "He's just trying to stop Daniel from bothering me." Is that what I really thought? I wondered.

Daphne smiled at me. "Look, if you're fine with it, then we're fine with it. You don't have to explain."

I tried to smile back, but my face felt wooden. *Was* I fine with it? Or was this part of the price I had to pay to keep our marriage together?

Luckily our food arrived then, giving me a chance to center my thoughts. I could still talk to them about Chrissy and the sleepwalking.

"There's something else I wanted to talk to you about," I said, as soon as the server withdrew.

Mia leaned forward. "It's about the ghost, isn't it? I knew it."

I picked up my fork and started playing with my salad. "Well ..."

Mia fist pumped. "Yes! You know, I still haven't forgiven you guys for having that séance without me. Or for not even telling me. You knew how much I wanted to meet Mad Martha. I would have loved doing that séance! I'm considering giving you the silent treatment."

"We could only be so lucky," Daphne said drily.

I was staring at Mia. "Wait. Did I talk about Mad Martha with you, too?"

Mia looked surprised. "Of course. It was all we talked about that summer. Well, that, and our nonexistent summer romances." She rolled her eyes. "Oh, the angst! To be a teenager again. But, wait," she brought her focus back to me. "How can you not remember that?"

I was silent. Daphne looked at me. "You'd better tell her."

Mia looked at both of us. "Tell me what?"

I sighed. Maybe I should just put up a billboard and be done with it. "After that night ... I lost my memory of that summer."

Mia stared at me. "Really? You don't remember anything? At all?"

"It's coming back, but there are still huge holes."

"What about that night? And does Daniel know?"

I shook my head vehemently. "No! And, don't tell him, either. I guess I had some sort of conversation with the cops that night that I also don't remember."

Mia sat back in her chair. "Wow. Well, just wow."

"Explains a lot, doesn't it?" Daphne said.

"Yeah, it sure does."

"What do you mean?" I asked.

Mia and Daphne looked at each other. "Just ... just the way you've been acting," Daphne said. "Not like the old Becca."

"And, why Daniel keeps pestering you," Mia piped in. "I mean, I know he had a crush on you and all that back then, but he's with someone now, and so are you. He's not one to, you know, cheat. Loyal to a fault."

Daphne rolled her eyes. "*Too* loyal."

Mia made a face. "Yeah, well, that's most definitely a conversation for another time. Over wine. But, now it all makes more sense. If you're not telling him what he wants to know, he's like a dog with a bone."

I held up my hand. "Okay, so first off, Daniel most certainly did *NOT* have a crush on me." At that, both Mia and Daphne burst out laughing. "He did NOT," I insisted. "Stop laughing, you two." Had I told them about Daniel standing me up? Maybe I ought to mention it now to prove he didn't have a crush on me. I also wanted to ask them what they meant about Daniel being "too loyal," but with both of them laughing the way they were, I didn't think the time was right.

"Okay, whatever," Mia said through her giggles. "Another conversation to be had over wine."

I wadded up empty paper sweetener packets and threw them at her. She ducked, still giggling.

"Secondly, and probably more importantly, are you telling me he's going to keep harassing me about that night until I tell him the truth about my memory?"

"Probably," Daphne said. "Especially now that your husband has stepped in."

"Daniel always did like a good challenge," Mia said. "Remember that date rape case a few years ago? Horrible. Guy slipped this girl a mickey in her drink at the bar, so she couldn't remember anything. He wasn't her actual date either, which made it more confusing. There seemed to be no leads, but Daniel didn't let that deter him. I still don't know how he was finally able to break that case."

I sunk down in my seat. "Great. Just great."

"Well, look on the bright side," Mia said. "You'll be able to spend all kinds of time with Daniel. That's what you always wanted, right?"

I shot her the evil eye. "Yeah, perfect pastime for a married woman."

Mia smirked. "Oh, that's right. So, I guess there is no bright side."

I picked up my fork and speared a piece of chicken, still glaring at Mia.

"But, back to the ghost," Mia said, grinning at me. "I want it all—the good, the bad, and the ugly. Let's hear it."

I took another bite of my Cobb salad, which was surprisingly good, mostly to give myself a moment to switch gears and try and figure out the best way to start. I was still trying to decide if I really wanted to disclose it all. There was no going back once I told them—did I really want them to know all of it?

Maybe some things are better off staying buried, the voice said.

I mentally shook my head, quieting it. No, I had to get to the bottom of what was happening, even if I didn't particularly like what I found.

"Chrissy is sleepwalking," I blurted out. Daphne and Mia looked surprised. "She never did this in New York," I explained. "But, it's actually more than sleepwalking. She's sleeptalking, too."

"What's she saying?" Daphne asked.

I sighed and dug around for another tissue to blow my nose again. "Let me start at the beginning."

I told them almost everything. Even about the Aunt Charlie dreams, which I wasn't intending to bring up, but they somehow seemed important when I started sharing it all.

The only thing I held back was how strange Chrissy had been acting around Stefan.

My friends listened quietly. Even Mia didn't interrupt. They simply let me talk and talk, until it had all just poured out of me.

When I finished, I sat back, feeling exhausted. It was like I had been vigorously exercising, rather than simply having a conversation. But I also felt a deep sense of relief—of lightness. I didn't realize how heavy a burden keeping all of that inside of me had become.

"Wow," Mia said finally. "I'm not sure I know where to start."

Daphne shook her head. "I'm not sure either."

"Well, I can help. Why did we pick *that* room to do the séance in, Daphne?"

Daphne poked at a few lone carrot slices on her nearly empty plate. Mia examined her empty iced-tea glass.

I looked at both of them. "Well, c'mon. You know I don't remember. Spill it."

Daphne and Mia looked at each other before Daphne finally met my eyes. "That's the room Mad Martha killed Nellie in, before hanging herself."

I stared at them, an ice-cold lump forming in my stomach. "*That's* the room? I let Chrissy sleep in *that* room?"

"Did you put her in that room, or did she choose it?" Daphne asked.

I shook my head. "It doesn't matter. I never should have let her be in there."

Which room could you have put her in, a little voice inquired. *Your room? The master bedroom? Aunt Charlie's office?*

And if you don't want her in that room anymore, where precisely are you planning to move her to? And what are you going to do about Stefan's office?

I rubbed my temples. This just kept getting worse and worse. "Why did we do the séance in the first place?"

Daphne sighed. "You'd been having dreams. About Mad Martha ..."

Mia interrupted. "I thought it was Nellie."

"Well, one of them. They were trying to communicate with you, but they couldn't."

"You kept hearing things too," Mia said. "Like someone walking around at night. But when you would get up to check, no one was there."

The salad in my stomach turned into a sour lump. "Old houses make noises," I said automatically, through numb lips.

Daphne paused. "You ... you were also becoming convinced that something was moving things around. You'd find your keys in the fridge, or your paintbrushes under the couch."

"Not to mention the headaches," Mia said. "You would wake up with these awful headaches."

I closed my eyes, a ghost of a headache flitting across my temples right then, as if to solidify the memories creeping slowly back in. "Aunt Charlie? Did she know?"

Daphne nodded. "Yes, after the séance. She knew about the forgetfulness and the headaches of course—she made you tea for both. And she also knew something else was going on, but she didn't want to interfere—she respected your space. I think you finally told her everything after I left that night, because the next day, you told me she was planning on doing something herself. She was going to bring a psychic to communicate with the ghosts, or cleanse the house, or something. I remember she never minded living with the ghosts—claimed they just kept her company. But who knows? Maybe after talking with you, she thought something else was in the house."

Something else. The cold lump in my stomach traveled up my spine, and I shivered.

"So, why that day? What made us do the séance?"

Daphne took a deep breath and looked at the table. "Because of what I saw." She raised her head and looked at me. "Look, both Mia and I thought it was entirely possible that the house was haunted. I had felt … something, on more than one occasion while I was there." She shivered. "But with your headaches and the forgetfulness—we weren't really sure what to believe."

"You were getting paranoid, too," Mia added. "Especially that last week or so. You were sure you were being watched. You didn't feel like you could trust anyone besides us. And it was clear you weren't sleeping well."

Daphne opened her mouth like she was going to say something, but then she suddenly shut it, shaking her head like she had changed her mind. I was about to question her when she started talking again. "Anyway, back to the séance. Before we did it, we were alone in the house. CB had taken off to hang out with the guys. I met him at the door when I was coming in. I'm pretty sure you never said anything to CB about any of this, even after the séance."

CB. I had forgotten he was there. But of course he was. He must have also been at the party the night Jessica disappeared.

Daphne continued. "Charlie had left to go drop some tea and herbs off to someone in another town. You and I were in the kitchen getting something to eat, when I got up to use the bathroom."

She swallowed, reached out to play with her fork. "I was walking through the living room, near the stairs, when something caught my attention. I'm still not sure if it was something I heard, or just felt, but I stopped and looked around. That was when I felt it—a pocket of cool air. I took a step forward, looking around, and that was when I finally looked up the stairs."

She stopped and took another deep breath. "It's hard to explain, but it was like this white puff of air. It was floating on the landing upstairs. I watched it, blinked, and it shot forward, toward the room we did the séance in, and disappeared."

A white puff of air. Like a scrap of white nightgown disappearing into a bedroom. I could taste the cold fear in my throat, and I gagged on it. I thought I might be physically sick.

Mia was looking at Daphne in awe. "Why did you agree to do a séance after *that*? I would have gotten the hell out of there!"

Daphne laughed, a bit self-consciously. "Well, yeah, that was one of my first thoughts. But the main thing going through my head was that Becca was right all along—there WAS something in the house. And if she was right about that, she was probably right about it trying to contact her."

"I saw that," I said through numb lips. "That first night. Remember, I told you all at the bar—I thought it was Chrissy's nightgown flowing behind her, as she went back into her room. But she wasn't wearing a white nightgown."

Daphne nodded unhappily.

"So, if the ghost is back," Mia said. "Maybe it has another message for you. Maybe we need to do another séance."

Both Daphne and I shook our heads. "One séance was enough, thank you," Daphne said.

"Yeah, but it may be important," Mia insisted. "Look, Chrissy is sleepwalking and having these cryptic conversations with you. This is serious. I think we need to do something."

"I'm not sure a séance will answer our questions," I said. "It's not like we got a real helpful answer before."

"Well, then maybe we bring a psychic to the house," Mia said.

Daphne groaned. "Not Antonia."

Mia looked defensive. "Why not her? She has the Gift."

"Who's Antonia?' I asked.

"She's a psychic. Or at least, that's what she calls herself," Daphne said.

"She IS a psychic," Mia said firmly. "She's even helped the police on a few cases."

"If you call bringing a lot of attention to yourself without actually getting a lot of results 'helping,'" Daphne said, putting air quotes around the word helping. "Then, sure, she's your gal."

Mia made a face. "I still think she could help. Plus, she and Charlie were friends."

"Yeah, well, Charlie had lots of friends," Daphne said, digging around in her purse. "As fun as this was, I'd better get going. My mom will be expecting me."

"Yeah, I'd better get going too," I said. As I had been vague about my plans with Chrissy, I didn't want to push it and have her get suspicious about what I'd been doing. As I reached for the check, I started sneezing.

Daphne glanced at me. "You know, you had allergies back when you were sixteen, too. Have you thought about getting some allergy medicine?"

I blew my nose. "Oh, allergies? I thought I was having a reaction to all the dust in the house. I didn't have allergies in New York."

"Do they even have anything green in New York to *give* you allergies?" Mia asked.

I frowned and waved the waitress over, so I could get a box for my half-eaten salad. "I never thought of that."

As the waitress came over, I noticed two women, both who appeared to be in their forties, staring at me from across the bar. They didn't look very happy. Actually, on closer examination, they were out-and-out glaring at me.

If looks could kill …

I leaned forward, trying to keep my head down so they couldn't see me. "Mia," I said quietly. "Why do I keep running into women in this town who seem to hate me?"

Mia looked up, startled. "What? Who hates you?"

"Well, I don't know if they hate me or not, but they sure glare at me," I nodded to the women.

Mia craned her neck to look over at them, and then snorted a dismissal. "Oh, that's just Brenda Tully and Annette Johnson. Don't worry about them."

"But, why would they look at me like that? I've never done anything to them. I don't even know them."

Mia fished out her wallet from her purse. "No, but your aunt did."

"Remember, you're living in The Witch's House now," Daphne said, counting out her cash. "You're going to get a lot of that."

"Yeah, half this town thinks Charlie did something to them—worked some sort of evil hocus pocus on them. The other half love her, sure she saved their health or marriage or something. I'm surprised no one has shown up to see if you're carrying on the family business," Mia said.

Christ. I made a face as I got my wallet out. That's all I needed—Stefan or Chrissy to answer the door and see one of Charlie's "clients" on the other side, looking for one of her "cures." I didn't even want to think about what Stefan would say. Talk about a distraction from getting the house ready for market.

"Well, look on the bright side," Daphne said, sliding out of the booth. "If you need a little extra cash to tide you over, you could always start up where Charlie left off."

"Yeah, yeah," I muttered, sliding out of the booth myself. Now would be the perfect time to tell them I needed to focus my time and energy on getting the house ready to sell, but somehow, I couldn't push the words past my lips.

Daphne smiled as she draped her purse over her shoulder. "I'm serious. I could help you if you want. I did some training with her."

I looked at Daphne in surprise. "You did?"

Daphne shrugged and started heading toward the entrance. "Just the healing part. Mostly herbs, and the tea variations. I've been studying a lot of healing modalities. When my mom first started getting sick, I wanted to help her. I discovered I had a knack for it. I take on clients myself from time to time, but I know folks would love to see a descendant of Charlie's take up the mantle. Even if it was only temporary."

"Not happening," I said as we went outside. Dark clouds had gathered, and the wind had picked up. The air felt thick and heavy and smelled like rain, even though no drops had fallen yet. I said my goodbyes and hurried to my car, which was parked in the street in a two-hour zone, digging in my purse for my keys.

"Bout time you showed up," a voice said, startling me so much that I dropped my keys. Daniel was lounging against the side of my car, arms crossed, looking relaxed … like he didn't have a care in the world. Of course, he would be there—like we had just conjured him up, talking about him over lunch.

I bent over to scoop up my keys, trying unsuccessfully to quash my irritation. I needed to be on my way, not wasting more time dealing with Daniel. "What now, Officer? Stalking me? How did you find me anyway? Or were you just planning to wait until my two hours were up, so you could give me a ticket?"

He didn't smile. "What are you hiding?"

I looked at him in surprise. "Hiding? What are you talking about?"

"Why else would you get your husband involved, if you weren't hiding something?"

"What makes you think that was my idea?"

He cocked his head. "So, it wasn't your idea to have him run interference with me?"

Thunder crackled from a distance. The wind picked up, rustling Daniel's hair.

I paused. Was it disrespectful to Stefan if I told Daniel the truth? I opened my mouth to lie, but somehow found the truth coming out instead. "No, it wasn't."

He didn't say anything, studying me with his dark-blue eyes. Like a cop. Or a predator.

I felt exposed standing there, with those penetrating eyes on me, like he could see all the way into my soul, laying bare all my secrets, even the ones I couldn't remember. A cold wind whipped around me, with just a hint of moisture. I shivered.

"You know he called the station, too," Daniel said, almost conversationally. "Put in a formal request that I don't question you without him."

"And, yet here you are," I said. "I see that worked out really well."

Daniel shrugged. "You're not under arrest, nor have you requested me to go through your attorney, so Stefan really doesn't have a leg to stand on." He paused and continued to study me. "But, he knows that. So why do you think he'd bother?" He said the words quietly, almost to himself.

I shrugged. "You'd have to ask him."

He straightened from the car, a hint of that predatory smile on his face. "Maybe I'll do that." He stepped closer. Even with rain in the air, I could smell the clean scent of his soap. I shivered again as another cold, wet wind whipped against me.

He noticed, and said, "You may want to head on home. Storm's a'brewing."

"Thanks, Officer Obvious. Appreciate the public service announcement."

He shot me a sideways smile, nodded, and sauntered down the street. More thunder crackled from the distance. I watched him go before turning to get into my car.

My phone buzzed right when I was about to put the key in the ignition. It was Chrissy—she was planning on making dinner, and wanted to know if I would stop and pick a few things up on my way home.

Chrissy. Sleeping in the same room where Mad Martha killed Nellie, and then herself. I groaned, gently hitting my head against the steering wheel. What on earth was I going to do?

Chapter 17

I texted back "Yes, I'll stop"—I needed to pick up some allergy medicine, and stock up on a few other things anyway. I hadn't counted on Stefan showing up when he did.

I pulled into the grocery store parking lot just as big, fat raindrops started plopping onto my windshield. I quickly ducked into the half-empty store.

As I rounded the corner into produce, I saw Rich, one of Daniel's friends who had been at the bar with us that night, putting apples into a bag. I moved closer, raising my hand to wave at him. He glanced in my direction, before deliberately turning his back on me and walking away.

I paused, my hand still up. I was sure he saw me. He'd looked right at me. So, why did he ignore me like that? Was he one of the people who wanted me to go back to New York? Was he only pretending to like me?

Or maybe he really hadn't seen me?

I dropped my hand and went back to filling my cart, pushing away the gnawing sensation that something was off. He probably hadn't seen me. I was reading too much into it.

I headed home as it began to pour. Great—not only was I going to get wet, but so were the groceries. Yet another reason to get our belongings unpacked—so we could use the garage as a garage instead of storage.

Once inside, I shook the water off and put the groceries away. Chrissy wandered in to examine what I'd bought, grunted an approval, and wandered right back out. I debated saying something to her about what I'd learned from my friends at lunch, but I still hadn't landed on the best way to start the conversation. Maybe I'd have my chance over dinner.

I had intended on spending the afternoon sorting through stuff and beginning the unpacking and packing process.

Instead, I found myself cleaning. Again. With a vengeance. Like I was trying to keep myself from thinking.

It didn't work.

Daphne's words kept running through my head. Was I okay with Stefan simply taking charge of my life without asking me what I wanted?

When did he start? Or had he always been like that, and I just hadn't noticed until now?

I thought back to when we first met. I was still reeling after my divorce. My first husband, Jake, an up-and-coming hotshot attorney whom my mother adored, had been cheating on me with his secretary. SO cliché, but somehow, it didn't make it any less painful.

I still remembered how it all went down. Jake worked long hours, and one night, I had decided to surprise him with dinner and maybe a little something extra. Walking through the wood-paneled, stately offices, my brand-new sexy heels clicked on the hardwood floors. I could smell the curry in the Indian takeout I carried, mixed with the smell of old books, leather furnishings, and new money.

His secretary wasn't at her desk, but that didn't surprise me. It was after seven p.m. I gently pushed open the door to his office, my naïve and innocent eyes expecting to see him hard at work behind his desk.

Instead, I saw him and his secretary on his desk, going at it like a couple of rowdy, half-dressed teenagers.

I stood there, in utter shock, watching them, the takeout in my hands. I had absolutely no clue. From that day on, I couldn't bear the smell of curry.

Jake had always had a bit of wild streak in him—thinking back, I probably shouldn't have been surprised he wasn't able to be faithful. Stefan, however, was the complete opposite— which was one of the reasons I was initially attracted to him.

Stefan was so *kind*. Well, eventually, he was. Not at first. When I started at the law firm, he basically ignored me unless he needed something, and then he would ask for it in a firm, clipped voice, without even looking at me. I was just one more assistant out of dozens.

But then one night, everything changed. I was working late, and I stopped by his office to drop off a file. He was still there, as well, so I tapped lightly on the door. He glanced up at me, and gestured for me to come in.

I moved to the desk to give him the file, when I saw him rub his face with his hands. He looked tired. No, exhausted was more accurate. His face was drawn, his eyes drooped, and he had a five o'clock shadow.

I paused at his desk, uncertain, wondering if I should say something. There was something vulnerable about him in that moment—a sadness, a loneliness.

Just as I felt.

He saw me standing there and looked up. "You're Rebecca, right?"

I nodded, taken aback that he actually knew my name.

He smiled then. "Late night for both of us."

His smile literally took my breath away. It lit up his entire face. In that moment, I saw what the other assistants were always swooning about in the break room.

I'm pretty sure I said something … for the life of me I'm not sure what. I was so completely lost in that smile—it made me feel like I was the only woman in the world. It had been a long time since a man had made me feel that way.

"You've probably missed dinner, too," he said. "Want to grab a quick bite?"

Over dinner that ended up lasting until the wee hours in the morning, I learned that he, too, was divorced. He, too, had a cheating wife. I felt like he understood what I had gone through, because he had gone through it, too.

And that was the start of our whirlwind romance. At first, we kept our relationship a secret, which made it that much more heady and romantic. Office romances were definitely frowned upon, and as a senior partner, Stefan was expected to set a good example for the rest of the staff. But it didn't take long before the gossip and rumors started flying—in retrospect, our relationship was so heated and intense at that point, we probably couldn't have been any more obvious if we had plastered it on a billboard—a passionate kiss in the break room while getting our morning coffee, sex on his desk during lunch and after hours (and one particularly memorable time in the stairwell at two in the afternoon—I don't think anyone saw us, but I can't be sure). After a month, Stefan was pressuring me to quit.

Initially, I resisted. How would I support myself? Although I was living in an apartment my parents owned and was paying them a token amount as rent, I still had to pay for utilities and food, and my meager salary barely covered even that. Stefan invited me to move in with him. But, he had a teenage daughter. How would she react to me living with them?

Easy, Stefan had said. We'll get married.

Any objection I had, he skillfully countered. Part of me thought I had lost my mind—was I really going to marry yet another lawyer, who I barely knew, who was a dozen years or so older than me, AND who had a teenager?

But, mostly, I was swept up in the romance and giddiness of it all. A hot, sexy, successful man wanted me. He had fallen in love with me. He had pursued me.

I finally understood the "making my head spin" and "sweeping me off my feet" sayings. I felt like I was dancing on air. I couldn't believe my good fortune. I must be the luckiest girl alive.

Fast forward to not even a year later. In a house alone … my husband absent.

No wonder I was spending the afternoon cleaning. I felt like a complete and utter failure.

Chapter 18

As promised, Chrissy did cook dinner—chicken parmigiana with homemade marinara sauce, gluten-free pasta and garlic bread, and a salad.

"Smells wonderful," I said, as I poured myself a glass of wine. And it did. But despite my afternoon cleaning and only eating half my salad for lunch, I wasn't all that hungry. I was preoccupied. How could I convince her to move out of her room, without telling her the truth? And, if she did, what if she wanted my old room? Did that mean I had to move into my aunt's bedroom? I still hadn't even opened the door. Argh. I could feel the knots growing in my stomach. I nibbled on the garlic bread, hoping it would settle the queasiness.

"You should try the chicken," she said pointedly, taking a bite herself. "It's really good."

"I'm sure it is," I said. I sipped my wine and ate some of the spaghetti with marinara sauce. "The sauce is wonderful."

"The chicken is better," she insisted.

I obediently cut a small piece and ate it. "You're right, it *is* good."

She looked appeased. I drank more wine.

"Chrissy," I began hesitantly. "What do you think about switching to a different bedroom?"

She looked at me suspiciously. "Why would I want to do that?"

"Well, I was thinking that room may be a better office for your dad," I said, surprised when it popped out of my mouth. I hadn't been thinking that at all, but now that I had voiced it, it really did sound like a pretty good idea.

She speared more chicken. "Where would I go?"

I broke off a piece of garlic bread and started crumbling it in my fingers. "Well, there's that room right next to yours …"

She eyed me suspiciously. "The room that's already set up as an office? Why doesn't Dad just set up his office there?"

The Magic Room? It was difficult to imagine Stefan setting up his briefs and files and holding legal conference calls in the same room Aunt Charlie cast her "magic spells." I could hardly say any of that to Chrissy though, and she did have a point about how the room was already set up. "Well … I thought if his office was at the end of the hallway, he would be less likely to be disturbed."

"But my room is bigger. I don't want a smaller room."

"It's not that much smaller."

"Smaller enough."

"I think they're probably closer to the same size than you think. Your room is a corner room, so it's shaped differently. It just looks bigger."

Chrissy coughed. "That's BS."

I swallowed. This was not going well. "What if you moved into my old room?"

She made a face. "Same problem. Your old room is smaller than mine, too. And where would you sleep?"

I played with my spaghetti. "Well, in the master bedroom."

She stared at me. "You haven't even opened the door to the master bedroom."

"Yeah, well, clearly I need to."

Her eyes narrowed suspiciously. "I don't understand. Why are you bringing this up now?"

Her question took me by surprise. "Ah …well …"

She interrupted me. "What happened today?"

Her tone sounded almost accusatory, like she knew I had seen my friends and Stefan wouldn't like it. Guilt rose up inside of me and I quickly looked away, not wanting her to see it on my face. But, almost immediately, I wanted to shake myself. What the hell was wrong with me? Chrissy is my stepdaughter. Stefan is my husband. Neither were my keeper. If I wanted to see my friends, I could go see my friends. I didn't need anyone's permission, for heaven's sake. I was an adult.

"Nothing happened," I said. "Your father needs an office and I need to figure out the best room to put him."

She threw her hands up in the air, dropping her fork so it landed on her plate with a clatter. "I don't believe this. Why don't you want me in my room?"

This was *really* not going well, but at least we were back on the room change and not on my earlier whereabouts. "I didn't say I didn't want you in your room …"

"Yes, you did. This is bull. I like my room. I don't want to move. Dad can set up his office in the room that already IS an actual office."

"But, I don't know if that room is good for you." The words were out of my mouth before I could stop them. I so wanted to crawl across the table and pluck them right out of the air—out of existence.

However, they stopped her tantrum. She looked at me, lowering her hands. Some of her long black hair had escaped the ponytail, and she blew the strands from her face. "What are you talking about, 'not good for me'?"

I took a deep breath. "You're sleepwalking," I answered cautiously, watching her closely to make sure I didn't set her off again. "As you pointed out, you didn't do that in New York, but here, you are. And I'm wondering if it might have something to do with the room."

"The room?" she burst out. "Are you serious? Maybe it's the house! Maybe we shouldn't have ever left New York."

I could feel my temper starting to rise, and I fought to keep it under control. "Look, I agree with you. I didn't want to leave New York either …"

"It's all your fault," she spat. "You're the one with the crazy aunt. Do you know what they called her? A witch. And they say this house is haunted. If your aunt never left you this house, we'd still be in New York."

"It's not my fault we had to move. Your dad's practice …"

She leapt to her feet, knocking the chair onto the floor. "Oh, spare me. This house was an out. If you didn't have it, he would have figured out a way for us to stay in New York. This is all your fault." Her eyes glistened as she held back tears, and she ran out of the room. I heard her footsteps all the way up the stairs, and a few seconds later, the slamming of her door.

"That went well," I said out loud to myself. I sighed and rubbed my face. Apparently, Chrissy wasn't going anywhere.

I surveyed the food on the kitchen table and sighed again. I picked up my wine, drained it, and got up to pour another glass. I forced myself to finish what I could from my plate, which was mainly the salad and garlic bread. Something didn't taste right in the chicken and pasta, so after a few bites, I threw most of what was left away. I packed up the leftovers and put them in the refrigerator.

I took another sip of wine as I studied the kitchen. It was truly a disaster. It appeared Chrissy had used every pot in the house. I could feel the beginnings of a headache start to crawl up the back of my head and into my temple.

Well, she did make dinner, so I guess it was only fair for me to do the cleanup. I took a last sip of wine before rolling up my sleeves and diving in. I didn't bother turning on the light, choosing instead to let the rays from the setting sun illuminate the kitchen.

"You didn't eat your chicken."

Startled, I dropped the pot I was scrubbing back into the soapy water with a plop. "My God, Chrissy, you about gave me a heart attack," I said, turning to face her.

She was standing at the door of the kitchen, wearing her red and blue sleep outfit, her long black hair pulled back in a loose, messy braid. It had stopped raining at some point, and twilight shone through the window. I had been so lost in my thoughts, I hadn't realized how dark it had gotten. Chrissy looked pale, almost ethereal, in the delicate grey light … like a lost soul from one of those teenage vampire books. But there was a childlike quality about her too, a vulnerable, bewildered innocence that made my heart break, although I couldn't explain why.

"You didn't eat your chicken," she said again, her voice somehow both plaintive and accusatory.

I picked up the pot and resumed scrubbing. "I actually did eat more. It was delicious. Leftovers are in the fridge, including what you didn't finish. I labeled it."

She took a step closer. "No, you didn't. You're lying."

I paused to drink my wine. "I'm not lying."

"Yes, you are."

I put my wine down, harder than I intended, and it made a clinking sound. "What, were you watching me? How do you know what I did after you left? And why are you making such a big deal about this? I told you it was delicious."

"I know," she said, sounding almost hysterical. "I made you chicken parmigiana and you didn't eat it. Why? Didn't you like it? Was it not up to your standards?"

I dropped the pot back into the water and turned to face her. "Chrissy, what on earth is wrong with you? There was nothing wrong with what you made. Thank you— I really appreciated you cooking tonight. After you got so angry about switching rooms, I lost my appetite, so I ate what I could. That's all. I'm sure I'll have leftovers tomorrow."

She stood there for a moment, stiffly, then, her face seemed to collapse in on itself. Her mouth worked for a minute, but nothing came out.

Was she having a stroke? What was going on with her? I ran toward her. "Chrissy, are you okay? Here, sit down. Let me get you some water."

"No ... I ... no, I'm fine," she said, backing away from me, her eyes glistening in the faint grey light. "Look, I'm ... I'm sorry. I didn't mean to yell. I guess I .... Dad told me to be nice to you, and I was trying to be nice and make you dinner, and I worked hard on it, and it all got ruined."

She seemed to be on the verge of tears—the lost, abandoned ten-year-old was back, and again I found myself wondering what could have been, if her mother hadn't been such a selfish, self-centered bitch, or if her father ...

I squelched the thought before I could finish it. Stefan did the best he could. He had to work to support them, after all, so there was only so much he could do. He couldn't be both a father and a mother.

I took a step closer to her, but she quickly darted out of the kitchen, like a frightened rabbit. I heard her scurry up the stairs and back into her bedroom, but this time, the door closed with a gentle click.

Teenagers. I sighed and went back to my dishes. Even the ones who had a decent childhood regularly lost their minds at that age. How could I expect anything more from Chrissy? Especially in this situation—uprooted from all her friends and everything familiar, and stuck in a new town, without her father, and with a clearly incompetent stepmother. I felt terribly helpless, and wished I could do something more for her— that she would *let* me help her more. I wondered if I would have a better idea of what to do if I had had children of my own.

I finished the dishes and went outside to sit on the porch. The air was cool and fresh after the rain. I gently rocked in the porch swing, watching the pine trees sway as I listened to the birds' chatter. A couple of rabbits hopped along the edge of the yard … oh man, they were probably eating the garden. I really needed to get back there. In the shadow of the trees, I saw what looked like a black cat watching me, tail twitching. Didn't Aunt Charlie have a black cat? Somewhere in the corners of my memory, I recalled Aunt Charlie laughingly calling it her "familiar." What was its name? I couldn't remember now.

Of course, I knew it wasn't the same cat. It couldn't be. That was fifteen years ago.

The cat's tail twitched, eyes watching me. It made me feel strangely comforted. Like I really wasn't alone.

I didn't stay out long. I didn't want to let my thoughts wander too much. So much had happened over the past couple of days—actually, so much had happened since we had arrived. Had it only been a week? Man, it felt like a month. Or a year. I was already feeling like a completely different person.

I wasn't sure if that was a good thing or not.

I took a few more sips of wine, relaxing in the peace, when I suddenly realized I had lost track of my phone. I made my way back inside to find it. I needed a refill anyway.

I dug my phone out of my purse and saw that Stefan called but hadn't left a message. He had, however, texted. I read it and immediately felt cold all over.

Hi babe. Sorry I missed you. Wanted to hear your voice. Hope you're being a good girl.

Chapter 19

Sipping my coffee the next morning, I kept seeing that text from Stefan in my head.

Hope you're being a good girl.

Stefan had never used that language with me before. Why was he doing it now?

Was it a warning? Did he know I had seen my friends yesterday despite his objections?

But, how could he?

Unless Chrissy said something to him.

But, she didn't know either. Unless she was following me around and spying on me.

Could I BE any more paranoid? I had to pull it together. This was getting ridiculous. Stefan was probably just trying to be funny, and it didn't come across well on text.

It's not like he was trying to control me. He wasn't like that.

I finished my coffee and went to pour myself another cup, making a brief stop to check my phone again. Last night, after I had calmed myself down, I had responded with *Of course. Miss you too.*

He hadn't responded since.

What I needed to do was something physical, I thought, as I filled up my mug. Get out of my head and focus on doing something productive. Like clean up The Magic Room and see if it would work as an office for Stefan.

Yes, that was it. The perfect focus for today.

But there was something I needed to do before I ended up knee-deep in paper, herbs, and dust. I opened a can of tuna, slipped on some flip-flops, and headed outside.

The air smelled fresh and clean after yesterday's rain. Water dripped from tree branches and the top of the roof. I sloshed through the tall wet grass (a reminder that I probably needed to mow the lawn as well), searching for any signs of the little black cat.

I checked the side of the house under the pines, which is where I had first seen it, but there was nothing there. I headed behind the house, trying to avoid staring at the overgrown, tangled garden. *Hey, at least things were growing back there,* I reasoned with myself.

I saw no signs of the cat. Had I imagined it? I went to the back stoop to leave the tuna just in case, when I saw it—a sunken hole in the garden.

It looked like a footprint, pointing toward the house, like someone was creeping into the backyard to peer into the downstairs window, and his foot slipped in the mud. I looked closer; were those streaks of mud in the grass next to the footprint where someone had tried to clean the mud off his shoe?

I stared at the dark, muddy gash, feeling the cold prickles of fear dance up my spine, listening to the dripping of water break the silence, along with a couple distant chirps from a sparrow.

Had someone been wandering around the house?

Could it have been Chrissy? Why would she be out back though? Could she have been sleepwalking again? Although the print didn't look like Chrissy's, to me. Then again, how could I know? I considered bringing out one of her shoes to compare, but the footprint wasn't all that clear or defined. Was it possible it wasn't even a footprint? That I was blowing everything out of proportion?

I looked around at the clouds hanging low and grey in the distance, brewing another storm, and at the trees that surrounded the house. The full weight of how isolated and alone we were hung as heavily on me as the angry-looking clouds.

It's probably nothing, I told myself. *It may not even be a footprint. Maybe it's from an animal. Or something else. And even it if was a footprint, it could easily be one of Chrissy's friends, as she screwed around outside. Or even from Chrissy herself.*

I left the tuna can on the stoop and headed back into the house, the quiet of the morning feeling ominous as it pressed against me.

Once inside, I took a few moments to pause and cup my suddenly-cold hands around my mug, warming them. Still cradling my cup, I took it to the window and stood there, drinking my coffee, looking at the corner of the garden where I had seen the footprint. If it *had* been a human, that person would have had a clear line of sight into the kitchen window.

I thought about how I had stood alone in the kitchen the night before, washing dishes, totally oblivious to the fact that there might have been someone outside watching me.

I shuddered. Okay. Imagining scenarios wasn't helpful. What *would* be helpful would be cleaning out The Magic Room. I had things to do. Enough of the maybe/maybe not footprint debate I was having with myself. It was surely nothing.

But … there were people in Redemption who wanted me gone …

I was being silly. I wasn't in a Lifetime movie, for goodness sake. Things like that didn't happen in real life. I picked up my coffee and left the kitchen.

The first thing I did in The Magic Room was pry open the window, letting in the clean, fresh air. Next, I got a bucket of water, a sponge, and a towel. While the entire house had been dusty, the Magic Room was the worst yet. I wondered when Aunt Charlie had last opened the door.

Files and notes were everywhere, along with dried flowers and herbs, and an ancient-looking Apple computer that (miracle of miracles!) still worked. Some of the stacks teetered precariously, making me wonder if maybe some magic spell actually kept them from falling.

I picked up a wet rag, intending on digging in, but instead found myself staring at the desk. I could see Aunt Charlie sitting behind it, sun-streaked brownish-blonde messy curls shoved behind her ears, a smudge of dirt on her cheek as she rummaged through the piles. "Where's Maggie's file? I just had it in front of me." How was she able to keep the details of her clients straight, being as unorganized as she was?

Suddenly, I was hit by a wave of grief so overwhelming and unexpected that I ended up sitting on the floor as tears spilled from my eyes. I could see Aunt Charlie peering up at me through tangled curls—she had the same crazy hair as me—explaining the different herbs and teas to me. "You have the gift, Becca," she would say. "The gift of healing. Whether it's through your art, or making the right tea, it's still a gift. Never forget that."

She was the only one who believed in me. She was the only one who supported whatever I wanted to do. She was the one who helped me step into Becca.

But now, Aunt Charlie was dead. And so was Becca. And I felt practically swallowed up by my grief about both.

When Stefan told me Aunt Charlie had died, I had felt nothing. Well, that wasn't true. I felt numb. I remember thinking I should feel something else, maybe relief that the source of my nightmares was finally gone, but there was nothing.

But sitting there in the Magic Room, feeling her presence all around me, smelling her in the dusty herbs and flowers, I finally admitted to myself how much she had meant to me. How much I missed her. And how I wished, oh I *so* wished, that things had been different.

Once I finally got my sobbing under control, having stuffed the rag in my mouth to keep Chrissy from hearing me, I took a minute to clean myself up in the bathroom. I still looked like I had had a good cry, but maybe I could blame my red face on the amount of dust in the room.

Straightening my shoulders, I headed back to the Magic Room. Nothing like a good cleaning to get myself back under control.

After removing the worst of the dust, I started going through everything. I found tea recipes and client notes. I had intended on tossing most of the files, especially from her clients, but between remembering the words Aunt Charlie had spoken to me, and Daphne's suggestion that I take over where Aunt Charlie had left off, I couldn't do it. I had no intention of becoming a healer and making teas for people, even for the short time we were in Redemption, but what harm could it do to hang onto the files? Maybe someone else, like Daphne, would want to take up the practice. What an amazing treasure I would be throwing away.

So, instead, I reorganized. There were filing cabinets, but they were filled with all sorts of things—stacks of magazines, fabric swatches (like there weren't enough down by the sewing machine), old calendars, accounting records from the nineties, faded photo albums, even, oddly enough, a stuffed bear—in addition to the client files and recipes. Once I got things in their proper places (and threw out what I *knew* wasn't needed), I discovered I actually had room for everything.

After a few hours, I took a break and went down to the kitchen for fresh coffee, since mine had grown cold. Chrissy was sitting at the table, looking tired and sullen as she stirred her limp-looking cereal. I tried talking to her, but she only shrugged and stared at her phone. Sighing, I went back up to continue with the cleaning. Maybe that night, I would make dinner for Chrissy, to try and make up for the failed meal the night before.

My head started pounding around lunchtime, so I took another break. I decided to have some of the leftovers, realizing I should have known better. My headaches were always worse when I skipped meals, and I definitely wasn't eating as well as I should have been.

By mid-afternoon, I had to stop. My headache was getting worse, in addition to feeling a little lightheaded and sick to my stomach. Even with the allergy medicine, I still found myself having a reaction as I battled all the dust in the house. On the plus side, I felt like I had made pretty good progress. And the best part was that I had found the headache tea, although it appeared to be so old, I wondered if it would still work at all. Luckily, I had also found the recipe, so maybe next I would tackle the garden, and start harvesting some fresh ingredients.

I took a shower to wash all the grime and dust off me, and was sitting in the kitchen with my tea, wondering where my phone went, when Chrissy walked in.

"I'm going out," she announced, looking at her phone.

I held my hand out, wincing a little at the pain in my head. "Wait a second. Where are you going? Are you going to be back for dinner?"

"Just out with friends. I don't know about dinner. I'll text you." She finally glanced at me and her eyes widened. "Are you okay?"

"I have a headache." I rubbed my temples. "So, it would be nice to know so I can better plan for dinner."

She stood in the middle of the kitchen, looking a little uncertain. "Do you want me to get you something? Maybe ibuprofen?"

I looked at her in surprise. She had never offered to help me before when I had a headache. I was going to refuse, but then changed my mind. "Yes, ibuprofen would be nice."

She went to fetch it, and I took a moment to look for my phone. If she was going to text me, I probably needed to find it.

Odd. I was sure I had left it on the counter this morning, but it wasn't there now. Had I taken it upstairs with me?

She returned with not only the ibuprofen, but also with a cool wash cloth, and helped me lay down on the couch. "Are you going to be okay?"

"I'll be fine. I probably breathed in too much dust and overdid it. Thanks."

She bit her lip as she looked down at me. I got the feeling she wanted to say something, but at the last minute, changed her mind. "Okay, see you later."

"Chrissy," I called out. "Just one more thing? Have you seen my phone?"

"Why would I know where your phone is?" She snapped. "Are you accusing me of stealing it?"

"What?" I said, taken aback. "No, I don't think you did anything with it. But I was hoping you could help me find it ..."

"I don't know where your phone is," she interrupted. "I haven't seen it. Okay? I gotta go." I heard her steps pound through the kitchen and the backdoor slam.

What was wrong with that girl? Had I been this crazy as a teenager? In that moment, all I wanted to do was pack her up and ship her back to New York and let her father deal with her.

Chapter 20

It wasn't just allergies after all. I ended up getting sick.

I spent the week feeling like crap. Headaches, dizziness, sick to my stomach … not constantly, but off and on, which made it even more frustrating, because the moment I thought I was getting better, another headache would sneak up on me.

Today had been particularly brutal, made worse because for the life of me, I couldn't find the ibuprofen. I didn't think I had used it all up, so where on earth had it gone?

I rubbed my temples as I sat in the kitchen with a bowl of chicken and rice soup, gluten-free crackers, half of a gluten-free chocolate cookie Chrissy had baked from scratch, and a pot of tea in front me. I had been trying to eat through the pain, but it hadn't been working. Neither had the tea, at least not as much as I remembered. I probably needed fresher ingredients.

The doorbell rang, causing me to jump and spill my soup. Chrissy? Had she forgotten her key? Since seeing that footprint in the garden, I had made a point of keeping the doors locked. It made me feel safer, even though I hadn't seen any evidence of someone hanging around.

The doorbell rang again, and I quickly glanced at my phone before getting up. (I had found it next to the sewing machine and a pile of fabric I was planning on moving to storage or getting rid of—why it was there, I had no clue.) No calls or texts from Chrissy. She too had been difficult all week, vacillating wildly between helping out, doing her part to prepare a few meals, and being concerned and caring about my headaches, to throwing a fit and storming out of the house.

I opened the front door to find Daniel and Chrissy on the porch. Chrissy was swaying back and forth, her eyes half-closed. Daniel had a firm grip on her arm, and I got the impression he was the one keeping her upright.

"Chrissy? What on earth …"

Chrissy turned her glassy, unfocused eyes on me. "I don't feel so well," she said, her speech slurred.

"Maybe we'd better get her inside," Daniel said.

I was still staring at Chrissy, trying to get my head around how I was going to handle the situation. "What? Oh yeah, good idea." I held the door open. "Maybe get her to the bathroom. It's right around …"

"I know where the bathroom is," Daniel said curtly, half-dragging Chrissy's unresponsive body across the living room and depositing her on the bathroom floor. She groaned and collapsed in a heap.

I rubbed my temples. The timing couldn't be worse. I could barely make myself tea—how could I possibly take care of Chrissy too?

Daniel came back out, his face flat and expressionless, and motioned me toward the door.

I followed. "Where did you find her?"

He turned to face me, his expression looking graver. "I didn't."

"What do you mean you didn't?"

He held up his hand to silence me. "Her friends had taken her to Aunt May's, I think to get some food into her, but she was so wasted she could barely sit at the table. One of the waitresses called me."

"Mia?"

He gave me a look. "No, not her."

I sighed, feeling my head pound. Behind me I could hear retching. Hopefully, she had made it into the toilet.

Daniel was watching me closely. "I think you should know her friends were pretty sober. Maybe she didn't pace herself at all, I don't know … but they seemed a little … worried about her."

I closed my eyes. Why wasn't Stefan home? What was I going to do with her?

"It's been stressful for her," I began. "The move and everything. Being a teenager. I guess … well, maybe it's been more stressful than we thought."

He shrugged. "It may not be anything more than that. But it probably wouldn't hurt to have her talk to someone. There are a couple of therapists in town who are quite good with teenagers. Let me know if you want their names."

I nodded, but inside I was thinking that Stefan would never go for that. I remembered his disdain when our friends in New York talked about their therapists. "Are you going to arrest her or give her a ticket or something?"

He shook his head. "Not this time. But see that it doesn't happen again."

I closed my eyes in relief, listening to Chrissy retch and groan behind me. Thank God I didn't have to deal with legal issues with her—at least not for the moment. I opened my eyes and smiled at Daniel. "Thanks. I appreciate it."

He nodded once. I thought he would leave then so I could deal with the mess behind me, but instead he lingered, studying me. I could feel myself growing warm under his gaze. Why was he looking at me like that? All of a sudden, I was conscious of the fact that I hadn't taken a shower in a few days. I was wearing yoga pants and a stained tee shirt. Daniel had a knack of stopping by when I was looking my worst.

"Are you okay?" he finally asked.

I was taken aback. "Yeah. As good as to be expected when the cops bring home your drunk sixteen-year-old stepdaughter."

He cocked his head. "I mean, are you feeling okay? You don't look well."

I half-smiled. "You always had a way with the ladies, didn't you?"

He groaned and rolled his eyes. "That's not what I meant. You look great, you always look great, I mean … " He paused and gave me a sheepish smile. "I'm making it worse, aren't I?"

I laughed. "Well, yeah. The good news is it's never too late to stop digging the hole."

He smiled then, a real smile, and I could almost feel my heart stop. God, I had almost forgotten how hot he was when he smiled. I had to blink a few times to refocus on what he was saying.

"What I meant is you don't look like you're feeling well. Are you?"

I was also conscious we were, for all practical purposes, alone in the house. Apart from a drunk teenager, of course. I swallowed and had to look away. "Well, ah, I do have a headache. I think I may be coming down with something. I haven't been feeling like myself all week."

"Are you going to be okay? Do you want me to call someone, Daphne maybe? To help with ..." he nodded toward the bathroom and Chrissy, which had gone silent. At least she had stopped throwing up, although I probably should go check on her and make sure she was okay.

"I'm fine, but thank you," I said. "I don't need to screw up anyone else's Saturday night." I smiled, trying to lighten the suddenly-charged mood. "Bummer you have to work tonight."

He took a step back as his lips twitched up in a smile. "Just doing my job." I got the feeling he felt it too, the energy between us, and was trying to soften it as well.

He backed away another step, so he was halfway out the door. "Okay, if you're sure. I'll be on my way."

I nodded and quietly closed the door behind him. It dawned on me then that I should maybe ask him about what may have been a footprint in the garden, but I was reluctant to call him back. It was probably nothing. I didn't want to waste his time.

So, why did it feel like I was making a big mistake, keeping it to myself?

Chapter 21

Over my morning coffee, I pondered my options.

After Daniel left the night before, I headed over to the bathroom. Chrissy was slumped over the toilet, passed out and snoring. I sighed. At least she hadn't made a mess.

I considered leaving her there—she was already asleep, and I wasn't entirely sure how cooperative she would be, or if I'd even be able to get her up the stairs if I woke her—but somehow, that didn't feel right to me, so after a lot of hauling and swearing, I got her on her feet and up the stairs. I undressed her, tossed her in the shower and turned the water on cold. After she regained consciousness (screaming at me the whole time), I forced her to drink as much water as I could, before dumping her into bed to sleep it off.

I headed to bed myself and slept better than I had expected. Better yet, I didn't have a headache when I woke. Maybe I was finally on the mend.

But that was where my good luck ended. What on earth was I going to do with Chrissy? And Stefan?

I needed to tell him. I knew that. This was bigger than the sleepwalking. I couldn't wait until he came home again.

But still, I hesitated. What was I going to say? *Stefan, the cops brought Chrissy home drunk last night.*

I rubbed my forehead. What a nightmare.

Well, first things first. I was here. I was Chrissy's stepmother and before I did anything else, I needed to deal with her.

I marched upstairs and into her room. As expected, she was still sleeping, in a sweaty tangle of blankets and sheets. I threw open the drapes, letting the early morning sun stream in.

"Rise and shine, sleepyhead."

Chrissy groaned and tried to bury her head in the sheets. "Go away," she muttered.

"I'm not going away. You're getting up now."

"Leave me alone," she snapped, burying her face in her pillow.

I started stripping the bed of blankets, sheets, and pillows. She whimpered and tried to cover her face with her hands. "Nope. Not letting you spend the day hungover in bed. You're getting up and getting some breakfast into you. And then we're going to talk about what happened last night."

She muttered something I couldn't hear and tried to curl up, hiding her face in her hands. "I'll give you ten minutes. If you're not downstairs, I'm coming back up. And you don't want to find out what I'm going to do to you then."

I went back down to the kitchen and started to assemble breakfast— toasting gluten-free bread and brewing green tea, which wasn't a bad hangover remedy.

I pulled the cereal out of the pantry and stopped, almost dropping the box. There was the bottle of ibuprofen. What in God's name was it doing there?

I reached out and plucked it out of the pantry. Well, I guess I at least knew where it was when I needed it next, and chances were Chrissy would need it pretty quickly.

But, still. How did it end up in the pantry behind the cereal?

"I'm here. Happy?" A voice croaked behind me. Chrissy slumped down on the table, holding her head in her hands.

"Not especially," I said, plopping the green tea in front of her. "Drink that. It will help. What do you want to eat?"

She peered at the mug from between her hands. "What is it?"

"It's green tea. It will help. What do you want to eat?"

She made a face, but dragged the mug toward her. "Ugh. Nothing."

"You need to eat something. You'll feel better. What about toast?"

She took a sip of tea, still making a face, and barely nodded at me. I put the toast in front of her and slid into a chair with my coffee.

I watched her pick at the toast and sip the tea. She looked awful—her eyes were puffy and bloodshot, her hair a tangled mess, sticking up every which way—but at least the color was starting to come back into her face.

I sipped my coffee. "Want to tell me what happened?"

She crumbled up a piece of toast. "No."

Deep breaths. "You do know what you did was illegal."

"So, what?"

"So, what? Chrissy, not only could you have ended up in jail, but you also could have ended up in the hospital. What happened? Why did you get so drunk?"

"I just did. It's no big deal."

"Do you have any idea how drunk you were? Do you even remember last night?"

"Of course, I remember," she said, but her eyes slid off me like she was lying. "I don't know why you're making such a big deal about this."

I wanted to throttle her. "Okay. If you don't think it's a big deal, let's call your father and tell him what happened. Together." I picked up my phone.

Her head shot up. "God, Rebecca, you can be such a bitch." She stood up so fast the chair toppled over. "You make such a big deal out of everything. So, what, I had a little too much to drink. So, what? *So, what?*" Her voice got louder and louder until she was practically shrieking at me as she ran out of the kitchen.

I thought about going after her, but then decided to give her a chance to calm down, and myself a chance to text Stefan.

We need to talk about Chrissy.

While I waited for an answer, I refilled my coffee. Maybe I ought to call him. Did I really want to text him this?

My phone beeped. Stefan had responded.

Is she okay?

Yes, she's fine, I texted back. *Hungover, but fine.*

Can it wait? I'm in the middle of something urgent.

I drummed my fingers. Could it wait? In theory, it probably could. For the moment anyway, she was fine. Safe. No legal trouble or health issues.

But, something didn't feel right. Chrissy was his daughter. Why wouldn't he want to talk about this now?

And, it was Sunday. What could possibly be so urgent? It wouldn't have anything to do with Sabrina …

"Rebecca?" a tentative voice came from behind me. Startled, I jumped, dropping my phone with a clatter, before turning around, a part of me glad for the interruption. Stefan was in New York to work, not to see Sabrina. A very chastened looking Chrissy stood in the kitchen doorway.

I pressed my hand against my heart, forcing my breaths to slow down. "Chrissy, you scared me."

"Sorry," she said, if anything looking even more unhappy.

I took another deep breath and forced a smile to my lips. "It's okay. Not a big deal. What is it?"

She bit her lip and looked away. "I'm sorry."

I bent over to scoop up my phone and put it on the table. "Are you ready to tell me what happened?"

She slowly came forward and slid into a chair. "I … I don't really know what happened. Everyone else was drinking beer, so I had one, too. I don't know how it got so out of control."

"Was this your first time drinking? Or did you drink back in New York, too?"

She swallowed and looked away. "I just wanted them to like me," she said, her voice dropping to a whisper. "Everything is so strange here. I miss my friends. I miss New York."

I sighed. "I miss it, too." But as soon as I said it, I wondered … did I really? Back in New York, things certainly seemed simpler, but was I actually any happier? "I know things have been rough for you, but this is just temporary. We'll be back in New York in no time." I forced the cheery note in my tone.

"I know," she said. "I shouldn't have done it. And I promise I won't do it again. I … know you need to tell Dad. But I learned my lesson. I won't do it again."

"He has to know, Chrissy. I can't keep this from him."

She rubbed an imaginary spot on the table. "I know."

I studied her. Things hadn't been easy for Chrissy since her mother waltzed out the door a few years ago. So, it certainly made sense, her acting out, and drinking too much. And it did seem like she had learned her lesson. Besides, I reasoned with myself, it's not like I wasn't doing the same thing at her age.

But ... something about her explanation and apology didn't feel right. I couldn't put my finger on it, but it just seemed ... disingenuous.

"Do you want more tea?" I finally asked.

She nodded, looking relieved. I got up to make more, telling myself my intuition about something being off was probably nothing. I hadn't been feeling good all week, so maybe I was just sensing things that weren't there. Chrissy made a mistake, which is easy enough to do at sixteen, and even easier to do when you've had an unhappy few years. Plus, she'd always made it clear she didn't like me, so of course any apology would sound "off," to me.

I snuck a look at her as I measured tea into the pot. She was staring at her phone, her hair completely obscuring her face, but even without seeing her expression, it was clear to me what she was feeling. In fact, her whole being seemed to vibrate with the energy of one single emotion ...

She was angry.

Chapter 22

The house was dark and still. Shadows stretched across the hallway, huge, dark, and twisted, seeming to suck the last bit of light into their depths.

Actually, everything looked distorted and crooked, like something out of a funhouse mirror.

This had to be a dream, I thought, which meant I was definitely staying out of the kitchen. I had no desire to see Aunt Charlie, or drink any of her tea.

Voices rose up from the stairs, sounding argumentative. Could Chrissy be down there? Who could she be arguing with?

And, did I *really* want to go down to find out?

Despite my misgivings, I found myself floating down the stairs. From the corner of my eye, I saw something flutter—a woman wearing an old-fashioned maid uniform dusted a lamp, her movements short and spasmodic. Her brown hair was pulled back in a messy bun, and topped with a little maid cap. She was pretty, in a wispy, waif-like way, but her face was pale, and she had black circles under her eyes. I could hear her muttering to herself.

"Where is it? Where did it go? I must find it. Where is it?"

I felt something stir inside me, watching her eyes scurry around the room, searching for whatever she was muttering about.

So familiar—what was it reminding me of?

"Who are you?" I asked.

She whirled around, her dark eyes wide and startled. "What are you doing here?" she hissed. "You can't be here."

"What are you talking about? This is my house."

She shook her head frantically, as she waved the duster at me. There was something strangely familiar about her, but I couldn't quite place that, either. "No, no, no. This is all wrong. All wrong. It can't happen again. It just can't."

I took a step closer. "What's all wrong? What can't happen again? I don't understand."

Her eyes were jerking and skittering around the room, like she was trying to look everywhere at once. "You have no idea what you've done. You must go. You're in danger here."

Danger. The word seemed to echo throughout the house as the cold tentacles of fear delicately stroked my spine. "Why am I in danger? In danger from what?"

Her eyes continued to dart madly around. "Don't you get it?" Her voice dropped to a whisper. "What you've awoken, by coming here? Now that it's awake, there's no putting it back!"

I was about to ask her what, exactly, was awake, when I suddenly realized I did recognize her. "Wait. Nellie??"

She gasped, both hands going to her mouth as she dropped her duster. "Oh no. You mustn't … "

"Nellie," another voice called out from another room. Nellie looked so frightened, I thought she might faint. "Oh, where is that child? Nellie?"

Nellie backed against the wall, her eyes round and desperate. She stared at me, pleading with me, to do *what*, I had no idea, but before I could figure it out, a woman walked into the room.

She was tall and regal, dressed in a high-buttoned, old-fashioned dress, her hair swept into a complicated up 'do. "There you are, Nellie. Why didn't you answer me? Did you find my locket?"

Nellie shook her head. "No … no ma'am," she stammered.

"It should be in my jewelry box. Where did it go? Careless girl, did you lose it?" She started to advance toward Nellie, threateningly, making Nellie cower even more.

"No … no ma'am. I'm looking. I'll find it!" Nellie gasped.

"You better," the woman hissed. "Or I'll dock your pay."

Nellie let out a frightened sort of squeak, and I found myself stepping forward. The woman's head snapped around, and she looked at me.

"You again," she said, her lip curling under. "You came back."

I found myself shrinking under that hot gaze. "You're Martha," I said.

"Did you lose your wits, girl? Of course I'm Martha. Who else would I be?"

I licked my suddenly-dry lips. "I … I just …"

She looked disdainfully at me. "Why I ever tried to help you, I have no idea. You're not much better than this idiot girl." She tilted her head toward Nellie. "I don't suppose you know where my locket is?"

I shook my head, starting to back up, icy fear sinking into the pit of my stomach.

She took a step toward me, her eyes glittering. "You wouldn't be lying to me now, would you?" She purred, her mouth twisting. "You didn't steal it, like you did my house, did you? That locket is powerful—more powerful than the likes of you would know what to do with."

I took another step back, as fear crawled into my gut. Martha advanced, her form stretching and distorting, resembling that painting, "The Scream." She opened her mouth, and began to shriek—"Where is it? Where is my locket? What did you do with it?"

I woke with a gasp, darting straight up in bed, my breathing harsh and loud in my ears. I could still taste the fear in my throat, as I struggled to get it under control.

And I thought the Aunt Charlie dreams were bad.

No question, as creepy as they were, I definitely preferred them to the Mad Martha/Nellie show.

Slowly, I calmed down. The sheets were twisted around me, sticky with sweat. I unwound myself and got out of bed. I wanted to go down to the kitchen and make myself a cup of tea, but the thought of running into Mad Martha and Nellie in the living room, or Aunt Charlie in the kitchen, kept me upstairs.

Instead, I went to the bathroom to splash some cool water on my face and fill my water glass. Not as satisfying as a cup of tea, but I could at least avoid running into any unwelcome visitors.

As I headed back to my room, I found myself hesitating in the hallway. The house was silent. Chrissy's door was closed. Everything seemed quiet and peaceful.

So, why did I have an absolutely nagging feeling to check on Chrissy?

She's fine, I told myself. *She's asleep, like you should be.*

But, still. Every other time I had been awakened by a nightmare, Chrissy had been up, and sleepwalking. Why would this time be any different?

Of course, those other times, I had been dreaming about Aunt Charlie. I had also heard Chrissy up and walking around, whereas right then, the house was as silent as a tomb.

Still, it wouldn't hurt to check in on her. Unless, of course, I woke her. For all I knew, that might start a screaming fit, even in the middle of the night. Her moods were completely impossible to predict, and I really preferred not to deal with a temper tantrum in the wake of the Nellie/Mad Martha dream.

I shook my head and walked toward my room. *I'm being silly,* I told myself. *She's sleeping.*

Shutting the door firmly behind me, I returned to bed. I was determined to get some more sleep.

I lay there for a while, watching the shadows from the trees play on the walls, and each time I'd drift off, I'd jerk awake with every creak and groan of the house, sure it was Mad Martha coming to ask me where her locket was, or Aunt Charlie holding a tea cup out to me. I was about to give up hope, when I finally drifted off into an uneasy slumber, haunted by confusing dreams of being chased by faceless shadows.

I awoke to a room bathed in yellow sunlight. Despite the dreams, I had slept longer than I had anticipated.

Not feeling entirely refreshed, I hauled myself out of bed. In the light of day, surrounded by the comforting warm sun, my fears from the night before seemed silly. Laughable even.

I went downstairs to make some coffee. Chrissy's door was still closed, which wasn't all that surprising, as she typically slept the morning away.

Coffee first, then breakfast. It was later than my usual wake up time, and I expected Chrissy to join me shortly.

The house was quiet, other than the ticking of the grandfather clock. I sat at the table, bathed in the warm sun, with my coffee and oatmeal. Maybe it was a good day to tackle the garden. Maybe I could also look for that cat, too. Something had been eating the tuna I was putting out. Of course, not just cats ate tuna. For all I knew, I could be feeding a raccoon, or even a skunk.

The minutes ticked by. I finished my breakfast and drank half the pot of coffee. No Chrissy.

The uneasiness I had felt the night before came creeping back. Maybe I should have checked on her after all. Surely, she was just still sleeping.

What else could it be?

Unless something WAS wrong, a little voice said. *Maybe she had been sleepwalking and fell and hit her head, or maybe she cut herself and was lying up there on her bedroom floor bleeding …*

I got up abruptly and headed upstairs. I kept telling myself I was being silly, but I knew I would feel much better once I saw her safe and sound in bed—even if she threw a fit for bothering her.

Her door was still shut. I gently knocked.

Silence.

I knocked again, louder, and called her name.

Still nothing.

The uneasiness inside me had morphed into a silent scream, and suddenly, I couldn't get the door open fast enough. I shoved it as hard as I could, banging it against the wall behind it as it swung open.

The room was empty.

I rushed in, still calling her name. Her bed was made—it didn't even look like she had slept in it. I turned around to check her closet, when I saw the words on the mirror. My knees buckled, and I would have fallen if I hadn't grabbed the back of the chair.

It's coming. Beware.

Chapter 23

I closed my eyes. My sixteen-year-old self collided with my thirty-one-year-old self. Dizziness swamped over me. I could almost smell the incense and burnt candles.

When I opened my eyes, the words were gone. All that was there was my own wild reflection.

Becca, get ahold of yourself, I told myself sternly. *You'll be no help to Chrissy otherwise.*

Just because the last time I saw a message like that, a different sixteen-year-old I knew disappeared, didn't mean it would happen again.

I took several slow, deep breaths while quickly scanning her room. Nothing appeared to be missing. I checked her closet. It all looked normal. Her suitcase was still there, shoved in the back corner

Okay, so at least on the surface, it didn't appear like she had run away, which of course, was a good thing.

Unless something else had happened to her.

It's coming. Beware.

I squeezed my eyes shut. Chances were high she had just snuck out of the house to go see her friends. Maybe she didn't even mean to sneak. Maybe she had every intention of telling me, but she didn't see me around, so she left a note.

A note. That reminded me to find my phone, to see if she had texted me. Or, heaven forbid, left a voicemail (as if she would ever be caught dead leaving a voicemail).

When could she have left? I racked my brain, trying to remember what time she had gone to bed. I knew it had been pretty early—shortly after dinner. She had still been recovering from her hangover. Maybe eight? Maybe a bit later? I honestly couldn't remember—I hadn't been paying attention. Stefan had texted me earlier to ask if the talk I wanted to have with him could wait until he arrived later that week, and I found myself feeling simultaneously overwhelmed (the house was nowhere near ready for him to see) and puzzled.

Was this normal behavior for a parent?

Granted, I was pretty new to the whole parenting business, but I was having trouble imaging myself having the same reaction if the roles were reversed.

On the other hand, maybe I should give Stefan a break. I knew how stressed he was with the law firm. Maybe he figured if there was something really wrong with Chrissy, I would insist we talk.

Still ... I couldn't help wondering if part of the reason why I was having so many issues with Chrissy was due to her father sometimes acting like he didn't care about her.

This isn't helping you find Chrissy.

Fair enough, I thought. What I needed to do was find my phone, to see if Chrissy had left me a message.

I went back downstairs and found it in the living room. No message from Chrissy. I tried calling, but it went to voicemail, so I texted her. "Where are you?"

There was no immediate response. I went into the kitchen and poured myself more coffee. If I didn't hear back from her, what should I do? Call the cops? The hospital? All of the above?

Should I even bother letting Stefan know?

I was debating calling and texting again when she texted me. "I'm fine. I'll be home soon."

I stared at the phone. That was her answer?

I texted her back. "No, that's not good enough. Where are you? I want you home NOW."

No response.

I restrained the urge to throw my phone across the room and went upstairs to get dressed instead. I'd had enough. I was going to go look for her. And I was going to drag her back home when I finally found her.

I pulled on jean shorts and a yellow tank top, and ran a comb through my hair before securing it with a ponytail. I went to get my phone, keys, and purse, and found two of the three.

My keys were missing. Again. For the second time in a week.

What was going on with me? Along with finding the ibuprofen in the pantry, I had found the cream standing on the plates (luckily it hadn't been there long enough to spoil) and a wet washcloth stuffed in the medicine cabinet.

Was my recent forgetfulness related to my other memory issues from fifteen years ago?

I really didn't have time to figure it out right then; I needed to locate my keys and track down Chrissy. Luckily, they were pretty easy to find, sitting on the washing machine. The last time I lost them, I found them in the freezer. I snatched them up and headed out.

It was only after I got in the car that I realized the flaw in my plan to bring Chrissy home. I had no idea where to look for her. It was one thing to imagine triumphantly finding her and watching her meekly get in the car. It was quite another to actually figure out where on earth she was.

She was a kid, so could I assume she had spent the night at someone's house?

Even if I could, I didn't know any of her friends.

I found myself driving to Aunt May's. It was where Daniel picked Chrissy up the other night, and as good a place as any to start my search.

The diner was buzzing with a healthy number of customers. Mia waved at me from across the room. Relieved, I waved back as I made my way to the counter to ask her for a coffee to go (not that I necessarily needed more coffee, but it gave me an excuse to talk to her).

Mia frowned, pouring my coffee as I talked. "I haven't seen her or any of the kids," she said. My heart sank, even though on some level, I had known it was a long shot.

"You could try Rocky's Pizza—that's a popular place. So is the movie theater by the mall. And, of course, out by the lake. And, The Rock."

The Rock. Of course.

Mia handed me my coffee, waving off my attempt to pay. "On the house. If I see her, I'll tell her to get in touch with you." Mia paused, as if framing her next words carefully. "I'm not saying you don't have a right to be worried. And, yes, you need to find her. But she texted you—so I'm sure she didn't disappear. She'll come home."

Didn't disappear? What did that mean? I wanted to ask more, but Mia had already turned away to deal with customers, and I needed to get back to my searching.

I checked out Rocky's Pizza, the movie theater, and the mall first. While I saw other kids, there was no sign of Chrissy.

I was about to go out to the lake, but somehow found myself turning off onto the road that led to The Rock instead.

As I wound my way up the hill, my emotions seesawed wildly—from worry and concern for Chrissy, to memories full of heartbreak, from years ago. I pulled into a little clearing, cut the engine, and just sat there.

It hadn't changed. The fire pit was still there, next to the big boulder that gave the clearing its name, and all the trees that surrounded the area. Broken glass glittered in the bright sun, along with empty beer cans, stacked logs, and more rocks.

I took my coffee, got out of the car, and walked over to the fire pit, staring into the mounds of ash and half-burned sticks. A monarch butterfly fluttered past as birds busily chirped and serenaded me. In the distance, a hawk circled lazily against the bright blue sky and heavy white clouds.

With the fire glowing, the music blaring, and the beer flowing, The Rock was the perfect place for teenagers to hang out at night.

If I closed my eyes, I could almost smell the smoke, and the freshly-cut burning wood mixed with the scent of mosquito repellent and burning citronella candles. The heat was hot on my face, which was motivation to drink more beer, the taste sour in my mouth. I never really cared for beer, but I would drink it out of politeness, or lack of better options.

I thought about the last time I was there, fifteen years prior. Music blared from car radios as I hung back by the fire, watching Mia and Jessica dance in a group of girls, bathed in the glow of the flames. CB joined them, beer in hand. I could tell he had had way too much to drink.

My own glass was empty. I headed over to the half-barrel tucked next to The Rock, on the opposite side of the fire pit.

Daniel was alone there next to the beer, leaning against The Rock. It didn't surprise me to see him there—he was the one who always brought the beer, although I was pretty sure Barry, whose dad owned all the car dealerships, was the one who paid for it.

When Daniel saw me approaching, he picked up the tap and gestured. I handed him my glass to fill.

"Why don't you ever dance?" he asked as he poured.

"Why don't you?" I countered. I really didn't want to get into how I looked like a lumbering elephant when I danced.

"Someone has to keep an eye on the beer," he said, handing me my glass back.

"I'd be glad to take over if you want to join in." I gestured with my beer.

"No, it's my cross to bear," he said. "Besides, I'd rather watch."

"Ha!" I snorted as I took a drink, making a slight face.

He saw it and laughed. "Don't like beer?"

"Not particularly," I wiped the foam from my mouth.

"What do you drink in New York?"

"Whatever our parents have in their liquor cabinets," I said. "Which is usually better than this."

"If you drink enough, I bet you'd be dancing."

"You'd lose that bet."

In the firelight, his eyes gleamed. "Is that a challenge?"

Before I could answer, Jessica fell into us. "Oh my God, I so need a beer," she giggled. "Bartender, a round for the house. We're celebrating."

Daniel plucked Jessica's glass and started to fill it. "Celebrating? What are we celebrating?"

Jessica waved her hands over her head. "Getting out of this damn town. I can't wait!" She looked at me as Daniel handed her the beer. "God, Becca, you're so lucky you don't live here."

"I second that," Mia said, dancing around me. "You too CB," she hiccuped as CB wedged himself in to refill his beer.

"Why don't you come with us to New York?" CB asked. He winked at me as Mia and Jessica screamed in excitement. "There's room. Especially at Becca's house. Her older brothers aren't living at home anymore, so there's two vacant bedrooms just sitting there waiting for you."

"Yeah, but I thought LA was better for modeling," Jessica said.

"Where do you think the fashion industry started, sweetheart?" CB said.

Jessica turned to me. "Oh my God. CB's right Do you think your parents would mind?"

I backed away, making an excuse about getting something out of the car.

"I'm serious Becca," Jessica called out, as CB started telling Mia about legal opportunities in New York. "I'd love to hang out with you in New York."

I was furious at CB. There was no way my parents would ever, EVER accept Jessica or Mia or anyone from Redemption in their apartment, and CB knew it. How could he dangle this in front of them? And then make me the bad guy for telling them no?

I was so going to kick his butt.

"Hey, slow down." Daniel said, catching up with me. "What was that about?"

I shook my head, pressing my lips together. I didn't like talking about my New York life when I was in Redemption. I wanted to pretend my New York life didn't exist—that at the end of summer, I didn't have to go back to being Rebecca, the girl who could dabble in painting but really needed to put her focus on landing the "right" husband and career. The girl who was admonished to smile more and talk less, because every time she talked, she realized no one had the faintest idea what she was trying to say.

A girl who would get so frustrated she wanted to scream, because maybe, if she screamed loud enough, people would finally hear her.

"Jessica is pretty set on going to California," Daniel said. "She's got cousins there or something."

His voice was so gentle, I found my eyes tearing up. He might as well have said, "You don't want to talk about your family. I get it." I opened my mouth to make some noncommittal comment, and instead found myself telling him the truth about my family and living in New York. How no matter how hard I tried, I always felt like I was a puzzle piece being forced into the wrong puzzle. How Aunt Charlie always felt more like my real mom than my mother did. How my mother and I had a dreadful fight before I came to Redemption, and the last thing I had screamed at her was how I wished Aunt Charlie was my real mother, instead of her. I could still see how white my mother had turned, so white for a moment I thought she was going to have a stroke. She had left the room without a word, and she and I hadn't spoken since.

How I was dreading seeing her again at the end of the summer.

And, now, CB with this ridiculous talk about bringing Jessica and Mia to my parent's apartment? Had he lost his mind?

He listened quietly as we walked, eventually finding ourselves in the woods sitting on an overturned log. After I finished my ranting, he shared his story. His dad had walked out years before, leaving him and his mother to fend for themselves. They had very little money, but over the years, Barry would often help—giving him food, clothes, shoes. A part of him was grateful for Barry, but truth be told, part of him resented his friend's charity.

I'm not sure how long we talked—hours it seemed like. Something shifted as we sat together. I could feel the energy change between us, his knee or arm brushing against mine.

I don't know what would have happened if we hadn't been interrupted, but CB suddenly burst in on us, his arm around a giggling and hiccupping Jessica. "There you are, Becca," he crowed. "We've got plans to make."

I glared at CB, feeling my anger rise up inside me again. Daniel intervened, saying we needed a refill, and should head back to the fire.

Daniel refilled all our beers for us. As he handed me mine, our fingers touched. I could feel a shock run up my arm. He leaned closer. "Want to meet here tomorrow?" His breath was warm on my cheek and had a faint, yeasty smell.

I nodded, not wanting to speak and draw attention to what he asked me. A part of me thought it was stupid—I was leaving in a few weeks. Did I really want to start something that would have to end so quickly?

The next day, he didn't show. I waited for almost an hour, wondering what had happened. Was something wrong? Should I call? Did he change his mind? Did he not say what I thought he did?

I stewed about it, not knowing what, if anything, I should do. Then, when I finally did see him again a few days later, not only did he completely ignore me, but he was with another girl. Deb, according to Mia, had an on again, off again thing with Daniel. "Looks like it's on again," she said, squinting at them sitting together on the pier, their legs dangling in the lake.

Now, years later, I was back walking around the fire pit to lean on The Rock, smelling the fresh, clean air that only hinted of smoke and ash. I wondered what on earth happened back then. Was it a miscommunication? Was he simply not interested? Did he wake up the next morning and have second thoughts? Or was he actually a jerk?

Should I bring it up? Or did it even matter? After all, he was engaged, and I was married. What would be the point?

I heard the car before I saw it, pulling slowly into the clearing and parking. A police car.

Daniel.

Of course.

Chapter 24

Of course Daniel would just show up, I thought, watching him get out of his car as if I had again conjured him up by mulling about our past.

He headed over to me. "Mia thought you'd be here," he called out.

I took a drink from my coffee, mostly to give myself a moment to pull myself back to the present. "And why are you looking for me?"

He stopped by one of the broken logs, and put his hands in his back pocket. "To tell you I dropped Chrissy off at home."

I looked sharply at him. "Is she drunk again?"

He shook his head. "No, but I thought she was. I found her up on the other side of town, by the Ford dealership. She was alone, and I watched her stumbling as she walked. I questioned her, and she appeared sober enough. But ... there seemed to be something wrong. I dropped her off at home, saw you weren't there, and figured you were looking for her, so I decided to come find you."

How the hell did she get way out there? With no car? Did someone drop her off and leave her there? I blew the air out of my cheeks. "Nice of Chrissy to let me know where she was. I could have gotten her."

He kicked a pebble, not meeting my eyes. "I got the feeling she didn't want you to know."

I shook my head and took another swallow of coffee. A crow cawed somewhere behind me, startling me, and I jumped, spilling a few drops on my shirt. "Christ. I guess I better go home and deal with her." I stared at the stain on my shirt and sighed. "Did she tell you what she was doing way out there? Alone?"

He shook his head, still not meeting my eyes. "Look, there's something else." He hesitated. "She didn't have on any shoes."

I stared at him, feeling like we had suddenly slid into the Twilight Zone. "No shoes?"

He shook his head. "It was why she was stumbling and falling down. Her feet were a bit of a mess."

Why didn't Chrissy have any shoes on? She couldn't have sleepwalked that far. Could she?

It's coming. Beware.

The sun went behind a cloud, giving the clearing an ominous feel. A cool breeze blew against me, causing me to shiver. I quickly drank more coffee, although it wasn't nearly as hot as before and didn't warm me up.

Daniel scuffed his foot against the ground again. "Did anyone ever tell you how this town got its name?"

I blinked. Had I fallen down a rabbit hole and not realized it? What did the name of the town have to do with Chrissy? "Ah, no."

He nodded and then looked up at the sky. The sun peeked out from behind a cloud, but there was no warmth behind it. "In the 1800s, this town was a lot like other small towns around here—more of a large farming community than anything else. By all accounts, it was perfectly normal. Then, the winter of 1888 happened."

"The Great Blizzard of 1888," I said softly.

Daniel nodded. "Yes. That blizzard hit New York and the East Coast. But, what you may not know is a few months before that, the entire Midwest was also hit with a massive blizzard. It was called "The Children's Blizzard," because hundreds of children died.

"Although Wisconsin didn't get the brunt of it—Minnesota and Nebraska were hit hardest—it was still pretty bad. Everyone basically hunkered down where they were. There was little to no travel between towns, which in those days, wasn't that uncommon during the winter months.

"Spring finally came and as the weather warmed up, traveling resumed. When people came here, I'm sure they expected the blizzard to have taken its toll, but they definitely weren't prepared for what they found."

Daniel paused. The sun dipped behind a cloud again, and I shivered.

"What did they find?" I asked.

He didn't answer right away, instead looking out over the horizon where the hawk continued making its lazy circles in the sky. "All the adults were gone."

I blinked. "Gone?"

"Gone."

"Like ... poof?"

He nodded. "Only the children were left."

"The children? What happened?"

He shrugged. "No one knows.

"What do you mean no one knows? What did the children say?"

"They didn't," he said simply.

"What do you mean they didn't?"

"They claimed they didn't know what happened—that they woke up and found their parents gone, along with the other adults."

Daniel's story sounded more and more bizarre by the second. "But, wasn't there an investigation?"

He held his hands up. "Sure, but you have to remember things were different back then. This was one of many small towns in Wisconsin. Life was a lot harder then, and most people were focused on staying alive. And, it's not against the law to disappear when you're an adult. As far as anyone could tell, there wasn't any sign of foul play. It was sort of like what happened in Roanoke, Virginia, except instead of an entire town disappearing, it was only the adults."

I was mystified. "Why have I never heard of this before?"

"Did you ever hear about Black River Falls, Wisconsin?"

I shook my head.

"There's a book about it called *Wisconsin Death Trip*. I have a copy if you want to look at it. It's a collection of newspaper articles and photos around the same time. It's like the entire town was gripped by madness—suicides, murder, violence—for years.

No one talked about that either. Back then, people tended to mind their own business."

The wind ruffled my hair, bringing with it the delicate scent of decay and death. "Back to Redemption—what happened to the children?"

"They took over the town, and the farming, and ended up doing better than people expected. Not all the children were little. There were quite a few teenagers, and as they had grown up here, they knew how to farm. Also, some adults—mostly relatives—moved in to help. Over time, the town actually began to grow and prosper. The children were the first to start calling it Redemption, and the name stuck. It certainly seemed like the town had been saved."

"This is just so weird," I mused into my coffee. "Are there any ideas about what happened?"

Daniel shrugged. "Some crazy theories, as you can imagine. There's a lot of Native American land around here, so probably the most popular theory is Redemption was built on old Native American burial grounds, and the adults were taken as payback. Revenge."

Oh God—could that be true? Was my house built on Native American burial grounds? Could that be the source of my ghost problems?

"Was it?"

"Was what?"

"The town. Was it built on Native American burial grounds?"

Daniel shook his head. "No one has found any evidence of that."

Somehow, I didn't feel all that relieved.

I cocked my head and studied Daniel. He seemed uncomfortable, and it didn't fit him well. Throughout the entire telling of the story, he had barely glanced at me. Instead, he alternated between staring at his feet scuffing the ground and watching the hawk soar overhead. "Why are you telling me this?" I finally asked.

He hesitated. The sun moved behind a cloud again, throwing his face into shadow. The smell of decay grew stronger. I wondered if there was a corpse rotting somewhere close by, and what exactly had died. "Redemption is … different. It's kind of hard to explain. It's almost like the town decides who it wants here and who it doesn't. If the town wants you, you stay. Even if you don't necessarily want to."

I thought about Celia, and the almost desperate look on her face when she talked about leaving. "Like Celia."

He nodded. "Celia isn't from here, I think she grew up in Illinois, but yeah, she's stuck here. Not only is she married to Barry, who isn't going anywhere, but they have two children. Redemption almost never lets its children go."

Almost never. I shivered. "What if the town doesn't want you?"

He stared directly at me. "Then you go," he said simply.

Mia's voice echoed in my head. *I'm sure she didn't disappear.* The coffee hardened into a lump in my stomach, and I swallowed hard to keep myself from throwing it up. "You mean disappear," I said, my voice coming out in a croak. Next to me, the crow cawed again.

He half-smiled. "It's normally not so dramatic. Usually people just up and move, sometimes rather abruptly. Or they want to move here, and somehow it just never works out so they can. You see this with some of the summer visitors. They start looking for a cottage or a house, and every deal falls through. But, yeah, sometimes they do simply disappear."

I thought I was going to be sick. "Are you trying to say Redemption doesn't want *us*?"

He paused and rubbed his neck. "I'm not sure. It's clear the town wanted Charlie here. The fact that your husband has spent almost no time here since your move makes me wonder if the town doesn't want *him*." He looked directly at me. "I don't know about you, though. Or Chrissy."

He didn't say anything more, but he didn't need to. I could almost hear his thoughts. *Watch yourself. And watch Chrissy.*

I felt cold and nauseous. Is that what my dreams were trying to tell me too? Is that what the message in the mirror meant? That we weren't wanted? That we should leave? Slowly, I stood up and brushed off my shorts. "I better go see about Chrissy. Thanks for getting her home."

He nodded as I picked my way across the fire pit. I found myself wondering, could that have been the reason why he stood me up when I was sixteen? Because he didn't know if Redemption wanted me or not?

When I drew close, he reached out, as if to touch me, but his hand simply hovered over my arm. "How are you feeling?"

I looked up, a bit startled. I found myself wanting to ask him why he was being so nice to me. And if I could trust him. "I've certainly had better days," I said instead.

A ghost of a smile crossed his lips. "I meant your headaches. You said you were coming down with something. Are you better?"

"I hope so. It's been a couple of days and I haven't had one." My recent forgetfulness was another story.

"I'm glad," he said, but his eyes lingered on mine. I felt a jolt of electricity move through me, and for a moment, everything else melted away and I was sixteen again. Would I make different choices this time around? Or was I cursed, stuck in the same cycle, doing the same things over and over?

I shivered again, although not from the cold.

He noticed, and stepped out of the way, breaking the spell. "I should let you go."

I nodded. "Thanks again," I said.

He inclined his head as I headed over to my car. I looked back at him as I got in. He was still standing in the same place, watching me go. He lifted his hand to wave goodbye as I started the car and headed for home.

My emotions were a mess. My dreams, the warning in the mirror, Chrissy sleepwalking, the story of Redemption, Daniel all collided in my head. I had no idea what to think about any of it. But, quite honestly, I had to set most of that aside. What I really needed to be doing was focusing on Chrissy.

Had she been sleepwalking again? I thought about that footprint in the garden—maybe that had been hers after all. But still, the other side of town was a long way to sleepwalk.

And she had her phone—if she were asleep, would she have grabbed her phone?

On the other hand, if she had snuck out, why hadn't she put her shoes on?

Neither option made any sense.

Or was something else going on with her? Something medical, maybe? She certainly hadn't been acting normally. Getting drunk, out-of-control mood swings ... maybe what I really needed to do was get her to a doctor.

Argh. I was just about to accelerate, knowing I really needed to get home to talk to her, when I saw *her*.

Trundling down the sidewalk in front of me, pushing her loaded shopping cart, was the homeless woman, still bundled up in her scarves and jackets. I could feel my heart speed up. "Nonsense," I told myself. "I'm in a car and she's walking. What could she do to me?"

Nevertheless, I found myself slowing down as I passed her. She turned to look at me, staring straight at me. Her eyes widened. I could see her lips move. "You know."

I quickly turned my head away to focus on my driving. It didn't necessarily mean anything. In fact, it probably meant nothing at all. She may not have even said anything. Maybe she was just yawning.

Regardless, the cold pit of fear that had been my constant companion since I discovered Chrissy missing that morning got even colder.

Pulling into the driveway, I shut the car off and ran to the front door. I found Chrissy in the kitchen, a bowl of cereal in front of her. Her hair was wet, like she had taken a shower, and she was dressed in a tee shirt and cut off sweat pants. Her feet were covered in thick socks.

She glanced up at me when I walked in, then quickly turned away. I took a deep breath, pulled out a chair, and sat down in front of her.

"Wanna tell me what happened?"

She didn't answer, twisting her hair with her finger.

"Chrissy. We need to talk about this." I wanted to scream, but forced myself to speak quietly. "I want to know what happened, and if we have to sit here all day until you tell me, then that's what we'll do."

"I don't want to talk about it," she said. She sounded hollow and unsure—like a sad little echo of her normal self.

"Tough. We're *going* to talk about it."

She didn't answer. Instead, she picked up her spoon and swirled it around her bowl.

I didn't say anything. I simply sat there and watched her play with her food. If that's what I had to do to get her to talk to me, then that is what I would do.

The house was silent except for the ticking of the grandfather clock. The dust motes danced in the sun rays that slanted through the window. Chrissy stirred her cereal, but didn't eat.

Finally, she sighed. "I don't really know what happened," she said softly.

I leaned closer. "What do you mean you don't know what happened? Were you sleepwalking?"

She looked up sharply. "I ... I don't know what happened."

"Okay, just start from the beginning. What do you remember?"

She looked out the window. "I ... I got a text. From one of my friends. She was going over to a friend's house and invited me, and I decided to go."

I sat back. "You snuck out."

She nodded.

I bit my tongue to keep myself from yelling at her. "Who was your friend?"

"You don't know her."

"I'd like to know her."

She made a face. "It's Brittany."

"Is she the girl who came over the other night?"

She nodded.

"So, how did you get to your friend's house?"

"Brittany picked me up."

The whole conversation felt like pulling teeth. "Whose house did you go to?"

"You don't know her."

I tightened my jaw. "I know that. But I want to. Look, Chrissy. This needs to change. I need to know who your friends are. I need to meet them, and I need their contact information. You can't do this anymore. What happened at this friend's house? Was there drinking?"

She didn't meet my eyes. "Just beer."

"Did *you* drink?"

"Not much. One or two maybe." She finally looked at me. "I wasn't drunk. Honest."

I almost believed her. "If you weren't drunk, then why didn't you call me to come get you? Why were you wandering around with no shoes on?"

She muttered something I couldn't hear into her cereal bowl.

I leaned closer. "I didn't hear you. What did you say?"

"I said, I don't know," she said loudly. "I don't know what happened!"

"What do you mean you don't know?"

"I … I just found myself wandering around."

I sat back. "Chrissy, you're making no sense."

Her jaw worked. "I must have fallen asleep because the next thing I knew, I was walking down the street."

"But you had your phone. How did you have your phone and not your shoes?"

She shrugged. "My phone was in my pocket."

I started rubbing my temples. "So, what you're saying is you sleepwalked again? And found yourself walking outside. Chrissy, do you have any idea how dangerous that is? You could have been attacked, or hit by a car, or God knows what else. I think we need to take you to a doctor."

"No!" For the first time that morning, she looked directly at me, an expression of horror on her face. "I don't need to see a doctor. I'm fine."

"You're *not* fine. You just said you're sleepwalking, and found yourself outside."

"I don't think I was sleepwalking."

"So, you *were* drunk?"

"No, I told you I only had a couple of beers."

"Chrissy, you can't have it both ways. Were you sleepwalking or were you drunk?"

"Neither! I … I don't know what happened. But I'm fine. I don't need to see a doctor."

I studied her, drumming my fingers on the table. Her agitation was definitely real, but was anything else? Was she out-and-out lying, or just not telling me the whole story?

"Okay," I finally said. "Your father is coming home this week and we can wait until he gets here to decide what to do. But Chrissy, we're all going to have a conversation about this. It's gone far enough."

She nodded and looked down. "I know," she said in a small voice.

I thought about saying something more. It felt like I should. But what?

Instead, I got up from the table and turned to leave the kitchen.

"Rebecca?" Chrissy said, her voice hesitant.

I stopped and turned around.

She still wasn't looking at me. In fact, she seemed to be focused on something behind me. "I'm … I'm sorry."

I was quiet for a moment. Everything about her, from her facial expression to her body language, screamed absolute misery. I felt sorry for her. But her father needed to know. I couldn't keep hiding all of it from him, no matter what her wishes were. "We can talk about it more with your father."

I turned to leave but then I thought of something. "And Chrissy?"

She still didn't look at me, but she dipped her head to indicate she was listening.

"Call me Becca."

Chapter 25

I sat back on my heels and stared at the bag of ground coffee.

There it was, in the bottom cupboard in front of the slow cooker.

Why the hell was it there? Who put it there? Was it me? Could I be the one misplacing all the things in the house? Maybe I was the one who should go to the doctor. Or, maybe it was Chrissy playing some sort of joke.

I took the coffee and went to make a pot. Perhaps I should talk to Chrissy about it. I had avoided the subject so far mostly because I wanted to pick my battles with her. Her moods swung so wildly, they were impossible to predict, and keeping her as calm as possible seemed to be the best way to keep the peace, at least until her father was back in the picture.

Stefan had texted the night before to let me know he had been able to get more done than he had anticipated, so he could join us early, and would arrive the following day. I had mixed emotions. On one hand, I was relieved he would be home sooner to help deal with Chrissy. I was also hoping he had wrapped things up faster because he had finally realized his child needed him, and had rearranged his schedule accordingly.

Secretly, I was also wishing maybe he realized how much he missed *me* as well, and couldn't wait for us to be together again.

But, another part of me dreaded having Stefan home. What would he say when he walked in and saw that I still hadn't done anything he had asked? Our stuff was still packed up, Aunt Charlie's belongings were still everywhere, and I hadn't even opened the door to Aunt Charlie's bedroom, much less moved us into it.

Would he be furious? Or would he understand? After all, it's not like I hadn't had my hands full, between getting sick and dealing with Chrissy.

And seeing your friends on the side, a little voice chimed in. *Including Daniel.*

I shivered, remembering the jolt of energy that flared between us at The Rock, before pushing that memory away.

Daniel couldn't be helped, I firmly told the little voice. If Chrissy hadn't gotten drunk or … disappeared, I wouldn't have seen him. And who cares that I *did* see him? Nothing happened.

Yes, blame the sixteen-year-old, the little voice said. I decided to ignore it and focus on the positive instead. Stefan was finally going to be with us. We were finally going to have that time to bond and become a family again. And he would even have an office to work in. I had at least managed to whip The Magic Room into shape. That would make Stefan happy.

Everything was looking up.

I poured myself a cup of coffee, boiled a couple of eggs to eat with gluten-free toast, and took everything to the table. After finishing breakfast, I had every intention of digging in and getting as much of Aunt Charlie's belongings packed away (and ours unpacked) as possible.

But, as I sat in my warm, homey kitchen, dappled in the bright-yellow sunlight, the sunflowers winking at me from the glass canisters on the counter tops (ah, how Aunt Charlie loved her sunflowers), I started to have second thoughts.

I had been so forgetful lately, misplacing all sorts of things … from my keys to the ibuprofen. Given that, was embarking on a massive reorganization of the house a smart move? What if I ended up making a bigger mess and no one was able to find anything?

That would definitely annoy Stefan.

In fact, the more I thought about it, the more I decided the prudent move would be to leave the house as it was, and instead, focus on cleaning up the studio. No one would care if I made a mess reorganizing the studio. It wasn't like we were trying to live in it.

Yes, that was definitely the way to go. Once Stefan was here, I could explain everything to him and make him understand. Maybe he would even realize how silly it was to unpack all of our New York belongings when we'd be moving back once we sold the house.

I finished my breakfast, topped off my coffee, and began the long walk upstairs to the attic, to the studio.

My footsteps slowed the closer I got to the top. It was hot. And musty. Dust, cobwebs, and bugs coated the creaky wooden steps. I passed a dried snake skin, too, as I climbed, and wondered why on earth a snake would shed its skin there.

I reached the top, took another deep breath, stepped through the archway, and gasped.

It was all bright sunlight and light wood. I had forgotten how huge the room was, with the high, pointed ceiling. Dusty windows lined both sides of the walls, which made it unbearably light, and unbearably hot. At the same time, all the natural light made it a perfect place to paint.

Memories came rushing back. The hours I spent there painting. How sure I was I would become a painter—no matter what my family, my mother thought. The encouragement and love from Aunt Charlie and my friends was all I needed.

They had believed in me. They had thought I was good enough to make it as a professional artist.

They hadn't thought the only way I could support myself was becoming someone I wasn't.

Grief overwhelmed me. Grief for the girl I was, the woman I had become, and how far apart those two were. How much time I had wasted. How much I had lost. I could feel the first stabs of a headache behind my eyes.

I slowly walked across the floor, the dust so thick I left footprints. Boxes, trunks, and old furniture was shoved against the walls under the windows, so I had to lean over them to wrench them open. Cool air rushed in, surprisingly cold on my wet cheeks. I realized I had been crying.

I methodically began to open all the windows, sneezing the whole time, before approaching the corner that had been carefully set up for me to paint. It still looked exactly the way it did when I had left. I ran my fingers over the dusty jars of paint, the stiff and dried brushes, my old sketch book. Stacks of my paintings were lined up against the wall. Two easels, one still covered with a dusty white cloth, stood on top of a grey drop cloth. A wooden chair covered with paint splotches faced the easels, as if it were studying them.

My chest literally ached as I stood there in what I once considered my "happy place." I felt so sick, I wondered if I should just forget about it and come back another day.

But, did I really think it would get any better? I sighed and scrubbed at my face. Baby steps. That was the ticket. Start small. Like tackling the dust. I could do that. I went downstairs for a bucket, mop, rags, and a Swiffer duster, changed into my oldest tee shirt, and dug in.

But no matter how hard I focused on the dust in front of me, my eyes kept drifting back to my paintings. What would I see when I finally looked at them? Would I like them? Would I see talent? Did I want to see talent, or would that just devastate me more—knowing I had squandered it?

Oh God, I had to stop. I threw myself into the cleaning, dusting, washing, and scrubbing. I was even able to ignore the pain in my head and my clogged sinuses, which I was sure I was making worse with all the dust.

From below, I heard a door slam. "Becca?" Chrissy called.

I sat back, ran my hand over my forehead, and promptly knocked something over, hearing it clatter as it fell. "Up here."

I heard her footsteps heavy on the stairs, and turned to see what had fallen. Some old photographs had spilled out of a carved wooden box with a rose on the lid, along with what looked like an old diary, yellow and brittle, and a heavy gold locket decorated with a jeweled rose. The petals looked like they were made with rubies and diamonds, the stem from emeralds. It was gorgeous. And instantly disturbing.

Where is my locket?

I rubbed my temples, trying to shut out Mad Martha's voice. This couldn't possibly be her locket. Could it?

Suddenly, I realized Chrissy had nearly reached the top of the steps. I quickly swept everything back into the box and hid it behind an old table just before she stepped into the room.

She wrinkled her nose and looked around. "Wow. What a mess."

I half-smiled. "Yeah it is."

Her eyes fell on the paintings set up in the corner. "Your aunt painted?"

I paused. I wanted to say "yes" and bundle her back downstairs before she asked any more questions. But instead, when I opened my mouth, I found myself saying something else entirely. "No, they're mine."

She almost looked impressed. "Really? Can I see?" She started walking toward the stack of paintings. I had to scramble to my feet to intercept her.

"Not now. Okay?"

She stopped, the expression on her face a mix of hurt and anger. "What? Am I not good enough? Only your *friends* can see them?"

Careful Becca. I didn't want to make the same mistake I did when she first heard the name Becca. I took a deep breath. "It's not that I mind you seeing them. It's just *I'm* not ready to see them yet. Can you understand that?"

She paused, looked at me, and then back at the paintings. "Yeah. Okay. Whatever."

I tried to hold back my relief. At least for the moment, I'd managed to avoid a fight. "Did you need anything?"

"I'm making lunch. Do you want any?"

"Um, sure." I was surprised. She hadn't offered to cook or pitch in since the night she got drunk. I wondered if this was her way of burying the hatchet.

"Okay, give me fifteen minutes." She turned to head back down the stairs.

When she was gone, I looked to where I had hidden the box. I wanted to examine it more closely, but it didn't feel like the time. Maybe after I ate. Eating would probably help my headache from getting any worse as well, keeping it from going beyond the dull pain it was at that point. I took a moment to blow my nose.

I headed to the bathroom to clean up and swallow a couple ibuprofen and a decongestant, and then went downstairs. Chrissy was just putting the finishing touches on tomato soup and grilled cheese sandwiches with tomato and bacon. It smelled wonderful.

Along with taking care of lunch, she even made an effort to have a conversation with me, finally sharing a bit about her new friends. Even though a part of me was suspicious of her motives, her dad *was* coming home tomorrow, and maybe she thought it would be a good idea to get on my good side. I pushed that thought away.

It didn't matter if her motives weren't completely pure; this was still a good sign. It was something to build on.

After lunch, I offered to clean up, so she could go join her friends. But before I did anything, I wanted one of the cookies she had made a few days ago. I opened the lid of the sunflower cookie jar only to find it empty.

A sense of dread uncurled itself in the pit of my stomach. The night before, there were still plenty left. What happened? Did I move them and not remember?

Chrissy breezed in as I was opening cupboards and peering into pots. "What are you doing?"

"Looking for the cookies," I said, picking the lid off the slow cooker. "Do you know what happened to them?"

"They're gone."

"What?" I jerked my head to look up at her, and ended up banging my head. "Ow. Gone? What are you talking about? There were a bunch left last night."

She shook her head. "No, there wasn't. I only saw two last night and I ate them."

I got to my feet, rubbing where I banged my head. "But that's not possible. I remember …" my voice trailed off.

Did I actually remember all those cookies? Was I sure?

Chrissy was staring at me, concern and alarm mingling on her face. "Becca? Are you okay?"

I shook my head, as if to clear it. "Yeah. I think so. I've also noticed things in odd places, like my keys and the coffee. Have you noticed anything?"

She shook her head, her expression turning suspicious. "Why would I touch your keys?"

"I didn't say you did. I was just asking if you knew anything about things not being where they belong."

"You always blame me for everything," she shouted, as she flounced out of the kitchen. "It's not my fault," I heard her yell as the back door slammed.

"I'm not blaming you," I said to an empty kitchen. "And why would I think it was your fault?" Sighing, I rubbed my head.

It was only later when I realized she never did answer the question.

***

The first thing I did when I returned to the studio was check to see if the box was still where I had left it. It was. As much as I wanted to take a closer look at the contents, especially that locket, a part of me still felt like it wasn't quite the right time. Instead, I finished cleaning the worst of the dust and grime. I also decided to keep the windows open to continue airing out the room. Eventually, once I cleaned out the boxes and other junk, I could turn the space into something really nice. Maybe it could be my office and studio, combined. I could move up the files and herbs from The Magic Room, too, and it could be a fabulous work place for me …

Wait a second. What was I thinking? I wasn't seriously considering getting back into painting again, was I? Never mind my aunt's herb and tea business. When would I have the time? I still had a ton of things to do to get this house ready to put on the market. Besides, chances were high we wouldn't be here long enough for me to turn this space into anything other than storage for all the boxes in the garage.

I vigorously dusted my hands together, like I was brushing all traitorous difficult thoughts off of me, and focused instead on collecting the cleaning supplies and cleaning myself up. I needed to turn my energy to the next day, and Stefan's homecoming.

I brought the rose box with me as well. After I had showered and changed into fresh clothes, I sat on my bed with the box in front of me.

Where is my locket?

Opening the box, I took the locket out. It had a rich, heavy feel to it. I ran my finger over the beautifully-etched diamond and ruby rose.

Still beautiful. And still somehow disturbing.

My logical mind argued with me. How on earth could a locket "feel" disturbing? It was a locket. It didn't emit "feelings." And it certainly couldn't feel that way just because it was probably Mad Martha's.

Could it?

Another part of me, a deeper part, knew why it felt disturbing.

That part knew the truth.

Cold prickles of fear covered my body. I was having trouble breathing.

"It's just a locket," I tried to tell myself. But the fear didn't go away. If anything, it just got worse.

Moving slowly, feeling almost like I was in a dream, I gently opened the latch with a small click.

Inside there were two pictures—a man and a woman. The man I didn't recognize, but the sour-looking woman with her hair in a bun wearing a buttoned- up, high-necked dress was a dead ringer for the woman in my dream.

Mad Martha.

Chapter 26

For a moment, all I could do was stare at that picture. Yes, it was definitely the woman from my dream.

That locket is more powerful than you can imagine.

I wanted to run screaming out of the room. Actually, remembering Daniel's story about Redemption, I wanted to run screaming out of the house, out of the town. Oh God, what were we living with?

Instead, I forced myself to pick up the pictures in the box. They were yellow with age, the edges curled under. More pictures of the woman in the locket, holding a baby, holding a baby with a man behind her—the same man from the locket, the woman sitting on a chair with the man and a young girl beside her, a baby in her lap.

I turned one of the pictures over. "Martha, Edward, and Helen, February 1910" scrawled in a spidery hand.

Mad Martha was real.

Until that moment, I realized a part of me had thought none of it was real—not Mad Martha, not Nellie, and certainly not the ghosts. I didn't even believe in ghosts.

Did I?

Gingerly, I picked up the diary and carefully opened it. The same spidery handwriting covered the brittle, yellow pages. I carefully flipped through the book, glancing at the entries.

The house is whispering to me again.

I dropped the book in horror. Oh God. It really *was* Mad Martha's diary. I didn't want any part of it.

On the other hand, it also meant I was in possession of the truth. Did I actually have a written account of her madness in my hands?

Would I finally find answers to what was happening in the house?

I picked up the diary, intending to read it downstairs with a pot of tea. Even though my headache had nearly drained away, thanks to the food, medicine, and shower, I thought some tea would hit the spot. First, though, I needed to hide the locket and the pictures. The last thing I wanted was for either Chrissy or Stefan to find them, before I had a chance to get to the bottom of everything.

But finding a hiding place was more difficult than I had first anticipated. There weren't that many places I could hide the box that I could be reasonably certain Stefan wouldn't stumble across. I finally decided to shove it in a pocket of my suitcase, which I then pushed to the back of the closet.

Downstairs, while the tea brewed, I searched for a book I could hide the diary in, if Chrissy surprised me while I was reading it. I settled myself with my tea and my phone on the couch in the family room—close enough where I could hear Chrissy come in either door.

January 2, 1913
Edward gave me a new diary for Christmas. "A new diary for a new beginning," he said as he handed it to me. I hope my smile didn't look as fake as it felt.

I know he means well. And he's trying to understand. But it's hard for him, especially when I don't understand myself what's happening.

Ever since Edward Jr. was born, I haven't been myself. I can't bring myself to touch him. How can this be? I'm his mother. I have to take care of him. I love him.

So why do I feel like if I touch him, something bad may happen to him? That I may hurt him?

I must be a terrible mother.

There he goes, crying again. And Helen is fussing, too. I'm just so tired. I don't know what to do. I just want to go to sleep.

I stopped reading. Did Mad Martha have postpartum depression? Or was I jumping the gun?

It certainly sounded like it, just from that first entry, and if she did, it might very well explain why she went mad.

I went back to reading. There were a number of pages—dated throughout most of January—detailing how depressed she was, how she couldn't cope. What a nightmare it must have been back then if she really did have postpartum depression.

January 28, 1913

Edward told me today he was hiring a new maid to help out. Her name is Nellie. She's young, Edward told me, but she's strong and eager to help. She'll be able to take over a lot of the maid duties, so Gertrude can focus all her attention on Edward Jr. and Helen, instead of trying to do both jobs. She'll be starting tomorrow.

He smiles as he tells me, but I can see the tension and disappointment behind it. He's unhappy with me. I've let him down. As both a wife and a mother.

And, instead of feeling relieved that he's getting me more help, all I want to do is crawl back into bed and cry. I'm so disappointed in myself. My mother, God rest her soul, would be so upset if she knew this is what I had turned into. This is not who she raised me to be.

What kind of mother can't pick up her infant son? What kind of monster am I?

January 29, 1913

Edward didn't tell me how pretty Nellie is. With her soft, doe eyes, creamy skin, full, luscious lips and silky brown hair, she reminds me a little of myself at that age.

I'm not sure how much I like that. None of our other help looks like her—Cook is soft and round with thick, heavy features, and Gertrude is all sharp angles with a hooked nose that reminds me of a bird's beak. We have one other servant who runs errands and pitches in wherever she's needed. I can't remember her name now, but she is a scrawny, ugly, little thing with red hair and freckles. A hard worker though.

But this Nellie …

I better go lie down and stop this nonsense. Supper is in a couple of hours and I need to look my best. Edward got me more help; he would think me most ungrateful if I don't make an effort.

I sipped my tea. The setup certainly lent itself to Edward having a bit of a dalliance on the side. If Martha really had been consumed with postpartum depression, the doe-eyed Nellie may have been too much temptation. He certainly wouldn't have been the first man to have had an affair with a maid.

Not that that excused his actions. But, all the pieces were starting to make an awful lot of sense.

I went back to reading. From the start, Martha had been suspicious of Nellie, and the relationship never improved.

February 23, 1913

Today, I walked into the drawing room only to find Nellie and Edward standing in the corner, way too close. They jumped apart when they saw me, and Nellie quickly left the room, mumbling that Gertrude needed her. When I asked Edward, he laughed at me, told me I was imagining things.

I know what I saw, but he's insistent. Asking me how would I know what I think I saw? I still can't touch my own child. Do I really know reality from fiction?

He has a point. I still can't bear to even be in the same room with my infant son, much less hold him like a good mother. But why won't Edward meet my eyes? And why are my instincts screaming that he's lying?

March 2, 1913

Why am I not getting better? No matter how much I rest, I just feel sicker and sicker. I don't know what's going on with me. Today, I was looking for Cook to make me tea, and I found Nellie in the kitchen. She seemed startled to see me. What was she doing in there? And where was Cook? There's something not right going on here. I must be more vigilant.

March 10, 1913

I think Nellie is poisoning me. She brought me my tea today, and I had only drunk half of it before I was hit with a raging headache and had to go lie down. As I headed off to bed, I passed one of the bedrooms and saw Nellie rocking Edward Jr. Why was Nellie rocking my baby? Where was Gertrude? I must talk to Edward about this.

March 11, 1913
I'm so upset I can barely write. I just told Edward what I suspected—that Nellie is poisoning me, but he only patted my hand and told me I needed my rest.

Rest? She's the one making me sick! But when I said that to Edward, he patiently reminded me I was sick before Nellie got here, that, in fact, Nellie was hired because I was sick.

But, why was she rocking my son then? He sighed and called for Cook to make me some tea.

I'm so confused now. Have I been sick that long? That can't be true. Did Nellie sneak in and poison me so we would hire her? Maybe I better lie down after all.

Why doesn't Edward believe me?

March 22, 1913
The house is whispering to me again. Edward still refuses to believe me. I know something is going on between them.

April 3, 1913
I had another raging headache today. I struggled out of bed to find Cook myself. I don't trust Nellie anymore. I know she's doing something to me. I know it! When I was walking to the kitchen I saw the four of them—Edward, Nellie, Edward Jr., and Helen, together in the garden. They looked like a family.

And that's when it hit me—Nellie wants to replace me. She wants my life.

She wants me dead.

As I stood there, watching them, my mouth hanging open, I heard the house whisper. "Yes, Martha," the whispers said. "Now what are you going to do about it?"

The back door slammed. "Becca, I'm home," Chrissy called out.

I quickly slipped the diary into the other book, stuck it in the bookcase, and stood up. She bounded into the family room and looked at me suspiciously. "Why are you in here?"

I smoothed my hands over my shorts. "So, this room is off limits to me?"

She took a step back, her expression uncertain. "Well, no … but you're never in here."

"First time for everything," I said briskly. "I'll go start dinner."

She moved back into the kitchen. "I can cook if you'd like."

Something jangled in the back of my head—something that felt like a warning. *I think Nellie is poisoning me.* "I can do it," I said quickly—maybe too quickly. Her eyes narrowed.

"What, don't you trust me?"

I opened my mouth, the words, "Why are you asking me if I trust you—shouldn't I trust you?" threatening to fly out. But, at the last moment, something stopped me.

The part of me that felt like asking that would be a very bad idea.

"I just wanted to give you a break. Your father is going to be home tomorrow, and I know he prefers your cooking to mine. But, what if we cooked together?" I forced a smile on my lips.

To my surprise, she agreed, although she didn't look all that convinced. Of course, to be fair, I probably didn't look all that convinced either.

She was civil, as we prepared the food together, answering questions and talking to me. I listened, but a part of me kept turning Martha's words over and over in my head. Martha, already suffering from postpartum stress, slipping into a deeper and deeper fog of suspicion and paranoia, feeling more and more isolated and alone.

How much was true and how much was her condition?

The Martha in my dream didn't look sick. Of course, I was being silly—this was a *dream* we were talking about, not reality. Martha was long dead.

On the other hand, she did seem paranoid in my dream.

I think Nellie is poisoning me.

I watched Chrissy chop peppers and mushrooms, her head bent over the cutting board, focused on the knife, her silky dark hair cascading against her smooth complexion.

She looked like an angel.

Chrissy, who was sleeping in the room where Martha murdered Nellie, and then killed herself. Chrissy, who was sleepwalking and sleeptalking.

Chrissy, with a knife in her hand.

I shivered.

She looked up at me. "Everything okay, Becca?"

She looked so innocent, so sweet—standing there in her white cut-off shorts and blue-and-white striped tee shirt. She's just a teenager, right? All teenagers are a little crazy, all those hormones coursing through their bodies.

She cocked her head, waiting for me to answer.

She's just a teenager.

Holding a knife.

I forced a smile. "Everything's fine."

Chapter 27

The front door slammed. Stefan was finally home.

I heard a thump as he dropped his suitcase, his deep voice greeting Chrissy.

I finished wiping the counter. This is what I wanted, right? From the moment we arrived in Redemption, all I had wanted was for him to be with us, regardless if it was in Redemption, or back in New York. Our fresh start.

So why wasn't I in there with Chrissy, greeting him? Why was I still in the kitchen, washing a clean counter, not feeling all that happy or excited?

Why did it suddenly feel like having him back with us was a bad idea?

Stefan walked in. "There you are, Rebecca."

I quickly dropped the washcloth into the sink and turned to give him a big smile, pushing my traitorous thoughts down. I was being silly—immersing myself in Mad Martha's journal probably wasn't all that healthy for me. "Yes, I was just finishing up. Welcome home."

He dipped his head to kiss my cheek. Over his shoulder, I could see Chrissy standing in the doorway, watching us with eyes that were as flat and cold as a snake's. I shivered.

Stefan glanced at me. "You cold?"

I tore my eyes away from Chrissy. "Probably a goose walked over my grave." I tried to keep my voice light, but the words felt awkward and heavy in the silence.

I think Nellie is poisoning me.

"Are you hungry?" I asked quickly, turning toward the fridge and shoving down all thoughts about Mad Martha. "Can I get you something to eat? Or drink?"

"I had something on the plane," Stefan said. He reached out and gently tugged me away from the fridge. "Is that the best welcome you've got for me?"

That snapped me out of my funk. What the hell was I thinking? Stefan was finally here, and we could start rebuilding our relationship. I definitely needed to stop reading Mad Martha's diary. I turned to him with a genuine smile on my face and gave him a real kiss.

"Ugh. Gross," Chrissy said crossly from the doorway. "Get a room."

Stefan chuckled. "We might just do that."

"God," Chrissy said, flouncing away.

"That's better," Stefan said nuzzling my neck. I could feel myself starting to melt into a pool of desire. "For a moment there, I thought maybe you weren't all that happy to see me."

My breath caught in my throat as hot desire froze into a block of ice. *How did he know what I had been thinking?* I forced a teasing smile on my face. "That's silly."

"Glad to hear it," he said, kissing my ear. "I'd hate to think you found something else to occupy your time while I was gone."

My stomach dropped with a thud. *Hope you're being a good girl.* "Why would you think that?" I kept my voice light.

"Well ..." he dropped his arms, his voice changing to one of disappointment. "I don't see much progress on the house."

And there it was. I swallowed hard, feeling a mixture of guilt and resentment. "I've been sick," I said, hating the note of defensiveness that had crept in. "Plus, a lot of stuff with Chrissy has been happening that we need to talk about."

He took a step back, leaning against the counter, and crossed his arms. "And that's it?"

Hope you're being a good girl. He couldn't possibly know who I had seen. Could he? Has Chrissy been spying on me? And why did I feel like I had to defend how I spent my time? "I got your office ready for you too," I said, thinking maybe it was a good time to focus on the positives. "And I cleaned up the studio, I mean the attic, so we have room for storage."

"Have you moved us into the master bedroom?"

"Ah ..." I looked away.

He sighed. "You see, this is why I wanted you to focus your time and energy on the house and not on creating relationships that are doomed to never go anywhere. There's still so much to get done."

"I *have* been focused on the house," I said, stung. "It's not my fault I got sick. That put me behind. And, Chrissy has taken a lot of time and energy. We need to talk to her …"

"So, that's really it?" he asked. "Chrissy and you being sick. Nothing else."

He was watching me so closely, it was almost like he knew I was lying to him. I swallowed hard. "That's what I said."

He stared at me for a minute longer, making me want to fidget, before relaxing his gaze and nodding. "All right then. So, what's going on with Chrissy?"

As thankful as I was to change the subject, I wasn't sure if this would make things better or worse. Nevertheless, it needed to be done. I took a deep breath, and let it all out—her getting drunk, her disappearing, and her mood swings.

But, I didn't tell him *everything*. I found myself curiously reluctant to talk about the sleepwalking. Maybe it was because my promise to Chrissy still lingered—so many adults had let her down—did I really want to be another one? Or maybe it was the way Stefan was watching me as I talked. There was something about the look in his eyes that made me uneasy.

I was being silly again. I needed to tell him everything. He was her father, after all.

But I didn't. And I certainly didn't share anything about Mad Martha or Nellie or the history of the town.

When I had finished, he took a deep breath. "Okay. I'm glad you told me. I'll talk to her." The way he said it, it sounded like the subject was closed. He would handle it. I didn't need to worry about it anymore.

That definitely didn't sit right with me. I opened my mouth to protest, and then closed it again.

She is his daughter, I reminded myself. And isn't that exactly what I wanted? For him to take charge so I didn't have to deal with it?

I watched him stride out of the room, biting my lip, somehow feeling like I hadn't done the right thing.

***

"You didn't do the right thing," Aunt Charlie said, bustling around the kitchen as she made tea.

I slumped over. "I knew it. I should have told him about the sleepwalking, too."

"That's not what I meant," Aunt Charlie said darkly. "You said too much."

I glanced up at her, a shadowy grey wisp in the kitchen. "But, he's her father. He needs to know."

"Does he? You sure about that?" She brought the tea to the table and pushed my sunflower mug in front of me. "You know what you need? To trust yourself. And to drink your tea." She nodded in the direction of the mug.

I gazed down into the tea, smelling the sweet, floral fragrance. I really wanted to drink it—I could feel my mouth start to water.

"Go on," Aunt Charlie said. "You know you want to."

I tore my gaze away from the mug and forced myself to look at her. She appeared as she always did. Nothing off or scary.

As I watched, she parted her lips to drink of her own tea, and I caught a gleam of a white tooth. A sharp, pointed tooth. Like a fang.

I sucked in my breath. Her eyes glittered as she gazed at me. "You're not going to drink your tea, are you?" she said, her mouth suddenly full of sharp, pointed teeth. "You were always stubborn. Just like my sister. Why are you insisting on doing this the hard way?"

"You're a monster," I gasped. "I can't drink that tea. You're probably poisoning me."

Suddenly, she was in my face, leaning across the table, moving as fast as a snake about to strike. "You don't know anything," she hissed, her tongue darting out, looking even more snake-like.

214

"I think Nellie is poisoning me," she said, but it wasn't her voice, it was Mad Martha's.

Her face melted, and Mad Martha was staring at me. "You think you know what's going on, but you have no idea," she rasped. "You don't even know where my locket is."

"But I do," I gasped.

Her lips stretched into a smile, more of a grimace really, full of teeth and madness. "Ha! You have no idea. You think I was crazy, don't you? That Nellie was a sweet, innocent thing. She was stealing Edward right from under my nose, and you believe her. Her! "

She leaned in even closer, so close I could smell her foul breath, as if something had died in her mouth. I was trapped in my seat. I couldn't move, couldn't breathe. "Beware," she hissed. "It's coming."

"What's coming?" I said, my mouth so dry I could barely push the words out.

Her smile grew wider, until all I saw were pointed teeth. "The evil that was done."

I sat straight up in bed, covered in sweat, my throat ragged with trapped screams. Next to me, Stefan muttered and rolled over in his sleep. I eyed him—how did he always manage to sleep through my nightmares? I didn't know if I felt envious or resentful.

I slid out of bed and padded my way to the door. I wasn't making the same mistake as last time. I was most definitely checking on Chrissy.

My heart sank as I stepped into the hallway. Chrissy's door was wide open. That wasn't a good sign.

I made my way down the hall and peeked into her room just in case—no Chrissy. The bed was empty, the covers flung off. That probably meant I needed to make my way downstairs. Taking a deep breath, and hoping I wouldn't run into Aunt Charlie, or even worse, Mad Martha, I hesitantly started down the steps.

Chrissy was in the family room, muttering to herself as she pawed through the bookshelf. For a moment, my heart became stuck in my throat. Was she looking for the diary? How did she even know about it? But then I realized she wasn't anywhere near where I had hidden the journal.

I cautiously approached her, until I could finally hear her words—"Where is it? I must find it. Where did it go?"

"Chrissy, maybe we should go to bed," I said, keeping my voice calm so I wouldn't startle her.

Her voice grew louder, more frantic. "Where is it? I must find it."

"We can look for it tomorrow," I said, putting my hand on her arm.

She shrugged me off, moving away from me, digging in the cushions of the sofa. "I have to find it."

There was something about her that was beginning to make the hairs on the back of my neck stand on end. She sounded exactly like Nellie had in my dream.

"Chrissy, we need to go to bed," I said, my voice loud and jarring in the stillness. I tried again to take her arm, and she whirled around on me, her face contorted in sudden rage.

"Leave me alone, you bitch," she hissed. "Don't touch me."

I took a few steps backward, startled by the vehemence in her voice. "Chrissy …"

"Stop calling me that. My name is not Chrissy."

Silence, except for the ticking of the grandfather clock that sounded like gongs in the stillness. I could almost feel my life draining away as I listened to that ominous ticking. I tried to swallow, but my mouth was completely dry. "Who are you then?" I found myself asking. *Oh God, don't say Nellie,* I thought a little desperately, trying to keep my breathing even, so I wouldn't hyperventilate and suffocate on my terror.

And, whatever you do, please don't ask me why I killed you again.

She gave me a disdainful look. "I don't have time for this."

Her voice had changed. It sounded older and darker. Ancient almost. I tried to swallow again. "Nellie?" I rasped, my voice barely over a whisper.

She turned back to the bookshelf. "Where is it? Where did you put it?"

I could barely form the words, my throat tight with terror. Oh dear God, what was going on? "Where is what?"

She spun back around. "What you stole," she practically screamed, her face contorted in rage. And, just as suddenly, her eyes rolled back up in her sockets, and she collapsed, like a pierced balloon, all the air rushing out.

I ran to her, knelt, and pulled her into my arms, saying her name over and over. The color had leached out of her face, leaving a very unhealthy, pale shade of grey in its place.

Should I call the hospital? At the very least, I needed to wake up Stefan, but at that moment, Chrissy stirred in my arms, her eyes fluttering open. "Becca …? What …?"

I hushed her. "It's okay, let's get you to bed. I'll get your father."

She struggled to sit up, focusing her eyes around the room. "Wait, why am I down here? Oh no, did it happen again?" Her face seemed to age right in front of me.

"Let's get you to bed," I said, helping her up. "I'll get your father."

"No!" But, even as she protested, she wilted against me. "I don't want to disturb him," she said weakly. "He has to get up early and work."

I started helping her up the stairs. "He can deal with it," I said shortly. "He needs to know."

She sagged against me, but didn't argue. I was already regretting not mentioning any of these episodes to him earlier. Now, how was I going to explain myself?

After helping her into bed, and getting her ibuprofen and a cool washcloth, I was just about to leave when she grasped my hand. "Becca, I just want to … thank you."

She looked like a sad little waif, lying there in the bed, her eyes huge and dark in her pale face, with her black hair spread over the pillow. I had to swallow a sudden lump in my throat. "You don't have to thank me. I'm here for you Chrissy, despite all our differences. I hope you know that."

If I had hoped it would lead to a bonding moment, I was sorely mistaken. She let go of me, squeezing her eyes shut and turning her face away to face the wall. "Do what you have to do," she said, her voice flat. "I'm fine, but if you want to wake him, go ahead."

I stood there for a moment, chewing my lip and debating my next steps. "He's your father," I finally said. "Don't you think he has a right to know?"

"Whatever," she muttered.

"I don't understand you," I said exasperated. "I'm trying to help. Why do you keep pushing me away?"

She jerked her head toward me, the fury on her face looking eerily like it did in the family room. "Did I ask for your help? No. I don't need it and I don't want it. Just go away."

I took a step back, shocked at the force of her rage. She glared at me one final time before turning back to the wall. Without another word, I turned to leave her room. As I closed the door, I heard a soft sound coming from her bed, like a sob.

Was she crying? Why?

I went back to my own bedroom and stared at Stefan, still fast asleep, his mouth slightly open in a snore. How could he sleep through everything? Didn't he sense, on some level, that there was a problem with his child?

I debated waking him. She was sixteen after all—did she really need her father comforting her in the middle of the night?

But, then I thought about that sob.

Where is it? I must find it.

Whatever was happening to her wasn't normal. Maybe it was nothing more than stress and hormones, but still, she should be evaluated by a professional. What if there was something seriously wrong with her? She was getting worse, not better.

I had to tell Stefan. It was getting out of control.

As gently as possible, I shook him. He jerked awake, flinging his hands up and nearly backhanding me.

"What's going on? What is it?" He barked, still half asleep.

"It's just me," I whispered. "Look, I'm sorry to wake you but Chrissy needs you."

He blinked at me, looking confused and disoriented. "Where am I?"

"Aunt Charlie's house."

He sat up slowly and rubbed his face. "What's going on? Why did you wake me?"

I took a deep breath. No going back now. "It's Chrissy. She's sleepwalking again."

He stared at me. "Sleepwalking? Chrissy doesn't sleepwalk."

"Well, she does now. She's in bed but Stefan, I think we need to get her some help."

He looked completely mystified. "Where is she sleepwalking?"

I sat heavily on the side of the bed. "Two times I found her in the family room. One time she was still in her bedroom." I decided to not say anything about the night she disappeared, as I wasn't clear what had happened, or if she even had been sleepwalking or not.

He ran his hand through his hair. "How do you know she's sleepwalking?"

"It's pretty obvious."

"What is she doing?"

I hesitated. Now it was getting dicey. How much do I share about the house's grisly past? Would he even take me seriously? Or would he think it was all too crazy, keeping Chrissy from getting the help she really needed?

"She ... well the first time she was throwing stuff on the floor in the family room. Tonight, she was just searching through the shelves, but she wasn't destroying anything."

"Are you sure she was sleepwalking?"

"Like I said, it's obvious if you see her."

"Is she saying anything?"

Where is it? I must find it.

I shrugged. "Yes, but it's nonsense." I couldn't believe how smoothly the lie came out. On the other hand, if you didn't believe in ghosts, it *was* nonsense.

He sighed and ran his hand through his hair. "Why didn't you tell me sooner?"

I picked at the edge of the quilt. "I ... I should have. But Chrissy asked me not to. And I was hoping it was just some phase—you know, hormones and stress—and that once she got settled in, she would stop. But, she's getting worse, not better. I think we should get her some help."

He sighed and flung the covers back. "I'd better go see her."

I watched him leave the bedroom with mixed feelings. I knew I had to tell him. I had no choice.

So, why did I have a gnawing feeling in my gut that I just made another big mistake?

I straightened the bed before getting back in. I laid on my back, stared at the ceiling, my thoughts whirling around.

Where is it? I must find it.

Was Chrissy being haunted by Nellie? It certainly was starting to seem that way. But, that would mean ghosts really *did* exist.

I didn't really believe in ghosts, did I?

Aunt Charlie in the kitchen, smiling her too-wide, too-pointed, smile.

Beware. It's coming.

I shivered, pulling the covers to my chin. Maybe the question I really should ask was how I could possibly convince Stefan that we had a ghost problem, knowing he wasn't a believer.

No, there was probably some other explanation for Chrissy's behavior—an explanation that had nothing to do with ghosts.

There had to be.

The minutes stretched out. What was taking Stefan so long? It felt like he had been in her room for an hour.

I was starting to drift off when the door creaked open and Stefan slid into bed. He curled up on his side, facing away from me, making sure he didn't touch me.

I was going to ask him about Chrissy, but something made me hold my tongue. There was something furtive about his movements, the way he slipped into bed, like he didn't want to alert me.

Maybe he didn't want to wake you, another voice said. *Maybe he's being a kind and compassionate husband.*

Maybe. But something didn't feel right.

Was I being paranoid? Or was there something else going

on?

Chapter 28

Sunlight streamed through the room. I blinked the sleep from my eyes as I looked at the clock. Later than normal—apparently my nocturnal activities had taken their toll.

Stefan's side of the bed was empty—no surprise there. Always an early riser, he had probably been up for hours, and was already hard at work in his office. I jumped out of bed, slipped on a pair of yoga pants and an oversized tee shirt, and padded my way downstairs to get my day started. Hopefully, Stefan wouldn't notice how late I'd slept in.

I walked into the kitchen, only to find Stefan and Chrissy standing very close together, whispering to each other. They sprang apart as soon as they saw me. "Rebecca, there you are," Stefan said, giving me a big smile. "Let me pour you a cup of coffee."

Chrissy backed away to lean against the counter, an unreadable expression on her face. Her outfit wasn't too inappropriate—cut off jean shorts and an oversized, off-the-shoulder hot-pink shirt with a black sports bra.

I felt the hairs on the back of my neck start to prickle. What were they talking about so secretively? Why did they act so guilty when I came in?

Today, I walked into the drawing room only to find Nellie and Edward standing in the corner, way too close. They jumped apart when they saw me, and Nellie quickly left the room, saying Gertrude needed her. When I asked Edward, he laughed at me, told me I was imagining things.

Why would that pop into my mind? Stefan is Chrissy's father—this wasn't a maid-employer situation.

But, if Nellie was haunting Chrissy …

Stefan handed me my coffee, a smile on his face that didn't quite reach his eyes. "I'm glad you're finally up."

My stomach tightened. "I'm usually up earlier," I said, hating the defensive note in my voice that I couldn't seem to stop. "I just overslept, after all the excitement last night."

From the corner of my eye, I saw Chrissy slink out of the kitchen, her expression still flat.

Stefan waved his hand. "It was a late night for everyone," he said, but there was a slight disapproving edge to his voice. He had managed to get up at a respectable time, after all. And so had Chrissy.

Yet another failure. At this rate, we were never going to get our marriage back on track.

"I've been thinking," he continued, not noticing me staring miserably into my coffee. "I think it's time for you to get a job."

My stomach sank even lower. "Why?" I asked. "We're going to be moving as soon as the house is sold."

"Just a temp job," he said. "What you used to do. Before we were married."

That was the last thing I wanted. "But, I thought the law firm was on better footing."

He made a face. "It is. After a lot of difficult choices. But, I'm still not able to pull money out the way I used to. And, with me being here, it's going to take longer to rebuild the practice." He noticed the disappointed expression on my face and added, "You *want* me here, don't you?"

"Of course," I said, wondering if what he was really saying was that this was somehow all my fault.

"And," he waved his hand around the kitchen. "We're not as far along with getting the house ready for market as I had anticipated. There's still a lot of work that needs to be done before we can sell it."

My fault again. "But, if I'm working, that's going to suck up my time," I said, trying to sound reasonable. "Wouldn't it make sense for me to focus all my energy on the house and not try to find a job, too?"

He gave me a look that clearly said *I've seen how fast you go when you're focusing all your energy on something.* "We need the money," he said flatly. "Look, we don't know how long it's going to take to finish the house or even how long it's going to sit on the market. It makes more sense for you to work, take some financial pressure off, and we'll work on the house in our free time."

I busied myself getting a spoon out to stir my coffee that didn't need to be stirred. A part of me wanted to defend myself. I was doing the best I could, I wanted to shout. It's been a really difficult few months, what with packing and moving across the country, to dealing with my past. And, that's on top of Chrissy and getting sick.

Why couldn't he see that?

But, a part of me felt like he was right. I should have gotten more done. Stefan has been working nonstop. Why haven't I? What was wrong with me? Unpacking our belongings would have made him happy. Moving our bedroom into the master bedroom would have made him happy. Why on earth did I try and convince myself otherwise? Didn't I want to make him happy? Didn't I want to save my marriage?

Or was I willing to face my family and friends as a two-time marriage loser, having to endure all the "I told you so's" for rushing into this one?

What a dreadful start to his homecoming.

"Hey," he said softly. He had moved from the counter to right behind me. He raised my chin with a finger. "We'll get through this. Okay? It's going to require some sacrifices. From all of us."

I nodded, knowing he was right, but still resisting. I tried one last plea. "What about the cooking and the cleaning? And the yard work? All of that needs to be done as well before we sell it."

"Chrissy can help. And, if we need to take a little more time, but it's not such a financial stress on all of us, then it's okay that it takes a little more time."

I noticed he didn't volunteer himself to help with those household chores. I quickly stomped down that thought. Stefan had been working overtime for months now. It wasn't fair to ask him to do more. I was the one who needed to step up here.

"I'm glad to hear you say Chrissy can help with the cooking and cleaning. I would love that. But I think she may need some time to take care of herself."

Stefan shot me a blank look. "Take care of herself? What are you talking about?"

I looked at him in surprise. "I'm talking about the sleepwalking and the drinking and everything else going on with her. We should make an appointment for her to see a doctor …"

He interrupted me. "She doesn't need a doctor. She's fine."

"How do you know? You're not a doctor."

"No, but I'm her father. I know my daughter and I know she's fine."

"Stefan, you didn't see her …."

He held up his hand. "Rebecca, that's enough. Just drop it."

Drop it? I stared at him. "Don't I get a say? I am her step-mother. And who has been taking care of her these past few weeks?"

"I said, that's enough." Stefan's voice cut through like a knife. His eyes narrowed. I could almost see the anger radiating off him. "That was a low blow," he said. "You know I couldn't be with her. But she *is* my daughter, and I have the final say."

I forced myself to take a breath. I had never seen him so angry. What could have triggered it? "Stefan, what's going on here?" I asked in a low voice. I had to press him. For Chrissy's sake.

He took a step backward. "What are you talking about? Nothing is going on. She's my daughter and I think I know best."

"This morning. In the kitchen. What was going on with you two?"

"Rebecca, what has gotten into you? We were just talking."

"But what were you talking about? What didn't you want me to hear?"

"Nothing," Stefan said. "Rebecca, where is this coming from? You're the one who wanted me to talk to her, right? So, I was talking to her. What do you think is going on?"

It's all in your head. I turned away and swallowed some coffee—as before, Stefan had fixed it perfectly.

He had a point. I did want him to talk to Chrissy. Lord knew she didn't trust me, so keeping it quiet between them made sense. Looking at it that way, *everything* I saw in the kitchen made sense. I could feel myself squirming a little, with shame and guilt. Honestly, what did I really think was going on? I was reading too much into Mad Martha's diary.

"I'm glad you're talking to Chrissy," I said at last. "But that doesn't mean she doesn't need a mother figure. Especially now. I know I'm not her mother, but I'm the closest thing she has to one right now. She needs me around."

"You can still be that and work," Stefan said. "Plenty of mothers work."

Yes, but Chrissy needs me, I wanted to protest. Instead, I swallowed those words almost as soon as I thought them. Did she really need me? I was the hated and resented stepmother. She certainly didn't act like she needed me.

In fact, Stefan was right. I didn't need to be here taking care of the house full-time either. All of this was just a bunch of excuses because I felt sick at the thought of forcing myself into a job I hated again.

I heard a paper rustle. "Yesterday, I picked up the local paper for you. It's on the table."

"Okay," I said, still studying my coffee. "I'll start looking after breakfast."

He paused. "It's not forever Rebecca. Six months, a year, year and a half at most. That's all we're talking. Okay?"

I finally looked up at him and tried to smile. "Of course. It's fine. I get it."

He nodded, refilling his coffee cup and headed out of the kitchen, leaving me alone with my thoughts.

* * *

Rubbing my forehead, I poured myself a glass of wine and headed out to the backyard. I was taking a break before starting dinner.

The moist, cool air kissed my cheek, smelling of green grass and growing plants. Ah, the grass. It was seriously overgrown and needed to be cut—when was I going to find the time? Or maybe I should talk to Stefan about getting Chrissy to do it.

The sun was starting its descent in the sky, but luckily, it wasn't low enough for the mosquitoes to be out yet. I headed over to sit on a bench overlooking the weedy and overgrown yard.

I was depressed and discouraged. It had been a frustrating day.

It all started with the Help Wanted ads. Combing through them, nothing had seemed right. I couldn't imagine myself in any of those positions.

That would have been dismal enough, but just as I threw the paper down in disgust, Stefan walked in.

He raised an eyebrow at me as he headed over to the coffee pot. "Problem?"

I blew the air out my cheeks and slumped over the table. "There's just not a lot of options."

"Oh?" He walked over to the table and started rifling through the paper. "I saw a lot of listings when I looked earlier. There were at least a couple I thought were promising. Maybe you missed them?"

I knew I hadn't missed anything. "Stefan," I began, and then paused. I didn't know how he was going to respond to what I wanted to say. "I was thinking ..." my voice trailed off.

He glanced up at me, a puzzled expression on his face. "Thinking? About what?"

"Well ..." *It's now or never, Becca.* "Maybe I'd like to look into doing something different."

His puzzlement seemed to deepen. "Different? Different than what?"

"Different than what I did before."

"I don't understand. What else are you qualified for?" His face seemed to change then. "Wait, you mean like go back to school? Rebecca, you know we can't afford that."

I didn't know if I wanted to laugh or cry. "So, you're saying I'm not qualified to do anything else? That I couldn't follow another path without going back to school?"

His eyes widened. "Oh, that's not what I meant." He pulled out a chair and sat down in front of me. "I'm listening. What are you thinking about doing?"

Was it my imagination or was he patronizing me? In that moment, I was feeling more like his wayward daughter and less like his wife and partner. "I was thinking about starting my own business."

He stared at me, flabbergasted. I don't think I had ever seen him so shocked. "Your own business? Doing what?" His voice dripped with disbelief.

I was starting to wish I had never started this conversation. "Well, my aunt had this business where she created custom teas and herbs for healing …"

"Teas? Are you serious?"

There was no way I was going to tell him about wanting to get back into painting now. "She had quite a profitable business going." My voice was getting smaller and smaller.

"What do you know about making teas?"

"I have her notes …"

But he was already shaking his head. "Honey, no." He put his hand over mine. "Look, this is my fault. I tried to protect you. I didn't want you to know how dire our financial situation is. But, this is silly. You can't start a business right now. You need money to start a business and we don't have it."

I stared at the table. "I know, but I thought …"

"Trust me, Rebecca. It's better for you, for all of us, if you just get a job. You have no experience making teas. You have no experience running a business. How can you possibly think you'll succeed?"

I was silent. The logical part of me knew he was right, but another part of me, a deeper part of me, rebelled. "I'll keep looking," I said, my voice so small and quiet I could barely hear it.

He let his breath out in a huge sigh and squeezed my hand. "I knew you'd come to your senses. Remember, the job is only temporary. And, if you're still interested in owning a business, once we're back in New York and on the other side of this setback, I'll see if I can find the time to teach you."

I nodded, trying to smile back. Finding a job was for the best. For everyone. I reached over to pull the paper back to me, hoping he would take the hint and leave.

He did.

I wasn't sure how long I sat there, re-reading the same ads over and over without anything sticking before I decided to just call it a day. Pour myself some wine, sit outside, and try and relax.

I had to stop feeling sorry for myself. It was time for me to grow up and get my act together. It was just a job. I needed to get over myself.

I saw movement in the corner of my eye. It was the black cat, creeping out of the woods, green eyes fixed on me. He slunk up to about ten feet away, and sat down, tail curling around his feet.

My mood lifted considerably as I watched him. Maybe things weren't as bleak as I thought they were.

My cell phone rang, causing me to jump. It was CB.

"You ignoring me now?" he asked in greeting.

"Oh, I'm so sorry. I didn't mean to not call you back. It's been crazy here."

"Crazy, huh? Now you're definitely in trouble. How could you not fill me in?"

I found myself glancing around, making sure I was alone. "It's complicated."

"Complicated? Did you do something naughty?"

"No! Not me. It's Chrissy."

"Chrissy? What's going on?"

I told him about Chrissy's drinking and the mood swings. I didn't mention her sleepwalking, or my finding Mad Martha's diary—they both seemed too long and complicated to get into, and I didn't want to stay on the phone that long. I also wanted to talk to him about the history of Redemption, and what Daniel had shared, but again, it felt like too much to get into right then.

"Is that all?"

I glanced around again. "Well ... Stefan's here. So, I can't stay on the phone long, but things are definitely ... strange."

"Well, that settles it. I think it's time for a visit."

I almost dropped the phone. "What? No."

His voice suddenly had an edge. "No? Don't you want to see me?"

"It's not that. But it's really not a good time. Maybe in a few weeks or a month? Give us a little time for Stefan to settle in?" My voice took on a pleading tone. The last thing I needed was a visit from CB, after Stefan specifically asked me not to have him.

He was silent. "Well, if you don't want me ..."

"It's not that. It's just not the right time."

"Who are you talking to?"

I almost dropped the phone again. Stefan was standing at the edge of the yard watching me. "I've got to go," I said as I hung up. From the corner of my eye, I saw the cat slink away.

"Just CB," I said, feeling defensive as I got up to move toward him.

Stefan studied me, his gaze flat. "You came out here to talk to CB?" He sounded skeptical.

"No. I was sitting out here taking a break before I made dinner, and he called. That's all."

He didn't look convinced. I tried to smile reassuringly as I went in to start cooking, hoping he wouldn't push the issue.

Luckily for me, he dropped it.

Chapter 29

I closed my laptop and rubbed my temples, willing my slight tension headache away. I hadn't been sleeping well, which most definitely was exacerbating my headaches. With every creak and groan of the house, I would jerk awake, sure it was Mad Martha or Nellie or Aunt Charlie wandering around. Or maybe it was Chrissy, sleepwalking again—a Chrissy who wasn't Chrissy, but someone else—someone older and darker. And, of course, once I was awake, I was tormented by thoughts of what to do about my future.

I sighed and rubbed my temples again. Maybe some tea would help. Or wine. Or chocolate. Luckily, the allergy medicine seemed to have taken care of my stuffy nose, so I at least had that to be grateful for.

It had been three days since Stefan moved back, and things still didn't feel quite right. He spent most of the time in his office, but still, his presence seemed to have shifted something … and not necessarily in a good way.

Chrissy was quiet. Remote, even. She mostly kept to herself, and the few times that she had to interact with either Stefan or me, she didn't say much. On one hand, it was nice we weren't constantly butting heads. But a part of me felt uncomfortable—in fact, as silly as it sounds, it felt almost like I was losing her. Yes, her constant pushback was exhausting, but it also made me feel like I had some sort of connection with her, albeit a challenging one. Since Stefan's return, I felt like I had no relationship at all with her.

The more I pursued outside employment opportunities, the more I felt like a failure. Nothing felt right. I spent time updating my resume, which somehow made everything even worse. My lousy track record neatly documented and laid out on paper for everyone to see … God. I was starting to wonder if I was even employable, much less if I'd ever be hired for a job that paid enough to support me without help from my husband or family. And Stefan's constant requests for updates only made everything worse, although I could tell he was trying to be supportive. He had even lined up a dinner date for us with some doctor and his wife who had "connections," and could presumably help me find a job. I was already dreading it.

I poured myself a glass of wine and opened the fridge. Hmmm, what to make? After poking around, I decided on turkey meatballs over zucchini noodles, and a salad. I pulled the ingredients out and started to organize.

Except I couldn't find my chef's knife. It wasn't in the knife block. It wasn't in the drying rack. It wasn't in the dishwasher—which was good, since I always hand-washed my knives. It wasn't in any of the other drawers. Where did it go?

A sense of unease started growing in my gut as I began opening random cupboards, even searching in odd places like behind the coffee maker. I had the knife yesterday, right? I tried to remember what I made for dinner—it was chicken and rice with veggies and a salad. Yes, I distinctly remembered chopping broccoli and an onion to sauté with the chicken.

This couldn't be happening again. How could I keep misplacing things?

Maybe Stefan or Chrissy had it. Although why either would need a chef's knife if they weren't being a chef was beyond me. If they didn't have it, maybe they knew where it was. Regardless, it was worth asking.

Neither of them was downstairs, so I headed to the second floor. I assumed Stefan was working and Chrissy would be in her room with her phone.

Chrissy's door was open a crack and I could hear the murmur of voices. Maybe she was watching something on her iPad. I knocked, calling her name, as I pushed open the door and found Stefan sitting on Chrissy's bed, Chrissy behind him, rubbing his shoulders.

My question about the knife died on my lips. "Stefan, I thought you were working. Why are you in here?"

Chrissy jumped off the bed, turning away from me as she moved to the dresser. Stefan stood up as well, a little too quickly, I thought. "I was just taking a break and thought I'd come talk to Chrissy."

So many words on the tip of my tongue. *Why was Chrissy giving you a massage, then? And if you wanted a break and a massage, why didn't you come to me?* Stefan had spent very little time with me since moving home, and most of that time was consumed by his grilling me about my employment progress.

Something was up. Every time I walked in on them, I felt like a third wheel. I definitely needed to have a conversation with him about it. And soon.

Chrissy turned toward me, flipping her hair behind her back. She wore very short, very tight black shorts I couldn't remember having seen before with a red tank top. Was it me, or had she been dressing even more skimpy since Stefan returned again? Something swung across her chest, catching my eye. I took a couple steps closer to get a better look.

It was Mad Martha's locket.

My blood froze.

Stop calling me that. My name is not Chrissy.

I strode across the floor and grabbed the locket. "Where did you get this?" I hissed.

Chrissy mouth fell open, her eyes round and shocked. "Ouch. Becca, you're hurting me."

"Answer me," I said, my voice louder, jerking her closer to me. "Where did you get this?"

"Geez, Becca, what's with you?" Chrissy whimpered.

"Rebecca," Stefan thundered from behind me. "Let go of her. What is going on?"

I ignored Stefan. "Take it off," I nearly yelled, shaking the locket. "Take it off right now."

Large hands grabbed me by the shoulders and wrestled me away from Chrissy. She backed away, her face white as she stared at me, her eyes round and huge in her face. For a second, I faltered, seeing the confused, lost child I comforted after her sleepwalking incidents. But, then, I saw it—a peek behind the curtain—the monster hiding behind the child.

Stefan gave me a quick shake as I started to lunge forward again. "Have you lost your mind? What has gotten into you?"

I struggled to free myself. "That locket isn't Chrissy's. She shouldn't have it."

Chrissy pressed the locket against her chest. "Then why did you give it to me?"

That stopped me cold. The sense of unease that had started prickling inside me when I couldn't find the knife froze into an icy ball of fear. "What are you talking about? I didn't give that to you."

My name is not Chrissy.

She continued pressing the locket into her flesh, but suddenly her expression began to change. No longer the frightened child, I could see something ancient and cunning beneath, just waiting for a chance to manipulate and twist the truth. The madness was sinking into her from that locket, and all I wanted was to snatch it away and destroy it. "You must have. It was on my pillow."

I shook my head. "No, that's not possible. I wouldn't give that to you." But I kept thinking about all the things that had gone missing, or that I had found in strange places. No, I wouldn't have given her the locket. I couldn't have. I felt sick with terror.

Was I losing my mind?

Stefan watched me carefully, like I was a wild animal, and he wasn't entirely sure what I was going to do. I wanted to tell him it wasn't me that was the problem— it was his daughter and that locket. "What's so important about that locket?" he asked.

I glanced over at Chrissy. Her hand was wrapped around the locket protectively, and she was still pressed against the wall. But a small, triumphant smile played around her lips, like she knew she had already won.

I wanted to scream in frustration. She was right. There was no way Stefan would believe me in that moment. I had to get that locket back.

"It's ... an antique. It's from my aunt," I said lamely.

Stefan stared at me incredulously. "All of this for an antique?" he asked.

I took a couple of steps away from Stefan and shrugged off his hold. He let go of me, letting his arms hang limply at his side. "It meant something," I muttered. "It was important to her."

Stefan opened his mouth like he was going to protest, but closed it without saying anything.

"Becca, do you want it back?" Chrissy asked, smug in her victory, sure her father would defend her keeping the locket.

"*Rebecca,*" Stefan corrected. In that moment, the cunning madness suddenly dissolved into the hurt, lost child underneath—a child who had no idea she was being used by ancient forces outside of her control. I could feel the anger building inside me, anger that was fast replacing the terror.

"It's okay, Stefan. She can call me Becca," I said quickly. "I don't mind."

Stefan frowned. "Your name is Rebecca."

I took a deep breath. I had lost this round, and I didn't feel like arguing anymore. My headache was back, and I needed to regroup and figure out my next step. "I have to go make dinner," I mumbled, backing out of the room.

It was only as I headed down the stairs that I remembered I had never asked them about the knife.

Chapter 30

"So," Daphne said, stirring her cappuccino. Her hair was loose around her face rather than in her customary ponytail, and she wore a red tee shirt that brought out both the red in her glasses and in her reddish-brown hair. Her eyes looked tired, but I still felt like she was fully focused on me. "What's this all about?"

We were sitting in a corner booth of the Brew House, a local coffee shop that roasted its own beans. Needless to say, it smelled heavenly, but I was too distraught to fully appreciate it.

I took a long sip of my large vanilla latte with an extra espresso shot. All the nights of broken sleep were starting to catch up with me, and the night before was especially bad. I couldn't stop thinking about Chrissy, and the locket, and most of all, how I was going to get it back from her. I wanted to know what it all meant—what all the signs had been telling me.

I didn't have a chance to do anything that morning, as Chrissy had basically stayed in her room. I knew I had to get out. I had to talk to someone. So, I reached out to Daphne.

But, what do I tell Stefan? Surely, he wouldn't begrudge me seeing one of my friends if he truly understood what was going on. But now was not the time for a big explanation. It felt easier for everyone to simply tell him I was going out to follow up on a few job leads. He was so engrossed in his work, he barely acknowledged me.

But as badly as I needed to talk things through with someone, I was still hesitant. Even knowing that Daphne was the ideal person to go to, seeing as how she already believed my house was haunted, I couldn't help but feel scared to admit it all. "You're going to think I'm nuts," I said as I looked up at her.

Daphne half-smiled. "I already know you're nuts. And yet, here I am."

I smiled back. I needed this, no matter what Stefan wanted, I needed time with my friends. I took one last look around—

there were only three customers, busy on their computers and phones—sitting on the opposite side of the coffee house. I took a deep breath.

"So much has happened," I said. "I'm not even sure where to start."

Daphne reached across the table to squeeze my hand. "Start at the beginning."

Where *was* the beginning? It was all so overwhelming. I didn't even know anymore.

I had to start somewhere. I opened my mouth and blurted out, "I found Mad Martha's locket. And her journal."

Daphne's mouth fell open. "What?"

"In the studio," I said. "In the middle of all the junk."

"So, it's real," Daphne said under her breath, almost like she was talking to herself.

"What's real?" I asked.

"The locket. Don't you … oh you probably don't remember."

I clutched my coffee cup with my suddenly cold fingers, feeling the heat without the warmth. "Remember what?"

Daphne sat back and sighed. "According to the story, shortly before, well, *that day,* Martha was going on and on about a locket. First, she said it was missing and blamed Nellie for misplacing it. Then, she said Nellie stole it and wanted her fired. The problem was …" Daphne paused, looked down at her cappuccino before meeting my eyes. "No one could remember her ever owning a locket."

I sat back, stunned. *Where is my locket? You did something with it. I know it.* "What? But, it must be her locket. It was with the journal, and her picture was in it."

Daphne looked surprised. "Her picture? How do you know what she looked like?"

"I, ah … there were photos," I said, barely stopping myself from saying I saw her in my dream.

"Photos, too?" Daphne sounded excited. "Did you bring them? Can I see them?"

I shook my head. "No. I can try and sneak them out to you. I don't want Stefan or Chrissy knowing about any of this."

"Wow. The locket exists," Daphne marveled again, almost like she was talking to herself. "And there's even a journal. Did you read it?"

I nodded. "It seemed Mad Martha really was mad. I think she was suffering from postpartum depression."

Daphne looked pensive, and then slowly nodded. "That makes sense actually. People always said she didn't seem right after her second child was born. Back then, they didn't know about postpartum depression, so it's no wonder she didn't get treated for it."

"But, that's not the worst of it," I said, glancing around the coffee house again. The girl who had served us was wiping down one of the tables near us. Was she listening? I tried to read her face, but she just looked tired and focused on the table, her blonde hair pulled back in a messy ponytail and her green apron stained with coffee. I leaned forward and lowered my voice. "I think there's something … bad, in that locket."

Daphne stared at me, her eyes wide and round behind her red glasses. "What do you mean "bad"?" she asked, dropping her voice.

I glanced around again. The girl had moved a table away. Maybe she wasn't listening. "Bad like evil."

Daphne continued to stare at me. "Maybe you'd better explain."

I sucked in my breath. I knew how crazy it sounded, but I *had* to trust someone. It was all too much to carry on my own. "I think Nellie is possessing Chrissy."

Daphne's mouth fell open. "What?"

"That's the only explanation I can think of."

"But … why do you think that?"

I ran my hand through my hair. "There's so many reasons. To start, when she sleepwalks, she doesn't *sound* like herself."

"Well, yeah. She's not herself. She's sleepwalking. It makes sense that she'd sound different."

"But, that last time she was sleepwalking, she was searching for something—I think it was the locket. And when I talked to her, using her name, she told me she wasn't Chrissy, and I should stop calling her that."

Daphne picked up her cappuccino, wrapping her long, white fingers around the delicate brown mug, but she didn't drink. "Did she tell you her name was Nellie?"

I ran my hand through my hair again. "Well, no. But when I called her Nellie, she didn't correct me."

Daphne studied me, her face impassive. "Okay. But, again, she was sleepwalking."

"That's the point! That's when Nellie *could* possess her."

Daphne opened her mouth and closed it. "Is that the only evidence you have that Nellie is possessing Chrissy?"

"Last night I saw her wearing the locket."

"How did she get it?"

I put my head in my hands and tugged my hair. "I ... I don't know. That's the even crazier part. She says I gave her the locket, but I *know* I didn't. After I found it, I hid it in my room. And I hid it in a place that would have been difficult for her to find ... unless Nellie told her."

Daphne held up a hand. "Wait a second. There are a few things here that don't make sense. Why would she lie about you giving her the locket? I don't understand."

I looked away. That waitress was talking to one of the customers, a studious looking woman with brown glasses, brown hair, and a black laptop. Was it my imagination, or did she look over at me? "She ... she claims I left it on her pillow."

"Could Stefan have left it there?"

I barked out a laugh. "No. He doesn't know anything about this. And he certainly wouldn't be rummaging around in my stuff."

"And *you* definitely didn't leave it on her pillow—you're sure?"

"I ... no."

Daphne looked at me suspiciously. "What does that mean?"

I sighed, looking down. "It means I don't think I did. I certainly don't remember doing that. But I've been losing things," I muttered into my coffee.

"You've been losing things?"

I still couldn't look at her. "Well, misplacing is probably a better word."

"Misplacing? What are you misplacing?"

I slunk lower in the booth. I couldn't tell her about the knife, which I still hadn't found. "My keys. The ibuprofen bottle. Other things."

"And you think you may have 'misplaced' the locket, putting it on her pillow?"

"Well, it's one theory," I said defensively. "But I can't believe I would do that. I mean, I use my keys all the time, so setting them down somewhere strange isn't out of the question. But I *hid* that locket. I wasn't carrying it around with me. So, how could I accidentally leave it somewhere?"

Daphne drummed her long, thin fingers against the table. "And you think the only way she would know where you hid it is if Nellie told her?"

"Well, yeah. I mean, sure, she could search my room, but that would take too long. Stefan's office is right next to our bedroom; he would surely hear or notice if she was digging around in there. And, how would she even know the locket existed to search for it? She doesn't know I found it. So, why would she even be searching my room in the first place? What would she be looking for?"

Daphne frowned. "That does make a certain amount of sense, but why would Nellie be possessing her? That was Mad Martha's locket—wouldn't Mad Martha be the one doing the possessing?"

That stopped me. I hadn't actually considered that. "Maybe the locket makes it easier for you to be possessed," I ventured.

Daphne started shaking her head, a confused look on her face. "But ... wait a second. Didn't you think Chrissy was possessed *before* she had the locket? None of this is making sense.

I don't understand—why are you so convinced Nellie is the one possessing Chrissy?"

Ah, the heart of the matter. Could I actually say it? Could I actually voice the thought that had been swirling around my head all night, not letting me sleep? I couldn't even believe I was really considering it, but the more I thought about the locket around Chrissy's neck, and what it all meant, the more sense it made. I looked around—the waitress was back behind the counter.

Daphne was waiting for me to respond, everything about her radiating calm nonjudgement. I had to take a chance. I had to talk this through.

Could I do it? Actually say, out loud, that I thought Chrissy was trying to seduce Stefan? Not as Chrissy of course, but as Nellie, as she possessed Chrissy's body?

I sucked in a deep breath. "Chrissy has been acting ... seductive."

Daphne raised an eyebrow. "She's sixteen. She's a walking hormonal mess."

I shook my head. "Not like that. She's ... She's ..."

"You guys want anything else?"

I jerked my head up. The waitress was standing there, looking at us. Actually, she was looking at me. How much had she heard? Had she been listening?

"Nothing, we're good," I said quickly.

She nodded and looked at Daphne. "We're good," I said louder.

Daphne glanced at me, and then up at the girl before indicating she could leave.

As soon as the girl was out of earshot, she leaned forward. "Becca, what is with you? Why were you so rude?"

"She was just trying to listen in on our conversation."

Daphne's eyes widened. "Becca, are you listening to yourself? What is going on? You're acting paranoid."

"I'm not paranoid! She was hanging around us on purpose—trying to hear what we were saying."

Daphne was silent for a moment. "Becca, seriously, what is going on with you? You're not acting like yourself. Do you remember the way you were fifteen years ago? About a week before Jessica disappeared? Exactly like this. Paranoid. And losing things. Like you are now."

I froze. My mouth worked, but nothing came out. I was like this before? What did that mean? A cold feeling of terror began to creep up my spine.

Was I being possessed, too?

Daphne reached over to squeeze my hand, which had gone cold. "It's going to be okay. I'm here for you. We'll figure this out."

My lips were numb, as my brain worked feverishly. If I was being possessed, it had to be by Mad Martha. And if I was possessed by Mad Martha and Chrissy was possessed by Nellie ...

That would mean they were trying to relive their dysfunctional relationship.

And that would mean ...

An image flashed in my head—Chrissy standing in her bedroom, bathed in moonlight. *Why did you kill me?*

Oh God. I couldn't even think it. And I definitely couldn't say it. Not to anyone—not even a good friend like Daphne. She would have no choice but to call the cops, as I would be admitting I was a danger ... to myself and to Chrissy.

Daphne was talking, but I had tuned her out. " ... other explanations. Have you seen a doctor? Has Chrissy?"

I slumped in my seat. "Stefan won't take Chrissy to a doctor."

"That doesn't mean you can't go."

I wanted to laugh. How could a doctor help with a possession? What I probably needed was a priest or exorcist.

Or maybe I needed to do that séance, after all.

Daphne squeezed my hand. "Let's take this one step at a time. I think seeing a doctor is the first thing to do."

I nodded, dropping her hand.

I wondered if I should just turn myself in to the cops. Or, maybe a mental hospital. Was that the safest, most prudent course of action? Maybe in the short term, but it wouldn't help Chrissy. Everyone would just think I was crazy. Stefan would *definitely* think I was crazy. And if he decided to stay in that house, then Chrissy wouldn't get the help she needed. She'd have no one. What would happen if the possession continued? Would both Mad Martha and Nellie try to possess her at the same time? Would she end up killing herself, if that happened?

I had to do something.

"Becca, are you okay?" Daphne waved her hand in front of my face. "Are you listening to me?"

I started to gather my things. "I'm sorry. I just remembered something I need to do. I'd better get going."

Daphne opened her mouth like she was going to say something else, and then clearly changed her mind. "Okay. I'll text you some doctor recommendations. And you'll let me know what the doc says, right?"

I nodded, just wanting to get out of there. I needed space to think and figure out what to do.

Daphne slid out the booth and walked with me to my car. She hugged me tight, and I inhaled scents of lemongrass and lavender. Such calm, relaxing scents. I so wished those scents would bring me peace, but I suspected nothing short of a miracle would do that right now. "We'll get through this. Call me."

I closed my eyes and, for a moment, leaned against her and let myself despair. A part of me was feeling guilty for not telling her everything. Maybe turning myself in really was the best move. Maybe that would break whatever spell or curse the house was under. I mean, if I was really possessed, would I be able to stop myself from doing what they wanted?

No. I had to go home and figure it all out. I would be very careful. But I *had* to get to the bottom of what was happening.

"I'll call you," I said as I slid into the car.

I considered my options as I drove. Over and over, my thoughts returned to the locket. That seemed to be the place to start. I couldn't help but feel the locket was accelerating whatever had already been put into motion, and if I could just get it back, maybe then things would calm down enough so I could safely leave the house without feeling like I was leaving Chrissy alone and unprotected.

I decided I'd worry about the rest once I actually found the locket. That was what needed my attention right then—find it, get it out of the house, and away from Chrissy.

I let myself in the front door. The house was quiet—so much so that I wondered if anyone was even home. I checked upstairs. Stefan was in his office, door closed, on a conference call. I peeked in, mouthed "Where's Chrissy?" He responded, "Out. How was the job hunt?"

I blinked. Job hunt?

Oh. My lie. I held my hands up in an "I don't know" gesture and then crossed my fingers.

He smiled, gave me the thumbs up. *Good girl. Glad you're on board. Trust me, this is for the best.*

I backed out of the room and closed the door before he could sense the truth and question me. I didn't have time for more lies. This was my chance.

I quietly opened her bedroom door, revealing an empty room. I had no idea how much time I had—Chrissy could be home any moment, or Stefan could suddenly decide he needed some refreshment, and head down to the kitchen.

I started with the dresser and her jewelry box. Nothing. Not surprising, but a little disappointing. I did a quick search through her closet and chest of drawers, but found nothing but clothes.

The nightstand didn't reveal much, either—a glass filled halfway with water, an earring, and her iPad. An uncomfortable feeling started buzzing around the back of my head. In New York, her room was full of personality—a unique blend of up-scale design elements and her cherished teddy bear collection. This room was bare of anything that said "Chrissy," other than her clothes.

Come to think of it, where *was* her teddy bear collection? Where was her modern asymmetrical black-and-white bedspread trimmed in hot-pink with matching pillows? Where was her massive nail polish collection? I saw only two colors on her dresser next to her jewelry box.

Why hadn't she moved her things in?

I headed over to the bed, which still sported its original homemade quilt. I halfheartedly checked under the pillows. Chrissy had said I left the locket on her pillow after all. Next, I ran my hands under the mattress.

And felt something hard.

My heart started to pound as I pulled it out. Could it be the locket? No, it didn't feel right.

It was the chef's knife.

I stared at it, my hand numb. My mouth dry, I could taste terror in the back of my throat.

Why in God's name was it hidden in Chrissy's room? Under her mattress?

Did she put it there?

Or did I?

Like when I put the locket in her room?

I felt dizzy and nauseous. I had to get out of that room before I fainted, or worse. I turned and lurched toward the door.

My knees buckled as I saw it.

Another message on the mirror—a message that wasn't there before, when I came in.

Different words, but still of smoke and blood.

Beware. It's here.

Chapter 31

When I finally regained my senses, I found myself huddled on the floor of Chrissy's room, still holding the knife. The words in the mirror were gone. The room was empty.

I had no idea what had happened. Did I faint? How long was I out?

From a distance, I could hear Stefan's soft murmurings, presumably because he was still on the phone. I couldn't have been out for that long. And Chrissy apparently wasn't home yet either, so no one was any the wiser about my actions, thank God. The last thing I wanted to do was explain myself.

I stumbled to my feet, my entire body shaking, and staggered out of Chrissy's room. As quietly as I could, I shut her door and made my way down the stairs to the kitchen.

I was shaking so hard, I could barely fill the tea kettle, and I splashed the water all over my shirt. I made a strong pot of tea, loading it up with sugar and cream, and sat at the table to drink it. Normally, I didn't put either of those ingredients in my tea, but I seemed to vaguely recall something about sugar being good for shock.

It took a while, but the shaking finally stopped. Slowly, I got myself back under control.

But, with that control came the realization that I had no idea what to do next.

I knew I still needed to find the locket. But if it wasn't in Chrissy's room, where was it? Did I need to search the entire house? That might take a while.

And if it did, what else might happen while I searched? Would Chrissy get worse? Would there be more sleepwalking incidents? Could those sleepwalking incidents turn violent?

Why did she hide a knife in her room? Was it to defend herself?

Or to attack?

I shivered violently, spilling my tea all over the table, before forcing myself to swallow more. I couldn't go there. Not if I wanted to be of any help to Chrissy.

Instead, I focused on the knife itself. What was I going to do with it? It's not like I could put it back where it belonged in the knife block—I might as well hoist a banner announcing I had been snooping in Chrissy's room. But, where else could I put it? Should I try to hide it somewhere in the kitchen? No, too risky. What if Chrissy found it again? Somewhere else in the house? No, what if Stefan accidentally stumbled upon it? How would I possibly explain that to him?

For lack of a better option, I finally wrapped it in a dish towel and buried it at the bottom of my purse. At least at that moment, it felt like the safest option.

With the knife secured, I turned my thoughts back to my next steps. Acting normal seemed like a good plan. I glanced at the clock. What would I normally be doing at this time? Ah, making dinner. Mechanically, I moved into the kitchen.

I decided I'd keep my eyes and ears open, and search for the locket whenever I could.

And I wouldn't sleep.

Sleeping meant dreaming. Sleeping meant possibly losing control.

Definitely better not to sleep. Besides, as a bonus, that also meant I wouldn't bump into Aunt Charlie and her tea, or Nellie, or Mad Martha.

"What are you doing?"

Stefan's voice jolted me from my thoughts, and I jumped, dropping the potato I was peeling. "God, Stefan, you scared me." I put my hand to my heart—tried to slow down my breathing. I'd had more than enough shocks for the day.

He took a couple of steps into the kitchen. "What are you doing?" he asked again, his voice quieter.

I fished the potato out of the sink to wash it off. "What do you think I'm doing? I'm making dinner."

"We're going out tonight. Don't you remember?"

I looked blankly at Stefan, as my brain slowly registered the fact that he was wearing pressed khaki pants and a crisp, button-down shirt—definitely dressier than what he normally wore, working from home. He had shaved as well, but there was a puffiness around his eyes that made him look tired. He sighed loudly. "The Ellisons'. Remember? To help you find a job."

Oh, God. I felt a sinking pit of dread in my stomach. Now I remembered. We were going to their house for dinner. Chrissy was at a friend's house.

Stefan made a point of looking at the clock. "You don't have a lot of time to get ready."

"Uh … right. I'll go now," I said, my gaze darting between Stefan, the clock, and my half-peeled potato. What do you do with a half-peeled potato? Would it keep in the fridge? Should I just throw it out? Maybe I'll try the fridge first. I opened the door.

Stefan took a step closer, his eyes narrowing. "Did you say you were following up on leads today?"

Did I? I couldn't remember anymore. It felt like a week had gone by since leaving Chrissy's room. I nodded, feeling like that was the safest answer.

He made a point of looking me up and down. "You wore *that* to look for jobs?"

Oh no. I quickly dropped my gaze to see what I was wearing. Green tee shirt. Jean shorts.

I closed my eyes and swallowed. Crap. What was I thinking when I left the house? Why didn't I dress up to see Daphne?

"I wasn't thinking," I said, which was the truth. How did other people keep all their lies straight?

"Rebecca, how do you expect to a get a job when you show up so … unprofessional?" He gestured at me.

I hung my head. "You're right. I should have thought it through."

"I know you don't want to get a job, but I thought you agreed. I thought you were on board with it."

"I was. I am. I'll do better," I said, trying to edge past him. "I'll go change."

He paused and cocked his head, studying me. "Did you actually job hunt today?"

My stomach flipped into a massive knot. I tried to swallow and couldn't. My harmless little lie that seemed like such a good idea earlier was starting to feel not-so-smart now. "Of course," I said, my voice sounding a bit strangled. "What else would I have been doing?"

"I don't know, Rebecca. What else *would* you have been doing?"

"Nothing," I said. "I really should get ready. We don't want to be late."

"You're right," he said. "Go get ready."

I turned to leave the kitchen when he called me back. "You didn't happen to run into anyone while you were out job hunting, did you?"

His eyes bore into mine. I licked my dry lips. "Of course not," I said, trying to interject a tone of lightness in my voice. "Why would you think that?"

He stared at me for another minute longer. "You better hurry," he said.

"Okay," I said and fled the kitchen.

I tore off my shirt and first ran into the bathroom for more deodorant as I was sweating. Why was I feeling so guilty? Just because I met Daphne for a coffee? She was my friend. Yes, I know he didn't want me "wasting my time" with my friends, but it was my time to waste. It wasn't like I was cheating on him.

Although … I pondered Stefan's reaction as I struggled to tame my hair that seemed to have somehow gone even more wild. He was acting a little like a jealous husband.

Was that what this was all about? Did he think I was seeing someone else? Like Daniel?

I thought about the way he was when they met at Aunt May's. He had been acting possessive then, too.

But, why? Did Chrissy say something?

I decided I couldn't figure that out right now. What I needed to do was focus on getting ready.

I threw on a yellow sundress, fixed my make-up and my hair as best I could, and hurried back downstairs.

He was waiting for me, an impatient look on his face, but all of that melted away when he saw me. "Much better." He took my hand and spun me around and gave me a wicked grin. "I can't wait to take it off of you when we get home."

I could feel the heat rising in my cheeks, partly from the picture that just popped up in my head, and partly from relief—it appeared he might be done grilling me about my day. His smile turned wicked and he ushered me out of the house. "We better go before I change my mind."

Dr. Ellison and his wife lived on the outskirts of town in a rustic two-story, four-bedroom house. The yard was exquisitely maintained and included a large bed of roses that framed one side of the house.

Inside, the house was equally impressive. It was decorated in a clean, understated way—dark wood—walnut, I thought, cream leather furniture, with splashes of red and orange pillows and throws. A vase of roses, presumably from the yard, stood on the mantle. It even smelled clean and understated—a combination of lemon furniture polish and cinnamon.

Stefan immediately set to work charming Sue, our hostess, while I wandered through the living room.

The doctor handed me a glass of wine as I admired a delicate crystal butterfly. "Thank you, Dr. Ellison."

"Call me Pete," he said.

Pete was tall and distinguished looking in a quiet way, with short, close-cropped brown hair and glasses. He looked more like a retired general than a doctor.

"You don't remember me, do you?"

I took a quick swallow of wine to hide my discomfort as I frantically racked my brain for something, anything.

He smiled kindly. "It's okay. I actually didn't expect you to."

I smiled back, the tension in my chest easing. "So, how do I know you?"

"I was your doctor during your hospital stay fifteen years ago."

What were the chances?

I glanced over my shoulder to see if Stefan was listening, but he seemed engrossed in his conversation with Sue. "So, I guess I should thank you for saving my life."

He smiled slightly as he shook his head. "No, that wasn't me. I took over once you were stable. Physically, that is." He paused, taking note of my puzzled expression. "I'm a psychiatrist."

Oh *great*. What the hell was I supposed to say to that? Forget talking to him about employment opportunities. How soon could I possibly talk Stefan into leaving? Maybe whisper something in his ear about how hot it was … so hot I thought I might need to start removing my dress.

"I didn't mean to make you feel uncomfortable, or bring up unpleasant memories," Pete said.

I tried to smile. "Yeah, well, I'm not particularly proud of that time of my life."

He shrugged. "You were young. And clearly you survived it."

"Yes, luckily."

He paused, sipping his wine. "So, how has it been being back in that house?"

"Fine." Was he really going to go there? God, what a nightmare. Hopefully, he would take the hint with how short my answers were and change the subject.

He didn't. "Have you seen the ghosts yet?"

I stared at him. He smiled slightly, like he was trying to soften his questions. "It's not like it's a big secret that the house is haunted."

"Yeah, well, there's no such thing as ghosts."

He cocked his head. "Even I've seen things there that have made me wonder."

I found myself intrigued despite myself. "Like what?"

"One day, I was dropping something off and was standing in the living room. Your aunt went in the kitchen to get something, and while I was standing there, I saw movement in the corner of my eye on the second floor. It was like this white … mist, I guess, that floated down the hallway and disappeared." He laughed a bit self-consciously. "When I asked your aunt about it, if there was anyone else in the house, she said it was Mad Martha."

I was surprised at how similar that story was to what Daphne saw in the house. Did Mad Martha make a point of showing herself to visitors throughout the years? "Yeah, I've heard stories like that before."

"How about you? Do you have any stories like that?"

The bit of a white nightgown disappearing into Chrissy's room. My mouth felt suddenly dry. I shook my head. "Not really."

His eyes narrowed from behind his glasses. "Not really?"

I swallowed more wine. This was just getting weirder and weirder. As if the conversation wasn't bad enough, the careful way he was watching me was really starting to get on my nerves. Had I said something to him years ago about seeing ghosts? Or forgetting things? Had I confessed the same things to him that I had to Daphne? "Well, sure. It's an old house and I've seen a few … odd things there. But nothing that can't be explained by a trick of the light or an overactive imagination."

He smiled, a smile that didn't reach the cold, almost predatory expression in his eyes. "Yes, there's no question that house plays tricks on the mind." He took a step closer to me and dropped his voice. "Are you sleeping okay? And how about your headaches? Do you still have them?"

I took a step backwards. This had gone far enough. "Hey, did I miss something?" I tried for a joking tone. "Don't I need an appointment for you to be asking these kinds of questions?"

Finally, he got the hint. He lifted his hands and backed away, a smile on his face that tried for reassuring, but felt patronizing. Christ, did I need to hit him over the head with a hammer? He must be a terrible psychiatrist to not understand body language—no wonder I didn't get any better after talking to him fifteen years ago. "Of course. Sorry, I wasn't trying to make you uncomfortable. Sometimes I get a little too carried away." He lowered his hands. "Would you like to come in and talk? I'm happy to make an appointment if you ever feel like you need to chat with someone."

"Hey, you two, dinner is ready," Sue called out in a cheerful voice. The perfect interruption. I could have kissed her.

I spent the rest of the evening making sure Pete never got another chance to talk to me alone. What in God's name had I said to him all those years ago? Why was he following up now? Had someone said something to him? Maybe Barry's wife, Celia? Or could it have been Daphne?

No, Daphne wouldn't have said anything.

Would she?

Time ticked by agonizingly slowly as we lingered over dinner, dessert, and coffee, before Stefan finally indicated that it was time to leave.

"How did your conversation with Pete go?" Stefan asked, once we were in the car. "Did he have any good leads for you?"

"Fine," I answered shortly. "How did you meet him?"

Stefan glanced at me, but I kept my head straight ahead, watching the taillights of the car in front of us.

"I was talking to one of the local attorneys here, asking him if there were any administrative positions open. He didn't know of any at the moment, but he thought Pete might have some leads for other jobs here in town. I called Pete and he invited us for dinner."

I turned my face away to stare out the side window. How likely was it that the attorney Stefan called just happened to give him the name of the psychiatrist who treated me fifteen years ago? Was this yet another person in Redemption who wished I would leave?

"Who was the attorney?" I asked.

"Does it matter?" Stefan asked. "Do you really think you know him?"

"I might."

Stefan paused. "I take it your conversation with Pete didn't go very well."

It wasn't lost on me that he didn't answer my question. How much should I push? And how much of the truth should I tell him? "It went fine," I said again.

"So, what did he say about employment leads?"

I gritted my teeth. "Nothing. We didn't talk about jobs."

"What? Why not? You know that was the reason we were meeting them tonight. How could you let this opportunity slip through your fingers?"

I sunk down in my seat, feeling like a failure for the second time that day. "It didn't come up," I said.

"Well, you should have brought it up." He sighed loudly. "What a wasted opportunity."

I didn't answer, just kept my eyes trained outside the window.

"Rebecca, do you *want* to find a job?"

I jerked my head in surprise to look at him. His attention was on the road, but he glanced at me with the corner of his eye. "Of course," I said, even though that was a lie. "Why would you think I don't?"

"Because it seems to me you're not taking this job hunt very seriously. Where did you go today?"

"Today? We just went to dinner."

He sighed loudly. "I meant this afternoon. What businesses did you go to? What jobs were you checking on?"

Oh no. "The coffee shop," I said, although the moment it was out of my mouth, I wondered if they were even hiring. "Although I don't think they're hiring right now," I amended, hoping to God I wasn't going to get caught in an even deeper lie. "And I went to a couple of retail stores." I crossed my fingers, praying he wouldn't ask which ones.

He was quiet for a few minutes, watching the cars across from us at a stop sign. "It's only temporary," he said, his voice gentle. "And we really do need the money."

"I know," I said. "I'm trying."

"Try harder." His tone was softer than his words though. I nodded and went back to staring out the window, hating how this simple, little lie kept getting bigger and bigger.

It was like he knew I wasn't telling the truth. And was trying to trip me up.

Why would he do that?

We had almost made it home when it suddenly occurred to me that he had never asked what Pete and I *had* talked about. I wondered why.

Chapter 32

I pulled into the grocery store parking lot, turned the car engine off, and massaged my face with my fingertips.

I was beyond exhausted. I hadn't slept in two days.

Instead, I laid awake both nights, listening to the creaking and groaning of the house and Stefan's deep breathing, while watching the hands slowly tick away on the clock. The first night, around two in the morning when I couldn't stand it any longer, I quietly got up to resume my search for the locket. After an hour of digging around in the family room, I heard footsteps on the stairs. Sure it was Chrissy, I shoved everything back in its place and went to stand near the window. Except it wasn't Chrissy. It was Stefan.

"What are you doing down here?" he asked, rubbing sleep from his face. His eyes were pools of dark shadows.

"I couldn't sleep," I said. "I was just getting some tea."

He looked around. "In the family room?"

"Do you want some?" I asked, making my way to the kitchen. He nodded, and I hurried past him.

After that, I decided it was too risky to search at night.

While I was fairly certain I hadn't sleepwalked, I worried that could change at any time. At least if I was awake, I was most definitely in control. Mad Martha couldn't possess me if I was awake. Right? It *had* to be right, because the alternative was unthinkable. Besides, I'm sure I would know it if I was being possessed during my waking hours.

So, as long as I continued my search for the locket, I wouldn't allow myself to sleep, with the exception of a quick cat nap here and there when I knew Chrissy was either out of the house, or with her father ... when I knew she was safe.

I scrubbed at my face again and reached for my now ever-present cup of coffee, before checking my purse again.

Yes, the knife was still there.

Oddly, it made me feel safer, having it there. I found myself reaching for it constantly throughout the day, almost like I was reassuring myself of its presence. It made no sense logistically, but somehow, it made me feel like I was in charge.

I slid out of the car and headed into the grocery store.

Along with checking (and double-checking) the knife in my purse, I had also become hyper-vigilant about what I ate and drank. I insisted on doing *all* the cooking. If I came downstairs to a pot of coffee, I would dump it out and make it fresh. I started eating only foods that I knew Stefan or Chrissy ate—I refused to touch anything that was typically "mine," especially if it was already open.

Mad Martha's words haunted my thoughts. *I think Nellie is poisoning me.*

In the mostly-empty store, I hunched over my cart, and furtively made my selections. I was glad there were so few people—the last thing I wanted was to run into someone I knew. I found myself peering down every aisle, my eyes quickly darting from side to side, to ensure I saw no one I recognized, or anyone glaring at me, before choosing an aisle.

Part of me wondered if I looked like a crazy person, peering up and down the aisles the way I was. I knew I should probably take a deep breath, and not worry about running into anyone. So, what if I did? So, what if that person was hostile? But the bigger part of me just wanted to get my groceries and go home.

I filled my cart, paid, and headed out of the store.

Becca.

The word was whispered, and I barely heard it over the automatic sliding door. I jerked to a stop, twisting my head to either side, trying to decipher where it had come from and who had spoken it. In front of the store was a display of outdoor furniture, including some clay fire pots and bird baths, but as far as I could see, there was no one there. A handful of cars were in the parking lot, and one lone grocery store employee rounded up carts. His back was to me, his entire focus on trying to jam as many carts as possible into a line in front of him.

I must have imagined it. My nerves were stretched nearly to the breaking point. I was going to have to do something, and soon. I needed sleep. I couldn't keep living this way.

Becca.

I quickly turned again, and saw a pile of rags in the corner that I had assumed was part of the outdoor furniture display slowly knit together to form a figure. The homeless woman.

I stumbled backwards a couple of steps as I tried to talk, but my mouth was dry with fear, and nothing came out.

She grinned at me, revealing a lack of teeth. "Becca," she hissed, creeping forward, her broken smile widening.

"No," I whimpered, backing away as she continued to skulk forward. I could smell the stink on her—something rotting and dead. "Go away."

"Becca. Beware. You're in danger."

Danger? My head snapped forward. Could this woman know something? "Danger? What do you mean?"

The homeless woman paused, looked uncertain, her smile wavering.

I took two steps toward her. "What do you mean I'm in danger?" I said, my voice getting louder. "What do you know? What do you know?"

She began to cower away from me, but I continued my advance on her. This was my chance. Maybe I would finally get some answers. "What do you know?" I said, my voice sounding more like a shriek. "Tell me!"

A hand grabbed my arm from behind. "Becca, what are you doing?"

I spun around, ready to battle. It was Daniel, staring at me, his brow furrowed.

I whirled back around, only to see the homeless woman shuffle back to the corner, back bent, muttering to herself. "I … she …"

Daniel gently started steering me away. "That's just old Maude. She's harmless."

Harmless? She certainly didn't *feel* harmless.

Daniel was looking closely at me. I forced myself to laugh. "I was having trouble understanding what she was saying to me."

"She was probably just asking you for food. Or money."

I ran my hand through my hair. "You're probably right."

Daniel continued to study me, his eyes filled with concern. He was still holding onto my arm, the warmth of his hand practically burning me. "Becca, are you okay?" he asked, his voice low.

Am I okay? I considered the question. I had a knife in my purse. I was afraid my stepdaughter, and maybe myself, were being possessed by ghosts. And I had just been momentarily convinced that a harmless homeless woman would have all the answers.

No, I didn't think I was okay at all.

"I … I haven't been sleeping very well," I finally said. "I guess I'm overtired. Not really thinking straight."

"Are you still having headaches?"

I nodded. The only thing keeping the headaches at bay was how much ibuprofen I was taking—every four hours like clockwork, I would pop a couple of pills.

"Have you seen a doctor?"

I jerked away, causing Daniel to let go of me. Daphne's voice echoed in my head. *Have they been talking?* "No. I'm sure it's nothing," I said. "There's just a lot going on right now. Stefan's here now, which is an adjustment. Chrissy, well, she's sixteen and you know what that's like. I'm looking for a job, and well …" I forced my mouth to close. *Becca, you're babbling*, I said to myself. "It's just a lot," I said again, feeling stupid.

He was watching me closely. "Yeah, I get that. What sort of job are you looking for?"

"Well, the last job I had was at a law office. Not sure I want to get back into it again though." Why did I say that? God, I needed to stop babbling.

"Why not?"

I shrugged. "It's been awhile. Not sure if anyone would be interested in hiring me anyhow."

"Have you talked to Bill?"

"Bill …?"

"Bill Drover."

I shook my head. "No. What does he do?"

There was a pause. I looked up. Daniel was studying me, his face still, an unreadable expression in his eyes. "He's an attorney in Milwaukee," he said neutrally.

Milwaukee? Why would Daniel tell me to go see an attorney in Milwaukee? Did he know something about the attorneys here in Redemption, like the one who had introduced Stefan to Pete? "That's a little further than I want to drive every day. Is he looking for an assistant?"

"Maybe," Daniel said. He looked like he was going to say more, but decided against it. "He's well-connected. He might know someone willing to give you a shot."

I nodded. "Oh. Thanks for the tip. I'll reach out." I tried to smile and feel grateful, but inside I felt sick at the mere thought. I *really* didn't want to work in the legal field again.

"Are the ghosts keeping you up?"

Ghosts? My whole body jerked. Oh God, he was talking to Daphne. "Why would you ask?"

Daniel reached a hand out but didn't touch me. "Relax. I'm joking."

"Oh," I tried to smile again. Of course, he was joking. What normal person *wouldn't* be, when asking about ghosts?

"But, since we're on the subject, have you seen anything … suspicious?'

"Suspicious? What do you mean?"

He gave me a sideways smile. "Well, I know that night at the bar, you were talking about some *ghostly* activities. I was just wondering if you had seen anything else?"

Get ahold of yourself Becca, I scolded myself. *You're jumping at shadows.* "Well, it's an old house," I said carefully.

"Does that mean you have?"

"What are you asking? Are you wanting to come interrogate Mad Martha?"

His smile widened into a grin. "You got me." Even though his mouth was smiling, his eyes were serious. "Think Mad Martha would cooperate?"

"It would certainly make all our lives easier if she did," I said. "Wouldn't it be great to finally get some answers?"

"That's for sure." He paused, studying me. "What would be your first question?"

I laughed. "I have so many questions, I'm not even sure where I'd begin."

"Try. What's just one?"

There was something about the way Daniel was looking at me, along with the barely-concealed eagerness in his voice, that had raised my suspicions. "Are you interrogating me now, Officer?" I asked.

He raised his hands. "Occupational hazard."

I tried to smile. *Jumping at shadows,* I told myself again.

He lowered his hands and stepped closer to me. "All kidding aside. I guess I am a little … concerned about you. Are you sure you're okay?"

The compassion in his voice made my eyes fill with tears, and I quickly turned away so he wouldn't see. Suddenly, I wanted more than anything to tell him everything. Maybe he could help. He knew my aunt, he knew the house, the town. I was so exhausted trying to carry all the burden alone. It would be such a relief to let someone else step in and help.

But then, I thought of Stefan, and how upset he would be with me if he found out. I already felt like I was walking on eggshells with him, trying to keep my lies straight and pretending to be job hunting. And Chrissy. Would she get the help she needed? No. And that meant I needed to do everything alone. I had to figure out a way to get that locket back. Once I did that, then maybe I could think about leaving the house for good.

"I'll be okay," I said.

Daniel took a step closer to me. He lifted his hand and gently pushed a strand of hair away from my face. "I want to help you, but I can't if you won't be honest with me," he said quietly.

My stomach dropped. Was I that easy to read? "What makes you think I'm not being honest?" I asked, trying to brazen it out.

He moved closer, put his mouth near my ear. His breath was warm against my neck. "I … don't trust your husband," he said.

I blinked, pulling back my head to look at him. He didn't trust Stefan? "What do you mean?"

He looked a little embarrassed as he shrugged. "Something doesn't add up with him," he said. "And … well, I also feel like you're holding something back from me. I want to help you, Becca."

I shook my head. There was nothing wrong with my marriage that finding that locket wouldn't fix. Well, finding that locket and a good night's sleep. Then I could stop lying to him and start looking for a job. Then I could get the house fixed up to sell, and all would be well.

"Stefan isn't the problem," I said.

Daniel leaped on it. "Then what is?"

I looked up at him, wishing I could stuff my words back into my mouth. His face was closer than I expected, his dark-blue eyes watching me intently. I could smell him—clean soap mixed with his distinct scent. I thought about telling him that Chrissy might be possessed by Nellie, and, maybe, that I was being possessed by Mad Martha. I could imagine the disbelief clouding his eyes—how he would slowly back away. Maybe he would even decide to take me in for more "questioning."

So much for "helping" me.

Maybe once I had the locket, I would feel differently. Maybe then I could tell him everything. But, for now, I needed to go it alone.

"It's … I'm not feeling well. I haven't been sleeping," I said.

His face fell. He looked so disappointed, I found myself saying in a rush, "Let me get some sleep and feel better. Once I do, we can talk, okay?"

He still looked disappointed. "I'm going to hold you to that, Becca," he said.

I nodded and turned to go—if nothing else, my cart was filled with things that really needed to be in a fridge—but he called me back. He looked pensive. "Just ... be careful, Becca."

Beware. It's here.

I shivered, even though the sun was warm against my shirt. He gave me a meaningful look, as if imploring me to come clean.

I deliberately turned my back to him and headed to my car. I could feel his eyes against me as I walked through the parking lot, but I refused to turn around.

Chapter 33

Stefan and Chrissy were in the kitchen making dinner when I got home.

"Perfect timing," Stefan said, taking the grocery bags from my limp fingers as I stood there in shock. "Relax. We'll take care of everything."

Relax? How could I possibly relax with Chrissy cooking dinner? I looked at the clock. How had it gotten so late?

She was busy chopping tomatoes, her back to me. As I watched, she turned her head and smiled at me—a secret, taunting smile. Her eyes gleamed with triumph.

There was no way I was leaving her alone in the kitchen while she prepared my food.

Stefan shoved a glass of wine into my hand. "Go lay down, Rebecca. Relax. We've got this."

"Actually, I don't mind," I said. "Why don't I finish up? You two have done enough."

"Nonsense," Stefan said. "You've been cooking since I've been here. It's our turn to treat you."

I didn't move. I couldn't tear my eyes from Chrissy chopping the tomatoes. She had painted her fingernails a bright red. The red from the tomatoes dripped down her fingers, soaked the cutting board.

Like blood.

Chrissy saw me watching her and her smile grew even broader. Her lips were red too, more red than normal. Did she have lipstick on? While I watched, her tongue darted out and she licked her lips, like a cat. I could see a hint of sharp, white teeth. She looked at me like a predator eying its prey.

I thought about the knife in my purse. Would I be able to grab it in time?

Stefan nudged me. "Rebecca, go sit down. Drink your wine."

"Stefan, why don't I finish up with Chrissy? I'm sure you have work to do."

Stefan sighed loudly, taking my arm and escorting me into the family room. "Don't be silly. We're good. Drink your wine and relax." He put his hands on my shoulders and not-so-gently pushed me onto the couch. My wine sloshed in my glass. "There. Sit there and enjoy yourself. Dinner will be ready soon." He walked back into the kitchen, humming to himself.

Now what should I do? I got up, feeling too anxious to sit, and started prowling around the family room. I had no intention of eating anything I hadn't made myself, but I didn't know how I would get through dinner. At least I still had my purse with me.

As I passed the window, I saw a movement in the shadows. It was the cat.

It leaped onto one of the garden chairs, and settled itself down in the seat, its green eyes focused directly on me.

Could the cat actually see me? It seemed like it.

Actually, a *lot* seemed different about the cat.

Its eyes narrowed as it stared. I felt like it was trying to send me a message. Like it was trying to warn me. But of what?

Could it sense the ghosts? Did it know the house was haunted?

Did it know something I didn't?

Cats were known to have been companions of witches, even familiars. Was this cat a familiar? Was it more than a cat?

I stared into its green eyes, trying to will it to share its secret knowledge with me.

Stefan called out that dinner was ready. So soon? I looked at the clock. It'd been over thirty minutes since I had gotten home. Again, I wondered where the time had gone.

I looked back outside, but the cat had disappeared.

Stefan poked his head into the family room. "Did you fall asleep? I said dinner was ready." The dark circles under his eyes looked more pronounced than usual—maybe because he hadn't shaved. Under normal circumstances, I would have found that scruffy look sexy, but in that moment, it just made him look exhausted.

"Yeah, I'm coming." I took one last look out the window, but all I saw were the overgrown weeds rustling in the breeze.

"You didn't drink your wine," Stefan said, his tone faintly accusatory, as I sat down at the table.

"I, ah …" How could I tell him I wasn't drinking it because I needed to stay awake? And I needed to stay awake because I didn't want the ghost of Mad Martha to possess me? I picked up my wine and took a small sip. He nodded as he reached for his own glass.

"You haven't been yourself," he remarked, as he and Chrissy helped themselves to beef tacos, chips, beans, and a salad.

"I haven't been feeling well," I said, carefully watching their actions. All the food couldn't be tainted, I reasoned. Maybe I could figure out what was safe and just eat that.

Stefan passed me the tacos. "What's wrong?"

I shrugged. "You know. Headaches. Not sleeping well." I tried to nonchalantly turn the platter, so I could help myself from the same area Stefan had.

"Maybe have more wine," Stefan nodded to my glass. "That might help you relax. Fall asleep tonight."

"Maybe," I agreed, moving my food around on the plate. I wanted to make sure both Chrissy and Stefan took a few bites before I ate anything.

Stefan leaned over and moved my wine glass closer to me. The red liquid gleamed in the light of the setting sun, and I instantly saw the image of Chrissy standing in the kitchen, hands dripping with tomato juice. With blood.

I shook my head to try and clear it, and picked up the glass to drink. A little wine shouldn't hurt. And I could always make a pot of coffee after dinner, which would help combat any sleepiness. Plus, if I didn't drink, Stefan was likely to hound me all night.

"You should eat too," Chrissy said. "I know how much you like tacos." She sat back in her chair, smiling that secret smile, but her eyes were flat, like polished stones. It didn't look like she had touched her food.

I moved the food around my plate. "I'm sure it's really good, but I'm not all that hungry. I had a late lunch."

"At least have a few bites," Chrissy urged. I could see the tips of her sharp white teeth against her bright red lips. I scooped a small bite of beans into my mouth. It would be more difficult to taint the beans, since they were served family style.

Stefan asked me about the job hunt. I did my best to frame my answer to make it sound like I was doing more than I was, while being vague enough to not contradict myself.

I was so tired of the lies.

I could tell he wasn't impressed with my progress, but he didn't say much—just pressed his lips together and started asking Chrissy about her plans that weekend. I took another drink of wine and continued to play with my food.

Something wasn't right. My head was feeling fuzzy. Could it be from the wine? Especially on an empty stomach? Maybe what I needed was a glass of water. I pushed my chair back to stand up, and the next thing I knew, I was on the floor.

"Rebecca," Stefan said, jumping out of his chair to help me. "Are you okay? What happened?"

"I'm dizzy," I said, but my mouth felt like it was full of cotton. Oh God, maybe the beans had been poisoned? Had Stefan eaten any? I couldn't remember. "Something is wrong," I tried to tell Stefan as he helped me up.

"Nothing is wrong, Rebecca, you just need some sleep." He wrapped an arm around my waist and started half-dragging me, half-carrying me out of the kitchen. "Chrissy, can you help?"

Chrissy ran to my other side as I struggled to get free, but my arms and legs weren't working right. "No, Stefan, I need a doctor. I need to go to the hospital," I tried to say. I didn't want Chrissy to touch me, and I tried to twist my body away from her.

"Rebecca, stop fighting," Stefan said firmly. He was dragging me up the staircase. I could see blackness on the edges of my vision. "If you're not careful, you're going to cause all of us to fall down the stairs."

My limbs felt like they were underwater. I was so dizzy. Black lines scribbled themselves across my vision. There was a roaring sound in my ears.

Stefan and Chrissy managed to get me into my room and unceremoniously dumped me on the bed. The room spun around. "Stefan," I begged, trying one last time. "Please call the hospital. There's something wrong with the beans ..."

"There's nothing wrong with the beans," Stefan scoffed. "You need to sleep. I know you haven't been sleeping, so I put something in your wine to help you. Stop fighting it, and just relax."

Stefan did this to me? I opened my mouth to protest, but the darkness swirled over and drowned me. My last thought was that Daniel had been right all along.

Chapter 34

"You're back." Aunt Charlie said as she scurried around the kitchen, presumably making tea. "Thank goodness."

I blinked as I stood at the doorway of the darkened kitchen. I had a strong feeling there was something wrong, that I shouldn't be there, but I couldn't put my finger on exactly what it was.

"Come. Sit. Have some tea. No time to waste."

I shook my head. "No tea." Definitely no tea. I was sure about that.

She paused, dropping her head and sighing. "You always were so stubborn. Well, at least you're honest about it. Not like the other ones."

"What other ones?"

She pursed her lips and flapped her hands, gesturing the non-importance. "It would be better for you if you drank your tea. Especially now."

There was that tickle at the back of my head again. *Something is wrong.*

"Why especially now?"

"Drink the tea. Everything will make more sense if you drink the tea."

I found myself moving to sit at the table despite myself. "Why are you so insistent on me drinking this tea?"

She busied herself with the tea and the cups, not looking at me. "It's difficult to explain."

"Try me."

She paused, clicked her tongue. "It reveals things," she finally said.

"Reveals things? Like what? My memory?"

She carried the mugs to the table, sitting across from me as she pushed my tea to me. It was in the same purple and white mug I had used all day for my coffee.

She picked up her tea. "Maybe. It reveals what it wants to reveal."

"Well, that's nice and vague," I grumbled.

She laughed. "This isn't an exact science, Becca." Then, she leaned forward, getting more serious. A dim light from the window streaked across her face, hollowing out her features and turning her skin a pale grey, making her look like a long-dead corpse. Her eyes glittered at me—black, bottomless pools set deep in the folds and crevices of her face. "Time IS ticking, Becca. Even as we speak, things are shifting, and eventually the decision will be out of your hands."

There it was again. *Something is wrong.* I stared at the dark liquid in the mug, smelling the spicy, sweet scent as it drifted up to me. My mouth watered. I wanted to drink it. I *needed* to drink it.

I looked back up at Aunt Charlie. She held her mug near her mouth, watching me carefully. She had chosen one of the sunflower mugs for herself, and the cheery yellow looked out of place against her grey and washed-out skin. As I watched, her lips parted, revealing a gleam of pointed teeth.

Icy-cold fear shot up my chest, and I backed away from her, the chair clattering to the ground, my feet tangling up in it so that I, too, fell on the floor in a heap.

Aunt Charlie sighed. "Becca, you really aren't making this easy for yourself."

From up above, I heard crashing sounds and a moaning. Aunt Charlie, her face pink and plump, looking more like the Aunt Charlie I had loved as a child, stared at the ceiling. "Mad Martha again. She won't drink her tea, either."

"Is Mad Martha really up there?" I asked, sitting on the floor and staring up at Aunt Charlie. She seemed to loom above me, growing bigger and wider even as I watched.

She sipped her tea. "Of course, dear. After all, we live in a haunted house." She laughed a little tinkle of a laugh.

Mad Martha. Something clicked in my head. I tried to lean forward, but was all tangled up in the chair and couldn't move. "Is Mad Martha haunting us? Is Nellie?" I hissed.

Aunt Charlie looked down at me. She was quite wide now, like a cartoon character who sucks in helium and turns into a giant balloon that floats away. "Of course they are. That's what they do."

That icy-cold fear turned into a pit in my stomach. I couldn't move. I could barely breathe. "Chrissy," I gasped, trying to force the words out. "*Is Nellie haunting Chrissy?*"

Aunt Charlie smiled, her lips blood red. Those bloody lips parted, revealing rows and rows of pointed white teeth. "Of course, dear," she said, a trickle of blood trailing down her chin. "Just like Mad Martha haunted you."

I woke up, a scream caught in my chest, completely tangled up in the sheets and covers. Next to me, Stefan groaned and rolled over on his side in his sleep.

In that moment, everything hit me like a freight train. Stefan drugging me. My dream. Mad Martha haunting me—Aunt Charlie used past tense—could that be why I had lost my memory fifteen years ago? Not because of an overdose, but because Mad Martha had possessed me, way back then? Oh God, oh God. I could feel myself starting to hyperventilate, panic filling my chest like a pack of rats. And what about Nellie haunting Chrissy? I had to go make sure she was okay. She could be sleepwalking right then, like she did after I woke from the other dreams. She could be in danger.

And Stefan. The sheer enormity of what he did to me finally sunk in. He *drugged* me. My own husband *drugged* me. I wanted to hurl myself out of bed and run screaming out into the night, and never come back.

Becca, stop it. I forced myself to quit thrashing around. Not only were the sheets a tangled mess, but I was soaked in sweat, so everything was sticking to me. If I didn't calm down, I was going to wake Stefan, and that was the last thing I wanted.

Instead, I stared at the ceiling and listened to my own harsh breathing and Stefan's snores. I could feel my heart pounding in my chest. Every part of me wanted to hurry, wanted to throw myself off the bed and as far away from Stefan as I could. But I had to be smart.

Finally, I had calmed myself enough to begin unraveling myself from the sheets, all the while wanting nothing more than to pounce on Stefan and scream at him. How could he do this to me? Normal husbands didn't drug their wives, even if they thought their wives really did need sleep. Daniel's voice echoed in my head—*I don't trust him.*

Daniel was clearly on to something.

Finally, I untangled myself and got out of bed. I would deal with Stefan later. I had more pressing issues that needed my attention. I had to go check on Chrissy.

I took a deep breath, straightened my nightshirt, and crept out into the hallway. The house was quiet and still—*too* quiet and still. Like it was waiting. And watching, the way a predator waits and watches, until the perfect time to pounce …

Okay, the whole thing was getting ridiculous—over the top. I had to pull myself together.

The hallway was quite dark. All the doors appeared to be shut, including Chrissy's, which was good. Hopefully, that meant she was fast asleep in her bed.

I crept down the hallway, trying to make as little noise as possible. If Chrissy was asleep, I didn't want to disturb her. I could just poke my head in, make sure she was safe in her bed, and then maybe head down to the kitchen for some coffee to keep me awake while I figured out a plan.

Or … maybe not the kitchen. I didn't think I could face seeing Aunt Charlie, sitting at the table, blood dripping down her chin as she told me to drink my tea.

As I drew closer to Chrissy's room, I saw that the door actually wasn't completely shut. It stood ajar by a few inches.

I stopped and studied the small opening. Did Chrissy ever keep the door open after she turned in for the night? Even if she didn't, it could be innocent—Chrissy could have gotten up in the middle of the night for some water, or to go to the bathroom, and simply forgot to close it all the way.

But, probably not.

I took a few steps forward, put my hand on the door, and gently pushed it open.

The room was empty.

I took a step inside, staring at the bed, willing her to be in there. But no, the covers were thrown back, revealing light-blue sheets and a head-sized indentation in her pillow. I could see a few long black hairs draped across the pillowcase.

It looked like she had been sound asleep and had just … gotten up.

I stepped back into the hall, trying to keep myself calm and my breathing even, and slowly opened the bathroom door. It was empty, too.

Crap. Where was she?

I stood in the hallway, straining to hear something in the silence other than the beating of my heart. Should I check the other rooms up there, before going downstairs? She hadn't gone into any of those rooms before. Or should I check the downstairs first?

It still could all be completely innocent, I told myself. Chrissy couldn't sleep and was sitting downstairs in the dark with a glass of water in front of her. That was why it was so quiet. Or maybe she couldn't sleep, went downstairs, and ended up falling asleep on the couch.

Maybe she wasn't sleepwalking.

But, I didn't believe any of it. I could feel the panic rising up inside me.

Oh God, what if she was waiting down there for me? In the dark? Possessed by Nellie? And as soon as I appeared …

Okay, I really had to pull myself together. Becoming hysterical wasn't going to help anyone, especially Chrissy.

I headed for the stairs, being careful to check behind every corner, every shadow. Maybe I should just turn on the lights? But, what if that startled Chrissy, and she fell, hitting her head …

I crept down the stairs, staying close to the wall, trying to watch everywhere at once.

There was no sign of Chrissy. The house was quiet and still.

I reached the bottom of the staircase and paused. It made sense to make my way into the family room. That was the room where I had found Chrissy both times before. But how would I get there? I really didn't want to walk through the kitchen, but the living room looked even more daunting. I could see dozens of hiding places in the hulking shadows and dark, twisted corners. Forget Chrissy, Mad Martha herself could be lying in wait, holding my knife …

Wait a minute. Where WAS my knife?

I thought back to my room. No, my purse wasn't in there. But, considering recent events and my possible forgetfulness, should I go back up and double-check?

Oh God, just the thought of Chrissy prowling around in the dark with my knife was causing me to hyperventilate. I forced myself to take some deep breaths.

Maybe I'd go through the kitchen and grab another knife. That seemed like the best scenario, but then again, we'd each have a knife, if I did, and would Chrissy, sleepwalking and possessed by Nellie, even respond to me holding a knife? Or would I be better off with my hands free?

Oh God. Okay, I had to make a decision. Otherwise, I would find myself spending the rest of the night at the bottom of the stairs, back pressed against the wall, jumping at every creak and groan.

I began to slowly ease my way through the living room, trying not to trip as I carefully wove my way through the menacing shadows. I felt like I was walking through a minefield that was just waiting to blow up in my face.

I had almost made it through when I banged my shin on the corner of the bookshelf. I nearly screamed as I bit down so hard on my lip, I could taste blood.

Pausing a moment to collect myself, I leaned against the wall and rubbed my shin. The living room was empty, but that observation did nothing to assuage my panic. Rather, I could feel it racing right below the surface of my skin, like thousands of little rat claws grappling to take hold.

I definitely needed to get myself under control.

After taking a few slow, deep breaths, I finally ventured away from the living room and into the family room.

And there was Chrissy.

She was standing completely still in the exact same spot that I found her the first time—right in front of the bookcase. Her long black hair hung like a silky curtain down her back—in the dim light, the blue highlights had disappeared. Her face was very pale, but serene. Her hands dangled loosely at her side, no knife in sight. She looked like a china doll—beautiful, peaceful, fragile, and very breakable.

I stared at her for a few minutes, struggling to get my head around how easy it had been to find her. I should have just walked in there in the first place, instead of getting caught up in all that worry about what she might be doing.

Clearly, finding her had been the easy part. What was I to do next? I stepped hesitantly into the room, and quietly called her name. She didn't move. I took a few more steps toward her. She remained still—so still, I had to look closely to see if she was breathing.

Maybe it would be possible to simply take her by the hand, lead her back to her bedroom, tuck her into bed, and just forget the whole thing. No conversation, no nothing. That would be ideal.

Quietly I drew closer, keeping my movements slow and measured. She stayed still, and I started to think maybe my plan would work out after all.

But then she stirred, ever so slightly. "You have a question for me," she said, her voice flat and emotionless.

I stopped. *Don't answer.* I could feel my entire being screaming at me. *Just take her by the hand and lead her upstairs.* But my mouth opened seemingly on its own accord, and I heard myself say, "I don't know what you're talking about."

Slowly, she turned toward me, her eyes distant and unfocused. "You shouldn't lie to me. I don't like it when people lie to me."

I stared at her, shivers running down my back. Her voice sounded nothing like a teenager—it was far, far older. Ancient sounding.

"Are you Nellie?" I hadn't meant to ask it; it *fell* out of my mouth.

The corners of her lips pulled up in a strange, distorted parody of a smile. "That's the question you're going to ask me? Seriously?"

On one hand, she sounded more like herself, but that somehow made the entire exchange all the creepier. "What should I ask, then?" I questioned, feeling like maybe what really needed questioning was my sanity. *Am I actually arguing with a sleepwalking teenager in the middle of the night?*

She turned her gaze back to the bookcase. "What about— where is the locket? Or ..." she paused, lifting her finger and dragging it across the book titles. "Or what is in that tea?"

I felt myself grow cold. "How do you know about the tea?"

She smiled her strange, secret smile again. "I know lots of things." She continued dragging her finger across the books spines, making a scratchy, ominous noise. "Like I know you're failing right now."

"I'm failing? At what?"

Her fingernail, back and forth, back and forth. "The first of three challenges."

"What on earth are you talking about?"

She finally turned toward me, and I sucked in my breath in horror. Her face was empty—expressionless—but there was something about her eyes, something that glittered behind the surface. Something dark. Something predatory. Something that *felt* like madness.

"Perhaps 'tests' is a better word than 'challenges.' Nonetheless, you are definitely failing." She took a step toward me, her movements jerky, like a puppet on a string, all the while her eyes shining with an unnatural, unholy glee. I found myself rooted to the spot, unable to move, or even breathe, as she continued to lurch toward me. "And, if you *do* fail ..." she said, so close I could smell her breath on my cheek, hot and fetid. She paused, and I watched her tongue flick out of her mouth like a snake about to strike. "If you do fail, you will die."

Suddenly, she gasped, her eyes rolling up in her sockets, her face turning completely white, and collapsed. Moving reflexively, I caught her before she hit the floor, and gently lowered her to the ground. Her eyes fluttered.

"What in God's name are you doing to her?"

I jumped. Stefan stood by the door, an expression of horror on his face.

"Stefan, this is what I was talking about. Chrissy was sleepwalking again."

"Get away from her."

"But, we have to make sure she's okay …"

"Get away from her!"

"But Stefan …'"

"Are you listening? *I said get away from her!*"

What Stefan was demanding finally penetrated through all the layers of fear and concern that overwhelmed me, and I slid backwards a few feet. Chrissy's eyes continued to flutter. "Stefan, this isn't normal. Usually she wakes up by now. We need to call …"

Stefan knelt beside Chrissy, but his eyes continued to bore into me. "What the hell did you do to her?"

I lifted my hands. "I didn't do anything to her. She was sleepwalking …"

"Chrissy doesn't sleepwalk."

"Yes, she does. She was doing it just now!"

Stefan was shaking his head. "You're lying again. All you've been doing is lying. What the hell is going on with you?"

"With me?" I squeaked in indignation. "I'm trying to help her!"

"No, you're not helping anything. You've been acting crazy ever since we moved here."

"What are you talking about? You're the one who drugged me last night."

"Of course I drugged you. I *had* to. I'm exhausted, and I *needed* sleep. I haven't had a decent night's sleep in I don't know how long, because I constantly worry about what you're going to do in the middle of the night."

I stared at him, a sense of horror starting to dawn on me. "What are you talking about?"

In answer, he held out his hand. My purse dangled from his fist. "This. You're carrying a knife in your purse."

My mouth went dry. I tried to lick my lips. Chrissy shifted slowly, and I saw her eyes open. "Chrissy had that knife under her bed. I took it to keep it safe."

He shook my purse at me. "You're trying to tell me you found a knife under Chrissy's bed, and your response was to hide it in your *purse*?"

I had to admit, it sounded ludicrous when he said it like that. "Well, I didn't want to put it back in the kitchen, because then it would have been obvious I had found it in her room."

"Obvious that you found it? Are you listening to yourself? Why *were* you in Chrissy's room, anyway?"

This was getting worse and worse. Chrissy was clearly awake and had pulled herself up to sit with her back against the couch as she watched us argue. "I was looking for that locket."

"Why were you looking for that?"

"I told you, it was Aunt Charlie's, and I wanted it back."

Stefan snorted in disgust. "I don't believe it. What's really the deal with that locket?"

There was no way I was going to choose that moment to explain everything—all about Mad Martha, and Nellie, and Chrissy being possessed. "Why should I tell you?" I yelled. "You drugged me!"

Stefan glared at me. "I put a half of a sleeping tablet in your wine. Not even a full dose. And I admitted it to you. If I really wanted to hurt you, do you think you'd be awake right now? And do you think I would have told you what I'd done?"

My stomach started to sink. That made a certain amount of sense, in a weird way. "Husbands don't drug their wives," I said.

"They do when their wife gives them no other option. You've been carrying a knife around in your purse. You tried to attack Chrissy the other day over that damn locket, and now I find you standing over her in the middle of the night. You're not sleeping. You've been lying to me about job hunting and God knows what else. You're forgetting things. You keep talking about crazy stuff like Chrissy sleepwalking. You're literally acting like a crazy person, Rebecca! I'm at my wits end. I thought if I could get you to sleep, maybe you'd start to see reason again."

"But you drugged me with sleeping pills that weren't even prescribed to me."

"Oh, yes they are."

Shocked, I stared at him. "What are you talking about? I've never had sleeping pills prescribed to me."

"Dr. Ellison prescribed them."

"Dr. Ellison? The guy we had dinner with, because you wanted him to help me find a job?"

Stefan snorted. "Don't tell me you didn't know he was a psychiatrist. That's really why we were there. I thought maybe if you talked to him, he could convince you to make an appointment with him. But that didn't happen, did it?"

My head was spinning. "What? You knew he was a psychiatrist? Why didn't you say something?"

Stefan sat heavily down on the floor. "Because I didn't want you to say 'no'." He paused and took a deep breath. "He's on his way over now."

My entire insides felt like they hit the floor. "Wait. What do you mean?"

Stefan was slowly shaking his head. "I didn't want to do this to you. I really didn't. But you're leaving me no choice. I don't trust you with Chrissy. I'm afraid of what you'll do to her."

Oh, no. I scrambled to my feet, panic fluttering inside me again. "Stefan, you don't understand. I'm trying to help her."

Stefan got up as well, mirroring my movements and keeping himself between Chrissy and me. "Oh, but I *do* understand." Chrissy remained motionless on the floor, her eyes flat and expressionless, as if she were watching a rather boring tennis match.

I was starting to feel desperate. "No, you don't. Chrissy was sleepwalking. Sleepwalking. And when she does, she's ... not herself."

"Again, Chrissy doesn't sleepwalk. And what do you mean, 'she's not herself'?"

"She's ..." I didn't want to say anything else, but I was feeling trapped, and scared. Outside, I could hear the wail of emergency sirens. Were they coming to the house? Were they coming for me? I saw Chrissy's head cock, like she heard them, too. She met my gaze, and smiled at me.

That hollow, creepy smile. My blood ran cold. Even though I knew it was a total long shot, it was better than the alternative—I had to at least try to convince Stefan. I couldn't let Mad Martha win.

"You know this house is haunted, right?" I said, my words tumbling out of me in a rush. The sirens were getting closer. "Aunt Charlie knew it was haunted when she bought it. Mad Martha, she was one of the ghosts, she killed Nellie, her maid, and then she killed herself. And I think when Chrissy sleepwalks, she's possessed by Nellie."

Stefan stared at me, his expression reflecting his utter disbelief. "Rebecca, are you listening to yourself?" Below him, Chrissy's smile grew wider.

"Yes! I know it sounds crazy, but you've got to believe me. Chrissy is in danger. That locket, that locket is Mad Martha's. And Chrissy has it. And the room, Chrissy's bedroom, that's where Mad Martha killed Nellie and herself! And I've seen things in there, back when I was sixteen, Daphne and I had a séance in that room ..." I was babbling. Behind me, the sirens had reached our house. I was out of time.

Stefan looked at me, a mixture of horror and pity on his face. "Rebecca, you need help. It's okay, I'm going to make sure you get it."

I heard pounding on the front door, and Stefan yelled for them to come in. Desperate, I looked down at Chrissy. The light slashed across her face, hollowing out her cheeks, making her look like a grinning skull. She met my eyes, and deep in their depths, I saw a gleam of triumphant madness.

I started to scream as I was tackled from behind.

Chapter 35

"You're awake," Dr. Ellison said, peering at me as he paged through a file. It was definitely "Dr. Ellison" now—no more "Just call me Pete" casualness.

I didn't answer, turning away to stare out the window.

He sighed. "Things would be better for you if you would talk to me."

Really? I thought. Better for me? *Or better for you?*

But I remained silent, staring out the window with a view of the grey sky and the back of the building next door. It was better than staring at the strips of depressing, yellow-flowered wallpaper that bordered the top and middle of the walls. Or the fading yellow curtain that limply hung around the window.

He sighed again, made a few scribbles in his file, and left.

I know he thought I was being stubborn, but in truth, I simply had nothing to say. I had no interest in talking through my thought processes—I could do that myself as I stared out the window, studying the peeling paint on the broken-down building next door. I didn't need to add insult to injury by having Dr. Ellison poking and prodding at me.

Had I imagined everything? Certainly not *everything*—Chrissy had clearly been sleepwalking. Hadn't she? How could I have made that up? Even if I had imagined or misunderstood what she had said, surely, she *was* sleepwalking?

The alternative was much more terrifying: what if it *had* all been me? What if I had been the one who had hidden the knife in Chrissy's room, and given her the locket? What if I had done it *all*?

I honestly didn't even know anymore. Stefan's voice, his expression that night … he truly seemed like a husband who was at the end of his rope trying to figure out what to do with a wife who *was* losing her mind.

And if that's what was happening—if I was losing my mind— would I even know it? Or would I have reacted precisely as I had—in utter confusion, blaming intangible things like ghosts and hauntings?

Was this what had happened to me before, in that same house, fifteen years ago? Was this why I still couldn't remember?

I felt like I was standing at the edge of an abyss. And I was terrified.

Who was it that said if you stare into the abyss, the abyss stares into you? Was it Nietzsche? Was the abyss staring into me right now?

Oh God. What have I done?

A nurse walked in to the room, holding a little tray. "Time for your meds."

When I didn't immediately respond, she thrust the paper container of pills in front of me and rattled them. "I said, time for your meds."

I looked down at the pills, and then up at her. She seemed familiar somehow. Her dyed blonde hair was pulled back in a tight ponytail, and her face was covered with thick foundation, which didn't hide the puffiness and exhaustion. Her eyes narrowed as she rattled the container again. "Such a princess, aren't you? Think you're too good to be here?"

There was something about her eyes—something almost malevolent, lurking behind the smeared eye shadow and clumped mascara. And just like that, it hit me— she was the woman who had yelled at me that night in the bar bathroom.

She smiled then—one of secrets and rage—almost like she realized I had finally recognized her. "I don't have all day. Take your meds."

There was no way I was taking anything from her. I pushed myself back against the bed and shook my head. Her smile widened.

"Are you refusing to take your meds?" There was a syrupy-sweet undertone to her voice, which worried me—she was clearly enjoying my refusal too much.

"I'm not taking anything from you," I said.

She practically grinned at me. "Oh, you will." With that, she turned on her heel and left the room.

I brought my knees up, wrapping my arms tightly around my legs, and began to rock. What was I going to do? I felt completely alone. Abandoned. And hopeless.

The door opened, and the nurse came back in. She smiled at me before triumphantly brandishing a hypodermic needle. Behind her, two unsmiling male orderlies slithered inside.

"We can do this the easy way or the hard way. It's your choice." She moved closer to me, gesturing to the male orderlies.

I drew myself up into a tighter ball. "I want to see Dr. Ellison."

"You can see him tomorrow," she said as she reached over to rub alcohol on my upper arm. I shied away. One of the orderlies grabbed my arm, while the other one held me from the other side as Nurse You're-Too-Good-For-Us jabbed the needle into my arm.

"Maybe tomorrow, you'll take your pills," she smirked, as the blackness washed over me.

***

"You're awake," Daphne said.

I stirred, trying to focus on her. My eyes felt gritty, like they were full of sand. How long had I been asleep? How long had I been in the hospital? What drugs—and how much of them— had they pumped into me?

Daphne looked worried. Her brow furrowed, as she drew her chair closer to me and took my hand. "How are you doing?"

"How long have I been here?" I croaked.

Daphne let go of my hand and went to pour me a glass of water. "Not very long. A day or two."

A day or two. It felt like I had been there forever, locked in a lifeless, grey dream world, while just on the other side of those walls, life carried on, all bright colors, loud noises, and fresh air.

She handed me a glass of water and waited for me to take a drink. The water was warm, but I drank gratefully. I hadn't realized just how dry my throat was.

"What happened?" she finally asked.

I looked away. The late afternoon sunlight slanted in my room, the bars creating shadows on the floor. Again, I studied the side of the tired-looking, red-bricked building I could see from my window.

How could I answer her? If I was being honest, I wasn't even sure myself what had happened. Was Mad Martha and Nellie to blame? Or was I simply losing my mind? And what about Chrissy? Was she okay?

Guilt, shame, and terror roiled around inside me, playing a massive tug of war. Not to mention feeling like a total loser—fifteen years after my last breakdown, I was once again back in the same hospital, presumably because I was having yet another breakdown.

God, I felt like crap.

Daphne hadn't said anything. I glanced at her from the corner of my eye. She waited patiently, still holding my hand, her face calm, but I could see the telltale stress lines around her eyes and mouth.

I took a deep breath. "I don't really know what happened. I thought ... well, it seemed so *clear* that Nellie had possessed Chrissy. But ..."

She gently squeezed my hand. "I thought you were going to call a doctor?"

I shrugged. "I was, but ... I don't know. Everything ended up happening so fast. After Stefan drugged me ..."

Daphne held up her hand. "Wait a second. Stefan drugged you?"

I nodded. "I wasn't sleeping. I *couldn't* sleep. I was so worried about ... well, the ghosts. I had to keep an eye on Chrissy. No one would believe me, and I know she's in trouble. I *know* it, Daphne. I can't even imagine what's happening to her now that I'm here, and she's alone in that house ..."

Daphne squeezed my hand. "Hey, hey. Breathe. You're getting yourself worked up again."

In my agitation, I had started to sit up in bed, but I collapsed back into the pillows. "You don't believe me. No one believes me. I don't know if I believe me."

"First thing's first: I think Chrissy is okay. I stopped by the house. Stefan answered the door and I talked to him briefly."

I turned my head to look at her. "Did you see Chrissy?"

She paused. "He said Chrissy was fine."

I leaned forward urgently. "But did you *see* her?"

She hesitated again. "Not really. A glance. But that doesn't mean anything."

I shook my head and looked back out the window. "You don't know."

"Look, I can try and see her if it's important to you. But, I'm sure she's fine. He is her father, after all."

Yeah, but Nellie thinks he's Edward. And where the hell is Mad Martha? I shook my head to clear my thoughts. Did I honestly still believe all of that was happening, even now, sitting in the hospital? I really didn't believe in ghosts, did I?

I didn't know *what* I believed. All I knew was that I still had this gnawing sensation inside of me that kept telling me Chrissy was in danger.

Daphne squeezed my hand again. "Tell me about Stefan drugging you."

I pressed my eyes shut. "He crushed sleeping pills in my wine that night. Or maybe it was just one sleeping pill. Well, it doesn't matter. When I woke up, Chrissy was sleepwalking again. Stefan found us downstairs, and, well …"

"He said you had a knife."

My eyes flew open. "Well yes, that was the chef's knife I couldn't find, but it's not like I was holding it! I found it in Chrissy's bedroom, under her mattress. Why did she have a knife in her room, Daphne? I put it in my purse, so nothing would happen."

Daphne didn't say anything for a moment. "I wish you had called me."

I slumped even further into my pillows, despair cascading over me. I felt completely and utterly alone. No one was going to save Chrissy. And it was all my fault. "Why? You don't believe me. Maybe I am crazy."

"You're not crazy."

I gave a short bark of laughter. "Certainly sounds like I am, even to me."

Daphne shook her head furiously. "No, I'm certain there's something else going on. That's why it's good you're here. You needed to get out of there. Get some objectivity, so we can figure out what's really happening. Not to mention, you need to see a doctor."

"Yeah, but I don't know if I trust him," I said morosely. "Stefan found him for me. But, it was all so weird ..." my voice trailed off as Daniel's words echoed in my head. *I don't trust your husband.*

Daphne squeezed my hand. "I don't trust anything happening here," she said softly.

"Could ... could Stefan be behind this?" I asked. "He did drug me that night, although it seems like he had a good reason. He thought I was crazy. And, in his defense, I kind of was acting crazy."

Daphne's eyes widened. "Are you defending him? For drugging you?"

I squirmed. "No. Yes. I don't know. I don't know anything anymore. When he explained it, he made so much sense."

Daphne was shaking her head. "No. You're not crazy."

"But, what alternative is there?" The words were barely out of my mouth when another thought struck me. "Wait a minute. Is it possible I've been drugged *the entire time?*"

"Who would have been drugging you?"

"I don't know, but is it possible?" I sat up, feeling the first surge of hope and excitement that I had felt in weeks. "Maybe it was someone who didn't want me here." I thought about that footprint outside. Maybe I *had* been stalked after all. I hadn't been imagining things. I wasn't crazy.

Daphne, however, didn't look convinced. "You think someone snuck into your house to drug your food?"

"Well, it makes the most sense. I mean, who else could it have been? Stefan? He wouldn't have done it. He's my husband."

"Who drugged your wine."

"Well, yes. That's true. But, how could he have done it? He was mostly in New York. Unless he only drugged food and drinks he knew only I would touch ... or told Chrissy to leave certain foods alone." I frowned. "No, that seems too complicated. But wait! Chrissy! Maybe it was Chrissy, when she was possessed by Nellie."

I grasped Daphne, nearly shaking her in my enthusiasm. "Don't you see? It makes total sense." All the strange and mismatched pieces of my time in Aunt Charlie's house clicked together. All those instincts I had about NOT eating food prepared by Chrissy ... it all fell into place.

Daphne sighed. "There were no drugs in your system."

"How do you know?"

"Because you were tested when you were first admitted, and it came back negative."

It felt like the air had been sucked right out of my lungs. No drugs in my system. Everything inside me deflated again.

I must be crazy. That was the only explanation.

Daphne looked like she was about to say something when the door opened, and Nurse Nasty walked in. I slunk down further in the bed, contemplating the fact that maybe Nurse Nasty was exactly who I deserved.

She saw Daphne sitting next to me and did a double-take. "What are ... oh of course you'd be here."

"Hello, Ellen," Daphne said stiffly. "Nice to see you, too."

Ellen? I perked my head up, looking between Daphne and the nurse. Nurse Ellen looked distinctly uncomfortable, and Daphne, I realized, looked sad.

"You two know each other?" I asked.

"Everyone knows everyone in Redemption," Nurse Ellen snapped. She glared at Daphne. "You have five more minutes before it's pill time." Whirling on her heel, she stalked out of the room.

I blinked. Daphne sighed.

"What's that all about?"

Daphne shook her head. "It's complicated. And it happened a long time ago."

"What happened a long time ago?"

Daphne sighed. "We were … involved."

I blinked. "Involved? But …" A number of thoughts collided in my head and I wasn't sure where to even start. Daphne took one look at my face and burst out laughing. "Yes, I'm gay."

"I … well, okay then," I said. "But, I actually saw her—Ellen—that night we were at the bar, and … she just went off on me. Started yelling that no one wanted me here and I should go back to New York."

Daphne looked even sadder, although a moment before, I didn't think that was possible. "Ellen is … confused," she said. "That's part of what happened years ago. But, I better go. I can tell you the story when you're out of here." She leaned over to give me a hug. "Don't listen to her—a lot of people in this town are happy you're here."

I tried to hug her back, but something didn't feel right. Here I was spilling my heart out to Daphne, but Daphne clearly had secrets of her own that I knew nothing about. Even back when we were teenagers, she could be so secretive. Could I trust her?

I quickly shoved those thoughts away. What on earth was wrong with me? Daphne was with me, right by my side, right then. She had never been anything but supportive of me. Why should I question her?

It was probably the drugs in my system making me paranoid. And the despair of being trapped in this awful hospital. Despite Daphne's optimistic words, I really didn't feel like I would ever get out.

Daphne straightened up to leave, but I reached out to grab her hand. "You will check on Chrissy, right? You don't mind?"

"I don't mind, if that will make you feel better."

I nodded. "Yes, thank you."

The door opened, and Nurse Ellen strode in, glaring at Daphne. "Time's up."

Daphne nodded, giving me one last wave as she backed out of the room.

Nurse Ellen didn't look at me as she flung the pill cup in front of me. I meekly took it, along with the water she offered me. She barely glanced at me before striding out of the room, her shoes making faint squeaks on the linoleum floor.

I gazed at the ceiling, trying not to let utter despair engulf me, before the pills did their work.

Chapter 36

"Someone's here to see you," the nurse said. I hadn't seen her before. She was a plump older woman, her brown hair streaked with grey, and pulled back in a tight bun. Thank goodness it wasn't Nurse Ellen.

"I don't want to see anyone," I muttered. Since Daphne's visit, I had fallen into something of a depression. Clearly, I couldn't trust my own mind, so what *could* I trust? Doctor "Call-me-Pete?" Nurse Ellen? Hardly. Even my very surroundings were called into question: if I couldn't trust my mind, could I trust that I actually *was* in a hospital? Or was I still back in Aunt Charlie's house, wandering the halls and mumbling to myself? Needless to say, I hadn't bathed, brushed my teeth, or combed my hair in days. I probably stank to high heaven. I had barely eaten. In my current condition, I wasn't fit to see anyone.

"I think you want to see this person," The nurse said, smoothing the wrinkles on the cover of my bed. She seemed like she would be better suited baking cookies for hordes of grandchildren than working in the psychiatric wing of a hospital. She smiled at me, a kind smile, before leaving the room.

I went back to staring out the window.

"Hi Becca," a deep, male voice said. I turned, but I instantly knew it was Daniel, before I even saw him. He pulled up a chair to my bed and sat down. "How are you feeling?"

"How do you think?" I asked tonelessly. I noticed Daniel was out of uniform, wearing jeans and a white Bud Light tee shirt. Did that make this a social call? I was too depressed and discouraged to care.

He paused. "Yeah, that was probably a dumb question. Are you feeling up to answering some questions?"

I sighed. "I don't have many answers."

"I actually think you might." He pulled his chair closer to me and showed me his phone. A part of me wanted to sidle away. I felt so disgusting, I didn't want Daniel anywhere near me, but

I told myself it didn't matter and stayed put. "Do you know this man?" he asked.

I glanced down at a picture of an older man wearing a dark suit, his thin, graying hair combed over a prominent bald spot. "Should I?"

"Just … do you know him?" Daniel asked gently.

I shook my head. "Who is he?"

Daniel paused. For a moment, I didn't think he was going to answer me, but then he did. "He's Charlie's lawyer."

Aunt Charlie's lawyer? I took a second look at the phone. "That doesn't look like the man who came to see me in New York," I said. "Does he have a partner? An associate?"

Daniel stuffed the phone back in his pocket. "He's one of a few lawyers in that firm."

"Oh, well that makes sense," I said, feeling oddly relieved, even though I wasn't sure why. Something had begun to tickle the back of my head, like a bad smell that you couldn't figure out the source. "I must have seen one of the other attorneys," I said.

"Undoubtedly," Daniel agreed. "Has anyone else come to see you?"

"Daphne."

"No one else?"

I glanced sideways at him. "Should someone else have come to see me?"

He put the phone away. "There's a lot of people pulling for you," he said.

I laughed, but there was no humor behind it. "I don't know how that's possible. I'm batshit crazy, apparently."

He opened his mouth, and closed it again, before finally saying. "I don't think you're crazy."

"You're definitely in the minority."

"You'd be surprised how many people don't think you're crazy."

I turned to look at him. "Are you seriously telling me people are more willing to believe that Aunt Charlie's house is haunted than that I've lost my mind? Since when do you believe in ghosts?"

He leaned forward. "Those aren't the only two possible explanations, Becca."

"I guess you didn't hear. My drug test came back negative." I went back to looking out the window. God, I felt gross. How could he stand to be in the same room with me, let alone sit right next to me?

"There may be something else going on entirely …"

"I can't remember the night Jessica disappeared," I said, my tone flat. A robin had alighted on the building next door. I focused all of my attention on the bird as it hopped around, so I didn't have to look at Daniel. I couldn't bear to see the disappointment I was sure would be all over his face. But, he deserved the truth. He was a good guy. I should have come clean the first time he came to the house.

All the lies I had told. I had practically choked on them. No more.

"I didn't want to tell you. I thought … well, I guess I thought it made me look guilty. Or something. But maybe I am guilty. Maybe I am crazy. Something certainly seems to be … unglued, in my brain." I sighed deeply, painfully. I didn't think I had ever felt as defeated in my life as I did in this moment. "I'm sorry."

"What are you sorry for?"

He sounded surprised, but I still couldn't bear to look at him. "I should have told you. I've let you down."

"Hey. Look at me." I glanced sideways at him, seeing him shift in his chair, leaning closer to me. "You didn't let me down. I had a feeling … well, I'm not completely surprised that you don't remember. But, there's more to the story here than even you know."

Despite myself, a tiny glimmer of hope lit up inside me. "What? What else could possibly be going on?"

He glanced around the hospital room, even though we were the only ones in there. "Look," he said quietly. "This isn't the time or place to get into everything, but things are not as they seem. Daphne came to see me …"

At that, I jerked my head up. "Daphne? Did she see Chrissy? Is Chrissy okay?"

Daniel picked up his hand as if to touch me, then dropped it back on the bed. "Chrissy is fine. For now. Look, you need to know that you have friends. People who believe in you, and who are digging into *all* of this, on your behalf."

He picked up his hand again, lifting it to my cheek, as if to caress my face, but again he paused, just inches from touching me. I could feel the heat from his fingers radiate onto my skin. A part of me longed to close my eyes and press my face against his hand, but I restrained myself. *He's engaged,* I reminded myself. Plus, technically I was still married, even if my husband had stuck me in the mental ward of a hospital and hadn't even been to see me. Not that I completely blamed Stefan.

"I have something for you," Daniel said, breaking the spell and dropping his hand. I could almost feel the cold rush in, where his hand had just lingered, and I closed my eyes briefly against the disappointment.

He reached into his pocket and pulled out a cell phone.

I stared at it, uncomprehending. "You're giving me a phone?"

He pressed it into my hand. "It's a burner. You know, one of those you pay cash for, and that doesn't have a contract? You're not supposed to have phones in here, so keep it hidden." He smiled, a little self-consciously. "Daphne's, Mia's, and my number are all on there, so don't get caught. I'd have some explaining to do."

I looked down at the phone. "I still don't understand. Why are you giving this to me?"

He leaned closer, nearly whispering in my ear. "Do you know what's happening here?"

I must have looked as confused as I felt, because he continued without waiting for me to answer. "You won't be staying here very long. And, since your calls are monitored and you can't have a cell, you have no way of letting us know if you're being transferred."

I blinked at him, feeling really stupid ... like I was missing something big. "Transferred? To where?"

"To an actual mental institute or clinic. Probably in the Milwaukee area, but who knows? This place is for temporary placement. It's not designed to be permanent."

"Wait ... what are you talking about? Temporary placement? Permanent? They can't just *move* me somewhere."

Daniel's face didn't change expression.

"Wait. *Can they?* How, Daniel? How is that legal?"

"Well, it's not. Not yet, anyway. They have to go to court to do it."

My head was spinning. "On what grounds? How can they just take me to court without my knowledge?" I started to pull the covers off. "I have to go. Where's Stefan? I need to talk to him."

Daniel placed his hand on my shoulder and gently pressed me back onto the bed. "You're not going anywhere."

"What do you mean I'm not going anywhere? I have to get myself discharged."

Daniel shook his head. "You can't. At least not right now. You've been involuntarily committed."

"*What?*"

He brushed his fingers against my lips. "Hush. Keep your voice down."

"But ... what is happening? I don't understand. How can they do that?"

"It's only temporary. That's why they need to go to court, if they want to make it permanent."

My breathing was loud in my ears. Blackness swarmed at the edges of my vision. The phrase "involuntarily committed" kept repeating itself over and over in my mind.

Had I really lost it?

From far away, a voice that didn't sound like me faintly asked, "On what grounds have I been committed?"

Daniel watched me carefully. "That you're a danger to yourself and others."

"I'm a danger ..." I couldn't even finish the thought. I wasn't a danger. I couldn't be a danger. I was trying to help Chrissy. Wasn't I?

"If you've tried … if you've tried to take your own life, you're automatically committed in order to be watched."

"Take my own life? I never tried anything of the sort!"

Had I? I thought back to that night. Chrissy sleepwalking, Stefan yelling at me about the knife in my purse. No, I did NOT try to commit suicide. That was the furthest thought from my mind.

Or, an ugly little voice whispered, *are you just not remembering?*

I shivered.

Daniel was talking, but I had missed what he said. I asked him to repeat it. "You didn't try and kill yourself? Or kill Chrissy?"

I pressed my fingers against my eyelids. "I … I don't think so. I don't remember that at all. Chrissy was sleepwalking again, and I was trying to help her. Stefan was the one who came in with the knife. I didn't have the knife, I didn't have anything. But what does Stefan say?"

Daniel was silent for a moment. "Becca, he's already filed papers. He's trying to have you committed. Permanently."

I felt like I had been slapped. "There must be some mistake," I said, my voice sounding far away again.

"There's no mistake."

"But … Oh God." I felt like my reality was cracking around me. "How could he do this? He hasn't spoken to me or visited me or anything." I slumped over, all the strength leaving me. "Could he be right? Maybe I did try something, and I just don't remember?"

"Becca, look at me."

I didn't want to, but something in his voice compelled me to raise my head slightly. He was staring intently at me. "I don't believe that, and neither should you."

"How can you not? It's not like this would be the first time I've lost my memory," I said bitterly.

He leaned forward, his voice urgent. "Have you been having blackouts? You said you don't remember an entire day. Is that what has been happening? Are you missing big chunks of time?"

I closed my eyes. "No. Nothing like what happened to me fifteen years ago. But, wait, would I remember missing big chunks of time? I don't know. I'm so confused." I rubbed my eyes again before opening them. "But, if it's not true, why would Stefan say that's what happened?"

Daniel's face got very still. "That's precisely the question I'd like to get the answer to."

Chapter 37

After Daniel left, I laid in bed, feeling the sharp edges of the cell phone through the thin pillow, and stared at the ceiling. Unsure where to hide it, I had shoved it under my pillow, although that was probably the worst place to put it. Thoughts of cell phone wave-induced brain cancer danced in my head, but I shoved them away. What did it even matter if I got brain cancer? I was most likely crazy, and my husband was actively working to keep me locked away in a mental institute for the rest of my life. A possible brain tumor seemed like the least of my worries.

Before he left, Daniel had asked me more questions. General questions about my marriage.

Was Stefan having an affair? Probably not, but who knows? Brittle, blonde Sabrina definitely wouldn't be kicking him out of her bed.

Was there money? I laughed. Hardly. We were broke, so there was no reason he couldn't simply divorce me. Half of nothing was still nothing. Yes, I did have a trust fund my grandparents had set up for all the grandchildren, but I couldn't access it until I was fifty-five.

Was I having an affair? Daniel didn't meet my eyes when he asked. My answer was flat. No.

Did Stefan have enemies? Did I? Not that I knew of.

Could I think of anything, anything at all, that might help? Not a thing.

Daniel frowned and glanced at his phone, telling me it was later than he thought, and he had to go. He was just about to step out when I found myself calling after him. "Why are you being so nice to me?"

That stopped him. He stepped back into the room and closed the door behind him, a puzzled expression on his face. "Why would you ask such a question?"

I paused. Did I really want to get into what happened fifteen years ago? How he had stood me up? Could I trust him? I felt like I could, but having married two men who had betrayed me, it was becoming clear to me that I wasn't the best judge of character. "I guess … well, you know, with what happened that summer …"

"Oh." The confusion cleared, but it was replaced by his professional "mask." "We were kids," he said briskly. "And it was a long time ago. It doesn't have any bearing on what's going on now."

I blinked at him. That seemed like an odd answer. I wondered if we had had a conversation about it that I just didn't remember yet. I wondered if I had been a bitch about it.

He glanced at his phone. "I've got to go, but I'll be in touch."

I nodded as the door gently closed behind him.

Pieces of the conversation danced through my head as I stared at the ceiling. I still didn't know if I could trust Daniel or not, but his questions did clarify one thing for me.

No, there was absolutely nothing I could think of, no reason why my husband would want to permanently commit me to a mental institute.

Unless he really did believe I was a danger to myself and others.

Despair settled around me like a thick cloak. How on earth was I going to live the rest of my life unable to trust my own thoughts? Unable to believe if what I was seeing or experiencing was real or not? What was I going to do? My husband had definitely abandoned me. The rest of my family wouldn't want anything to do with me either—the stigma of having a crazy daughter? I was already such a disappointment to my mother. I couldn't even imagine how she would react when she heard the news.

My life rolled out in front of me: a series of quiet, uneventful days filled with doctor visits and drugs. Lots and lots of drugs.

No meaning. No friends. No family. No connections. No purpose. No fun.

No life.

I would simply be lost, locked away in my own private hell. Maybe CB would visit, if he'd remember.

I couldn't even cry. I felt too empty even for that.

Did Redemption hate me so much that it had to make me go crazy, to drive me away? The words stung. God, I hated my life.

The only small comfort I could find was in the fact that, if I *was* a danger, I was actually in the safest place I could be. I certainly didn't want to be responsible for hurting anyone, especially Chrissy. Despite our rocky relationship, I truly wanted to protect her.

Maybe, with me in the hospital, whatever weird spell that was in the house would finally be broken.

Daniel's voice floated through my brain. *Chrissy is fine. For now.* What did he mean by that? Was Chrissy not actually fine, and he didn't want to tell me? I felt the stirring of some ominous dread penetrate the fog of my depression. If there was something wrong with Chrissy, what could I possibly do about it? Who would even believe me, if I tried to get her help?

The grandmotherly nurse walked in with the pill tray. "Ready for your meds?" she asked.

I nodded listlessly. She pressed the button on the frame to slowly raise the bed. I thought about the cell phone under the pillow, and pressed myself back to keep it from sliding out. Just because there was no hope for me didn't mean I had to throw my friends under the bus.

She handed me my meds and a cup of water. I swallowed them, moving stiffly and automatically, almost like a mannequin.

"Think you can eat a little dinner tonight?" She asked, peering over her dark-framed glasses to study me.

I tried to smile. "I'll do what I can." Although I already knew I wouldn't be able to swallow a bite.

As soon as she left, I lowered the bed to its flat position and continued staring at the ceiling, lost in my dark thoughts.

"About time you got here."

I blinked. I was back in Aunt Charlie's kitchen. Aunt Charlie stood behind the stove, clattering pots and pans, making a racket.

"How did I get here?"

Aunt Charlie snorted. "You don't want to know. You have no idea what I had to do to get you here."

The kitchen was dark except for a faint light that outlined Aunt Charlie as she bustled about. The appliances looked like hunched shadows, ready to pounce the moment I turned my back. I licked my lips. My mouth was so dry, it felt like my tongue was cracking. I could feel the fear start to curl up in my stomach.

"I don't want tea," I said.

"You don't know what you want," she said, bringing the mugs over to the table. Even though I hadn't been aware of moving, I found myself sitting in my usual chair across from my aunt.

She slid the mug over to me. "Drink," she said.

I looked at the tea, but didn't touch it. "Aren't I still in the hospital?"

She picked up her mug and blew on it. "Where else do you think you'd be?"

"Then how did I get here? Did something happen with Chrissy? Is she sleepwalking?" I gripped the side of the table. Oh God, this would all be for nothing if everything I believed about Mad Martha and Nellie were true.

"Chrissy is fine. For now."

I sucked in my breath. "That's what Daniel said. What does that mean? For now?"

She gestured toward the tea. "If you want to know, you have to drink."

I stared at the tea. It looked as black as ink. I looked back at Aunt Charlie. She was watching me, her eyes as black as the tea.

"Are you trying to poison me?"

"I'm trying to help you," she said. Her lips parted, showing a mouth full of white, pointed teeth—so white, especially in contrast to her red mouth.

"I … I don't trust you. You can't be my Aunt Charlie."

"You have to trust someone, Becca." She took a sip of tea and it started to dribble down her chin. Why did it suddenly look like blood in the dim light?

"You're a monster," I said.

Yes, it *was* blood running down her chin again, and dribbling onto the table. She smiled widely, showing rows and rows of sharp teeth, now stained red. "How can you be sure?"

I tried to back away from the table, but found I couldn't move. "I ... just ..." How on earth could I answer that? Because you look like a monster? All teeth and blood?

She banged her mug on the table and leaned forward. "Who told you I was a monster? My sister? Your mother? And why did you believe it, all of these years?"

"I ... uh ..."

"Do you really remember me as a monster?" She banged her hand on the table, rattling the mugs. "Do you?"

I tore my gaze away to stare at the table. "No," I said, my voice small.

She leaned back in her chair. "You know what I think? I think you don't have the slightest idea who the real monsters even are in your life. If you truly, truly believe that I'm a monster, then don't drink the tea, and spend the rest of your life locked in a mental ward. But, if you believe I'm not ..." she paused and nodded at the mug.

I peered into the mug. The tea was so black, almost sludge-like. How could something that looked like tar possibly be good for me? But, then I caught a whiff—it smelled like honey and cinnamon and apples.

My mouth watered. I wanted that tea.

I glanced back up at Aunt Charlie. Her eyes were pools of black, her lips bright red. Blood stained her chin.

There was no way I was going to drink that tea.

She must have seen it in my face, because she sighed deeply. "It's your choice, Becca. If you want to spend the rest of your life in a mental institution, that's your choice. But ..." she held up a finger that sported a very long, curved, and pointy fingernail. It almost looked like a claw. I found myself wondering how she was even able to make tea with that fingernail. "But, there's one thing you should know. I can't come back. This will be the last time you ever see me ... *if* you don't drink the tea."

"What do you mean you can't come back?"

She shrugged. "This is it. Your last chance. Things have moved even faster than I had anticipated, and I've run out of time. You have one more chance to drink the tea. One more chance to stop the madness you're living in. One more chance to stop the *real* monsters from ruining your life. And, if you still refuse ..." she let her voice trail off ominously.

I tried to swallow, but my mouth was too dry. I could taste the fear in the back of my throat. "Then what?"

She leaned forward and leveled those coal-black eyes on me. "You're trapped in an institution. Until the day you die."

I wanted to back away, but again, I couldn't move. I felt like a rabbit hypnotized by a snake about to strike. Actually, her eyes did look like snake eyes. Her tongue even darted out, a forked tongue, and licked the blood from her lips.

I tore my eyes away and forced myself to look at that tea. Could I really drink it? Tea from a monster?

I thought about how safe and loved I had always felt in her house. Was she really a monster? Or was she right—that I didn't know who to trust? After all, my first husband cheated on me, and my second husband was trying to get me committed. Clearly, I wasn't such a great judge of character.

And, really, what did I have to lose? I was set to spend the rest of my life in a mental institute, as it was. Did it really matter one way or another?

And, what if Aunt Charlie was right?

I hadn't drunk the tea and look where I ended up. How much worse could it get if I actually *did* drink it?

Quickly, before I could change my mind, I lunged forward and grabbed the mug. It was heavier than I expected, and I spilled half of it as I brought it to my lips and drank deeply.

It tasted as sweet as it smelled. Honey and clover and cinnamon. Of being sixteen again and having your life stretched out ahead of you, full of excitement and possibility.

It tasted of hope.

From the corner of my eye, I could see Aunt Charlie nodding. "I knew you'd come through." She looked like Aunt Charlie again—no more blood or teeth or black eyes.

I dropped the mug on the table, wiped my mouth, and started to scream. Fire burned inside me, starting in my stomach and shooting out through my throat. The pain was intense. I fell, writhing, to the ground.

"You lied to me," I gasped. From a great height, I could see Aunt Charlie peer down at me, her face a little sad.

"Truth has a price," she said quietly. "I wish you didn't have to pay it."

I could feel the fire raging out of control inside me. I opened my mouth, expecting flames and smoke to come pouring out … and woke up gasping in the hospital bed.

I sat up, blinking in the dim light, trying to get my bearings. What just happened? Why did I drink that tea? Was Chrissy safe?

I rubbed my chest. I could still feel the burning, but it was slowly dying down. My hands shaking, I reached over to find the water pitcher, almost knocking it and the glass to the ground in my haste.

My hands trembled so much, the water sloshed as I poured a glass and brought it to my lips to drink. It was so cool … so good. I drank it greedily, and it spilled down my chin. It reminded me of the blood on Aunt Charlie's chin and I shivered, but I didn't stop drinking.

I poured myself a second glass and drank that too. And then I realized I was absolutely starving. I couldn't remember the last time I had felt hunger. Or, for that matter, the last time I ate more than a few bites to satisfy the nurses. Would I even make it to breakfast? Could I call down to the kitchen and get something sent up right then?

My eyes finally adjusted to the dim light, and I realized there was still a covered dinner tray in my room. Why was it still there? They always collected the trays after meal time. Nevertheless, I swung my legs out of bed and pulled it toward me. Spaghetti and meatballs. Garlic bread. Salad. Broccoli. Brownie.

Surprisingly, it was still somewhat warm. I picked up a fork and ate every bite, even the limp, lukewarm broccoli.

I was finishing the last few bites when I realized that for the first time in a long time, I felt clear. Normal. Like myself. The drugs they had me on made me feel strange and disconnected. Like I was in a bubble. I hated that feeling, but I had been so discouraged and depressed, I couldn't even muster up the energy to fight it.

But, now I felt fresh and clean. Like the drugs had been flushed from my system.

Or, thinking of the post-tea fire in my body, maybe they had been burned up.

Of course, the tea wasn't real. It was part of my dreams.

Right?

Along with the tea burning up the drugs, it had also burned off the clouds of confusion that had muddled my thinking for so long. Suddenly, everything was crystal-clear to me.

I wasn't crazy. I had never been crazy.

But, that didn't mean there wasn't something evil living in my house.

I finished eating and got back in bed. I lay on my back, feeling the cell phone press against my head, and began to plan.

It was high time for me and Stefan to have a heart-to-heart.

Chapter 38

I paused by the entrance to the common area to give myself a chance to survey the scene and plot my next move.

Not only had I eaten that morning again, but I had also showered, and was dressed in a clean gown. The grandmotherly nurse was on duty, and she had been ecstatic to see the change in me as she changed my bed sheets. I had pretended to take my meds, but spat them out as soon as the nurse left the room. She barely looked at me after she handed me the cup and the water, so it was easier to pull off than I had expected.

My next move was to figure out my escape plan. The problem: I had no idea what to do. I didn't know where my clothes were—a quick search of my room revealed nothing in the way of personal effects. How could I have *nothing* there? I had arrived with clothes, didn't I? So where did they go?

It was almost like I no longer existed. I wasn't Rebecca *or* Becca—but something in between. An insubstantial ghost.

I didn't like it.

The common area had about a dozen or so patients milling about, supervised by two nurses. A large console television was set up against one end of a room. Four people watched the Weather Channel, their eyes blank and staring, from faded blue couches. An overweight, balding, middle-aged man paced next to the window. A teenage boy crouched against the wall, his head in his hand, his black hair greasy and matted. Another three people sat at various round tables, attempting to do some sort of art project.

Although the last thing I felt like doing was art, I headed for one of the empty tables. Large sheets of drawing paper, along with a variety of colored pens, markers, and paints were scattered across the surface. One half-finished painting was in front of one of the chairs. I took the seat next to it, glancing at it. A distorted face was shoved in what looked like a box. I quickly looked away.

I pulled an empty piece of paper toward me and stared at it. Should I draw something? What? Maybe I could just sit, staring at the paper. No one would think that was weird—I was in a mental ward, after all. Maybe it would even be expected, with the drugs (they thought) they had me on.

Someone sat down in the seat next to me, the one with the disturbing painting in front of it. I glanced at her without raising my head. She wore a gown like I had on. Definitely a patient.

"You're new here."

She said it factually, like she was commenting on the weather. She was young, with long, blonde hair hanging straight down her back like a waterfall. Her eyes were a clear sky-blue, framed with thick lashes. With her high cheekbones and full lips, she looked familiar, but I couldn't place her.

"I am," I said.

She nodded, reaching for a paintbrush and plastic set of watercolor paints, the kind made for children. "I can tell," she said.

"How long have you been here?"

She shrugged, dipping her brush in the water. "We're all here for as long as we need to be."

Well. That wasn't terribly helpful. I looked back at the array of drawing utensils in front of me and selected a blue-colored pencil.

"Who decides how long we need to be here?"

She shrugged again. "Depends."

Okay then. Tentatively, I drew a line on the piece of paper. It felt awkward and uncomfortable. God, the hospital was the last place I wanted to be when I tried to rediscover my inner artist. Why did I sit down with all this art paraphernalia in front of me, when I could have been mindlessly staring at the Weather Channel?

"Have you ever noticed how busy it is here during the day?" she asked. I glanced at her, but she was hunched over, focused on her painting.

I drew another line. "I guess."

She nodded, as if to herself. "Yes, very busy during the day. Lots of people going in and out. How can anyone keep track of all the people going in and out? Not like at night. At night, it's very quiet. Everyone sleeps. Or should be sleeping."

I wasn't entirely sure how to answer her, or whether she even required an answer. I continued my drawing. It was starting to resemble a bird. "That's true."

She sat back and studied her painting. "Yes, daytime is definitely busier. People can get lost during the day. Much easier than at night."

I had no idea where she was going with what she was saying, so I continued to focus on my bird. It was looking a little deranged. Man, I really seemed to have lost the touch.

The girl stood up and wandered away. She reminded me of a waif, lost and alone in a strange and cruel place. I made a few more half-hearted attempts to fix my bird before idly glancing at the girl's painting.

I gasped, my pencil dropping from my hand.

Below the box with the head, jagged, red and black letters read, "The evil that was done."

I quickly twisted around, looking for her, but I didn't see her anywhere. Where could she have gone? Did she wander away to her room?

I got up to try and follow her, when it suddenly hit me who she reminded me of. Jessica. She reminded me of Jessica.

* * *

"Are you sure this is going to work?"

Mia and Daphne were both in my room, door closed. After the Jessica waif had disappeared, I had frantically started searching the room and the hallways, when one of the nurses stopped me. "Are you okay, dear?"

"There was a patient, a girl, painting next to me. Did you see her?"

The nurse frowned. She was tall and very thin with a hooked, beak-like nose. "I don't remember anyone sitting next to you, but I wasn't in the room the whole time. Why don't we sit down?"

"No, I ..." I tried to argue, but the nurse had a firm grip on my arm and led me to a chair. I wanted to protest, but at the last moment tightly closed my mouth. The last thing I wanted was more drugs pumped into me, and if I made too much of a fuss, I suspected the nurses would be all too happy to give me a shot.

"Should I get you some water?" she asked, once I was safely seated. I nodded. She studied me for a moment, probably to make sure I wasn't going anywhere, before walking away.

I took a deep breath to calm myself and looked around. The chair I was sitting in had a view of the hallway, so I craned my neck to see if I could catch a glimpse of the Jessica waif wandering down the hallway, but there was no one who looked even remotely like her.

"Here you go, dear." The nurse was back, handing me a cup of water. I took it and obediently drank, my eyes never leaving the hallway. A bearded male patient was arguing with a nurse, getting more and more agitated, until she finally signaled to a couple of male orderlies to quiet him. A little further down, a couple of doctors went about their rounds. A janitor swished a broom across the hallway. Nurses went in and out of rooms. A family in street clothes walked next to an older woman as she slowly paced down the hall.

The Jessica waif was right; it was pretty busy. At the far end of the hall, two people finished signing in and waved at the orderly behind the glass. He barely glanced at them as he pushed a button to unlock the door. One was holding a large plastic pot of flowers and struggled a bit getting through the door. The orderly ignored them.

How easy *would* it be to leave, I wondered? Especially if you were wearing street clothes. And were part of a group.

An older, grey-haired woman wearing cream pants and a short-sleeved, blue-striped shirt approached the door. The orderly glanced up and pushed the clipboard at her. She signed out.

The agitated patient in the hallway suddenly turned violent, yelling and lashing out. The orderly guarding the door looked up, completely fixated on the scene, ignoring the woman trying to get out. She pushed the clipboard at him. Again, without looking at it, he pushed the button to let her out.

I started to smile. Could it really be that simple?

"Sometimes simple is best," I said to Daphne. "Too complicated can also mean too many things can go wrong."

"Completely agree," Mia said, rubbing her hands gleefully. She looked excited. Daphne looked skeptical.

"You honestly think all you need to do is put on some street clothes and they'll let you walk out of here?" Daphne asked.

I shrugged. "Why not? It's not a prison. It's an understaffed holding wing at a regular hospital. From what I can tell, that locked door exists to help keep the patients contained, so they don't run amok in the rest of the hospital. Not everyone is here against their will like I am. It seems to me most of the people are here voluntarily, and they designed this place with that in mind."

"Doesn't that mean they're watching you even more?" Daphne asked.

I shrugged. "I haven't noticed. Of course, I didn't leave my room until today, and I've been careful to move slowly, like I'm still drugged up. Honestly? I think they've forgotten I'm here against my will."

Mia flopped down on the bed next to me. "And besides, she has us here to help create a distraction to make sure it works."

Daphne shook her head. "It just seems ... too easy."

"I signed in twice," Mia said. "He didn't notice. How hard would this be?"

"Look," I said. "How many times have we seen people do something really outrageous and get away with it? If you walk in expecting something to happen, most of the time, that's exactly what happens. So, if I walk out with you like I'm a visitor and expect to be let out, that's likely exactly what will happen."

Daphne didn't look convinced.

Mia plopped a duffle bag on my lap. "So, what's the plan?"

I opened it and started rifling through. Underneath a couple of magazines was a pair of jean shorts, socks, underwear, tennis shoes, and a pink tee shirt. I also found a mound of black hair, which turned out to be a wig.

"There's a baseball hat in there too," Mia said, as I studied the wig. "Your hair is pretty ... different. I thought a wig might help."

"The wig looks like your hair," I said.

"Duh," she said. "I signed in twice, too. You're going to be me leaving, remember?"

I glanced up. Mia was wearing a pink tee shirt, although hers was a lighter pink with the words "Keep Calm and Drink Wine" on it in white. She also had a University of Wisconsin baseball cap on. All of a sudden, I understood where Daphne was coming from.

"Daphne was right," I said. "This is stupid. There's no way anyone is going to think I'm you."

"As you pointed out, that orderly is barely glancing at people coming and going." Mia said. "I'm not sure if he even looked at me, so why would he remember me? Besides, I'm going to stay behind. You get dressed and leave with Daphne, and I'll be the distraction. And, in case anyone remembers that Daphne walked in with a cute dark-haired chick, well, there you are."

"A cute *short* dark-haired chick," I retorted. "I'm about a foot taller than you."

"I told you this was a stupid idea," Daphne groaned.

"Well, we needed to do something to cover up Becca's hair," Mia said. "That might cause a second look. And she needs to sign out as me. So it makes sense to have her look as much like me as possible."

I took a deep breath. Was I really going to do this? Staring at Mia, I was starting to get a bad feeling. Maybe I should stay put and figure out a better way—a legal way—to get out.

But then I thought of Chrissy. And that giant ticking clock inside me. Something *was* wrong. I needed to get out.

"So, when are we going to do this?" Daphne asked. "Right now? Or ..."

I glanced at the clock. "They come with meds at around 5 o'clock. It's quarter to four now, so yeah. If we're going to do this, let's do it now."

I collected the clothes and headed for the bathroom to change. I had no sooner shut the door when I heard the door open to my room. "Where's Rebecca?" a voice snapped, and my heart sank.

It was Nurse Ellen.

I hadn't seen her earlier and had been hoping it was her day off. No such luck.

I heard Mia tell her I was in the bathroom.

"How long is she going to be in there?" Nurse Ellen definitely sounded impatient. Crap, now what would I do? I stared helplessly around the bathroom as I held my clothes. I needed to hide them, but where? While the bathroom was relatively roomy and had lots of metal handles everywhere, it was also pretty sparse: a bathtub, sink, toilet, and cupboard above the toilet, which held a pink plastic bin, some extra gloves, and disinfectant. I shoved my clothes behind the pink plastic bin, trying to be as quiet as possible, before flushing the toilet, washing my hands and opening the door.

Nurse Ellen was standing by the door to the room, arms crossed, a displeased expression on her face. Mia and Daphne were sitting on the bed. Daphne was staring out the window.

"There you are," Nurse Ellen said. "Let's go."

I didn't move. "Go where?"

Nurse Ellen frowned even deeper. "To see Dr. Ellison. Where do you think?" She turned to Mia and Daphne sitting on the bed, and my heart jumped into my mouth. My cell was sitting there in the middle of the bed. Oh God, was she going to confiscate it? "You two might as well leave," she said.

Mia and Daphne looked startled. "Ah ..." Daphne started to say, but I interrupted.

"Dr. Ellison always comes here to see me, though. I thought he wasn't seeing me today."

Nurse Ellen tapped her foot. "He only did that because you didn't leave your bed before. But, now that you're up and walking around, he wants to see you in his office."

I didn't see how I could possibly get out of seeing the doctor without drawing unwanted attention to myself, so I started shuffling forward.

Mia reached out to touch my hand. "No worries, we can wait until you're done."

"It's a waste of your time," Nurse Ellen said. "Who knows how long she'll be with the doctor, and then it will be time for meds."

"That's okay," Mia said firmly. "We'll wait."

"Suit yourself," Nurse Ellen snapped, turning on her heel and striding out of the room. I looked back at Mia and Daphne before walking out the door—Daphne looked worried, but Mia winked at me.

Nurse Ellen appeared to be in a particularly foul mood, muttering to herself as she strode down the hall. I had to hurry to keep up since I really had no idea where I was going. She finally stopped in front of a door, knocked and pushed it open, and left without looking at me.

Hesitantly, I approached the door. I hoped I would be able to find my way back on my own.

Dr. Ellison was behind a desk, shuffling papers, but he looked up and smiled at me. "Ah, Rebecca. So good to see you walking around. Come in." He stood up and gestured for me to sit in one of the two chairs in front of his desk.

I sat in the hard, wooden chair, trying not to fidget. How fast could I make this without raising his suspicion?

The room was small and cramped. There was no couch, just a big messy desk, a lamp, and the two wooden chairs. The walls were painted with what I imagined to be a soothing blue with yellow accents, although, because there were no windows, the effect felt more claustrophobic than comforting.

He leaned back in his chair, tenting his fingers. "Are you ready to talk about what happened?"

Oh no. He looked like he was settling in for a long conversation. I dropped my gaze to the coffee mug on his desk. It featured a cartoon picture of a cow standing in the middle of a field with the words "outstanding in my field" below it. It reminded me of my dream the night before, drinking tea with Aunt Charlie. I shivered.

The doctor noticed and leaned forward. "Are you cold? I can turn up the heat in here."

I shook my head. "I'm fine."

He settled back in his chair. "Tell me about that night."

I fiddled with my hospital gown. "There's nothing to tell. Clearly, I wasn't in my right mind."

"Tell me how it seemed from your standpoint."

This wasn't going well. I really didn't want to get into a big discussion about my mental health. "I woke up and saw Chrissy wasn't in her room. I found her downstairs and I thought she had been sleepwalking, but I guess she hadn't been. All I was trying to do was get her back to her bed."

The doctor nodded slightly. "And the knife."

"I didn't have it."

"Your husband says otherwise."

I bit my lip. "It's true I had put it in my purse. But, I didn't have my purse with me when I was talking to Chrissy."

He nodded again, and jotted a few notes. "What else?"

"Stefan came down and … and he started yelling at me. And then you showed up."

"Do you remember why Stefan was yelling at you?"

"He said I was a danger to Chrissy, but I wasn't. I was just trying to get her back to bed."

Dr. Ellison took a few more notes. "Anything else?"

I shook my head.

"You don't remember threatening Stefan?"

I made a face. "No." I said, and clamped my mouth closed before I could say "because I didn't threaten him." I figured the less confrontational I was, the better.

Dr. Ellison pursed his lips. "What about Chrissy?"

"What about Chrissy?'

"Do you remember threatening her?"

"No." *Because I didn't threaten her either.*

I could feel myself wanting to lash out and protest my innocence, but I forced myself to stay calm and breathe. If I wasn't careful, I was going to get myself sedated.

Dr. Ellison peered at me over his glasses. "That's not the story I got from Stefan and Chrissy."

Chrissy too? Oh boy. Although it made sense that she would back him up. After all, he was her father. And if she were possessed by Nellie, she would probably lie just to make more trouble for me. I decided to try a different tact.

"I ... I'm tired, Dr. Ellison. Can we talk about this tomorrow?"

He took his glasses off to study me. "I think we should talk about this now."

I went back to plucking at my gown. "Things are still ... a blur. And I'm really tired. It's been a long day."

He opened his mouth, as if to protest, then closed it. "I think you're right. Let's pick this back up tomorrow, after you've had a chance to rest and think about things some more."

Fat chance, I thought grimly, but I nodded as I rose to my feet. He called my name as I was turning to the door and I looked back at him.

"Good job today," he smiled at me. "You've had a big breakthrough."

You have no idea, I thought, but I nodded again and left.

After a few missed turns and some help from a couple of nurses, I made my way back to my room. Mia and Daphne were still there, thank God.

"You won't believe it," Mia hissed as soon as I closed the door, but no sooner had I shut it, when someone wrestled it open from the other side. Nurse Ellen. Of course.

"Your meds," she snapped, muscling her way in. I took a couple of steps back.

"The doctor said I had a breakthrough," I said hesitantly. I wasn't completely sure if I could fool her with the pills.

She smiled. It wasn't a very nice smile. "I know." She held out the paper container and a glass of water. "I have your new prescription right here."

Oh crap. I slowly reached for the container and the water. Her smile widened, looking even nastier, if that was even possible.

I tossed the pills into my mouth. My first thought was to hide them under my tongue but at the last moment I jammed them between my lower teeth and gum. I took a gulp of the water, making a big deal out of swallowing it.

I went to hand back the glass, but she didn't move. "Open your mouth," she said.

Oh God. This was what I was afraid of. I opened my mouth, praying I had hidden the pills well enough.

She peered inside. "Lift your tongue," she ordered.

Thanking God for the impulse that kept me from using my tongue, I lifted my tongue.

She nodded, apparently satisfied, and took my glass away from me. "Doesn't make sense for your friends to stay. You're not going to be worth much very soon." She turned on her heel and left the room.

I quickly whirled around so my back was to the door and spit the pills out. "We don't have much time," I hissed, heading to the bathroom. "If she thinks those meds are going to knock me out, she's going to be back here soon."

"Becca, maybe we shouldn't do this now," Daphne started to say, but I shook my head.

"No, I have to get out of here. Now. I can't wait any longer. " The ticking in my head was so loud I could barely think—all I could hear was "go, go, go." As I shut the bathroom door, I heard Mia say to Daphne, "What on earth did you see in that witch?"

I hurriedly stripped off my gown, then dug the clothes and wig out of the cabinet. I was glad Mia had brought that silly wig, after all. It would be more difficult for Nurse Ellen to spot me with that wig on.

Roughly, I pulled the clothes on. In my haste, I got tangled in the shorts and nearly lost my balance. "Becca, get ahold of yourself," I muttered as I struggled to right myself.

Finally, finally, I was dressed. It felt like it had taken hours. Quickly, I pulled my hair back and arranged the wig on my head. I didn't have a mirror, so I had to feel around to make sure I had tucked up all my hair. I slapped the baseball cap on and was about to open the door, when I spied my hospital gown on the floor. Not completely understanding the impulse but doing it anyway, I scooped my hospital gown off the floor and shoved it in the cabinet where I had hidden my clothes before opening the door.

Mia was standing in front of the door and Daphne was still on the bed. They both did a double take. "Wow," Mia said. "You look nothing like yourself."

I fretted with the wig. "Is it straight? There's no mirror in the bathroom."

Daphne got off the bed and came toward me. "Here, let me." She adjusted the wig and the hat, taking a moment to walk around me and check me from all sides. "Okay, that should work."

"No one is going to recognize you," Mia said. "We just need to get you out of the room."

"Yeah, that's the tricky part." I scooped up the duffle bag from the bed. The ticking in my head had become a gong. I had to get out. "Any suggestions? I could just …"

"Hold on," Mia interrupted. "Turn on the light in the bathroom and close the door." She rolled her eyes at my questioning look. "How else am I going to pretend you're in the bathroom?"

"Oh, makes sense," I said, as Daphne crossed the room to do what Mia suggested.

"Daphne, you leave first," Mia continued. "Once the coast is clear, let Becca know and she can slip out. I'll wait here. And I'll do my best to keep them from realizing you're missing, Becca. Hopefully, if they think they just lost track of you, it will buy us some time."

"I think you missed your calling," I said. "I know you wanted to be Erin Brockovich, but you should have been a spy or something."

"Naw," Mia said cheerfully, although her smiled faded slightly when I mentioned Erin Brockovich. "I'm more of a *Mission Impossible* or *Ocean's Eleven* girl."

Daphne shook her head as she approached the door. "I have a bad feeling about this."

"That's Star Wars," Mia said cheerfully.

"Are you sure?" I asked. "I think that's Raiders of the Lost Ark."

"Oh, you might be right. Still Harrison Ford though," Mia said.

Daphne blew out air in exasperation. "I wasn't making a movie reference. It's what I feel."

"If it makes you feel any better, I have a bad feeling too," I said. "But I have a worse feeling about staying here."

"Ready?" Mia asked, positioning herself to stand behind the door as it opened. Daphne nodded, and Mia opened the door.

Daphne stepped out and looked around. I think she was trying to be casual, but her entire body was stiff and jerky. I heard Mia hiss "relax" at her. Daphne scowled, and gave me a quick nod.

I took a deep breath. Mia whispered to me: "Remember, whatever you do, don't stop. Just head straight to the door and sign out."

I nodded, took a second deep breath, and stepped into the hallway.

I don't know what I was expecting—maybe an alarm to go off or one of the nurses to yell, "There she is, grab her before she escapes!"—but absolutely nothing happened. A glassy-eyed woman with dark, stringy hair lurched by me, hand trailing on the opposite wall. Down the hallway by the nurse's station, two nurses appeared to be doing paperwork, completely oblivious to their surroundings.

I turned and started walking down the hallway, Daphne next to me. "Slow down," she muttered. "We're not in any hurry. And hunch over."

I slowed my pace and bent my head, letting the dark hair from the wig cover my face. A nurse passed us going the other way, and I quickly angled my head away ... but she completely ignored me.

"Remember, you have every right to leave," Daphne murmured. "Just act like you have total confidence in what you're doing."

Easier said than done. Thinking about this escape plan and actually doing it were two completely different things. I sucked in a breath and squared my shoulders, repeating to myself, "I have every right to leave. I have every right to leave."

I could see the doorway just up ahead. Almost there. God, it was agonizing how long it took. I felt like I was going to hyperventilate, so I focused on slowing down my breathing.

From behind I heard a shout. "Daphne." It was Nurse Ellen. Daphne gasped, and I could see her face grow paler. "Keep going," she muttered. "Whatever you do, don't stop."

Nurse Ellen called her name again, sounding more frustrated. Daphne stopped and turned. "What is it?" she said, her voice tart.

"Are you leaving?" Nurse Ellen asked.

"What does it look like?" Daphne snapped.

Even though I had my head down and hadn't stopped, I could still hear their conversation.

"You might want to rethink visiting Rebecca," Nurse Ellen said. "I don't think your visits are helping, and they may even be setting her back."

I finally, finally, reached the desk that manned the door. The orderly was bent over, in front of a computer.

"What are you talking about?" Daphne demanded. "She looked great to me."

I opened my mouth to say, "Signing out," but all that came out was a squeak. I closed my mouth, swallowed hard, and tried again. "Signing out."

"Where did you go to medical school again?" Nurse Ellen asked. "Oh. That's right. You didn't."

Without looking at me, the orderly thrust a clipboard at me. I reached for the pen and saw my hand shake badly. I dropped my hand to the desk to steady it.

"That has nothing to do with anything and you know it," Daphne said.

"Oh, so you *do* think you're qualified to diagnose Rebecca?" Nurse Ellen said, sarcasm dripping from her voice.

"Don't be absurd," Daphne said. "I didn't say anything of the kind."

It seemed to take forever before I found Mia's name and signed out. My hand shook so hard the scribbled name was barely legible. I swallowed hard, and silently handed the clipboard back. The orderly took it without looking at me.

"Then," Nurse Ellen said, a syrupy sweetness dripping from her words. "As Rebecca's friend, I'm sure you'll agree with me you should do what's best for her. And *not* visiting her would definitely be better for her."

Oh God, this was taking forever. What if Mia came out right now and Nurse Ellen saw her? I could feel myself starting to hyperventilate again, and fought to get my breathing under control.

The orderly barely glanced at the clipboard. He put it down and slowly, oh-so-slowly, reached for the buzzer.

"Whatever," Daphne snapped. "All I ask is you do your job with her."

"Are you implying that I don't?" Nurse Ellen's voice had a dangerous tone to it. Oh Daphne, *what are you doing*?

Finally, the orderly hit the buzzer. I lunged for the door before I could stop myself. *Careful, Becca. Remember, you have every right to leave.* I pushed it open, stepped out, and kept walking.

Oh my God, it worked! I could barely believe it. I kept walking, sure I was going to hear Nurse Ellen behind me, yelling at me to stop.

The only problem was, I had no idea how to actually get out of the hospital. I followed the hallway and found myself at a bank of elevators. Not sure what else to do, I pressed down.

Could I find my way out without Daphne? Would I be able to find her outside?

The elevators seemed to take forever. Should I take the stairs? What if Nurse Ellen came running out? Would I still be able to get out of there?

Bing. The doors to one of the elevators slowly opened up. A man wearing a white doctor's coat with glasses and a black beard stood inside, staring at his phone.

"Let's go," Daphne was behind me, breathing hard. She didn't have to ask me twice. I quickly stepped into the elevator. Daphne hit the first floor. Slowly, the elevator doors closed. I kept waiting to see Nurse Ellen running down the hallway yelling that I was getting away, but the hallway stayed empty.

The doors closed. The elevator began to descend.

I glanced sideways at Daphne. Her lips were pressed tightly together, but I could still hear her breathing. I wanted to ask her what happened, and what about Mia, but with the doctor hovering next to us, maniacally texting on his phone, I didn't dare.

The elevator crawled its way down, stopping two more times before finally getting to the first floor. Each time it stopped, my heart jumped in my throat, sure Nurse Ellen would be on the other side, waving a needle at me. But, no. At one stop, a father and daughter got on, the daughter happily talking about her baby sister. A nurse pushing an older woman in a wheelchair joined us on the second stop. The nurse smiled as she angled the wheelchair into the elevator. I squished myself in the corner and forced myself to focus on my breathing.

Finally, the elevator stopped on the first floor. I waited as it slowly opened, and the nurse backed the woman in the wheelchair out. Daphne strode out next to me, and I had to hurry to follow her.

"Mia?" I asked in a low voice.

Daphne gave a quick shake to her head. "We brought separate cars."

I nodded and didn't say anything more. Daphne led me through the maze of hospital corridors, past the gift shop and the welcome desk. I eyed one of the nurses who was on the phone, but she seemed completely focused on her computer screen as she talked.

No one came running after us. In fact, no one paid the slightest attention to us.

Finally, we made it through the outside doors and into the parking lot, and I visibly sagged with relief.

Daphne continued at the same pace. "We're not safe yet," she muttered. I hurried to catch up.

The sun was still bright, but starting to sink in the sky, casting long shadows on the parking lot. The air smelled like gas and hot asphalt. I never smelled anything so sweet.

Daphne led me to a silver minivan that seemed to sparkle in the sun. A raven stood on the roof, twisting its head and eyeing me.

"The Raven is about rebirth," Daphne said as she unlocked the door. "He helps with transitions by casting light into darkness."

Instead of flying away as I approached, the raven watched me get into the van. "Seems appropriate."

Daphne nodded. "A good omen."

It wasn't until we were safely driving down the highway that Daphne spoke. "I thought I was going to have a heart attack in there."

"You and me both," I said, removing the hat and wig and ruffling my now-sweaty hair. "Think Mia is okay?"

Daphne glanced at the rear-view mirror. "She'll be fine," she said, but her voice didn't sound all that convinced.

I looked out the window at the trees rushing by, hoping against hope that Mia wouldn't get into any trouble for helping me.

"So, now what?" Daphne asked, cutting into my thoughts.

"Home," I said.

Daphne's eyes widened. "You don't mean Charlie's house?"

I rubbed my head and shook out my curls: even though I had just washed it that morning, it still felt greasy. Actually, my whole body felt that way—like the hospital had left a disgusting layer of film on my skin. I couldn't wait to take a proper shower. "Of course I mean Aunt Charlie's house. What other house do I own in Redemption?"

"Yes ... but ... you *do* know Stefan is there, right?"

"I should hope so. I'm counting on it."

"What? But ..." Daphne stuttered before she finally got herself under control. "Becca, we just got you out. Don't you think the hospital has already called him? He's probably waiting for you—maybe with the police."

I shrugged. "Good. That would save me from calling them."

Daphne looked at me, aghast. "But, they'll take you right back to the hospital."

I turned to her. "Stefan set me up. You know that, right? This was all a big set up. He wanted to get me committed."

"And he succeeded. Why on earth would you give him a second bite of that apple?"

"What else am I going to do? If what you say is true, and the hospital is already taking steps to get me back, don't you think the police will eventually show up at your house too? And Mia's? Where am I going to go? I don't have any money—I'm sure my bank accounts are frozen, or at least being watched. I guess I could call my parents for a loan, but wouldn't the police think to check with them too? And Stefan has probably already poisoned them against me. Realistically—how long am I really going to last on the run, before I'm caught?"

"That's why you should have fought this legally," Daphne said.

I barked a laugh. "Stefan is a lawyer! He planned this. Although I still don't know why." I turned away to stare out the window. I had no idea what was going on, but what I did know was Chrissy was there, alone, in that house. I wasn't going to abandon her. "The worst part is how easily I fell into his trap. Like an idiot."

I could feel Daphne's eyes on me. "You're not an idiot. What Stefan did isn't normal—why would it have ever occurred to you that your husband would try to get you committed? It doesn't make any sense."

"And here I thought my first husband was a rotten pig. He just cheated on me."

Daphne laughed. "I shouldn't laugh …"

"No, you should," I said. "It IS laughable … if it wasn't so tragic."

"Yeah, well." She took a deep breath. "Okay, I understand why you didn't want to fight this legally. But do you really think showing up at the house and confronting him is your best bet? Do you honestly think you're going to be able to trick him or something?"

"I'm hoping it's 'or something'."

She glanced at me and shook her head. "How are you even going to get *in* the house? What if he changed the locks?"

"He probably didn't think about the entrance to the basement," I said. "You can't see the door anymore, from the outside. It's completely overgrown."

"You don't think it's locked?"

I shrugged. "Aunt Charlie always kept a key hidden in the garden in case she ever locked herself out. I imagine it's still there."

Daphne pulled off the highway and took one of the side streets. "So, you're going to sneak in? And then what?"

"With a little luck, finally get to the bottom of what's been going on," I said.

Chapter 39

I crouched in the woods, in the same place where I first saw the black cat, and watched the house slowly disappear under the velvety darkness of the night.

I was waiting for the exact right moment. I wasn't even sure what that moment would be, but I had a feeling I would know it when it showed up.

About fifteen minutes previous, a cop (not Daniel) had come by the house. Stefan stood on the front step to talk to him. After a few minutes, Stefan went back inside, and the cop walked around the house, peering around the yard. I had pressed myself into the ground, behind a large log. He didn't see me.

After we had left the hospital, we made a quick stop at a Walmart Superstore where Daphne had bought me an olive-green tee shirt with a mosquito and the words "Wisconsin's State Bird" on it (if I was going to be sneaking into my house, I needed a different shirt than that hot-pink one), a towel, a flashlight, a couple of protein bars, trail mix, almonds, and two large bottles of water. I swapped shirts in the car while she drove me to a small, empty park. It was about a mile away from Aunt Charlie's house, if I used the forest trails. It had been years since I had tried to find my way on those trails, but I trusted I would figure it out. I still had the burner phone in my pocket, but I had switched it to vibrate.

The forest was quiet. All I could hear was the sound of my own breathing and the chirping of a few birds. There was a damp, woodsy smell in the air, which was heavenly, after the sterility of the hospital. I had forgotten how fresh and good the smell of the woods was.

I knew I was taking a big risk going to the house, but I had no choice. I had to confront Stefan. I had to trust that I would be granted enough time to sneak in through the basement, find Stefan, and get him to confess before he was able to call the cops. How I would do that, I hadn't a clue. I had never stood up to him before. I hadn't dared. Because if I had stood up to him, that would mean I wasn't a perfect wife and stepmother.

And it had been very important to me to be that. Because if I was, then Stefan would love me and take care of me.

God, I felt like such an idiot. A gullible, stupid idiot.

It was easier than I remembered, finding my way back to Aunt Charlie's house. Once there, I eased my way closer until I found the perfect hiding place—behind a large log that provided me with cover, where I could see both the house and the road. I arranged the towel and sat on it, grateful for Daphne's foresight. When she had first handed it to me at the store, I had looked at her like she was crazy … but the dampness of the ground would have been pretty uncomfortable without it. I ate my dinner, sat, and waited.

I watched as the sunlight slowly drained from the sky, lengthening the shadows before dimming them. One by one, the lights went on and off in the house. Off in the kitchen. On in Chrissy's room. On then off in the bathroom. On in Stefan's office.

I paused to make sure the lights stayed off downstairs in the kitchen, and on in Chrissy's room and Stefan's office, before slowly easing myself out from my hiding place and quietly making my way to the house.

A bat swooped across my path, and I jerked to a stop. My aunt's voice popped into my head. "Bats are an omen of change. And death." I shivered.

I hadn't seen the black cat, but I had felt its presence more than once. Each time, I whirled around, certain I could feel its eyes on me, but nothing was there. At least nothing I could see. It was somehow comforting—like a friend watching over me, protectively. As I picked my way through the backyard, I pretended to be that cat, silently stalking as I moved through the overgrown weeds and grass.

It was easier than I had expected to locate both the key and the door to the basement. It was almost like the house itself *wanted* me back … welcomed me back. As I cleared away the vines and unlocked the door, I truly felt—deep in my bones— that I was home.

This *was* my home. And, just like that, I realized I wasn't going to leave it again.

Quietly, I eased the door open just enough to slip inside. In the stillness of the night, it sounded so loud. Were the windows open upstairs? Had they heard it, or was I being super-sensitive? Both Stefan and Chrissy always worked with background noise—Stefan usually played music or kept the news on. Hopefully, he was so busy focusing on whatever he was working on, he wasn't paying attention to much else.

I eased the door shut, and fumbled around for the flashlight. The basement smelled damp and musty, reminding me to get a dehumidifier.

I clicked the flashlight on, and waited for my eyes to adjust. From what I could see, it was as I remembered—cement walls, cement floor, the furnace and water heater next to one wall, stacks of boxes and what looked like broken furniture piled everywhere, and lots of spider webs. I also remembered all over again how much I didn't like the basement—how uncomfortable I always felt down here.

I had to walk down a set of rickety wooden steps to reach the floor, before weaving my way to another set of steps that led up to main house.

The stairs creaked as I slowly mounted the first. Oh God, I hoped Stefan really was still upstairs—that he hadn't wandered down into the kitchen for a drink. I tried to calm my nerves, reminding myself that the whole house creaked. I was sure he wouldn't be able to differentiate the sound of the basement steps from all the other creaks and groans.

Finally, I reached the top. I clicked off the flashlight and listened. I couldn't hear anything on the other side of the door. This of course didn't guarantee that no one was there, but if someone was, he or she was being awfully quiet. Or, I just couldn't hear him or her over my pounding heart.

I stayed there, listening and hearing nothing but my own harsh breathing and heartbeat for what felt like hours. *This is stupid,* I told myself. *I can't stand here forever.*

I put my hand on the doorknob, and gently turned. It let out a squeak, which stopped my heart, but I heard nothing in response on the other side.

I pushed the door open. It was dark and quiet. I carefully closed the door, slipped my cell phone out of my pocket, and pressed a preprogrammed number. It rang once, and was then silent. I slipped it into my pocket and arranged my shirt over it, before making my way to the upstairs staircase. I stayed near the wall, where the steps didn't creak as I mounted them.

Chrissy's door was shut. I could see the light beneath it. She was probably listening to music, or watching a video. Stefan's door was mostly closed, but not shut. Light poured out into the hallway, along with the faint sounds of Rolling Stone's "Sympathy for the Devil."

I approached the room, carefully stepping around the floorboard that I knew creaked, and took a deep breath, before gently pushing his door open.

Stefan was sitting behind the desk, furiously typing. He glanced up before doing a double-take. He smiled. It wasn't a welcoming smile.

"Well, well, well," he said, finishing whatever it was he was typing and then closing his laptop. "I figured you would turn up sooner or later. How did you get in?"

"Does it matter?" I asked.

He shrugged. "Not particularly. It's not like you'll have another chance, after this."

"What's that supposed to mean?"

He leaned back in his chair and laced his hands behind his head. "Just that once I call the police, this will all be over for good. You won't be sneaking out of the hospital a second time."

I struggled to swallow, my mouth feeling dry. "Why are you doing this to me, Stefan? I'm your wife. We made vows to each other. Why would you betray me like this?"

"My wife," he said, his voice dripping with contempt. "My wife who tried to stab my daughter."

My eyes widened. "I did no such thing."

He dropped his hands from behind his head. "Really? Then why did I find a knife in your purse?"

This wasn't going exactly like I had imagined in my head. But, honestly, what did I think was going to happen? He would see me and confess all as Daphne recorded it? Like I was in a bad television movie? They don't hand out partnerships at big New York law firms just because you look good in a suit. Of course Stefan would be on his guard with me.

I stepped into the room, moving so my back was against the wall and positioning myself so I could still see the door. The last thing I wanted was for Chrissy to sneak up behind me. "The knife was in my purse, which was in another room when you found Chrissy and me together." I spread my hands out wide. "How could I stab her when the knife was in a completely different room?"

A small tick started above his eye. "No, it wasn't. You had your purse with you."

"You brought the knife into the room," I hissed.

He stared at me for a moment and then started to laugh. "What? Are you recording me, or something? Rebecca, I don't know what you've been telling your cop boyfriend, but you tried to attack both of us that night. With a knife. And you also tried to kill yourself."

Oh God. Did I really think I could match wits with a lawyer? There was no way I was going to be able to make him admit the truth. I really was an idiot. My mouth was so dry. Why did I think this was a good idea? Daphne was right. I should have just tried to make a run for it.

He reached for his cell phone. "As fun as this conversation is, it's probably time to get you back to the hospital. You look like you could use your meds."

Becca think! This is your one chance to finally stand up to Stefan. Are you really going to blow it cowering in a corner while he smugly sits there in complete control of the situation?

In complete control of YOU?

I straightened my back. Absolutely not. If I had to go down, I was going to go down fighting. I quickly ran through the conversation, trying to see if there was something, anything, I could use against him.

I was starting to despair when Stefan's words floated through my head. *I don't know what you're telling your cop boyfriend.* Why would he bring that up? Why would he care what I was telling him? It wasn't much, but at this point I was pretty desperate.

"What do you mean my 'cop boyfriend'?" I asked. "If you're talking about Daniel, he's not my boyfriend. What does he have to do with anything?"

Stefan picked up the cell phone. "Don't act so innocent. You know he's investigating me."

"Why would he do that?"

"Why the hell should I know? Probably because you're screwing him."

I shook my head. "Why do you care if he investigates you or not? If it's true that I have lost my mind, then why do you care what he does?"

Stefan didn't say anything. He didn't move, except for that twitch above his eye.

I sucked in my breath and stepped forward. "You *do* have something to hide. You bastard. What is Daniel going to find? What is it?" I put my hands on his desk and leaned over it. "You and I both know what happened that night. You had the knife, not me. I didn't attack anyone, and I certainly didn't try and commit suicide. Why are you lying about it? Why are you doing this to me? Why are you trying to make me think I'm losing my mind?"

He glared at me and jerked backwards. "You went crazy all on your own, just like you did fifteen years ago. It has nothing to do with me." Although he sounded sure of himself, he couldn't meet my eyes. Instead, he seemed to be focusing on my shoulder.

I gave him a slow smile and started shaking my head. "No."

He looked startled. "No?"

"No. I'm not crazy. I didn't go crazy fifteen years ago and I didn't go crazy now. You're hiding something. I wonder what it is."

Rage suddenly contorted his face. "Tell that to the courts. I have documents that prove you're insane. And if you think anyone is going to believe you, you're even crazier than I thought. Now, if you'll excuse me, this conversation is over. I'm calling the cops."

"No," I said, taking a swipe at his phone. But he was too fast, jumping to his feet and backing away from me. He pressed the phone to his ear, his eyes never leaving mine. "Hello? Yes, I'd like to report a break-in. Rebecca McMurray is here. Send the cops. Yes, I think she is dangerous. Please hurry." He ended the call and smiled. A cold, empty smile. "As I said, this will be all over soon." His eyes shifted, focusing on something behind me. "Chrissy. You may want to say goodbye to your *stepmother*. I doubt you'll be seeing her again after this."

I whirled around. Chrissy stood by the door. She looked absolutely dreadful. Her hair hung in greasy strands around her pale, pinched face. She wore her normal sleep shirt and shorts, but they were stained and wrinkled. Idly, I wondered when she had last bathed, or eaten a decent meal. Her sleep outfit hung loosely on her, like she'd lost weight. There was a shiftiness in her eyes that reminded me of a starving, feral cat.

I took a step toward her. "Chrissy? Are you okay?"

Chrissy's dark eyes stared at me listlessly, like she didn't even recognize who I was. I spun back to Stefan. "What the hell did you do to your daughter? What is wrong with her?"

Stefan started shuffling papers on his desk. "There's nothing wrong with her. Quit trying to take the focus off of you."

I turned back to Chrissy, and took a few steps toward her. Her dark eyes, so huge in her face, just stared at me. "Chrissy, it's okay. You can tell me what's going on. I'll believe you." *Oh God*, I thought. I'm too late. My worst fears had come true—whatever was going on between Mad Martha and Nellie had erupted and shredded Chrissy's psyche in the process. I mentally kicked myself. Why did I let myself stay so long in the hospital? I should have broken out sooner. For her.

Stefan pushed me aside as he headed to the door. "Better enjoy your freedom while you can." He brushed by Chrissy, who didn't move.

I reached out and lightly touched her face, her dark eyes never leaving mine, before I rushed after him. "Stefan, what is wrong with you? Can't you see there is something seriously wrong with your daughter?"

"You're just trying to save yourself from going back to the mental hospital," he said over his shoulder as he headed down the stairs.

"This isn't about me," I yelled, running after him. "It's about Chrissy. She needs help."

"She's fine," Stefan said, as he reached the bottom of the staircase and strode over to the front door, flinging it open. "She's here, Officers."

Two cops I didn't recognize stepped inside. Stefan pointed to me, huddled halfway down the staircase. "There she is."

I pressed my back against the wall. Trapped. Now what? One of the cops slowly came toward me. "Ma'am. You're going to need to come with us. Would you come down the stairs?"

I shook my head. "You don't understand," I said. "There's something wrong with my stepdaughter. That's why I'm here."

"More of your delusions," Stefan snapped. "She tried to kill Chrissy again, Officers. My daughter is not safe with her in this house."

"No. That's not true," I said, as one of the officers reached up to grab my arm. He jerked it so roughly, I thought he was going to pull it out of my socket. I let out a little scream, partly from pain and partly from frustration, as he began hauling me down the stairs. "Officers, please. Just look at Chrissy. She needs help. I didn't touch her. I would never hurt her."

"Ma'am, it would be better if you didn't struggle," the officer said, as I broke free and tried to run. He tackled me from behind and pressed me against the floor. I could feel my cell phone digging painfully into my thigh, and my eyes filled with tears, wondering if Daphne could hear everything that was happening. *I should have listened to you, Daphne.* I sent her the message mentally, as the cop yanked my hands behind me to handcuff me. I gasped as pain shot through my shoulder. They hauled me to my feet, as I continued to struggle. My eyes focused on Chrissy standing on the stairs, looking like a ghost herself.

I blinked the tears out of my eyes. "Chrissy," I begged. "Tell them the truth. I would never hurt you. You know I wouldn't."

"Will you never stop? Officers, get her out of here. Can you see how much she's traumatized my daughter?"

"Chrissy, please," I begged. My voice broke. I knew it was all over, that I would never get out of the mental hospital, but in that moment, what I *needed* was to hear the truth from Chrissy's mouth.

Chrissy just stared at me, with those empty, dark eyes.

I could feel the tears start to rise up again, and I closed my eyes as the cops dragged me to the door.

"Stop." It was Chrissy's voice, the voice of a sixteen-year-old, yet full of power. The cops paused. I opened my eyes.

Stefan stared at his daughter. "Chrissy ..." he began.

"I said stop," she said, and took a step down the stairs. "Becca never attacked me or tried to kill me. She didn't try to kill my father either. Or herself."

Stefan's mouth dropped open. "Chrissy ..."

She ignored him and took another step down the stairs. "My dad set this whole thing up. He wanted her to think she was crazy. He even made me help."

I briefly closed my eyes. Of course he made her help. Suddenly, everything that had happened, all of Chrissy's wild mood swings and unpredictable actions, made a lot more sense.

I could feel the cops loosen their grip on my arms. Stefan took a step forward. "Chrissy, stop right now." He turned to the cops, who were suddenly a bit more interested in him. "Look, she's clearly not herself, after what's happened tonight. After what her stepmother put her through. She doesn't know what she's saying."

"Oh, but I do, father," Chrissy said, taking another step down the stairs. "And even more than that, I have proof."

Stefan gasped. "Proof? What proof?" He started to stride forward to his daughter, but both cops let go of me and grabbed him instead.

Chrissy smiled then, and took another step down the stairs, revealing papers clutched in her hand. "You want Becca's inheritance. That's why you *did* all of this." She shook her hand at her father, who could only gape at her.

"My inheritance," I broke in, completely puzzled. "What inheritance? I only have a trust fund from my grandparents. I can't even touch that until I'm fifty-five."

"Not that inheritance," Daniel said, stepping through the front door. "The one from your aunt."

"Aunt Charlie?" I looked wildly between Daniel, Chrissy, and Stefan. "Are you talking about this house? Stefan, you wanted *this house* so badly, you tried to have me committed? And why are you here?" I asked Daniel.

Daniel nodded to Chrissy. "She called me. We've been in contact."

Stefan's eyes narrowed. "You've been talking to the police?" he growled, his voice dangerously quiet. One of the cops holding him tightened his grip.

"She's a key witness," Daniel said, stepping in front of Stefan. "And you're under arrest."

"Wait," I said, bewildered, as the two cops took the handcuffs off me and put them on Stefan. "Stefan, I don't understand. Why did you want this house?"

"He didn't want the house," Daniel said. "At least, not just the house. He wanted the trust fund Charlie set up for you."

"Aunt Charlie set up a trust fund? For me?"

But no one was paying any attention to me anymore. Stefan was glaring at his daughter, his eyes so full of hatred and disgust, she shrank against the wall. I took a step forward to go to her, but Daniel held a hand out. "Not now," he said gently. "Chrissy needs to come with us. There're things we need to do. But you're safe now. You can stay here."

"But," I said as the cops dragged Stefan out. I had so many questions, with little hope for answers, at least at that point. Daniel held a hand out to Chrissy, gently coaxing her. Hesitantly, she reached out to take it.

Daniel turned to me. "Get some sleep," he said softly. "We'll talk soon."

I nodded as he started to lead Chrissy to the door, but she paused in front of me.

She lifted her chin, but kept her eyes from meeting mine. "I'm sorry, Becca," she said weakly.

I took a deep breath. "You saved me, Chrissy. And, in the end, you did the right thing," I said. "Thank you." As she turned away, I reached my hand out to stop her. "But why? Why did you turn on your dad?"

She dropped her gaze to the floor and started to walk away from me. I thought she wasn't going to answer, but then I heard her voice, so soft I almost missed it.

"I drank the tea."

Chapter 40

I was on my knees, covered in dirt, planting marigolds, when a voice behind me made me jump.

"Looks like you're getting the garden under control."

I sat back on my heels and looked up, shielding my eyes from the sun. "You startled me."

"Sorry." It was Daniel. I recognized him immediately, even without seeing his face, thanks to the sun in my eyes.

I stood up, my back and knees protesting after being crouched over for so long, and took off my gardening gloves. "Being out here—with the plants and the dirt—has been healing," I said, putting a hand to my lower back and stretching.

"I can imagine," he said.

"Can I get you something to drink? Some lemonade? Or maybe iced tea?"

"I can't stay too long, but a glass of lemonade would definitely hit the spot," he said. I saw he was wearing his uniform, indicating an official visit.

I led the way to the back porch. I had fixed it up with some new outdoor furniture—a table with an umbrella, and four comfy chairs. The lemonade was already on the table in a glass pitcher, along with a couple of clean glasses.

"Am I interrupting?" Daniel asked, as I filled one of the glasses to hand to him.

I shook my head. "Daphne has been keeping an eye on me. She's developed a habit of popping in nearly every day. And if she doesn't come up, then Mia does." I gestured to the chair and seated myself. "It's easier if I just plan in advance."

He nodded and took a sip. "How are you doing?"

I shrugged. "About as well as can be expected, I think." I decided not to mention I still had trouble sleeping at night, and if I did happen to doze off, I would be tormented with nightmares where Stefan was chasing me around the house with a knife. The doctor—my NEW doctor, NOT Dr. "Just-Call-

Me-Pete"—told me they would pass in time. She also had prescribed me some sleeping pills, but I wasn't ready to use them
yet. And even though I had gotten rid of all of Stefan's clothes
and belongings, I still occasionally felt his presence lurking in
the house, especially in the dark stillness of night. I wondered if
moving to my aunt's bedroom would stop all of that.

We were silent for a moment. I watched a couple of chickadees land on the birdfeeder.

"It looks like the state of New York is going to extradite Stefan," Daniel said finally. "The embezzlement charges appear to
be a stronger case."

I made a face. "Of course, embezzling millions from a law
firm definitely takes precedence over intentionally driving your
wife mad, so you can involuntarily commit her and take her inheritance. Not to mention forcing your sixteen-year-old daughter to take part in it. That makes perfect sense."

He sighed. "I know it looks bad, but it wasn't just the law
firm. He also stole directly from dozens of wealthy individuals,
some of them the firm's clients. And your case isn't as rock solid. He never tried to kill you. The evidence we do have makes
that clear. And the fact that a side effect of your allergy meds is
paranoia ... well, it weakens the case even further. Quite honestly, the case against Chrissy is more damning than the case
against him. She actually admitted to drugging you on two oc-
casions. Stefan has wisely lawyered up."

"What about Chrissy's testimony against him? Doesn't that
count for something?"

Daniel shrugged. "What about it? He's claiming she's a confused teenager who was out to get you. And she's got very
little proof backing up her side of the story—not even texts she
claimed they exchanged. He must have deleted them off her
phone. And your paranoia escalated the situation. His lawyer
is arguing that clearly, he never should have left you two alone
together for so long, but that's hardly a crime."

A sparrow joined the chickadees on the bird feeder, who
immediately began squawking at the intruder. The sparrow ignored them. "So, he gets away with it?"

"He's hardly getting away with anything. If Chrissy hadn't turned on him, we never would have been able to seize his laptop and personal files. Those records are what's going to put him away for a long time in New York."

I watched the birds continue their squabbling by the bird feeder. "Still doesn't *feel* ... right, somehow. And there's still so much I don't know. Like how he was able to get his hands on my medical records from fifteen years ago. Isn't HIPPA supposed to prevent that?"

"There are a lot of things he shouldn't have been able to do. How was he able to trick Aunt Charlie's attorney into thinking he was telling you about your inheritance, when he was really telling that woman who impersonated you?"

"Sabrina." I spat the name out. "I always knew there was something off with her."

Daniel half-smiled. "Well, she's getting her comeuppance now. She's up to her neck in all of this."

"I suppose," I said morosely, playing with my lemonade glass. "I just feel like such a fool. How could I have fallen for all of this?"

Daniel put his glass down and leaned across the table to grasp my hand. "Hey. Look at me." I reluctantly raised my face. His dark-blue eyes were intense. "Don't even go there. There are a lot of people to blame for this, starting with that doctor fifteen years ago who suspected you might have had an adverse reaction to your allergy medicine, and didn't follow through."

"Well, to be fair, maybe he did tell me in the hospital, and I blocked it out, along with everything else that happened," I said.

Daniel looked skeptical. "Maybe. But it still feels sloppy to me."

"And, in New York, I wasn't on allergy medicine when I met and married Stefan. I didn't have allergies in New York. How would he know I would have allergies here? And that I would have that reaction to the medicine? Or was that just a lucky break?"

Daniel's eyes got a little darker. "He knew. Although he shouldn't have been able to access your medical records. If you hadn't started taking that brand on your own, Chrissy was supposed to secretly swap it out."

I closed my eyes. It was worse than I had imagined. How could he have pretended to be in love with me to my face, and plan all of that behind my back? "Did he also know about Mad Martha and Nellie?" My voice sounded strangled.

Daniel paused. "We're not sure about that, although everyone is assuming that was the case. He had access to the stories about Mad Martha and Nellie, and he was definitely coaching Chrissy to gaslight you. It makes sense that the whole thing was a setup. What other explanation could there be? After all, ghosts don't exist, right?" He smiled as he said it, but it seemed forced.

Could it all have been an act? I thought of Chrissy's empty eyes when she was sleepwalking, and the horror on her face when she woke up and I told her she had been sleepwalking. Was she really that good of an actor? I thought of the locket, the journal. Could all of that have been a massive setup designed to play into my fears, just so Stefan could get what he wanted?

Or was there something else going on? Something ... more sinister?

I drank the tea.

"I feel like a complete idiot." I said. "Our entire relationship was one giant lie and I had no idea. How did I fall for someone who only wanted me because he thought he could get my grandparents' Trust? He must have thought he won the lottery when he got notice about Aunt Charlie passing. He probably thought that was a much easier inheritance to get his hands on."

Daniel squeezed my hand. "He fooled a lot of people, Becca. Including his own daughter."

His hand was warm, and I could feel electric tingles where he touched me. I stared into his eyes, wishing with all my heart that things had been different. Maybe if Jessica had never disappeared that night, maybe if I hadn't drunk so much I ended up with alcohol poisoning ... but there was no sense going there. What's done was done. And for all I knew, he was never all that interested in me in the first place. He was still engaged, after all. Plus, I was batting oh-for-two—actually, I was possibly in the negatives, at that point. Starting another relationship was the last thing I needed.

He seemed to sense my discouragement, and removed his hand from mine. After the warmth of his fingers, my skin felt so cold, I shivered.

"I can't even imagine how Chrissy felt," I said, rubbing the place where his hand was, and trying not to think about how alone I was. "Her own father had one, ONE, one-way ticket to Ecuador. She's only sixteen. Where on earth did he think she was going to live, while he hid in Ecuador?"

Daniel slid back in his chair, distancing himself from me. "It looks like he had reached out to his ex-wife, to have her take custody. It also looks like he was planning to leave her money— we found a safety deposit box in her name full of cash. While Wisconsin doesn't have any clear emancipation laws for minors, she's sixteen. If one of her parents had given consent, she may have been able to simply stay here in this house."

I stared at him. "Really?"

He shrugged. "Legally, it's possible. If he had managed to have you involuntarily committed, and had taken ownership of the house, and if his ex had refused to take custody, he could have drawn up the necessary paperwork for her to stay here. You wouldn't have been able to contest anything. But, when he actually became a fugitive, I don't know what would have happened."

"Wow," I said. "I ... just wow. I mean, I've had a lot of time to think about how ruthless he was, but that seems harsh even for him."

"Yeah, he's a real peach. Abandoning his own daughter, in-voluntarily committing his wife, framing his lover. Keep in mind there was no ticket for Sabrina either. Imagine her shock when she realized he not only wasn't planning to take her, but that he had set up a paper trail that led straight to her."

"Karma is a bitch," I said.

He inclined his head. "That it is."

A blue jay landed on the bird feeder, cawing loudly and scattering the other birds who angrily chirped back. "Where is Chrissy now?"

"With social services." He saw the expression on my face and lifted his hands in supplication. "Everyone knows that's not a good place for her, but we don't have any other options. Her mother isn't responding to us and her father is in jail. Stefan is beyond furious that Chrissy turned on him, and wants nothing to do with her, so he won't talk. And we've been trying to track down other family members, but it hasn't been easy. Chrissy seems to be too depressed to do much of anything except the bare minimum to stay alive."

I could feel my heart breaking. Stefan had told me that he was an only child and both his parents were dead. I had no idea if that was true. I thought Stefan's ex had a brother and a mother somewhere, but I had never met or even talked to them. I had no idea where they lived, or even their names. And, of course, that could have all been a lie, too. In fact, it would be smart if I just assumed everything Stefan had told me from the beginning was a lie.

Although, to be fair, Stefan wasn't the only one who had lied in this relationship. I had lied as well. Right from the beginning, I had lied about who I was, and then I spent our entire short marriage trying to convince both him and myself that I was something I wasn't.

All because I wanted him to take care of me.

I lied because I believed the lie I was told my whole life: that I couldn't take care of myself.

I still wasn't sure if I could. But at least now, I'm willing to try.

I thought about Chrissy and what it had cost her to betray her own father—the only parent who had been willing to take care of her. I thought I was alone. What she felt must have been ten times—no hundreds of times—worse.

"What if I take her?" I found myself saying. Daniel looked at me in surprise.

"You? Uh, no. That's not a good idea."

"Why? I'm her stepmother."

"Did you forget the part where she colluded with her father to involuntary commit you?"

I dropped my gaze to the glass table, seeing the rings our lemonade glasses had left. "It's not like she tried to kill me," I said.

"No, but she DID try and drug you. Remember those cookies she baked? She admitted to drugging them, with the same thing Stefan had been putting in your coffee. He wasn't sure you'd still react the way you did fifteen years ago to the allergy meds, and thought a little extra kick wouldn't hurt."

"She threw those cookies away," I said, thinking back. "That was when I was so sick. And clearly, she was feeling guilty about it. You brought her home drunk after she baked those cookies."

"Yeah, well. Not a good idea to have her in your house."

I sighed. "She's not going to hurt me, Daniel. All she had to do is keep her mouth shut at the end, and she couldn't. She's not like her father."

"Yeah, well. I don't think the courts are going to agree with you."

"Maybe not." But, maybe there was something I could do to help her.

Daniel drained his lemonade glass and placed it on the table. "I better get back to work."

I nodded and stood up as well. "Thanks for stopping by," I said. It sounded so final, but I knew I was being silly. We both lived there, in Redemption ... of course I would see him again.

Except he was still engaged.

"Of course. You're planning on staying, right?"

I looked around the yard. The garden was still a bit wild, but I was starting to tame it. It was a blaze of colors, everything blooming. "Aunt Charlie wanted me here. And, I'm starting to feel like she was right." Not to mention the fact that I wasn't even sure if my parents would want me back in New York, after all the drama I'd caused. Appearances were important to them, and I had pretty much failed in that category.

He studied me for a long moment. I felt something pass between us, something that had no name. I found myself thinking about what he said in the hospital—should I bring up what happened between us fifteen years ago again? Or did it even matter? Maybe all of it was in my head—he certainly didn't seem to be interested in me. Before I could figure out what to do, he was turning to go.

He had almost disappeared around the corner of the house when I called him back. "I never properly thanked you. For what you did. If it wasn't for you …"

"It was my pleasure," he interrupted. "Don't even think about it. I'm just glad it worked out the way it did."

I half-smiled. "Too bad I wasn't able to really help you."

He cocked his head. "What do you mean?"

"Well, this all started because you wanted to pick my brain over Jessica. But, my memory of that night never returned."

"Oh that," he smiled slightly as he turned to leave. "Probably just as well. I'm sure she just ran away."

Ran away. Something about the way he said it didn't sound right. And the way the trees and the branches rustled as he walked away, it almost sounded like laughter.

I shook my head to go back to my gardening. Of course she ran away. I was letting my thoughts get the better of me. What else could have happened to her?

A Note From Michele

Want to know what happened to Jessica? I've got your covered. Keep going with book 2, *This Happened to Jessica.*

Fifteen years ago, 16-year-old Jessica vanished, never to be seen again. Can Becca, the last person who saw her, discover the truth before it's too late?

Grab your copy right here:

https://www.amazon.com/dp/B07H38DL8W

****

You can also check out exclusive bonus content for *It Began With a Lie,* including a short story called *The Missing,* which takes place in 1888, right after the adults disappeared. Here's the link and QR code:

https://MPWNovels.com/r/q/itbegan-bonus

The bonus content reveals hints, clues, and sneak peeks you won't get just by reading the books, so you'll definitely want to take a look. You're going to discover a side of Redemption that is only available here.

***

If you enjoyed *It Began With a Lie,* it would be wonderful if you would take a few minutes to leave a review and rating on Amazon:

amazon.com/dp/B07DT8ZTN3/#customerReviews

Goodreads:

goodreads.com/book/show/40577287-it-began-with-a-lie
or Bookbub:
bookbub.com/books/it-began-with-a-lie-by-michele-pariza-wacek

(Feel free to follow me on any of those platforms as well.) I thank you and other readers will thank you (as your reviews will help other readers find my books.)

All my series are interrelated and interconnected. Along with my psychological thrillers, I also have a cozy mystery series that takes place in the 1990s and stars Aunt Charlie. (It's called the Charlie Kingsley Mysteries series.)

You can learn more about Redemption and my other series at https://MPWNovels.com. You'll also discover a lot of other fun stuff such as giveaways, puzzles, recipes and more.

I've also included a sneak peek of *This Happened to Jessica*, just turn the page to get started.

Chapter 1 - Jessica

"Haven't you been moping around long enough?"

I blinked. "Excuse me?"

The older woman standing on my front porch straightened herself to her full height, which was none too high. The best way to describe her was round—round face, round glasses, round bosom, round belly. Her silver-grey hair was cut short, and it 'poofed' around her face like a dandelion gone to seed. She looked like a stereotypical grandmother, except for her sharp eyes, which peered out at me from behind black-rimmed frames. She smelled like a combination of mothballs and chamomile. "I said, haven't you been moping around long enough?"

"Uh," I wasn't sure how to answer her. It was true I hadn't been doing much other than recovering from what Stefan, my now-estranged husband, had done to me, but I had no idea how in the world she would know this. "Do I know you?"

She snorted in exasperation. "Of course you do. You're Becca, Charlie's niece. Where on earth are your manners? Are you going to invite me in or what?"

"Well, yeah, but ... who are you?"

"Pat."

She continued staring at me with those sharp little bird eyes, clearly waiting for the invitation. I still had no idea who Pat was but found myself relenting under her gaze. She did seem harmless enough. I backed away from the door so she could come in. She snorted again, plainly miffed at how long it had taken, and bustled her way straight to the kitchen. I hurried after her.

"Why don't you have water simmering?" she exclaimed as she entered the kitchen. "Did you forget everything Charlie taught you?"

Before I could properly frame an answer, she began banging away in the kitchen, filling the tea kettle with water and bringing out the teapot and cups.

I moved into the kitchen to help her. "So, you knew my aunt?"

She slammed a drawer shut. "Of course I knew your aunt. Who in this town didn't know her? She treated me for years—thyroid and insomnia. You probably saw all of that in her files."

Oh. So that's what this was about. Since the whole blowup with Stefan, I've had various folks reach out to me, assuming I would be taking over Aunt Charlie's business. But, quite honestly, I was still figuring out what I wanted to do.

Her birdlike eyes studied me for a moment. "You don't remember me, do you? I watched you grow up, you know. Saw you every summer you were here."

"I *think* I remember you," I said, even though it was a lie. Great. Yet another memory lost to me. "It was just a long time ago."

She let out a rusty chuckle. "Not that long ago. But I guess for someone your age, it seems that way." She went back to digging in my drawers for tea. "Is this all you have?" she snapped, holding up one of my store-bought boxes.

I swallowed. "For now."

"Hmph." Muttering something about how she could have stayed home for store-bought tea, she prepared a couple of mugs for us and took them to the butcher-block table.

I found myself trailing after her, feeling like things had somehow gotten flipped around, reversing our roles. She was the host and I was the guest. But as I sat down in front of her, I felt the sadness that was never very far from my consciousness rise up inside me, nearly swamping me in its intensity.

She reminded me of Aunt Charlie. This is precisely how Aunt Charlie would have acted.

I so wished she was the one making tea for us.

Pat pushed the mug over to me, spilling a little in the process. I took it and held it, focusing on its warmth in my hands to keep the tears from spilling over.

God, I was still such an emotional mess. I was starting to wonder if I would ever feel like myself again or if what happened had permanently destroyed some essential piece of me.

Pat blew noisily over the tea to cool it. "You haven't answered me yet."

I blinked at her. "Sorry. What haven't I answered?"

She rolled her eyes. "Are you finished moping?"

I picked up my tea and held it near my lips, but I didn't drink. Instead, I breathed in the scent of oranges and cinnamon. "I didn't realize I was moping."

"Well, what else would you call it? There's no tea in here and no one's heard from you. We're all waiting for you to get up and running."

I took a deep breath. "I don't know if I'm going to be starting Aunt Charlie's business up again."

She looked aghast. "Of course you are! What else are you going to do?"

"I'm not sure yet."

She put her tea down with a bang, sloshing more of it on the table. "What are you talking about? You have the gift! Charlie always said you'd take over."

I closed my eyes. *Thanks, Aunt Charlie. It would have been nice if you had mentioned that to me.* "She and I never talked about it. I'm still trying to figure out what I want to do."

Pat waved her hand at me. "Pshaw. You don't need to figure anything out. You're an artist and a healer. You've just got to stop moping and get back to work."

Am I? Pat sounded so confident. I wished I could soak it up.

"I haven't been the same since I ran out of the tea Charlie made for me. You can start by making me another batch. I haven't slept right in months." She began to gather her things and rose to her feet. "You young people, always trying to 'find yourself' or some such nonsense. I tell you, in my day, we never had the luxury of all that fooling around. We did what we had to do, and we were happy about it."

She started toward the door, still berating my generation's lack of work ethic. I followed, wondering if I should try and interrupt her to let her know I didn't have a clue how to prepare tea for her (or anyone, really).

As she opened the door, she called over her shoulder, "I'll be back in a week. That should give you plenty of time to get that tea together."

"Uh," I tried to interrupt, but she wasn't paying any attention. "A week is more than enough time. More than enough. If Charlie was here, she'd have it back in a couple of days. Maybe less. Young people. What are they doing with their time?"

"I don't know ..." I tried to interrupt as she headed out the door, but she waved a finger at me.

"A week is plenty of time. Bring it to my house when you have it."

"But I don't know where you live," I said, my voice trailing off as I watched her march toward her car.

Good thing I kept Aunt Charlie's files. I guess it wouldn't kill me to poke around to see what I could come up with. Creating a tea or two didn't have to mean I was starting up Aunt Charlie's business.

I was about to close the door when I saw Daphne walking up the street. I waved and waited for her.

"I suppose you want tea, too," I said, as I let Daphne in.

"You're finally making Charlie's teas?" she asked.

I sighed again as I led her to the kitchen. "You sound like Pat."

She sat down at the kitchen table. "Oh, is that what she wanted?"

It was amazing how quickly Daphne and I had resumed our close friendship. We first became friends fifteen years ago when I used to spend the summers here with Aunt Charlie, and since I'd returned six weeks ago, we've picked right up where we'd left off—almost like there hadn't been a gap at all. I don't know what I would have done without her these past few weeks. She'd been my lifeline.

I went to make a fresh cup for Daphne as she fingered the tea bags. "Store-bought tea? Oh, Becca. Tsk, tsk. Pat surely thought Aunt Charlie was rolling in her grave."

"Something like that."

Daphne removed her sunglasses and adjusted her reddish-brown ponytail. She had a long, almost horsy face with plain, strong features, a thin mouth and that pale white skin and freckles that are so common in redheads.

"It's kind of hot for tea," Daphne said as I put a fresh mug in front of her.

"A little heat never stopped Aunt Charlie."

Daphne's lips curled up into a tiny, sad smile. "That's true." She picked up her mug to blow on it. "Any news?"

I shook my head. "Stefan still refuses to sign the divorce papers."

"Bastard."

I definitely seconded that.

"What about Chrissy? Has she talked to him yet?"

I bobbed my tea bag a few times before removing it from the mug. "I'm not sure, but if I had to guess, I would say no."

Chrissy, Stefan's sixteen-year-old daughter, and my stepdaughter, had been the unwilling pawn in her father's scheme to bilk me of an inheritance I didn't even know I had. Aunt Charlie had left it to me, along with the house. It wasn't enough to live on for the rest of my life, no–but it would definitely keep the bills paid and food on the table while I figured out what I wanted to do.

At least … it would once it had been restored. Before being arrested, Stefan had managed to drain a chunk of it, and the authorities were still sorting out where he had stashed all the money he stole. I kept telling myself it was all going to be okay—the house was paid for and the small amount of money I did have access to could pay the bills for the next couple of months, which should be more than enough time to get my trust fund sorted out.

As hurtful as Stefan had been to me, it was still nothing compared to what he had done to his daughter. Needless to say, the fact that Chrissy had turned on him in the end didn't help their father-daughter relationship at all. Even though my case against him was weak and he was actually being held in New York on much more serious charges, Stefan wasn't someone who would 'forgive and forget.'

"Are you seeing her?" Daphne asked.

I nodded. "Tomorrow. She's coming over to spend the night."

Daphne opened her mouth before closing it firmly and sipping her tea instead.

I appreciated her silence. We had had this argument around Chrissy many times before.

In the couple of weeks since the night Stefan had been arrested, Daphne had been my biggest supporter and cheerleader. She brought me food, held me as I cried, and helped me remove every reminder of Stefan from the house. She and Mia, my other best friend, had even arranged to have a shaman energetically cleanse the house. She was my rock.

But, when it came to Chrissy, we sat squarely on opposite sides. While she could understand why I didn't necessarily want to have the book thrown at Chrissy, it made no sense to Daphne why I was willing to re-establish a relationship with my step-daughter.

Mia, another of my close friends from fifteen years ago, had been the one to help me with Chrissy. Just like my friendship with Daphne, Mia and I started right back up where we had left off. Unlike Daphne, though, Mia understood why I wanted to rebuild my relationship with Chrissy. She had helped navigate the legal system to find a family willing to let Chrissy stay with them until she graduated from high school. They also didn't mind accommodating my request to work on things with my stepdaughter.

Honestly, I couldn't really explain why I wanted to continue being Chrissy's stepmother. Nor did I understand the part of me that wouldn't have minded Chrissy moving back into the house.

Daphne was right. In the beginning, she *had* conspired with her father to steal my inheritance. She *had* hurt me, physically, emotionally, and mentally. And, it was true—I had no guarantees she wouldn't try it again.

But she was also the one who saved me, and I had no intention of giving up on her.

That didn't mean she wasn't giving up on herself. The last time I had seen her, she was like a shadow of the girl she once was. She looked like she hadn't slept in weeks. Her clothes were wrinkled and stained and hung on her now too-thin body awkwardly. But, worst of all, she refused to look at me. She mostly just stared down at the ground, or off into the distance.

Margot, her foster mother, told me Chrissy was like that all the time, now. Barely eating, barely talking unless answering a direct question. They had started taking her to a therapist.

Chrissy's lack of family made me think of mine. Growing up, I had Aunt Charlie. She loved me and believed in me. I had my parents, of course, and two brothers who were quite a bit older. But that hadn't stopped my parents from trying one last time for a little girl. They must have been so joyful when I was born, their dreams having come true.

But somehow, as much as I had longed to be close to my mother, I always had this vague sense that I wasn't the daughter she had longed for—that I was a disappointment. I could never shake the feeling that my mother would have preferred a different little girl.

With Aunt Charlie, however, I never felt that way. I always felt loved and accepted and supported when I was with her.

Chrissy didn't have an Aunt Charlie. Chrissy didn't have anyone. And I would be damned if I didn't do what I could to be the one person in her corner.

Daphne was talking but I had missed what she said. I asked her if she could repeat it.

"I asked what you're doing Saturday night. A group of us are getting together."

"Um. I'm not sure," I said. "Who's going?" As much as I was ready for some fun—hell, I was long overdue for some fun!—I also had no desire to run into Daniel and his fiancé.

I had only seen Daniel once in the past three weeks and that was in passing at the courthouse. He was clearly on duty so a hasty wave in my direction was our only interaction. I had done my best to steer clear of any social situations where I might run into him. I didn't think I could bear seeing him with his fiancé.

Daphne seemed to read my thoughts. "For dinner, it's just us girls—Mia, Celia, maybe Janey. After dinner, well, who knows? But you can always leave after we eat, if you want."

I groaned. "Celia? I'm the last person she wants to spend the evening with, I'm sure."

I had only met Celia once, at a bar a couple of months ago. She was married to Barry, Daniel's childhood friend. She hadn't been shy in letting me know what she thought of me.

Daphne waved her hand. "That's just Celia. She's like that with everyone. She'll warm up. Eventually."

I snorted. "Yeah, right."

"So, can I count you in?"

I paused, taking a moment to gaze out the window. The marigolds were a fiery golden wave in the late afternoon sun. As painful as it would be to see Daniel and Gwyn together, I was ready to start getting my life back. "Okay," I said.

"Yes!" Daphne did a little fist pump. "About time we get you out of this house."

"Oh God, yes," I said. "I'm ready for some fun. But enough about me. How is your mother doing? Any improvement?"

Daphne's mother was a recluse. She suffered from numerous confusing ailments, which meant that no doctor yet had been able to come to an accurate diagnosis. I listened to Daphne share the latest challenges—most notably, her mother now had unexplainable knee pain, which not only kept her from sleeping through the night, but also limited her mobility. And that, of course, meant more work for Daphne.

Daphne glanced at the kitchen clock. "Oh, I didn't realize it was getting so late. I didn't mean to go on and on."

"Anytime," I said. "Not like you haven't listened to me do the same. Do you want something to take home for dinner? I made a couple of casseroles yesterday with all the zucchini I dug out of the garden. It's been growing like weeds out there. Do you want one? Then you don't have to worry about dinner tonight."

"No, no, I couldn't."

"Nonsense." I headed for the fridge over Daphne's protests. I wasn't much of a cook, but there was something healing about spending time in the kitchen making food. It was the same in the garden. And besides, Daphne had done a lot for me over the past few weeks. I was happy to do this small thing for her.

"Well, if you're sure," she said. I could see the relief in her eyes as she accepted the casserole. "Thank you, Becca." I felt for her. I knew she was under a tremendous amount of stress with her mother, even though she rarely complained.

"Of course I'm sure," I said. "Although I make no promises about how good it is."

She laughed. "I'm sure it's fine."

I walked her to the door, waving as she cut across the yard that led to her home. She waved back before hurrying along the path.

I watched her path long after she disappeared around the corner before softly closing the door. The house was so quiet. The only sound was the ticking of the grandfather clock.

Just like that, I was alone. Rattling around in a cavernous, creaky house with only the ghosts of my past to keep me company.

All by myself. Again.

Chapter 2 - Jessica

I wandered back into the kitchen to clean up the tea things and start thinking about dinner. I considered popping the left-over casserole in the oven, but I wasn't all that hungry. Instead, I poured a glass of wine and went to sit on the back porch.

It was easier being alone during the day. With the sun out, the birds happily chirping and the squirrels and rabbits playing, I didn't really feel all that alone. I could happily lose hours of time puttering around outside, or cleaning and reorganizing the house, eliminating every trace of Stefan.

But as the day waned into late afternoon, things became more and more difficult.

Dinnertime was the worst.

I definitely hadn't quite gotten the hang of dinnertime.

Even during the brief time that I was single back in New York, between marriages, I'd rarely had dinner by myself. If I wasn't working through it, I'd be with friends at happy hour drinking my dinner and, if I was lucky, nibbling on snacks.

I didn't even know how to cook for just one person. I'd either make too much and have leftovers for days or keep it simple with sandwiches and salads.

I sipped my wine and gazed around the garden. It had taken hours, and I wasn't done yet, but it was so much better. It was a riot of color and fragrance—roses, sunflowers, black-eyed susans, petunias, daisies, geraniums, marigolds and more, along with a huge variety of herbs (Aunt Charlie even had a special spot reserved for dandelions and other 'weeds' that were good for teas) and a few vegetables. If I stayed, I was planning on expanding the vegetable section of the garden the following year. There's nothing better than making meals with fresh vegetables.

As the sun sank lower I found myself searching the yard for Oscar, the black cat who had appeared a few weeks ago and promptly adopted me. I had no idea where he came from or who he belonged to and although he didn't appear to be feral, he also wasn't exactly a pet either.

There had been more than a few nights when the loneliness became almost unbearable. The little cat would silently appear, usually sitting in front of the window, tail curled around himself, dark green eyes watching me.

At first, I would sit at the window next to the cat to eat. Eventually, I started opening the back door. Oscar would saunter in, sniff at the food I would leave for him, eat a few bites and then leap up to sit at the table with me. After dinner, he would saunter back outside.

As the cat became my dinner companion, I decided he needed a better name than 'cat.' 'Oscar' popped into my head, and he seemed to approve.

If dinner was bad, the nights were even worse. Although I no longer dreamed of Mad Martha and Nellie (my resident ghosts) or of Aunt Charlie making me tar-like tea, I still had trouble sleeping. And when I would finally fall into a restless doze, I'd dream of Stefan chasing me around the house, usually with a knife. No matter how many doors I opened, I never could find my way out. Sometimes, I dreamed of Chrissy, too … standing like a statue in the family room with her cold, empty eyes.

Maybe it wasn't such a good idea to have Chrissy spend the night with me tomorrow after all. She would have to sleep in her old bedroom—which also happened to be the center of the hauntings from back in the early 1900's when Mad Martha killed Nellie and then herself in that same room.

I knew Chrissy liked that room though, and I wanted her to feel welcomed and wanted, so I cleaned it—physically and energetically–with the shaman. He had assured me that the room was no longer haunted, and was fine for Chrissy (or anyone) to be in.

But, still. Maybe I needed to rethink this plan.

I took another sip of wine and looked around the yard. No sign of the cat. It was beginning to get dark, and I needed to start dinner, yet I didn't move. I just sat there, hoping against hope that I'd see Oscar silently appear from the shadows. Instead the disappointment rose in my chest.

I didn't want to go into that dark, empty house alone.

But, as the late afternoon sun slowly turned into twilight and Oscar still didn't appear, I finally decided I couldn't wait any longer. I picked up my empty wine glass and headed for the door.

The noise was soft—grass rustling, a snapped twig. I quickly looked around, hope blooming inside me. "Oscar?"

No sign of the cat. I bit my lip as I gazed around. Did I imagine it? Or was it some other animal?

I heard the noise again. This time it sounded more like a footstep, and I froze. An image popped into my head—a footprint. I had been out in the garden early one more morning a few weeks ago and there it was, pressed into the mud. I never did figure out where it had come from. Chrissy? One of Chrissy's friends? A couple of neighborhood kids playing a prank?

Or maybe something more sinister.

I was suddenly aware of how alone I really was; no close neighbors, not even a dog. No one would hear a thing, should something happen.

Even if I screamed.

A cold lump of fear rose in my throat practically choking me.

What should I do? Make a run for it? Try and hide? Maybe find a weapon? My eyes swept the backyard again but I saw nothing. Crap. To make matters even worse, I had left my cell phone in the house.

Crunch. Another footstep. Definitely human. Oh God. Fighting the panic rising inside, I quietly took a few steps toward the large rose bush planted near the house. Maybe I could hide behind it until I saw who was there.

A shadow appeared off to the side. I sucked in my breath. The bush was too far away to get behind in time. I was just going to have to brazen it out.

The shadow came into focus, and I felt my body sag with relief. "CB! You nearly scared me to death! What are you doing here?"

CB grinned at me. "Hey cos. Nice to see you, too."

"I didn't mean ... I'm so glad to see you!" I ran over to give him a hug. I *was* happy to see him. Not only because I liked hanging out with him, but also because I wasn't alone anymore.

CB was my only cousin on my mom's side, but we had basically been raised together. Born just five days apart, we looked like brother and sister. We both had reddish-blondish-brown hair although mine was heavier on the red. His hazel eyes had more green in them whereas my eyes would often change from green to brown to gold. We both were on the slender side, but with CB that slightness simply made him look more feminine. He had always had more than his share of admirers from both sexes although he himself was open to whoever ended up in his bed, especially if that person was very attractive or very rich ... even better if both.

"You've lost weight," he said accusingly. "You were never this thin in New York."

"I also thought I had a happy marriage when I was in New York."

He clucked his tongue. "Maybe it's time to come back. Show off the new you? Thin is always in." He waggled his eyebrows.

I laughed. "You can never be too rich or too thin."

"Exactly! See, you remember. You haven't been corrupted living in this backwards country. At least, not yet. We'll need to act fast though. When are you coming back to New York?"

"You know, it's past five o'clock and you don't have any wine."

He widened his eyes. "You're right. Travesty!"

"We better get that rectified immediately."

He gestured with his arm in a broad flourish. "Lead the way."

I moved to open the side door and gestured at him to go inside. "How long are you staying?"

"Hmmm. A week. Give or take."

That sounded like CB. He was the essence of a social butterfly, flitting in and out of people's lives, often without much fanfare. He didn't have a job, or at least not a traditional one. It was always a mystery how he paid for his lifestyle as he never seemed to be hurting for money. Privately, I thought it was a combination of his wealthy male and female 'friends,' and his mother.

He wandered through the downstairs as I poured him his wine and refilled my own. "You haven't changed much, have you?"

I shook my head as I handed him his glass. "It still feels like Aunt Charlie's house to me."

He took a sip. "Ugh," he said. "We're definitely going to have to work on your wine palate. That's certainly gone downhill."

"You'll be amazed at how much better it tastes after you've had a glass or two."

He laughed. "Touché." He took another sip, narrowing his eyes at me from over the rim. "As good of a distraction as this is, you didn't answer my question about when you're leaving this place. And I'm wondering what that means."

I sighed and took a drink myself. "It means I don't know, CB."

"Ah." He nodded as he leaned against the counter. "But there's nothing here for you. Why would you stay?"

"There's nothing in New York for me either," I said, "except a higher cost of living. How would I support myself?"

"What are you talking about? You have money." He gestured around the kitchen. "Just sell this and you'll be set."

I snorted. Sometimes I wondered how CB had made it this far in life. "Set for how long?"

"Long enough to snag yourself another man."

"Oh no," I took a step backward, holding my hands out. "Two ex-husbands are two more than I ever wanted."

"Third time's a charm."

"Unless it's not." I shook my head. "I tried the husband thing and it didn't work. I need to figure out another way to support myself that doesn't require relying on anyone else."

CB rolled his eyes. "How noble. And ridiculous. You have a life in New York. Just come back. I'm sure it will all work out."

"I know this will come as a shock to you, but here in the real world, planning is considered a good thing. Especially when it comes to finances. Not all of us are blessed to live like Kramer in *Seinfeld*."

"Whatever." He finished his wine and picked up the bottle to pour another glass. "So, what have you done with the place? I think I need the tour. Although what I've seen so far has been less than impressive. It looks like you haven't changed a thing."

"That's not exactly true," I said, following him as he headed for the stairs. "I got rid of the sewing machine."

"You can't even sew," he scoffed. "And, besides, it probably didn't even work."

"That's beside the point. I also got rid of that hideous lamp in the living room."

"Chalk one up for the good side."

I followed him up the stairs, relieved he had changed the subject. I didn't want to share the real reason why I was afraid to move back to New York. My parents had always been my financial back up. They hadn't approved of me marrying Stefan as fast as I had and I couldn't bear to face them now that my marriage had blown up in such a spectacular way. I couldn't go back to them now, hat in hand, after everything that had happened. No, I was going to have to figure this out myself.

We had almost reached the top of the steps when it suddenly occurred to me that I didn't know where he was going to sleep. When we stayed here as kids, he had always slept in Chrissy's room. While I supposed he could sleep there tonight, where was I going to put him tomorrow when Chrissy was here? Come to think of it, what was I supposed to DO with him when Chrissy was here? It was supposed to be a girl's night in. Maybe I ought to reschedule. And while I'm at it, rethink the wisdom of putting Chrissy back in that bedroom.

He poked his head in Chrissy's room. "Aw, that's sweet of you to have my room ready for me."

I cleared my throat. "Actually, it's not for you. It's for Chrissy."

He turned to look at me in surprise. "Chrissy? I thought she was with a foster family."

"She is. But, I'm trying to rebuild a relationship with her. She's actually coming over tomorrow night for a sleepover."

CB peered over his shoulder at me, his face surprised. "Is that wise?"

I sighed. "Don't start, CB. If I don't help her, who will?"

He made a face. "Your funeral. Whatever. Clearly you're not listening to me about anything. I'll make myself scarce tomorrow night so you can have your little girl's party."

"You don't have to do that," I said, touched by his offer. "I can reschedule."

He turned away to saunter down the hall. "Don't bother. I wouldn't mind seeing some of the old gang while I'm here anyway." He poked his head in what Aunt Charlie used to call the Magic Room, that had (briefly) been Stefan's office. With the help of Daphne, I had restored it back to its Magic Room's roots and was now using it for my own office.

He nodded as he took in the cleared-off desk, my laptop, the fresh flowers from the garden, the window open behind the desk and the light-green curtains covered with a daisy pattern dancing with the fresh breeze. "You taking over the healing practice?"

I stifled a second sigh. What was going on today? Was I somehow cursed to have the same conversations over and over? "Why would I do that? I have no training in it."

"Yes, you do," he said, moving away from the door. "I remember her explaining herbs and healing when we were kids. I'm sure it would come back pretty fast. Just study her files and you'll be fine."

I opened my mouth to argue with him, and then shut it. Now that he mentioned it, I did recall Aunt Charlie constantly feeding me information about the different herbs and their health benefits. And he was right about her files. But, still. If I was serious about it, I really ought to go back to school.

CB moved to the next room and poked his head in. "Why are you still sleeping in here?"

I went over to stand next to him. "Because it still feels like my room."

He looked at me in disbelief. "Well, yeah. When you were a teenager. But now you're an adult, and this is YOUR house. Why aren't you sleeping in the master bedroom?"

I shifted uncomfortably. Stefan had asked the same thing, and I really didn't have a good answer. Yes, part of it was that I felt more comfortable in the same room I had slept in when I was younger. And there was no question I still thought of the house as Aunt Charlie's, rather than mine.

But, neither of those answers explained why I hadn't even opened the door to The Room—otherwise known as Aunt Charlie's bedroom—yet.

An image from my dreams flashed in my head. Aunt Charlie in the kitchen, telling me to drink the tea, her white pointed teeth glinting in the moonlight while blood ran down her chin. I shivered despite the warmth of the house. Did I honestly think I would run into Aunt Charlie's ghost in The Room?

It just seemed safer keeping the door closed.

CB watched me for a moment, then deliberately walked over to Aunt Charlie's bedroom. "What do you think we'll find in there, hmmm?" he said teasingly.

"No, CB. Don't."

He put his hand on the doorknob. "Think her *corpse* is in there? Or maybe ..." he turned and waggled his eyebrows at me. "Her *ghost*."

My stomach dropped as I took a few steps toward him, putting my hand on his arm to stop him. "CB, it's not funny. Let's go back down to the kitchen. You need more wine and I should start dinner."

"Of course it's funny. You should be sleeping in here. It's silly that you aren't." He started to turn the doorknob.

A panicky feeling fluttered in my chest and I squeezed his arm. "You're probably right, but ... I'm just not ready. Okay? You know what I've been through. Can you just indulge me? Please?" I looked up at him imploringly, knowing he always had trouble resisting my puppy eyes.

He studied me for a moment then turned away from the door. "It's true I could use a refill. I don't know about you cooking for me though. Are you trying to kill me?"

The sweet feeling of relief bloomed inside me and I beamed at CB. "I've actually gotten pretty good at cooking. C'mon, let me show you."

I led the way back downstairs, squishing down the little voice inside that wanted to know what the heck was so wrong with me that the simple act of opening a bedroom door nearly caused me an anxiety attack.

* * *

CB swept into the kitchen and struck a pose. "How do I look?"

I whistled approvingly. "Very dapper."

He rolled his eyes. "Wasn't going for dapper." He wore dark, raw denim skinny jeans and a Burberry striped navy and white fitted polo.

"Well, you do know you're going to be the best dressed person in all of Redemption tonight," I said. "Including women."

"And yet again, I'm reminded of why it's taken me so long to visit," he said. "What are you waiting for? Pour me a glass of wine."

I reluctantly reached for a glass. "I figured you'd be leaving."

He widened his eyes in mock horror. "I couldn't leave without seeing my niece now, could I?"

Oh great. Chrissy was supposed to be here in the next half hour or so. I had really hoped CB would be out of the house by then. I was also hoping he would honor his promise about not returning until morning and decided to mention it again.

"I'm sure I can find *someone* who will take me in, since my cousin is so heartlessly kicking me out," he said with a wink.

"No doubt someone in Redemption would let you sleep on his (or her!) couch," I said.

He laughed. "The couch isn't precisely what I had in mind, but maybe that could be fun, too."

I handed him his wine. "Try not to get into too much trouble."

He winked. "Oh, but where's the fun in that?"

The doorbell rang. I felt my mouth go dry. CB was difficult to predict at the best of times, and after listening to more than a few passive-aggressive taunts in relation to Chrissy in the past 24 hours, I really hoped he wouldn't end up sabotaging my efforts at reconciliation.

CB set his wine down. "Well, well. It looks like the woman of the hour is here."

I made a face at him. "Just behave. Okay?"

He laughed. "Again, I ask ... where is the fun in that?"

I moved past him to answer the door, wanting to beg him to be good. I also considered simply pushing him out the door as I pulled Chrissy in. Typically, less was more when dealing with CB, so I resisted both of those urges.

Chrissy stood on the porch, holding a backpack, her eyes cast down. Normally, I would have been alarmed at her appearance—dark circles under her eyes, dull, lank hair hanging limply around her pale, nearly gaunt face—but instead, I was completely transfixed by the girl standing behind her.

Long, thick, wavy blonde hair framed a narrow, elegant face with jutting, high cheekbones, full lips, and huge, dark-green eyes.

I was staring at the spitting image of Jessica.

Want to keep reading? Grab your copy of **This Happened to Jessica** here:

https://www.amazon.com/dp/B07H38DL8W/

More Secrets of Redemption series:
It Began With a Lie (Book 1)
This Happened to Jessica (Book 2)
The Evil That Was Done (Book 3)
The Summoning (Book 4)
The Reckoning (Book 5)
The Girl Who Wasn't There (Book 6)
The Room at the Top of the Stairs (Book 7 coming soon)
The Secret Diary of Helen Blackstone (free novella)

Charlie Kingsley Mysteries:
A Grave Error (a free prequel novella)
Ice Cold Murder (Book 2)
Murder Next Door (Book 3)
Murder Among Friends (Book 4)
The Murder of Sleepy Hollow (Book 5)
Red Hot Murder (Book 6)
A Wedding to Murder For (novella)
Loch Ness Murder (novella)

Standalone books:
Today I'll See Her (free novella or purchase with bonus content)
The Taking
The Third Nanny
Mirror Image
The Stolen Twin

Access your free exclusive bonus scenes from *It Began With a Lie* right here:
https://MPWNovels.com/r/itbegan-bonus

Acknowledgements

It's a team effort to birth a book, and I'd like to take a moment to thank everyone who helped.

My writer friends, Hilary Dartt and Stacy Gold, for reading early versions and providing me with invaluable feedback. My wonderful editor, Megan Yakovich, who is always so patient with me. My designer, Erin Ferree Stratton, who has helped bring my books to life with her cover designs.

And, of course, a story wouldn't be a story without research, and I'm so grateful to my friends who have so generously provided me with their expertise over the years: Dr. Mark Moss, Andrea J. Lee, and Steve Eck. Any mistakes are mine and mine alone.

Last but certainly not least, to my husband Paul, for his love and support during this sometimes-painful birthing process.

About Michele

A USA Today Bestselling, award-winning author, Michele taught herself to read at 3 years old because she wanted to write stories so badly. It took some time (and some detours) but she does spend much of her time writing stories now. Mystery stories, to be exact. They're clean and twisty, and range from psychological thrillers to cozies, with a dash of romance and supernatural thrown into the mix. If that wasn't enough, she posts lots of fun things on her blog, including short stories, puzzles, recipes and more, at MPWNovels.com.

Michele grew up in Wisconsin, (hence why all her books take place there), and still visits regularly, but she herself escaped the cold and now lives in the mountains of Prescott, Arizona with her husband and southern squirrel hunter Cassie.

When she's not writing, she's usually reading, hanging out with her dog, or watching the Food Network and imagining she's an awesome cook. (Spoiler alert, she's not. Luckily for the whole family, Mr. PW is in charge of the cooking.)

Made in United States
North Haven, CT
19 November 2023

44256626R00209